THE GEORGIAN HOUSE

THE GEORGIAN HOUSE
A Tale in Four Parts

By
FRANK SWINNERTON

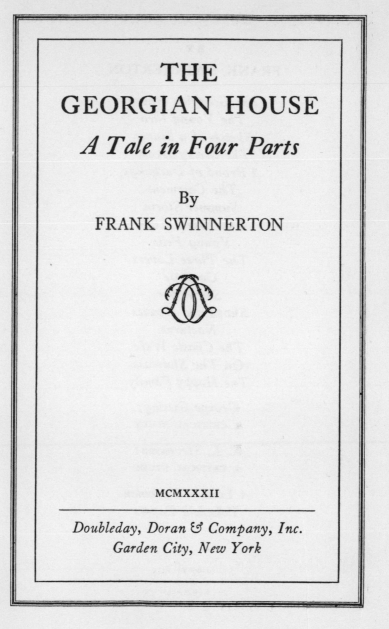

MCMXXXII

Doubleday, Doran & Company, Inc.
Garden City, New York

PRINTED AT THE *Country Life Press*, GARDEN CITY, N. Y., U. S. A.

CONTENTS

PART ONE
THE SCENE IS SET

CHAPTER ONE
SANDERSFOLD

ONCE upon a time, Sandersfold was a village; and this village, partly of the seventeenth, and partly of the eighteenth century, still lies intact, very nearly unspoilt, in the heart of the growing town. The village consisted of a single wide street, running east and west, at a distance of about ten miles from the English Channel. The town, spick and span, well stocked with villas, shops, cottages, and kitchen gardens, is the home of ten thousand prosperous persons. It has no large industries, but thrives upon the amenities of the neighbourhood. Young ladies bring parties of friends from adjacent coastal resorts to visit one or other of ye olde tea shoppes of Sandersfold; and upon summer afternoons the High Street is littered with every kind of small motorcar, each of which has its own method of dropping oil upon the elderly paving.

One end of this High Street divides in order sedately to embrace an old, short-spired grey stone church. The church is not at all beautiful, but it has a slaty reticence, and it dominates the street. Sandersfold natives are impressed by that reticence. Also, they have learned to regard the church—and its antiquity—as an asset to the town. They think it perhaps keeps a protective eye upon their doings, as if, magisterially, it takes the chair for each day's domestic inquisition.

If the church guards the High Street from one end, and surveys its activity, so at the other, or eastern, end do a couple of secular buildings, both of the eighteenth century.

3

The first of these buildings—the one upon the south side —is a respectable hotel (the Lion), which has a fine Georgian front and a useful Edwardian back. It stands at the corner of High Street and Larch Street with an air of success and open honesty. Its proprietress, Mrs. Settle, is so competent that the Lion is in reality the best-managed establishment in the town. Mrs. Settle is known facetiously to old residents as "the Lioness" and her husband, less impressive, is "the whelp-consort." No wonder the same faces are seen, night after night, all the year round, in its dining room.

Immediately opposite to the hotel, across the High Street, and on one corner of Eden Street, is a vermilion-painted garage, before which, as if they were totem posts, are several gay, moon-faced petrol pumps. The garage is managed by the whelp-consort, and you can almost hear the hearts of old residents throbbing with anger as they come in sight of it. In contrast, upon the other corner of Eden Street, fronting the High Street and glancing diagonally at the Lion, is the third most striking piece of architecture in Sandersfold. It never frowns, but remains quite composedly tolerant of everything in the world save the shockingly bright garage, which it ignores by means of an almost totally blind wall. It is a flat, plain, three-storied Georgian house built of reddish brown brick. It has ten large windows overlooking the High Street, four upon each of the upper floors, and one upon each side of a very wide, massive dark green front door with a small brass knocker, a large brass knob, and a cavernous letter box. A single step lifts this door above the level of the street; and above the door is an arched fanlight of irresistible beauty.

The house has no name. It is known in the town as "Mr. Starling's house." Before the days of Mr. Starling it was "Miss Strange's"; and before that nothing at all.

Nobody—not even the income tax collector—has ever dared to give it a number. For two hundred years it has stood as it now stands, solid, discreet, imposingly unpretentious. Its owner, who has not been abroad for some months, has no existence for the majority of dwellers in Sandersfold; but casual visitors to the town often stop to admire the house, ask the name of the people who live in it, and peep slyly out of the corners of their eyes in case anything is to be seen of the interior through one of those deceptively blank windows. Nothing is to be seen.

2

Two or three years ago, upon a late spring afternoon, two women were standing together at the corner of High Street and Larch Street, where there is another old wall, this time a part of the hotel premises. One of the women held a large grey-striped shopping bag, and was rather stout and heavily built; the other was smaller, with sharp cheekbones and rapid, not always quite genial, grey eyes. Mrs. Teviot and Mrs. Lax. Mrs. Teviot was the taller. She had once been a big woman, but she had ceased to hold herself upright, and her figure had spread. She now drooped rather listlessly, clutching her shopping bag, which pulled her shoulder down by its weight. Her face was square and pale. Her dark coat was closely fastened at the neck and went right down to her ankles. Her hat, of purple velvet, hung over her brow, and seemed like a disguise.

Mrs. Lax was without fat of any kind. She was lean and small, with a thin, dry voice, which did not, however, sound either cracked or disagreeable. She, too, wore a long coat that reached to her ankles, and her hat, carelessly and comically askew, was of black straw. All her movements were restless, and the expression upon her thin lips was impatient and dissatisfied. Both women were obviously poor, but comfortably poor. Both looked as if they had savings, as if their husbands were in work, and as if there were money to spare in their households for wireless, the gramophone, trips to the seaside, and easy, thrifty, enjoyable shopping. Neither was pressed for time.

Their heads were bent. They were talking in low, intimate tones; gossiping.

"Well, I believe she did," said Mrs. Lax. "In fact, I'm *sure* she did. Else why should she say she never?"

"George is *sure* he saw her," answered Mrs. Teviot. "And——"

"*He* wouldn't know," interrupted Mrs. Lax. "He's as blind as a bat. Them glasses! All covered in grease and dirt." They grimaced ruefully at each other. Mrs. Teviot laughed internally. The sound resembled the almost inaudible clucking of a hen. She did not defend George's sight or his glasses. But she continued:

"I don't like the way she's been running *after* the boy. It's like her, though. She was wild to get married. Always on to Fred, she was——"

"They're all the same," said Mrs. Lax. "Think being married means reading books all day, and the pictures in the evening, and kissing and cuddling. . . . They soon find out. Then they wish they was girls again, laughing and screaming. She's no worse than Doris and Vera. If as bad."

Mrs. Teviot did not answer. She had a way of being silent. "Thinking the more," some people said. The truth was that Mrs. Teviot's husband was a nervous talker, who exhausted himself in verbosity. Silence gave Mrs. Teviot great domestic advantage. She did not so much chill exuberance as sit upon it.

"Now, *Vera*——" began Mrs. Lax. Then she checked herself. "I won't say another word about Vera. I'm sick and tired of Vera. Ideas, and—well! All I can say is that some of these girls could do with a good thrashing."

"Who'd give it to them?" wondered Mrs. Teviot, speculatively. "Not the men, *I* know."

"Soft," sighed Mrs. Lax. "Have you been to Tucker's?"

Mrs. Teviot slightly lifted her bag.

"That young fellow there . . . He goes with Elsie Lodge."

"Mm. *She's* nice," said Mrs. Lax.

"Yes; but did you hear that about her dad?" Mrs. Teviot opened her eyes very wide. "He's give in his notice. He says he's going to Australia."

"Him?" Mrs. Lax was extraordinarily contemptuous. "Fine handy man *he* is. I got him to come and look at my stove. He covered the place in soot; and then I had to get Ted Rudd to do it prop'ly!" She laughed, a little high, mirthful laugh, wholly good-natured. "They want *men* in Australia. Not old handy Jacks!"

At this moment the High Street presented a typical picture of an English country town. It was crowded with motorcars; many pedestrians strolled in the last hot rays of the setting sun or looked in at the shop windows; and a rosy-faced policeman in his light grey helmet kept an eye upon those motorists who steered waveringly through the traffic. Larch Street had been empty; but in a moment a girl came quickly from some unnoticed quarter, passed the two women, smiled rather condescendingly, and continued upon her way across the High Street and down Eden Street, along by the high wall of Mr. Starling's house and garden.

The girl walked well. She had a light, slim figure; and her costume of russet brown tweed was the kind of thing that many English ladies of all ages wear in the country. She carried no bag, but swung her arms a little. The two women ceased their gossip and stood in silence, watching that quick step. They were very critical. Although the stout woman smiled cordially enough at the moment of greeting, her smile had instantly vanished, and the expression upon her face was now one of mere appraisement.

"Who's that, then?" asked Mrs. Lax, in a dry voice. A little mysterious smile—similar in bafflingness to the smile of the Mona Lisa, but rather less attractive—played upon her lips.

"Her? That's Miss Holpen. In the Crescent." Mrs. Teviot gave her friend a meaning glance. The Crescent implied a large house, possibly understaffed, but inhabited by unquestioned "gentry."

"Where's she going, then?" Mrs. Lax's tone was sharper.

The stout woman shook her head. She seemed to consider.

"Well, I expect it's old Miss Furze," she suggested. "Her in Grange Road. She's the only one I can think of. That big house on the corner."

"Mm." Mrs. Lax murmured. "I know. I used to see her at the Socials. She don't go now, pore old lady. She's nice. Miss Holpen don't go there, does she?"

"Shouldn't think so." Mrs. Teviot shifted her shopping bag to the other hand and smiled. "Thinks too much of herself. Well, *I* think she does. Her brother's solicitor up there——" She jerked her head along the High Street. Above some of the shops there were offices.

"Oh, yes," said Mrs. Lax, quickly. "I know *him*." Her tone was particularly dry.

"He's nice," protested Mrs. Teviot. "What d'you mean?"

Mrs. Lax turned and looked over at the Georgian house. Her lips were pressed close together.

"Oh, nothing," she said.

"Well, he's *got* to go there!" cried Mrs. Teviot, unconsciously speaking aloud. "I mean, Mr. Starling being ill——" She was vehemently hushed by Mrs. Lax. "Sh-sh-sh!" More quietly, she went on: "They say he won't get better. And as for *her*——"

Mrs. Lax interrupted in a whisper:

"I never said anything. I never said a word. And I didn't mean anything, either."

"Yes, you did. You meant he went to see *her*."

"No, I didn't! I was thinking of his father. You don't remember him, do you? He was a fine big man with a black beard."

"I used to see him. Not to speak to. He come to see Mrs. Mansard when I worked there."

"Yes, Mrs. Mansard," confirmed Mrs. Lax, with a peculiar nod.

"That wasn't anything."

"No, only he went there."

"Well, he come two or three times a week when Mr. Mansard was ill. It was to get her signatures or something. I was with the children, see."

"Yes, her signatures," said Mrs. Lax.

The two women exchanged a long glance. The bafflingness of Mrs. Lax's enigmatic smile was intensified. She had thoughts. Mrs. Teviot also had thoughts; but hers travelled more slowly, with less malice.

"I never see anything," she added, firmly.

"Have you ever seen *her?*" asked Mrs. Lax, with the faintest inclination of her head towards the house opposite.

"Well, *seen* her." Mrs. Teviot scrupulously did not claim acquaintance. "Of course, I often used to see *him*. Before he was ill. Mrs. Jones goes there——"

"Yes, I know. She sometimes tells me something about them. Mrs. Sims tells her. The maid."

At that moment the big green door of the Georgian house opened. A tall young man appeared. A tall, thin young man, rather sleek, with a small dark moustache, and a glittering ring upon his little finger. He was evidently letting himself out of the house. Although he seemed preoccupied, he did not fail to glance over at the two women on the other corner. But without appearing to recognize either, he walked quickly along the High Street towards the old grey church, a decided figure in his well-tailored black suit and hard felt hat and heavily winged stiff collar. As he went, five o'clock struck somewhere in the neighbourhood.

"Never saw us," said Mrs. Lax, under her breath.

"Yes, he did," answered Mrs. Teviot. "He sees everything."

"Well, I know. When he wants to. He'd see the King all right." There was a faint pause, during which Mrs. Lax seemed to think of some odd fact. She became more generous. "But he's very good-looking," she said. "All the young ladies like him."

They both ceased talking in order to observe the quick steps of young Mr. Leonard Holpen as he returned to his office.

"Funny our seeing both of them," suggested Mrs. Teviot. "So near, I mean. You could tell they was brother and sister, couldn't you."

"Yes. And funny our seeing him coming out of *there,*" added Mrs. Lax, drily.

Mrs. Teviot's white face became expressionless.

"Everything's funny," she observed. "If you look for it." She was stealing side glances under her conspiratorial hat in the direction of the Georgian house. Not one of the windows escaped. But all were blank. Then her tone changed. "Well, I must be getting on. Charley's got his choir practice tonight." She smiled broadly for the first time, with an air of proud fondness.

"What a little man!" answered Mrs. Lax, her eyelids flickering responsively, and her pointed teeth showing amiably for an instant. "I suppose I must get my Harold something for his supper."

They still stood, half smiling, unready to part. There was so much to tell in Sandersfold. Although the life there was slow, it never stood still. The sun was sinking in a red glow somewhere behind the church, which was silhouetted against the radiance. Mrs. Teviot drew attention to the picture.

"Pretty," she said, with appreciation. "Like a Christmas card."

3

Lettice Holpen, in common with many other modern girls, was self-conscious. She could not help seeing herself as others (if they were romantic half-wits) might see her. She was not at all simple-minded; and yet she pretended a good deal. On this afternoon, bracing herself against the unavoidable scrutiny of Mrs. Teviot and her friend, she had smiled graciously at them with the object of impressing. She had imagined what they would say of her. But only for an instant of amusement. You couldn't really tell, she thought, what women of that sort felt and said when they were alone. Sometimes you wished you could! But, on the other hand, perhaps it was as well you could not. Was it? Or not?

In person Lettice was very nearly as dark, and was quite as slim, as her brother; but even for her sex she was less tall proportionately than he. She was twenty-three—five years his junior. She had begun to grow her hair, which until lately had been shingled; and little dark bunches of it projected from under the soft brim of her hat. Large grey eyes, set well apart above a delicately chiselled nose and straight flat cheeks, gave no hint of warmth in her nature; and the thinness of her lips might have been disagreeable if, when parted, the lips had not fastidiously disclosed very pretty teeth. Coldness, pride, and a good deal of causticity might be read in the face by an unfriendly observer. One more kind could hardly have missed signs of great sensitiveness, conscious frustration, and a power of loving deeply and resenting at sight.

She was not, as Mrs. Teviot had supposed, visiting Miss Furze (an old lady—said generally to be rather a dear, and a great reader, but in fact much more than a dear, and no great reader, except of character). She was going for a brisk solitary walk. If you went straight down Larch Street and Eden Street, and continued past the entrance to the Sports Ground, you presently found yourself in a narrow meandering lane arched with the leafy boughs of beech, oak, birch, and chestnut. The lane straggled north, west, and southwest for a couple of miles, dangerously cut the main road, became a bridle path, and led round to Sandersfold railway station. But its chief attraction for Lettice was that it was little-frequented.

Hedges grew high above her head as she walked, imprisoning the hot, spicy air of the late afternoon. In the trees a never-ending loveliness of bird song made the most melodious clamour in the world. Shadows were long and deep; shafts of fervid sunlight pierced gaps in the hedge; the greenness of the leaves was yet unspoilt by summer dust. It was a lane for leisurely, responsive walking; but Lettice upon this occasion was unconscious of all the afternoon's delights. The corners of her mouth drooped. Her eyes were dark. She looked bitter, cold, ungovernable. And then, an instant later, mocking, demure, unscrupulously charming. With a breathless smile she hastened her step; with a renewed and tremendous frown she came abruptly to a stand in the middle of the lane.

She was not happy. Sometimes her unhappiness carried her to the verge of hysteria. But when she forced herself to face the truth she was convinced that her unhappiness was in good part only boredom. It was also due to the smothering effects of her home life; for her mother was an inert, greedily vain woman who believed herself to be fascinating, who performed before visitors and sulked when alone. Her brother was engrossed in his own affairs. Lettice had society, friends (of a sort), intelligence, but no special talent and no liberty. And the reason for her present agitated walk was that a prospect of escape seemed about to offer itself. Would that, too, fail her?

Impulsively Lettice turned round and retraced her steps. Her eyes were full of tears. She realized that in the whole town of Sandersfold there was nobody who could really help her. She had no friends. Those whom she called friends were no more than companions to whom she closed her heart. She never spoke naturally to them— always with a forced aristocratic note, as if strangers were listening. When she was with them she acted continuously. Even with her brother, although at times they were almost intimate, she was not at ease. The two sparred self-consciously in public (playing brother and sister!) and hardly spoke of personal matters when others were not present. In the end they denied each other confidence, because, like the rest, they were frightened of sincerity. It seemed so old-fashioned, so humourless. And at all costs one must maintain an air of detachment, of amusement, of "irony," lest one should reveal oneself for general contempt as an ignorant, bewildered, and (more terrifying than all) commonplace person.

In her sudden retreat Lettice reached home sooner

than she had expected to do. She lived in one of a row
of respectably pretentious houses built in the antique
fashion. Wooden beams zigzagged across the upper stories
of the house; red tiles hung picturesquely over the upper
windows; all windows were latticed casements. It was a
pretty house, and was roomy; but it faced north, and the
front rooms were all cold and cheerless except in the
height of summer. Only in the rooms at the back of the
house could one feel light-hearted, and these rooms had
been appropriated by Mrs. Holpen. Lettice's bedroom, to
which she now mounted, was on the north side, and it
chilled her. She took one glance at its bleak, grey-dis-
tempered walls, and at the sparse æsthetic wooden furniture, and fled downstairs.

The room she entered was unfortunately no more en-
livening, for the Holpens were moderns who believed in
an absence of clutter. And while the absence of clutter is
admirably hygienic, there can be no doubt that the frig-
idly furnished house is intended for a homeless generation. When (if ever) homes again become popular, clutter
will return. Here, before Lettice, all was select. All was
sparse. The very books upon those severe bookshelves had
cold winds blowing through them, and were present as
miniature lozenges in the larger design. The room was
high; the casement curtains were exiguous; the floor was
parquet, with one or two dwarfed rugs of dirty reds and
dull blues; the walls were vast expanses of buffness in
which occasional small pictures looked like postage stamps.
All was as cordial as an empty classroom.

With a sigh Lettice set a chair out of the draught
and picked up an illustrated journal. She idly glanced at
the photographs of people of whom she had never heard,
and noticed what the women were wearing. Impatient,
she threw down the journal, stood for a moment in deep
thought with her hands joined and pressed against her

lips, and went out of the room again, towards a curtained alcove in the hall, where the telephone stood. Here she paused; and while she paused the thrilling noise of the telephone bell quite close to her ear made her heart jump and her cheeks flush. With an effort to be calm, she lifted the receiver.

At once, her expression changed to one of nonchalance. "Oh, it's you," she said, coolly. "What? Yes? Yes?" Her brother's voice sounded distinctly in her ear.

"Let? Look here, Starling's dying. Henty's just phoned. I dunno when I shall get home. I shall go down there— may have to hang about. Tell Mother, will you?"

"Yes. Give my love to Ruth——"

"I may not see her. Don't expect I shall."

There was a click in Lettice's ear. Her brother had rung off.

That was odd! Leonard wasn't his usual self. A little breathless, wasn't he? Why should he say that he probably would not see Ruth? Of course he'd see her. Why had he to go at all? Lettice's mind jumped. Leonard, Ruth, old Starling. Money, love, death. Anything in it? She whistled under her breath. She no longer had any inclination to use the telephone upon her own account. Curiosity absorbed her.

"I wonder if there *is!*" she reflected aloud. "Might be. It would explain a lot. I don't know anything about him. Or her. What cool fishes they both are!"

Humming, Lettice returned to the room she had left. She was much more interested in life than she had been five minutes before.

4

Having telephoned to Lettice, Leonard Holpen rose from his desk and passed into the general office. Here an elderly

man and a youth were bending over a large plan of Sandersfold. The clerk's forefinger was tapping the plan, and
as he looked gravely up, the forefinger continued mechanically to tap the air. Burgess was always tapping something. When he could not tap the waistcoat of a listener,
he tapped his own desk, and when, as it were, off duty, the
finger still functioned. It was a long white finger, skilled
in the law.

But Leonard knew the finger too familiarly to show
respect for it.

"I may be back. Don't wait," he said, shortly.

"Very good, sir," said Burgess. His light eyes gleamed
in a withered old face that was unpleasantly reddish in
hue. His wig, so painstakingly brushed, stood out from
the nape of his neck. He listened attentively as if he were
so deaf that he only pretended to hear. That was a mannerism; he was not at all deaf.

The door closed behind Leonard. He was out upon the
gloomy stairs, treading with care. From below came the
sound of traffic. A moment later he was in the High
Street, pushing his way through a crowd. His eyes flew
everywhere as he walked, but he kept his head low. It was
Leonard's belief that to be a successful solicitor one must
always seem busy, and always seem to sweep aside great
preoccupations in order to give one's whole attention to
the client of the moment. Busy; but never *too* busy. By
strange chance this was his fortune. He was a success.
He was more successful than his father had been. But
his father had been of the older generation, with the older
generation's pleasures and preferences.

Only a short space had passed since the message from
Dr. Henty had reached him; and he was already at Mr.
Starling's house, knocking at the wide green door. He
did not look as if he had hurried. When he was admitted
to the house he spoke no word to Sims, the elderly maid,

but hung his hat upon the rack and went straight into the room upon the right-hand side of the square hall.

"Dr. Henty's there, sir. And Miss Coulevain. And the nurse."

"Nothing happened?"

"No, sir. The doctor said he was unconscious."

Sims would have continued talking if Leonard had not nodded sharply and dismissingly. Quelled, she withdrew, leaving Leonard alone in the big room. He knew how to get rid of anybody.

It was a room as different from any in his mother's house as could be imagined. Its furnishing was not so much old as elderly. A large green carpet covered the floor; the walls were panelled in light-coloured wood; in the open hearth a small fire glowed. There were one or two large, rather sombre oil paintings, and a bearskin rug before the fire looked warm and inviting. Upon the high mantelpiece an old dull-faced clock tick-tocked. And on a low chair near by was curled a black cat, apparently fast asleep, but in reality engaged in surreptitious examination of the newcomer.

Leonard ignored Peter; but he smoothed his hair with both hands. He then rubbed his hands with his white handkerchief. In this lofty room he lost an inch or two of height; but he had grace, and looked well here as elsewhere because not one of his features was disproportionate or insignificant. The forehead was high and straight; the head was narrow; the mouth under that small dark moustache was expressive, thin-lipped, and indicative of determination. Like his sister, Leonard had grey eyes; but they were less widely opened than hers. They had a way of concentrating suddenly, piercingly; but whether they did in fact pierce to the truth, or whether this abrupt fixedness was merely a mannerism, only Leonard (if anybody) knew. The concentration was often effective with nervous persons, whom it considerably flustered.

It showed itself now. Leonard was listening intently. He stood in the centre of the room, his body bent forward, his head slightly upon one side. As the nervous rubbing of his hands had proved, he was not completely at ease in this house; but although at the moment he was rigid as a startled cat, he was (again catlike) ready at the slightest sound to relax and adjust himself to a new situation. Seen thus, he revealed himself as a very alert young man who thought quickly and did not easily lose his head. There was something in him still of that immaturity which never fails to charm us in the physically beautiful person.

No sound at all came from within the house. With a faint sigh Peter stretched his legs and drew them softly together again in a sleepy embrace. Leonard went to the window, looking idly out of it, but standing in such a way that he could instantly turn towards the door if anybody should enter. Was that a sound? He was smiling watchfully as the door opened again, and tall old Dr. Henty came in, breathing a little hard, and showing by his strained eyes that he was not unmoved by what had just happened.

"Well, Leonard, my boy . . . He's gone." He craned elaborately over his shoulder at the closed door and continued in his wheezy whisper: "I thought you should be here . . . in case he came to, and wanted you. But he went like a bird: never opened his eyes. Sorry to have brought you for nothing——"

"Quite all right, Doctor. Anything I can do?"

"No, no, no, no." Dr. Henty drew in his breath. "No." Then he sighed. "Well, I'll get along. I'll just see *her* again."

"I'll wait," said Leonard.

"Eh?" grunted the doctor.

"As I'm here."

Dr. Henty shrugged, grimacing. He was a big rosy-faced Irishman, like a picture of John Bull; and he was short of breath. You could hear him panting as he walked along the street upon warm days. After dinner, over port, like Sir Robert Walpole he "talked bawdy, so that all could join in"; but he had a soft, kind heart, and a medical skill which was never blunted or inept. He had been present at Leonard's birth, at Lettice's birth, and at the death of their father. But he was now too bluff for Mrs. Holpen, who shuddered at the mention of his name, and said, "That awful noisy man. He's like a draught and a crowd."

"I'll just go and see——" began Dr. Henty. Then opened the door. Before he could close it again behind him, he saw Ruth Coulevain descending the stairs from the room where Thomas Starling lay dead.

She was very pale, but very composed. Her head reached to just above the doctor's great shoulder, so that from a slight advantage in height he saw clearly the whiteness of her face and brow and the curious dead straightness of her fair hair. He observed with more than professional exactness the consequences of the strain which she had endured—the increased height of her cheek-bones, the enhanced size and darkness of her eyes. An inscrutable quiet face, he felt; the face of one who would suffer great pain without crying out. A good patient. And a good nurse.

"By Jove, you're a brave woman," he said, bluntly. "You've made a great fight for him. We're unlucky. Eh? You're feeling all right, are you? Not faint? That's good. We'll do all we can, you know. Now, here's a friend to see you and speak a word of sympathy; and then I'll take him away with me. Come here, and I'll show you."

He held her arm lightly above the elbow (but it was a stiff arm, and inflexible), and brought her into the room.

For an instant Ruth seemed hardly to see her visitor, as if she were still possibly a little dazed by what had happened, as if she walked in a dream, as if she were blind. Then, with the slightest air of constraint, she greeted him.

"Oh, yes," she said, slowly. "How kind of you. Won't you . . . both sit down?"

"No, my dear young lady. We're not staying to bother you——"

"Only to help," interjected Leonard. "If we can." He fixed his penetrating gaze upon her.

"You must have a rest," wheezed the doctor. "You need a good rest."

Ruth shook her head, replying to Leonard, ignoring the doctor.

"No," she said quietly.

The hand Leonard held was cold. It was lifeless. He was forced to relinquish it, and stood, as if discomfited, looking at Ruth.

"No, no," breathed Dr. Henty. "Nothing at all, nothing at all. You need nothing . . . except a good night's rest."

He drew Leonard by the arm, impatient to be gone. But Leonard quietly, almost desperately, resisted that firm hand.

"Shall I ask Lettice to come to you?"

A shaken head—unmistakably decided.

"Come, Leonard," wheezed the doctor.

They were gone. Ruth, hearing the sound of their footsteps and the closing of the front door, stared straight before her. In the large room, increasingly sombre as daylight faded, shadows spread about her. She became for that instant a child, forlorn, delicate, and shrinking. And

yet so still that her resoluteness could not be misread.
She was dressed in clothes that seemed black, and her
pallor gleamed like alabaster in the twilight.

Darkness fell. Peter stirred again. A slight rasping
noise in the fireplace caused Ruth to move thither, to
kneel before the fire, mechanically to replace a fallen coal;
and, once kneeling, she stayed there lost in reverie.

5

For an hour Leonard sat alone in his office upon the first
floor of that house in the High Street. The door of the
big green safe was opened. His desk bore a number of
papers, each one of which he laboriously scrutinized. All
were deeds, letters, and drafts in which the name of
Thomas Starling occurred. There were deeds relating to
the purchase of the Georgian house; there were letters
addressed to Leonard's father, and to Leonard himself;
there were drafts of several documents, including no
fewer than three wills. And it was upon these last that
Leonard pored.

In the first, Mr. Starling had designed to leave his
property to a nephew, Philip Spears; but some hieroglyphs
in old Mr. Holpen's hand recorded the date, ten years
distant, upon which this will, which was properly exe-
cuted, had been superseded by another. The second was
no more than a draft. It had never been signed. There
were gaps in it, and pencilled queries. Evidently drawn at
the time of the other's supersession, it had granted small
legacies to individuals (nothing to Philip Spears); but
after directing that his property should be realized, Mr.
Starling had planned to bequeath the capital sum to the
town of Sandersfold, "for the improvement of its amenities and the reduction of its burdens."

The old man's mind had evidently changed before the

new will had been completed. There had been some violent reason for the proposed cancellation of the first will—some anger, or quarrel, of which Leonard knew nothing. His mind registered its accustomed note: this second will was one of reaction. Having no other person in view, Mr. Starling had resolved to disappoint Philip Spears. Why? Leonard did not know. Who *was* Philip Spears? *Where* was he? He must find out these things. But from whom? Probably Burgess. He did not want to ask Burgess. Perhaps he would have to do so. That was always the difficulty with an old clerk—he knew too much. He showed that he knew his own power. It was a constant reminder to Leonard of his own youthfulness. Damn!

Whatever the angry impulse, the old man had never signed his second will. Again, why? Leonard recalled that obstinate face, clean-shaven, with the wide, swollen lips and prominent eyes beneath an almost hairless brow. Hideous old devil! Hideous, repulsive, magnetic. He had always found it hard to deal with Mr. Starling. So, perhaps, had others. Including his father? That father with the big black beard, and the secrets, the scent of cigars and wine . . . A bigger man than you'll ever be. That so? A bigger rogue . . . Honour thy father and thy mother—what hypocrisy, when one knew a little about them! Yes, and there were a few things to know about Laurence Holpen, thought his son. . . .

So much for the remote past. It was outside Leonard's personal experience. It could be guessed and rumoured; no more. His own attention had been seized about three months ago, when the old man had sent for him. They had discussed a new and decisive will. Ah! Those had been exciting days! Days when Leonard had masked a thousand secrets. Even to think of them made him stir and push papers restlessly about, and clench his fists and set his teeth.

From the rough notes under his hand the young solicitor knew that Mr. Starling had wished to leave everything
"to my dear friend Ruth Coulevain." But the draft of
this new will had never been approved. Had Leonard
been too speedy in its preparation? A sick man, obstinate
and resistant . . . In vain had Leonard, in the most
casual manner, reminded him that it needed signature.
In vain had he more clearly pressed for instructions.
"Later . . . later . . . Presently . . ." At last, in a
snarl, "Good God, I'm not going to die yet, man!"

He had tried a new method. He had stayed away from
the house. He had not been sent for. He had told Dr.
Henty about the will—that was the reason for the doctor's telephone message;—and there had been no result.
Why? With puckered brow Leonard turned over the
one completed will and the two drafts. At last he pushed
them aside and stood erect.

"Damn!" he cried. "Damned old swine! Just like him!
Just like him!" For an instant it seemed as if his anger
and impatience would carry him into unmeasured abuse;
but his face changed. He ceased to fume. Instead, his
shoulders raised, his hands half lifted as though he were
appealing to a judge, he exclaimed: "Yes; but what am
I to *do?*"

Some moments later he swept all the papers together
into their tin box, which he locked and lodged in his great
green safe. As if he flew from perplexity, he made his
way down the wooden stairs and out into the High Street,
which was now, at seven o'clock, silent for the night.
A few lamps gleamed; one or two girls loitered, exchang-
ing chaff with hatless country youths in plus fours and
scarves after the University style; but the town was muffled in solitude. Leonard's steps caused echoes to ring
as he strode along.

He passed the Lion, and looked across at the Georgian

house. It was in darkness. No light was visible anywhere. With an ejaculation he went onward, his pace erratic, his arms swinging. At last he reached the Crescent, and the house in which he lived with his mother and sister. And here he no longer troubled to hide the turbulence of his mood, but (believing himself to be unobserved) strode into the bare drawing room, sank into a chair, and struck his clenched fist into the open palm of the other hand.

"Damn!" he cried, full of spite, and showing his teeth. "Damn! Damn! Damn! The blasted crook!"

"Hello!" he heard, in Lettice's cool, artificially pitched voice of amusement with everything. "Naughty! Naughty! It sounds as if you were *quite* cross."

Unseen, she had been sitting in the shadow over by the window, and must have watched his arrival. Leonard started. For a moment he could not control himself.

"Cross, by Jove!" he muttered. "I'm mad!"

"Da-ahling!"

"Oh, shut up!" He jumped up and walked across the room.

"Who's the blasted crook, then?" She still watched. "Burgess? I always knew it!"

"Old Starling."

"What, is he better?"

"Eh? Oh, no, he's dead all right. And I hope he likes it."

"*What* a Christian! Yes, dear. Continue! What about Ruth?"

"Ruth? That's just what *I'm* wondering," growled Leonard.

"*I* see. D'you mean she's taking it badly?"

"What? Oh, she's splendid, of course. I hardly saw her. I don't know what *she* thinks."

"She want to see me?"

"No."

Lettice's brows were raised as her brother snarled the word at her.

"What did you mean, then?" Lettice came nearer and leant against the edge of a table, watching him. "Aren't you being a bit mysterious about Ruth, my poor dear?"

"Yes, I meant to be," muttered Leonard, with his head down. His hand was at the heel of his shoe—a mere gesture of impatience. He had recovered his temper. "I'm damned if I know where she stands."

"Or where *you* stand, perhaps? Does it matter?"

Leonard checked a quick retort. He fixed his eyes upon Lettice. The eyes contracted in his characteristic stare. She remained calm, staring back in cool inquiry.

"Yes, or where *I* stand," agreed Leonard. He pretended to ignore her. Then, in an altered tone of pretended lightness, he said: "But, as you say, it doesn't matter. Nothing matters much, in this blasted world. I'm going to have a whisky. How long's dinner?"

He sprang up. Lettice, smiling drily, watched him go out of the room and heard his impetuous steps upon the stairs. But she knew the impetuousness was assumed for the purpose either of deceiving or of intriguing herself, and was much perplexed.

CHAPTER TWO

PHILIP

EARLY one Wednesday morning, about a month later, the Strand (which is never quite deserted, even on Sundays) was awakening into general life. Great red omnibuses, crowded with office-goers, roared along to east and west; the pavements were hidden by the dark masses of pedestrians who came from Waterloo Bridge and Charing Cross. Horse-drawn carts, heavily laden with goods, dawdled; private cars were still able to whip about among the slower traffic, stampeding those who crossed the road, and avoiding the central islands with breath-taking skill. And the sun was already obscured by grimy clouds, which hung low over the river and threatened to swamp the city.

Two very young men, not yet out of their teens, bowler-hatted and neatly, but not at all fashionably, clothed were standing at the shuttered doorway of a bookseller's shop on the north side of the Strand, between Southampton Street and Bedford Street. They were not eager customers, waiting to buy modern masterpieces, but booksellers' assistants who had arrived too punctually. Near them stood three other men, rougher as to clothing, chatting quietly, but ignoring the two who were by the door. Both these young men were looking attentively and anxiously aloft at the brimming grey clouds.

"Bet it rains," one of them was dejectedly saying.

"It would," agreed the other. "Just 'cause Sussex are at the Oval."

It was the week before Whitsun; and in the week

before Whitsun Sussex always play Surrey at cricket upon that miracle of greensward in the heart of London known as the Oval. It was unlikely that either Jenkins or Maddox would ever see this match, unless he chanced to be out of a situation; but both took profound interest in it, and both knew the names and cricketing histories of all the players engaged. They would follow the score daily. They would feel jovial or wretched, according to the progress of the game. And this although they had never seen Sussex in the field (a sight for the gods), and had seen Surrey, the home county, perhaps only three or four times in their lives, when both were schoolboys.

"Jack Hobbs won't get a century," remarked Jenkins. "Not against Sussex."

"Why not?" demanded Maddox, hotly. "He might."

"Bet you!" exclaimed Jenkins. "He never does. He can't!"

But he said that because he did not want Hobbs to get a century against Sussex (the county which Jenkins, whose parents were Welsh, had adopted), and not because he really believed Hobbs incapable of getting a century against any team in the world.

"Bet you!" cried Maddox. "Hullo, here's old misery." He was still boiling a little at the insult to Hobbs, but was slightly intimidated by the knowledge that many celebrated batsmen left early when Sussex were in form.

They saw approaching them a man who was taller and a good deal older than themselves. He was rather shabbily dressed, but with care. His collar was white, his plain blue tie unsoiled, his soft felt hat well-brushed. He was probably about thirty-five years of age, thin and brown-faced, very bright eyes. But the eyes, if clear, were melancholy; and his lips were pressed close together, as if at some time he had repressed a cry of pain so despairing as to call for bitter self-control. He carried himself without address, but was neither weedy nor furtive; and although he smiled in greeting the two boys and the packers, his coming did not enliven the waiting party.

Nobody spoke for a moment or two. All looked up and down the Strand rather constrainedly, or else at the lowering clouds. And whenever Maddox looked up he sighed, at the vision of a drenched pitch, derelict stumps, deserted benches, and a wasted game. He shivered.

Presently the boys exchanged what was less a glance than a common exclamatory jerking of the head in face of unnatural silence.

"Going away for Whitsun, Mr. Brown?" asked Jenkins, the readier of the two.

Mr. Brown looked drily at his questioner, shaking his head.

"No," he answered, with composure.

"Oh, *I* am," continued Jenkins, with false brightness. "Motor coach. I'm going home. Get there Saturday night, start back Monday afternoon. Down to Plymouth."

"Plymouth," murmured Mr. Brown, to show that he had heard.

"Ever been there?" Jenkins was red-headed, quick, and daring. His blue eyes were as sharp as knives. He was the cleverer of the boys, and the more promising; but Maddox, less quick, had the better head, and a tenacious memory for titles, authors, and publishers.

"No," answered Mr. Brown. "Never."

You might have heard the two boys groaning with exasperation. How could one converse with a man who had so leaden a tongue? But Jenkins persisted.

"Ought to go, you know. Fine place. Sir Francis Drake; and ships—my God, I've never seen so many ships. Ever seen ships like that, Mr. Brown?"

Mr. Brown smiled. Both boys felt a quickened interest when he smiled. He seemed to come alive.

"Yes, I've seen quite a lot of them. At Liverpool and Bristol. Both good ports."

"Any more?" demanded Maddox. "Southampton?"

Mr. Brown smiled more deeply.

"Yes, and Amsterdam and Toulon," he said, teasingly.

"Goo' lord," murmured Jenkins, impressed. "Been abroad, then, Mr. Brown . . ."

Again that smile. Not helpful, but pleasant. The man was as cold as a fish! thought Jenkins. And as stubborn as a horse that won't go.

"Yes," admitted Mr. Brown. "I've been abroad."

"Far? America?" They were both quite excited, awaiting his answer.

"Yes. America," he agreed. "And here's Mr. Dexter," he added, briskly, as if (for all his smile) he were relieved to escape further questioning.

They all turned to greet Mr. Dexter, who was striding like a giant parson through the crowds; and a moment later were inside the shop.

Here, tier upon tier, laden with unsold new books, ghostly in the darkness, shelves rose from floor to ceiling until they were swallowed in vague shadows. A fearsome monument to the perverse industry of mankind, to the optimism of publishers, the facile ecstasy of critics, the incredulity of the public. The waiters separated. For all, the day had begun, on the Wednesday before Whitsun.

2

It was not until half an hour later that Mr. Brown, who was checking some books ordered by a customer in Burma, heard his name called by Jenkins.

"Mr. Brown! Mr. Dexter, please."

Thoughtfully, Mr. Brown made his way to the small glass-windowed cage which Mr. Dexter used as his private

office. He found his employer seated at a desk, still surrounded by correspondence.

"Oh, yes, Philip . . . I wanted . . ." Mr. Dexter
thrust two unopened letters and a torn covering envelope
into Mr. Brown's hand. He did not look up. "These are
for you."

The lean cheeks of Mr. Brown glowed. He took the
letters; did not examine them; waited coolly.

"That's all," snapped Mr. Dexter. He kept his eyes
down, as if he were busy; but when Mr. Brown had
turned to leave, he was subjected to a scrutiny that was
long and patient. He knew nothing of it.

One of the letters Mr. Brown put straight into his
breast pocket as soon as he reached the bench at which
he had been working. The second he examined curiously,
turning it over two or three times before laying it along
with its companion. The covering envelope, which was
addressed personally to Mr. Dexter, and, in rough capitals
such as an ignorant person might use, was marked
PRIVATE, he tore into small pieces and threw into a waste-
paper basket near at hand. The melancholy of his expression deepened. He slowly and lifelessly resumed the
task upon which he had been engaged.

Mr. Brown had been in the shop longer than either of
the two boys. He knew where every book was to be
found. He knew titles and authors unfamiliar to both
boys, quick and intelligent though they were. And although, between themselves, they called Mr. Dexter "Old
Coughdrop" and "Dearly Beloved Brethren," or, more
simply, "Dex," and Mr. Brown "Old Misery," "Dismal
Jimmy," and "Dick Deadeye," they respected both of
their seniors. The young lady cashier, Amy Sparkle, they
called "Sister," but Sister had no eyes for young boys, as
she had rather obviously hinted.

"You know why, don't you?" Jenkins had whispered

to Maddox. "No, I mean—because she's grown out of
them. My dear sir, the woman's fifty——"

"Rot!" Maddox had been incredulous.

"Well, thirty, then."

Who could tell? Sister was overwhelmingly ladylike,
fair, with frizzy hair and globular, gooseberry-like bluish
grey eyes, and a height of five feet eight inches. She did
not make up, spent large sections of her days on manicure,
spoke filleted English, and cocked an approving eye upon
Mr. Brown. She tried persistently to engage him in conversation. And her age was quite certainly less than the
lower of Jenkins's estimates.

Mr. Brown was never impolite to Miss Sparkle. On
the contrary, his manner was everything that could be
wished, except flirtatious. "He's what *you'll* never be,"
Sister had once said reprovingly to an impertinent Jenkins. "A gentleman." "God help him!" Jenkins had
ribaldly rejoined. "What a waxwork!" He had not meant
this. "No, but seriously, Miss Sparkle, don't you think
he's a bit queer in the napper? I mean, when he looks
at you——"

"Ooh! When he looks at you, it goes all through you!"
sighed Sister.

"*Goo* on!" encouraged Jenkins.

"Lovely!" she added.

"Like that, eh? Well, look here, Miss Sparkle, why
don't you marry him? Make a man of him! There's your
job in life."

There had been no answer but an expressive look; but
Sister had ideas upon the subject of matrimony which
she never mentioned to a soul. Or rather, she *had* had
ideas. They were slipping nowadays into ideals. Soon they
would be dreams. And at last fantasy.

Mr. Brown went out to his lunch at two o'clock, when
the lunch-hour business was over, and before the two-

hours-for-lunch customers arrived. He walked through some of the streets behind the Strand to an obscure corner where, at this hour, a Tarratonga Tea Company's depot was almost empty. Here, with a book propped against the sugar bowl, it was his habit to eat frugally. But today he had something else to read. There were two letters.

The familiar one he read first. It was a scrawl. Impossible to guess at the writer's age in years; although not impossible to guess at her character.

Dear Flup [it said]. You are a mean thing not to write me. When you going to write. I guessed youd surely write this week, but you haven't. Mr. Parker came over yesterday in his new Packard, and took me a drive. It was swell. He never said he was coming. Just the same as ever. Oh well if you wont write you wont but its time you did, and I expect it would be all the same if I was sick. I can't say more now I'm busy. Love. Phoebe xxx. Write!!!

The other, in an unknown hand, bore a postmark which had been so nearly obliterated that he could not decipher it. The letter, upon stiff paper, was of a surprising nature. It ran:

Dear Sir. We regret to inform you that Mr. Thomas Starling died a week ago, on April 10th, and according to a will in our possession he bequeathed his entire estate to yourself. This estate is considerable, and we shall be glad if you will get into touch with us as soon as possible after receipt of this letter. We are sending it to an address found among Mr. Starling's papers, and trust it will reach you safely and without delay. We are, yours faithfully, HOLPEN AND GRANT, Leonard Holpen.

The letter had been forwarded from Cleveland, Ohio, and was addressed to Philip Spears, Esqre.

A deep flush overspread the face of Mr. Brown. He looked stupidly at the letter before him, seeing the words in a blur. The hand which held the letter shook slightly. Presently, as if he were resolved to dream no longer, he folded the two sheets and replaced them in their respective envelopes, which he then restored to his breast pocket. From his demeanour it would have been impossible to guess that in two minutes his fortune had entirely changed.

3

Now there were long stretches of green. Philip could see the soft shapes of distant elms. The sunlight was glancing upon water. In a garden two girls in white frocks ran about like marionettes in pursuit of an invisible tennis ball. In fleeting glances he made himself acquainted with his fellow passengers, four elderly ladies who (succumbing to that fatal allure of the smoking carriage for smoke-hating elderly ladies) were glaring and wrinkling their noses at a little old man whose pipe was as nearly foul as it could be. The little old man had no teeth, so that he was forced to hold his pipe all the time between grimy fingers; and when he inhaled, his yellow cheeks sank in like pockets. His nose was red. A youth, bareheaded and flannel-bagged, sprawled across the carriage. When the elderly ladies had done looking scathingly at the smoker, they looked with loathing at the unmannerly youth. Backwards and forwards went their eyes, as charged with voluptuous hatred as those of characters in a novel by Lawrence.

Now, for a time, the landscape was wholly green. At one point stumps were pitched in the middle of a large shaven meadow, a flag drooped from its pole above a rustic pavilion. Philip caught a glimpse of white-flannelled figures. That was past. In this lovely corner of England everything was richly and delicately verdure-clad, from the soft curves of the rising ground to the innumerable winding rows of trees that hid slowly running streamlets. Aloft the sky was cloudless, a deep and glowing blue. Philip could imagine the skylark mounting thither, lustily singing above the chorus from all the birds hidden in those old trees. Once, when the train was halted, panting, at a small wayside station, he really could hear that shower of song. Unguarded, his lips parted. He was now all eagerness, a poet amid the earthly malcontents with whom he rode.

Half an hour later, as the train paused again in Sandersfold station, he again heard the lark. This time he could see, against the sparkle of sunlight, the hovering speck that was filling the air with sound. Half dazzled from looking upward, he could not at once find his way; for he had never before visited the town. Even when he could again see, the sun-drenched station yard, which was quite ugly, seemed to him to be romantically beautiful. So it remained forever in his memory. He sauntered forth along the white road towards the centre of the town, taking the right-hand fork which led him to Cross Street, and at last to that end of the High Street which lies beyond the church. The strange enchanting scent of the place filled his nostrils. His heart was like water.

It was not until Philip had passed the church that he saw the High Street of Sandersfold. When he did so, he stood looking down towards the Lion and the Georgian house with great attentiveness; for upon this day, when the High Street was gay with cars, when the sunlight warmed the old brick and painted plaster of elderly buildings to a ruddier glow, and when flags and sun blinds added vivacity to the scene, the town was like an exile's memory of England.

He found himself unexpectedly at the foot of a steep

flight of very dark stairs. The stairs, oaken and uncarpeted, were worn deep by the tread of innumerable feet; the handrail was broad and low, as if it had been made for a generation of short men. A moment later he had passed a solid door and was confronting an elderly man with a curiously reddish yellow withered face. The man stared at him from light, rather evasive eyes, and raised a forefinger, as if to say, "Remind me of your name, sir. I'll get it in a moment——" There was a silence.

You could tell that Burgess was very old and that his teeth and hair were not his own. How old was he? Fabulously old and decayed. His coat was rusty; his manner furtively ceremonious. He was like a man who had died and been restored to life with death still claiming him. In those pale eyes and the wrinkles about them could be read an acquaintance with many secrets, all stale, all melancholy. The forefinger slowly beckoned. Philip shrank slightly.

Then, following that finger, he entered the front office which looked down upon the busy street. It was grey, old, and shabby, but less cavernous than the room he had left. For the first time he saw the young solicitor, Leonard Holpen.

4

He realized at once that the chair in which he sat was upon a lower level than Leonard's and that he was made to face the light. It might have been thus in the time of Leonard's father, and he remained grave. But while he knew that he was being examined, he was quite free to return that examination, because Leonard was avoiding formality. Indeed Philip was immediately interested in the younger man's easy manner, which took the shape of a pleasant lightness. It did not captivate him; but it kept the conversation agreeable.

This young man was hardly taller than himself, a little sleek. His hands were white, and a ring was upon one finger (Philip's hands were ringless). His collar was stiff and spruce. A small dark moustache emphasized the excellent line of his upper lip. His eyes were quick. Philip decided that he was intelligent, fairly straight, but of a peculiarly nervous temperament. In comparison Philip appeared phlegmatic. He was only more reserved.

"Well, Mr. Spears," Leonard began. He pushed a box of cigarettes across the desk and watched Philip's lean brown hand as it took a cigarette at random. The hand was steady. Leonard thought: "Hm. An oyster." He was already, therefore, at a disadvantage. The moves would all have to come from himself. "But pleasant enough, pleasant enough . . ." He smiled; he was cordial; cordiality spread about him like a perfume. "I expect you'd like me to give you a rough notion of what we've got to deal with. You knew Mr. Starling, I think?"

He seemed—like an English radio announcer—to introduce a subtle unctuous murmur between each sentence— "m-m"—as if to emphasize the genteel casualness of his utterance. Really to impress the listener, but with what object he did not precisely know.

"You *had* met him?" he continued, cocking his trim head and smiling.

"Long ago," said Philip. "Yes, I knew him." He was quizzically puzzled at such a question.

"Oh, really. Of course, he *changed* a good deal. . . . Well, I must explain to you that the will we're acting on was made a good many years ago. Twenty, as a matter of fact. Everything's left to you. It's quite clear. Your mother was Mr. Starling's sister, wasn't she?"

A sudden quick light came into Leonard's eyes. They grew very intense. He fixed them directly upon Philip.

"Yes." Philip did not stir under that gaze. His hands,

lightly clasped as he sat back in the leather armchair, were still. Smoke drifted from the end of his cigarette. There was a pause. Leonard seemed a little disappointed.

"Ah, well. . . . She's dead, isn't she? Fourteen years? *I* see." Leonard sat back in turn. He was silent, turning over in his mind the next approach he was to make. The corners of his mouth were drawn down. "So you're really the nearest relative. I mean, if there had been *no* will. . . . It's not important, but it simplifies. Yes, it simplifies. Now, as you probably remember, Mr. Starling lived here in Sandersfold for a good many years. He lived in the same house. And he died there, as you've been told. . . . Everything's perfectly in order. I've been through all the papers. His house, and a considerable sum of money—all quite straightforward. I've been in touch with his brokers. Apparently the estate consists of about sixty thousand pounds in investments, most of them gilt-edged. There's some minor property. And the house, of course. Call it seventy-five thousand all told. There'll be death duties, and so on. Horribly heavy, as I expect you know. What they think they're doing—— I mean, it may be ten thousand pounds. Frightful, isn't it! But I expect you'd like to examine the papers at your leisure. I've got copies here, ready for you; and anything I can do——"

Leonard smiled. It was still an agreeable smile, not conceited, but complacent, showing practice. It exposed his teeth, which were perfect; and it warmed his eyes, which were grey and clear under firm black eyebrows. Philip noticed for the first time a little ironic nick at the corner of one of those brows. He, too, smiled faintly. It is not difficult to like one who brings good tidings.

"Are there any complications?" Philip asked. "Any conditions, or—I should say, are there legacies . . . even implied?"

At the word "complications," Leonard's brows had lifted amusedly. And as Philip slowly completed his inquiry a smile deepened. He shook his head.

"No, no. It's all yours," he pleasantly said. "At least——"

"Yes?" prompted Philip. For Leonard's teeth were showing again, not in a real smile, but in some embarrassment. He waited.

"There's no complications," insisted Leonard. "Nothing that concerns you at all. May I be quite frank? Your uncle took into his house—— Of course, you realize one doesn't want to be misunderstood—— Your uncle took into his house a young woman—perhaps his mistress, perhaps a housekeeper . . ." He lifted his shoulders. "What can one say?"

"She's still there?" asked Philip.

"You know something about it, perhaps?"

"Nothing."

"She's still there. In fact I persuaded her to stay there. You have no responsibility at all to her. But she was dependent on your uncle; she runs the place admirably; and in fact she hadn't anywhere else to go."

"What age?" asked Philip.

The elaborate nonchalance of his companion was heightened. He again saw the white teeth and the nick by the black brow. For the first time Leonard made a single laughing sound—it was not a laugh.

"My dear Mr. Spears!" he exclaimed. "I'm a bachelor!"

"You prefer not to speculate," commented Philip, drily. "Do you think my uncle intended to leave something to her?"

"He hasn't done so, at any rate."

Philip saw a curious expression pass across the face of the young solicitor. Nonchalance had gone; laughter had gone. The expression might have hinted a cruelty in his nature.

"She's still there," observed Philip. "I shall see her, shan't I!"

Leonard looked fixedly at him. The glance was speculative, almost admiring. It was as if he had become conscious of Philip's power of determination. This glance held something different from the easy affability at which Leonard had aimed in greeting his new and extremely fortunate client. It implied the interest of man in man.

"Yes, you'll see her," he agreed, in an altered voice. "Oh, decidedly."

"Now?" asked Philip.

"Shall we go? We shall be expected. Now, is there anything more you'd like me to explain? There are the papers—copies, for the moment." He touched a large envelope which lay upon the desk. "The originals are in my safe. I shall have to see you again to go into details; but that will do when you've made your examination. I've got all the title deeds; and the brokers have got all the stock receipts and things. The whole business is thoroughly plain and straightforward—thoroughly healthy, I should call it."

He smiled again, and Philip rose. Philip did not say anything further; and, after waiting an instant for some response, Leonard turned to get his hat, which was hanging upon a peg behind him. Philip, observing the dingy, low-ceilinged room, with its large green safe and two rows of black tin boxes, realized that one could, quite unperceived, watch from the window all that passed for some distance along the pavement on the opposite side of the High Street. Thoughtfully he began to survey a little of that brightness; and when he again turned to the room it was to find himself looking straight into smiling eyes that were almost precisely upon a level with his own.

5

As they entered the Georgian house, Philip felt as if he had come home. Whereas most houses resemble one another, and are made different only by their occupants, this one had a character—a lofty warmth, a dignity, a beauty—of its own. You stepped into it and were enwrapped in its cordial embrace, as if you had known it for all your life. Instinctively Philip stretched out his hand and touched one of the walls, as if he caressed an old and well-loved possession. A little sound escaped his lips, that was neither a sigh nor a grunt, but an inarticulate greeting. Before him was a wide staircase, finely lighted by a large window upon a landing from which the staircase appeared to divide. This window instantly created an air of spaciousness. One looked up, one breathed; one glanced beyond the staircase along a passage to a plain door, painted in cream. And above this door was a fanlight similar to the fanlight over the front door. To right and left of the visitors were rooms; and as Leonard motioned him to enter that to the right hand, Philip was conscious of a sunlit quietness that had long been absent from his life. He stopped dead as he entered the room, and stood there, unconsciously framed in the doorway.

Ruth was standing by the fire, her face towards him, fair and pale, but with her head high. She saw a tall man with a brown, thin, clean-shaven face; a man who looked quietly but unsmilingly at her. Then, before he stepped forward, she saw him look past her, at the fire, and at the cat Peter, who washed a paw, sitting upon the hearthrug. She saw the sunlight fall upon his face, warming it; while Philip, perhaps a little confused or puzzled, advanced slowly, his hand offered.

"How d'you do," he said. A very cold voice, almost

expressionless. A cool hand. Nothing more to remember.

"D'you do," echoed Ruth, in a whisper. It sounded hoarse. She did not move.

"Mr. Spears thought he would like to come and see the house at once," announced Leonard, easily. "As we supposed he would, of course. Mr. Spears, this is Miss Coulevain, who for so long acted as housekeeper to Mr. Starling——"

Now Philip's thoughtful eyes had returned to Ruth, and he was noticing her appearance. She was very erect, rather tall, very white. She had very straight fair hair, which she wore shingled. Her age might have been thirty or more, possibly less. No, he thought, quite thirty. Her eyes, which he had expected to find blue, were a light, clear brown. Her nose was short and blunt; and her lips thin. What passed in her mind was unguessable, for she had a calm that seemed to him almost frigid. They were two cold people—on the surface. He had the impression of somebody who was by nature silent (and therefore enigmatic). Whether the silence was a concealment, he could not determine. And so these two silent people examined each other, while Leonard, half smiling as if in enjoyment of a discomfiture, looked on. As for Peter the cat, he ceased washing and began interestedly to be aware that there was a stranger present.

Peter's curiosity overmastered his excessive vanity. It became necessary for him to investigate. As though he said, "Who on earth is this? Where did they find him? Rather interesting," he rose languidly and strolled over to Philip—a large black cat with a fine tail and, ordinarily, much contempt for dog and man. This stranger attracted him. He sniffed at his shoes, at the knee of his trouser, at the hand which Philip extended. Apparently satisfied, he pressed his shoulder against Philip's leg, waving his

tail. At this Leonard laughed, and Peter, resentful of
ridicule, turned his head away from Leonard in aversion
while Philip stroked his beautiful fur.

"Shall we go?" asked Leonard.

They passed from this large room to another one,
across the wide hall, where the furniture was formal and
elderly, but not old. It was obviously a dining room in
which, at need, a large party could be entertained; and
there was a coldness here that contrasted with the inviting
comfort they had just left. But it was a fine room, for all
that, and shone with a kind of portly richness.

"In the old days, Mr. Starling entertained a lot," Leonard said.

"Not latterly?" asked Philip.

"No." There was a pause. Ruth added:

"He was ill a long time."

"But before that——" Leonard began. He stopped.

"I haven't used this room at all," said Ruth. "It's so
large and solemn. It's better in the winter."

Philip, about to respond, noticed that Peter was with
them, as if he, too, were resolved to tour the house. What
a dignified cat! He sat between Philip and his mistress,
the long tail, like a black ostrich feather, extended straight
behind him, his golden eyes steadily gazing around. Philip
again stooped to caress that noble head, unconscious of
an exchange of looks between Ruth and Leonard.

"Now we'll look at the library," suggested Leonard.
"The room behind this. It opens on the garden, d'you
see . . ."

He led the way, showing a masterful acquaintance with
the house. At times, it seemed to Philip, he behaved as
if he wished to ignore or to repress their companion. Was
there a reason? Clearly; but *what* reason? If the house
had been hers, would not his manner have been different?
That also was an indication of character, not to be under-

valued. Philip began to go deeper into the mind of this debonair fellow. There was more to be understood. Well?

When at last they entered the third room and saw the garden beyond, he could not restrain a murmur of pleasure. The sunshine and a light breeze caused every leaf to shimmer and glitter brilliantly; while a great lawn, old and marvellously smooth, stretched away from rose beds in which the first blooms were even now beginning to scent the air. It was a lovely sight. As the French windows stood wide open, Philip went straight towards them, and at last stood amazedly with the garden before him.

He did not know how long he had been there when he turned; but when at last he was recalled to knowledge of his companions, he saw Leonard coolly smiling, and Ruth with her cheeks deeply flushed. Not cold, then! Not quite the person of that first greeting. What had happened? They were disregarding himself. Whatever had provoked the smile and the flush concerned themselves alone.

"May we go into the garden?" Philip asked, addressing, not Leonard, but Ruth.

Without speaking, she went forward and down the single step towards the lawn. It was as Philip had wished. He stepped up to Leonard.

"I should like to have a talk with Miss Coulevain before I go," he said.

"Oh, yes." He was aware of a fixed interrogative scrutiny. Another change. An unfriendliness, the public schoolboy's attitude to one not of his own sort. "Oh, yes," answered Leonard. "Why not immediately?"

"I should like that. But first of all a question for *you*. What, exactly, is her position here?"

The watchful eyes moved quickly. Philip was so close to him that he could see the slightest change of expression. There was a hardening in the depths. But Leonard was adroit. He said, almost as if he had not hesitated:

"That's for you to decide. At present she's staying because I asked her to. It seemed better that the place——"

"Yes." Philip's tone was not at all impatient. "I should have said 'what *was* her position?'"

"She was Mr. Starling's housekeeper," replied Leonard.

"A little while ago weren't you rather more ambiguous?"

"Was I? I ought not to have been. He was an invalid."

"For two years?"

"I know nothing at all about their relations."

Philip did not answer. He was thinking. At last:

"I don't know. Ask her." The smile returned to Leonard's face. It was not friendly, decided Philip. It held malice, a kind of cruelty. There was more there than he understood. He must discover the truth.

"I *will* ask her," he promised. And smiled in his turn. He could see from the slight upward jerk of that sleek head that Leonard was in some doubt as to the personality of his new client. But he did not try either to explain himself or still further to baffle the young solicitor. They parted with mutual caution. Leonard ran after Ruth, spoke a few words to her, and returned.

"When can I see you again?" he asked. "Are you proposing to stay here?"

"No, I'm going back to London. I'll come down again on Tuesday. Shall we say Tuesday?"

"Splendid. I'll expect you."

They shook hands, half in liking, and with warmth, half with suspicion and dissatisfaction. A moment later Leonard was gone, and Philip slowly followed Ruth into the garden, where she stood, hatless, looking up, the sun upon her cheeks.

CHAPTER THREE

THE VIRGIN HEART

EXACTLY parallel with the High Street of Sandersfold is Hillington Avenue, where the houses are of solid red brick and the residents of solid respectability. Hillington Avenue is not quite as "classical" (to use a word now popular in England) as the Crescent; but it has every other thoroughfare in the town ignominiously beaten. It is very trimly kept. Its north, and inferior, side is broken by three turnings which lead to open land; the south side is a single long row of large houses. But each house is detached from its fellows; each has a name instead of a number; and each has fully half an acre of ground about it. Indeed the long gardens at the back of these houses quite hem in the shorter gardens of shopkeepers on the north side of the High Street.

At the Hawthorns, a big house lying towards the centre of Hillington Avenue, live the Davitts. Mr. Davitt is a deaf and quarrelsome man of sixty-five, very hale and bristling, who tramps about Sandersfold with a thick stick and a red face, so frightening any vagrants he meets that they incontinently take to the fields. When they do this, Mr. Davitt stands watching them, and gripping his stick, his Adam's apple working, while he utters internal rumblings similar to the growls of a dog. He then tramps on, glaring at cows and sheep in the meadows as if they were trespassers in his garden. When he is at home, Mr. Davitt (who is a retired builder and contractor from

London) busies himself with a stamp album and a card game which as he plays it is misnamed Patience.

His wife, Mrs. Davitt, is not quarrelsome. She is lugubrious. Having abandoned everything else in life, she has embraced old age before that was necessary. She cannot be more than fifty-five but behaves as if she were eighty, sitting much by the fire, knitting, peeping over her spectacles, shivering in spite of shawls and plumpness, and pretending to be as deaf as her husband. If her daughters did not tease her, she would be full of resigned melancholy, and would probably live to be a hundred. As it is, she is decidedly fretful, and feels that she might go at any minute.

The daughters are Rose, Susan, and Rachel. All bright girls of marriageable age, who chatter from morning to night about what they have seen, done, heard, and read in the newspapers. They are all completely devoted to one object—the well-being of their brother Henry. He is the apple of every female eye at the Hawthorns. He is seven-and-twenty, is very slim and fair, has a golden curl, slightly pouting lips, and a manner which shows him to be quite used to feminine admiration. He plays games well, can score against mediocre bowling in summer and mediocre goal-keeping in winter, and sings tenor in the choir and at socials. He has hardly any vices. He drinks abstemiously, smokes in moderation, is strictly chaste, and tries to tell the truth without making enemies of all about him. And he has literary ambitions. In his desk upstairs are poems, little notes, and the beginnings of two or three novels. Only his father finds any fault with Henry, who works dutifully in a large bank at Seahampton, on the coast. And what Mr. Davitt says can be ignored, since it is always so highly peppered as to be unacceptable. His words are:

"By God, he's the worst girl of the lot!"

It is to escape his family that Mr. Davitt tramps the
district. And as he tramps the district in season and out
of season, he knows more about it than any other man.
He notices a great deal. He is dangerous to every secret
meeting, every premeditated theft of wood, every piece of
public sharp practice. Although he is not on the Town
Council he can make his presence felt; and as his voice
(which he likes to hear) is a loud one, the things he ob-
serves have a way of becoming inconveniently known. It
is as though he were the Conscience of Sandersfold. One
cannot imagine him asleep.

But in spite of an expressed contempt for girls, James
Davitt loves his daughters. He loves them so much that
he has forced his protectiveness upon them. They remain
semi-domestic. Trooping about as a sort of indivisible
trinity, they invariably troop home again. Very shrewd
observers shake their heads over Rose, Susan, and Rachel.
Miss Furze, the old deaf lady who lives in Grange Road
(one step down from Hillington Avenue in the size and
class of its houses), shakes her head. She does not say
anything. She is too wise to say anything. Very old ladies
who talk much are ga-ga; but the knowledges, human
and divine, which virtuous old ladies carry hidden behind
their wrinkled ivory-coloured foreheads, and under their
antediluvian lace caps, would astonish outspoken members
of the passing generation. Had Miss Furze's thoughts
been revealed to her friends, the effect would have been
sensational.

2

Old ladies fall into a way of imagining the lives of
others. Miss Furze, who could not walk far without growing tired, spent many hours of her day alone. She had
opportunities for remembering all that had been said to
her, and piecing it together, not unkindly or maliciously,

but with the realism that accompanies detachment from self-interest. Although still alive, she was nothing but an observer. A recording angel. Her acquaintance was fairly large; the number of her intimates was small; through one or another she learned most of what happened in Sandersfold.

Upon this afternoon, when everything was quiet and sunny and lovely, she was sitting in her front window (it was wide open) drowsing in the warm shadow. The road was quite broad, and she could see some distance along it—past all the discreet windows and the small front gardens, to where a doctor's car stood before the door of No. 47. Miss Furze was anxious. In No. 47 lived an old and dear friend, now very ill. The sight of that car took Miss Furze back nearly sixty years. She sat very still, recalling the past, hearing old sounds and speeches in her head, smelling half-forgotten scents, her heart expanding with emotion, the lids of her eyes like little sunblinds sinking until one could imagine that she had fallen asleep.

It was not so. Miss Furze was wide awake. But when one thinks of secrets one hides one's thoughts; and old memories, even when they are painful, have a sweetness that cannot be shared, on a day in early summer, with one's neighbours. Birds twittered, leaves stirred; Miss Furze sat there unconscious of them. She could not hear their message. She could only watch that motionless car outside No. 47, and wonder.

And just then she caught sight of three figures, side by side, who passed the house of sickness, looking up at it with curiosity, turning to each other as if to comment upon the car and the quiet windows. Miss Furze leant slightly forward, her hand raised from her knee, upon which it had rested. Her cap gleamed; the white shawl about her shoulders glistened with the movement. A smile turned the corners of her lips. For at that moment Dr.

Bartholomew, a new smart young practitioner who had
begun to establish himself in place of old Dr. Dawes,
lately retired, came out of No. 47.

The three girls stopped. Miss Furze could see their
faces turned directly to the doctor. Three flower faces.
No coquetry—or very little. Only concern, eagerness to
learn good news. She smiled again. Her eyes softened.
The girls would come presently and tell her what the
doctor had said. What was he saying? She tried to
imagine it. She tried to imagine what he was *thinking*.
For of course he was not saying what he thought. Nobody did that.

In vain. Sighing, she could read nothing. He was talking to the girls—not to one of them, but to all—looking
quickly and noncommittally from one to the other. She
imagined his tone. "Yes, very poorly," he was saying (she
pretended). "Oh, we haven't given up hope yet. Of
course, he is old . . ." Yes, that was true. To a young
doctor one old person, one old patient, was very much like
another—a survival, to be aided, eased; but having so
little life still in him that it is almost of a corpse that one
thinks. And this was a young doctor. Young people have
no memories. All the associations of a lifetime mean
nothing to their raw young minds, so actively creating a
past for themselves.

This doctor looked at all the girls in turn, and did not,
could not, feel for one of them any emotion other than
pleasant courtesy. A man, and they were three girls:
nothing else. His love, his passion for some other woman,
was hidden, was masked. Or he was cold. There was no
distance in his manner. It was easy, friendly, but quite
impersonal. He was dark and quiet—not her own doctor,
who was Dr. Henty—but she knew he had a very sober
way of looking at one while speaking or listening. He
raised his hat; he stepped into his car; he drove off to his

next patient. The three girls continued their walk, not looking back at the doctor, not glancing at each other with any quickness, calm and cheerful, but apparently expectant of nothing but the daily round. Were ever girls as unromantic as these appeared? The smile faded from Miss Furze's lips. She looked critically at the three. A moment later they were in the room.

All, like their brother, were fair. They dressed very much alike. All were in plain costumes of dark blue, or dark green, with plain hats that still had small brims to shield the eyes. They were not tall—indeed one, Susan, was rather short—but they were all slim and boyish in figure. A stranger might have said: "Let me see, which are you? Susan or Rose?" and might have received the answer: "I'm Rachel." But owing to the habit which they had of talking nonsense, this reply might be untrue, and made for the purpose of teasing. The only person they did not tease was Henry. His vanity was sacred to them all.

Miss Furze did not kiss the girls, or suffer them to kiss her. She sat upright in her chair. Being more alert, she seemed thinner and older; the soft play of expression upon her face, which had filled it with life, became a keenness. She did not ask to be told of what the doctor had said. It was Rose who came forward and gave the news.

"Alicia. Mr. Hawke is very ill. Did you know? We saw the doctor just now. He's got a temperature. The doctor seemed quite hopeful——"

"It's his business to be hopeful," said Miss Furze, looking into the pretty round face that was so near her own. "Tom Hawke's an old man."

"The doctor says there's no *immediate* danger."

He says . . . he says . . . thought Miss Furze. But he *knows*. She took Rose's fingers in her hand and pressed them. In her low voice she said: "I've been watching his car. I saw you meet him. I knew you'd come in. Good girl. He's dying. How's your mother?"

"O-oh!" cried Susan, the short sister, in a disgusted tone. "She's sitting by the fire, reading *Queechy*. My dear! Imagine! *Queechy!*"

The others laughed a little at the memory of their mother.

"And Henry's been transferred to another branch!" burst out Rachel. "He's going to leave home. It's a better job. Near London."

"Near *London!*" almost shouted Susan. "Just think of it!"

"Not awfully near," corrected Rose, who, being the youngest of the sisters, was guardian to the others.

"No, but near enough," Susan retorted. "I'm going to offer to keep house for him. Only he's got no money, poor boy."

"You could do nothing better," said Miss Furze, with firmness. "Ask your father——"

"Hooo! Ask *Father!*" exclaimed Susan. There was some more laughter. "Father's awful. Really he is. He stamps and shouts as if he was a currified old Colonel."

"Worse—a General!" stormed Rachel. "No, I mean a Major. If you're a General you've cooled down."

"The truth is, he's got nothing to worry about," said Rose. "It's his whole trouble. If only he had something to worry about he'd be happy. But even the state of the country doesn't trouble him, because all his money is in property."

"But surely . . ." hesitated Miss Furze. "Surely he thinks of *others.*"

Rose gave her a smiling glance.

"With rage and contempt," she explained.

"*Screams* of rage," enlarged Rachel.

"But no sympathy. I was thinking of personal trouble. If Henry were ill——"

"*Rose!*" came in a chorus from the other two. That was too terrible a supposition. Susan went on: "If Henry doesn't take me to keep house for him——"

"*And* me!" cried Rachel. All three girls laughed. They looked very pretty. Their faces were unpainted; their clothes neat and unsuggestive; their eyes clear and shining; their teeth uniformly white and regular. Miss Furze shivered slightly.

"What about you, Rose?" she asked in a soft voice.

Rose smiled down into her face.

"Don't worry," she said, calmly. "Henry won't take any of us. He couldn't be bothered. He says we stupefy him. He says we bawl. And last night he said he thought women were *all* bores."

"Ha!" exclaimed Rachel. "That's because of Lettice Holpen!"

"Lettice?" Both Miss Furze and Rose turned quickly upon her. Rachel, nodding slowly and with meaning, looked from one to the other.

"Lettice!" she repeated. "How do I know? Well, I know this: he's frightened of her. Do you think she's got designs on him? Rather awful if she has. I mean, *Henry!* Well, my dears, he ran like a hare——"

"Oh, Rachel!"

"I tell you he did. He caught sight of her——"

As if at a signal (but there had been no signal), Rachel stopped in the middle of her disclosure. She had become aware of the fact that she was talking loudly. For a moment nobody said anything. The girls were wonderstruck. It was not that they doubted Henry's attractiveness. Nor that they were shocked at the thought of somebody pursuing him. Their wonder related to Lettice. And Henry's flight. Miss Furze's face wore an expression such as it might have had if she had just passed the gas works.

"Lettice hasn't been to see me for a long time," said Miss Furze, apparently with the object of breaking the silence. "You must tell her I miss her."

"We're going to call this afternoon. Have you heard about the new arrival?" It was Rose who spoke for them all. "A Mr. Spears. A mystery. That Miss Coulevain is still there. Mother's very upset about it. Doesn't think it ought to be. We've told her nobody thinks anything of that, nowadays."

"They think just as much," remarked Miss Furze. "In fact, more. But they say they think nothing of it. It's an excuse to keep on talking about it."

"Oh, I don't think they really think——" Rose stopped, seeing Miss Furze's expression, and smiled.

"I shall go and call," said Miss Furze. "That's what *I* think."

They all gathered about her, once again, wonderstruck. How simple-minded they were!

"You really *are marvellous,* Alicia!" impetuously exclaimed Rachel. "You *will* tell us what it's like there, won't you! I wish they'd let us play tennis on that lawn."

"When I was a girl I used to go to tea there with Miss Strange. She had the house before Mr. Starling. She was a little thing who always wore her bonnet. We used to think she went to bed in it. She was thought very old-fashioned forty years ago. Doesn't that seem amusing! We used to sit on the lawn under a mulberry tree. It was ever so quiet, and Miss Strange used to tell me about how she first heard of such things as the Reform Bill when *she* was a young girl. I like that house."

"We can never get in," complained Rose. "It's forbidden. And tempting," she added, half laughing.

"Perhaps now," suggested Miss Furze, encouragingly.

"But Miss Coulevain——" began Rose. Then she laughed outright. "Yes, of course, we shall never go. Once a doubtful character always under a cloud. Or else——" She raised her brows in mischief. "Perhaps this Mr. Spears will get married."

"Oh, Rose! I've thought of something *awful!*" shouted Susan. "What if he married Miss C.! What would Mother do then, poor thing!"

They stared at one another, faced with a tremendous social problem.

"He might marry one of yourselves," hastily added Miss Furze. "That would be *much* nicer." She smiled, with, however, a thoughtful glance in the direction of Rose, who was her favourite.

"He jolly well won't!" cried Rachel, with a dark frown. "I'll take care of that. Breaking up the happy home!"

3

As the Davitt girls, on their way to the Crescent, crossed Sandersfold High Street, they say Mrs. Settle, the proprietress of the Lion, shaking hands with some people in a car. A large, prosperous figure in black silk, the face a little florid, the hair a dark grey. They knew her, and smiled, but did not speak. Instead, without examining the travellers, they passed, and continued along Larch Street. Only when they were some yards farther upon their way did Rose, who had been thinking quietly, glance back with curiosity at the Georgian house. There, at the door, stood a stranger. She had no more than a glimpse of him. He was tall and rather thin, and he had a thin brown face. That was all she noticed. He was coming out of the house, his head thoughtfully lowered.

"He might marry one of yourselves," Alicia Furze had

said. Rose knew perfectly well which one of them Miss Furze had in mind.

Soon they reached the Crescent, where all the houses were large, detached, and pseudo-antique. They had ample gardens fore and aft, and the situation was countrified, since the houses backed on to open meadows. The Davitts gathered under the porch of the Holpens' house, talking in whispers, as if they were carol singers and oppressed by the fear that their noisiness might disgust nervous Mrs. Holpen.

"I hope Lettice is at home," mouthed Rachel. "Won't it be *awful*——"

"Sh," whispered Susan.

They waited. There was a long silence. Then a rustling. A black-dressed maid, in very correct style, drew open the door. Her severity cowed the Davitts, who were in the habit of answering the front door for themselves, without ceremony; and they trooped into the house as if they were a party of schoolgirls visiting a museum.

4

"D'you know Alicia's going to call on this new man at Mr. Starling's?"

"No-o-oh!" All the incredulity in the world was in Lettice's gay response. "What fun! When's she going? I'd love to be there. I *must* be there!"

The Davitt girls sighed enviously over their tea. They had forgotten that Lettice, through her brother, "knew" Miss Coulevain. It gave her instant advantage. She would see Mr. Spears.

"What does Leonard think of him?" asked Rose, remembering the glimpse she had had.

"Oh, my dear, don't ask me! Leonard's impossible. He's

full of business these days. *Too* provoking. He never has
a minute. I *begged* him to tell me what the man was like.
He said he was a tough nut. Of course that made me
furious! All I could get out of him was, 'He's an oyster.' "

"Well!" Three simultaneous cries of astonishment
greeted the disclosure. The Davitts laughed delightedly.
Even Lettice sparkled in fun.

"He sounds like a dark horse," observed Rose, demurely.

Lettice laughed aloud at that. Not a merry laugh, but
a rather indulgent one. She did not really like Rose, who
sometimes showed disconcerting candour.

"My dear!" cried Susan—forgetting what Rachel had
told them a few minutes earlier. "What *do* you think!
Henry's been transferred to London——"

"Transferred!"

"And we're all going to keep house for him, and pro-
tect him from *dangerous women.*"

Rose, terrified by these words, looked quickly away
from Lettice. She did not, in consequence, observe any
change of expression in her friend's face. She hardly
heard the ejaculation "transferred!" but only the artificially heightened *"No-o-oh!"* which was spoken in an appropriately breathless voice. Then Susan plunged into a
full account of what had happened. The first moment of
constraint was passed. Rose could breathe again.

"Such a good thing!" Lettice said. "When does he go?"

She froze them by her coolness. The news almost
ceased to be marvellous. It became a trivial incident,
quickly caught up into general gossip about tennis parties,
London, dresses, something Rachel had seen in the local
newspaper. Half an hour passed. The teacups were empty;
the cakes had been eaten. Still Mrs. Holpen did not appear.
One of the girls inquired after her.

"Oh, Mother's in her room. She thinks she's ill. She

won't come down." Lettice stared at the clock. "You know what she is, my dear."

"Heavens! We must fly!" cried Susan, following that sinister glance, and instantly oppressed by a sensitive fear that they had outstayed their welcome.

When they were going home, Rachel said to her sisters: "Did you see Lettice's face when Susan dropped that brick?"

"What brick?" demanded Susan.

"Henry, you idiot!" hissed Rachel. "She was—I didn't feel she was hurt. It was more as if she were angry. As if you'd snatched something. She sort of seethed. *You* know."

"I don't believe a word of it!" protested Susan, hotly. "It wasn't a brick. She's our friend, and she's got a right to know our news——"

"She didn't think much of it——"

"And she was as cool as anything. Wasn't she, Rose! And Henry *didn't* run away. It's beastly of you to say such a thing. Particularly about *Henry.*"

Rachel was abashed. They walked homeward in silence. Only Rose, in whose mind several unmastered thoughts were jigging about and cannoning against each other as one feels that dancing gnats must do, remained of her own opinion. She had ignored Susan's appeal. She thought that Lettice, though her heart was breaking, would still be able to deceive all three of them. She did not think Lettice's heart was breaking. But Rachel's earlier hint had given her an intuition concerning Lettice. And she was uncertain about Henry. For the first time consciously, she was doubting him. Also she could not check stealthy memories. Unnoticed by the others, Rose frowned thoughtfully. She had not been born the day before yesterday.

It was at home that the Davitt girls received the greatest shock of all; for when they arrived, and when they unceremoniously burst into the drawing room just as they came from out of doors, the first person they saw was Philip Spears.

5

What happened to the others, Rose did not know. Her heart gave a little jump. She recognized him at once as the man she had seen leaving the Georgian house. Recognized and liked him. She liked his thin brown cheeks and the dark eyes that looked so kind and intelligent. She had a sense of his strangeness, a foreign unobtrusiveness of movement, his very sweet smile, the small, thin, and very dark hands. When he spoke, she liked the gentleness of his voice.

"Here's my girls," growled Mr. Davitt, whose face was redder than ever with suppressed excitement. He was rolling about in his chair, with a kind of grandeur, proud to have a visitor who was his own friend, and no mere local and habitual caller. "It'll take you some time to tell them apart. Can't always do it, myself, haha. This is Rose; she's the one who looks after the others. This is Susan, who's kind to her father. And this is Rachel——"

"Who isn't," said Rachel. "How d'you do. Father hasn't told us who *you* are, but we guess." She was the least shy of the girls, almost bluff in manner, but not disagreeably so. She had a way of planting her feet apart, like a ship captain.

Rose saw Philip smile again at the friendly words, as if they had given him extreme pleasure, and moved a little away. She, too, was smiling. In this big, ugly room, with its old-fashioned wall paper and large engravings, her father seemed wholly "right." He was a big man, much bigger than Philip. His outspokenness was less than roughness. He had a big white moustache which overhung large lips and large, rather discoloured teeth. His eyes were small and rather bloodshot. But as he sat there in an armchair made for his comfort he was very substantial, very reliable, like a house of his own building.

"I'm glad you've come here, Flup," he said, in his loud voice. "By God, I feel the need of male companionship. I'll tell you all about the place. All the fads and wanglings. You don't guess the half of them."

"Father's the man to tell you," said Rachel, abruptly. She was at the door, about to depart; and Rose saw that Susan was also there, standing timidly, as if aware that she was untidy and still hatted. In a moment they were gone. Rose was alone with her father and the newcomer.

"It's a great piece of luck for me," Philip said. He turned to Rose, admiring her fresh prettiness and the open candour of her expression. She was indeed appropriately named, for she was like a flower that was passing from bud to bloom, still with the morning sweetness unspoiled. "Your father and I are old friends," he added.

"He's a very secret man," she answered, a little breathlessly. "For we've never heard of you until you came to Sandersfold."

"I have to be secret," grumbled Mr. Davitt. "Things get shouted here. And that's a word of advice to you, Flup. Keep a still tongue!"

"I'll do my best," Philip assured him.

The two exchanged a meaning look. When Rose saw Philip smile again, her lips trembled. She thought: "He's unhappy. It's something that happened. . . . Father knows about it. Father likes him. He's quite different. He's never been so cordial with anybody. And he knows. It's happiness he needs. He needs——" Without completing that thought, so inexperienced was she, Rose glanced again at Philip's hands. Something in their slen-

derness affected her strangely. She could not take her
eyes from their delicate beauty.

"Yes, a still tongue," repeated Mr. Davitt, in an altered,
ruminative tone. "Until you know where you are. Who's
your friend . . ." He nodded. "This place is full of old
women. I'm one of them. I've degenerated, Flup. I'm a
cantankerous old bore. Ask Rose, here——"

Rose smiled. Her father pressed for her comment.

"Isn't that so, Rose?" he persisted.

"You don't always do yourself justice, Father," she
suggested.

"Hm. How could I? Who does? Now, I used to be a
clever fellow. I seized my chances. I looked for 'em—
you know that. But I've grown deaf. I'm old. I'm bad-
tempered. And I know it. Maybe there's a poison in my
blood. Funny thing, Flup; if a young man talks about
himself it's held to be interesting . . . self-revelation.
It isn't. It's drivel, often as not. But an old fellow's
a noted bore. He talks about his ailments, I suppose. I
don't. I talk about the stupidity I see all round me. People
don't like it."

"They think you mean it, Father," said Rose.

"Well, I do!" Mr. Davitt bristled. His red face was like
the setting sun.

"He hasn't got any troubles, Mr. Spears," explained
Rose. "He interferes, and tells people their faults. Of
course *we* love him."

"Hm. I don't know so much about that," grunted Mr.
Davitt. "Flup, sometimes I could box their ears. No respect. No reverence. I'm so exasperated with them all.
Little silly doings. It's the narrow life here. Mind you,
there isn't a thing about this place I don't know. I know
the parsons and the shopkeepers; I know the poachers
and the policeman. I know who lives where, and why
and how. Nothing else to do. I ought never to have re-

tired from trade. *They* made me—said I was getting plethoric. I know which of the women are chaste, and which of the men are solvent. Not many of them." He gave a short, gruff laugh. "But you'll be a godsend to me, Flup. At the end of a month you'll be hiding from me. I'll tell you everything. I'll put you wise. Everything!"

"I wish you'd tell us how you came to know Mr. Spears," murmured Rose.

"Eh?" Her father shot her the glance he reserved for vagrants. "Well, that's an old story; and if I told you I don't think you'd be any the wiser. Mr. Spears will tell you himself, one day."

"Will you?"

Rose looked at Philip, but not at his face. She could not raise her eyes so far. But her father drowned that half-audible question, rushing out with another, like an October breeze.

"How does England strike you, after all this time, Flup? More like America? D'you like America? Sounds some sort of a place, with all the shootings and lootings. England's more like America now, isn't it?"

So he had been in America! She listened.

"It's still England," Philip said, quietly enough. "And though you see all the faults of Sandersfold, I expect you know there are some virtues in it, James."

"Hm. Old virtues. New faults."

Both his hearers shook their heads. They did not believe him.

"Not as happy as it used to be," suggested Philip.

"Damned taxation. Pauperizing the idle poor. Young people all girls and girlies."

Rose, glancing quickly at Philip, received a surprise. She saw him exchange a look with her father, saw one of his eyelids quiver. Then she saw the grim beam upon her father's face. How they understood each other! How envious she was of such an understanding! She had made a discovery. It was that her father, seen truly, was not the man she had in her own mind portrayed as a domestic tyrant with qualities.

"Well, you didn't promise to tell me, Mr. Spears," she ventured, feeling bold. "How you and Father came to know each other so well. And we none the wiser."

"I will," he said. "Of course. If I can remember. I wonder if I can."

"Thank you." Rose smiled in return; but her eyes were darker.

There seemed to be less light in the room. She felt her heart beating more rapidly, and her fingers were pressed tightly together. She could see the long fingers of Philip's hands extended upon the arms of his chair, and she had the assurance that he was about to rise. But he did not move, and those long fingers held her thoughts so strongly that she was unable to see anything else in the darkening room.

It was as though she felt Philip's hands clasping her own hands, as if she desired with breathless vehemence that they might caress her, that she might carry them to her cheeks and her breast. Memory of Alicia Furze's words was unconscious, but their meaning was present as an underthought. Rose knew that the blood was slowly creeping to her cheeks. She had never been so tongue-tied, so embarrassed, so burningly secret. She knew only that she must not, could not, stir lest she should in some way reveal the emotion which was causing her to tremble. With no further word spoken between them, and no more than a glance exchanged, she had fallen in love with the newcomer to Sandersfold.

She could only sit with hands and knees pressed together, too agitated to move, and too unversed in disguise to restrain the eagerness of her attention to all that passed between two men who were strangers to her. A faint smile caused her lips to part and her eyes to glow.

So the afternoon ended.

CHAPTER FOUR

EPILOGUE

PHILIP walked in the gathering dusk. Instead of turning homeward, he struck off blindly, until he found himself in that long winding lane along which Lettice had hastened, long ago, intending by accident to meet Henry Davitt. The leaves about him were very thick. Thrushes sang, and smaller birds chattered as the day declined. All was still, so that he was entirely solitary. Sometimes he loitered, sometimes he strode along with impatience. He hardly knew what he was doing or where he was going.

He had not been pleased to encounter James Davitt. The sight of that robust figure, with the red face and slightly bloodshot eyes and twitching white moustache, had stricken him. They had come face to face in the High Street, had stared, had turned cold, had come together eagerly, after a dozen years of lost acquaintance. It had been, for Philip, a shock. He had believed that in Sandersfold, so small a town, and one so remote from his every early haunt, he would be unknown. He had been wrong.

"Good God!" he thought, as he now walked alone. "Every house in the place . . ." The thought made him pause, made perspiration start about his eyes.

Vaguely he looked about him. The road was quite grey; the heavy foliage was like a softly swaying cloak about the scene. He responded to its reassurance, feeling once again secret. But his mind ran busily onward. James would be silent, a friend. . . . Philip bit his lip. He had friends. There were two of them—one Sam Dexter, the bookseller; the other James Davitt. Any more? None. None. He could have made friends. He knew that he attracted men and women: why, then, shun them as he had done? It was too late to change his temper. The old openness had gone.

He had thought to forget everything. Here, in this retreat, to discover his genius, and make his home, and grow old in peace. Had he really hoped to grow old in peace? Well, here was James Davitt, very much older, but as active, and as full of surprise, as ever. And James was his friend. James's home, that pretty girl who had such a gentle manner, and James himself, would be ever near. Was he not thankful? Thankful, but disconcerted. The meeting had been another reminder that nothing in life ever stood still. You were building and making all the time, or were being moulded by circumstance, or were sinking, sinking into despairing oblivion. Had not the peace he had proposed for himself been an acceptance of living death?

Here Philip came to a pause, standing pensive in the middle of the road. He was quite alone in this beautiful quiet. The tender shadows enveloped him. He was so still that a little wren, darting mouselike in the hedge, sang its song; and at the sound of that thrilling cascade of music Philip unconsciously smiled. In spite of these troubled perplexities, he had never been so happy, and so free from care, as now. Had he not everything to make him happy?

When his walk was resumed, his heels made sharp noises upon the surface of the road. And very soon he came out upon a broad thoroughfare, followed its hard surface, and found his way back to the town.

Lights were now to be seen in the windows of some

of the houses. Not the cottages, which were curiously dark, as if they had been deserted, but the larger houses. There, within, oblivious of all that might pass out of doors, men and women were absorbed in their own concerns. Everyone indifferent to Philip's fortunes, save as they provided material for talk and reconsideration. Presently he would pass the Davitts' home. James, those girls, the warmth and heavy dulness of massive furniture. . . . Well, was he sorry to have made that entry? It was a home; he felt such kindness and unaffected friendliness there that his own sensitiveness, which may have been excessive, was appeased. Still, light-hearted, Philip re-entered the High Street, passed the church, saw the lighted shops, and went onward. His spirits leapt as he reached his new home. Smiling again, in pride, he entered it, using his new key with a jubilant sense of delight.

2

His dinner eaten alone, Philip walked straight into the library, which had become already his favourite room. It was not only for the sake of the tall and well-laden shelves, for these he had hardly begun to explore. It was in part for the tall doorway which opened directly upon the garden, and for the pale clear light from the northern sky that was now visible through the open door. He could see the early stars and the dark foliage of the mulberry tree; he could relish the heavy evening scent of the roses after the sun had warmed them to ecstasy; he could stand in the window, all those aged books behind him, and look into the mysterious shadow, breathing deeply. As he did this, jubilation became thankfulness. His heart swelled.

But as the darkness increased, Philip turned within. He closed the long door and drew the heavy curtains across it. Then, lighting only a little fireside lamp, he seated himself and lay back, his eyes half closed, lost in reverie.

He had been sitting thus for perhaps a quarter of an hour, when a faint sound caught his ear. The door had been softly opened. It was strange to see it move and then gradually show a faint streak of light from the passage beyond. The light threw into relief the figure of Ruth Coulevain. She stood in the doorway for an instant, hesitating. At last she entered the room, Philip all the time lying back in his chair, curiously pleased by the sense that he was dreaming.

"Mr. Spears." He heard a low voice calling him by name.

Then it was no dream.

"Come in, Miss Coulevain." He rose as he spoke. Both stood in the darkness.

"I'm not disturbing you?" came that subdued voice.

"No. I thought you were a ghost."

"There are no ghosts here," she answered seriously. "Nobody has ever seen one."

"No *bad* ghosts. But you can't pretend that this house is ordinary bricks and mortar."

"You are fanciful." There was a pause. "Mr. Spears, I heard you come in here. I was in the small sitting room. I hoped you would come in there. I wanted to speak to you."

"Won't you sit down?"

"I'd rather stand."

"Please."

She came forward, not into the small beam which the light cast, but near enough to him to be faintly visible. He could see her outline against the dark material of the chair cover. Her face was a pale blur. Now that she was seated, everything was quite silent, and she apparently found that she could not speak.

"How extraordinary!" thought Philip. "What does she want?" Sitting there—he could just distinguish her hands, which he thought must be clasped—so tensely quiet.

"So you don't believe there are any ghosts?" he asked, to break that chill silence.

She made an effort.

"No. I hope there aren't any."

"Because of what they might do?"

"Because of what they may have seen."

"I don't believe they're supposed to tell tales. But I wasn't thinking so much of groaning martyrs and walking nuns. Rather of an atmosphere of friendliness here. You don't feel that?"

"No. I've never felt it. I'm not imaginative."

It was a full stop. "By Jove," thought Philip; "this is uphill work. If I could see her, it might be easier. I suppose she's melancholy. Naturally. A young woman; no society, for I've hardly spoken to her, and I can't remember that I've ever seen her go out or come in. That's peculiar. Neither out nor in. Now what the devil is she like?" He had a mental picture, recalled from his first encounter and their walk and talk in the garden upon that day, far in the past, when he had first come to Sandersfold. But only of straight fair hair, and unexpectedly brown eyes, and a manner of reserve and self-assurance. Nothing more personal, none of the tantalizing childishness with which all the other women he had ever known had at times charmed him. Self-command . . . coolness . . . a withdrawing from the least encounter that was not purely formal . . . very much the housekeeper, he thought. More in it than that, perhaps. Self-protection as well. Better so. How would he have managed somebody skittish? Say a Miss Sparkle. Yet Miss Sparkle was a good girl. . . .

"I wonder if you are finding it very dull here, Miss Coulevain," he said, rather abruptly. He could have sworn that she started at his speech.

"Oh, no——" It was like a cry of distress. "No, no."

"I suppose you're used to the life."

"Yes, I don't want to change . . . I don't want to change *anything*."

"That's very lucky for me," said Philip.

"*You* don't?"

"No." He was a little puzzled by the intensity of her manner, but he spoke smilingly. He heard a sigh of relief. So loud—was the woman an actress? It was not impossible, with that serious manner. Who could blame a young woman—at once a lady and a servant—for acting a little?

"That was what I wanted to see you about," she continued with a return to almost frigid self-possession.

"Oh, please! I thought we quite understood one another. Didn't we agree?"

"Yes, but I—— Excuse me, I'm not quite well. Something has happened that—— I had the impression that you might not want me to stay much longer."

"But how strange!" cried Philip. "Something as to myself?"

She had difficulty in replying. At last:

"No, I was given to understand—I was reminded that you only made the arrangement with me as a temporary thing. It was suggested that you might want to rearrange everything."

"Reminded!" "Suggested!" "Given to understand!" What ambiguities were here!

"Whoever told you that was quite wrong. Was it Mr. Holpen?"

She hesitated.

"Well, yes, it was."

"Extraordinary. What on earth made him say a thing like that? It's quite absurd."

She began to speak in a dry tone of desperation.

"Oh, please don't let him know that I've spoken to you. He'd think—— I felt I must ask you at once. I don't want to leave here. I don't. I don't. It's very important to me. Of course it's always for you to say——"

Philip was still thinking about Leonard Holpen's cheek. He hardly heard what she said. Like other sensitive men, he resented interference with a furiousness out of proportion to its significance. And so, irritated, he took two or three steps which brought him directly in front of Ruth. She was sitting straight upright in that chair. He could imagine that she had been crying.

"Look here," he said. "You and I will have a talk. If you want to go, you'll tell me. If I ever want you to go, I'll tell *you*. That clear? Otherwise you stay. I shall tell you if there's anything I don't like; and you'll tell me if I am inconsiderate or troublesome. I want you to feel free and happy—not merely a servant, and certainly not in constant fear of dismissal. I know that fear too well. I've been a very poor man; and once poor always poor——"

"I know." The words forced themselves from her lips.

"You know. It is in one's bones. Very well, if you understand, it's all clear. Nobody who works for me is ever going to be uncomfortable if I can help it. I may by accident be miserly. Or extravagant. You can check me. Please do so. But, whatever you do, never take somebody else's opinion of my wishes as true. Come to me, as you've done. It's not difficult."

She rose, and they stood facing one another.

"I've been poor, too," she said quickly. "I was starving when Mr. Starling found me and brought me here. That's what frightened me. It was meant to do so. I can't . . .

I can't go back to that. I'd do something—I'd steal, even —rather than go back to it."

"So would I," murmured Philip, responding to her suppressed fierceness. *"Almost* anything," he amended. "Not steal."

"Anything. Anything," she repeated very urgently.

"No, you wouldn't," he insisted. "I can tell that you're self-reliant. You've got pride."

"None!" she cried. "I'd have gone on my knees to you."

"It wouldn't have had any effect. And so you wouldn't have done it."

She was caught by that warm firmness of tone.

"Yes, I *have* got pride," she agreed, thoughtfully. "But not in the sense you have it. I can see you wouldn't plead for anything. You don't like other people to plead. You're cold." She stepped back from him. "I shouldn't have gone on my knees to you. I should have known it would be no good."

"That was what I said," Philip reminded her.

"Yes. It's true. I didn't realize it. I do now. I could go on my knees to some people. Not to anybody I respected."

"I hope you'll never have to do it," observed Philip, smiling. "To anybody."

She turned away, as ghostlike as ever in the room's dimness.

"Thank you," she said. "I'm very grateful to you. I'm glad I interrupted you."

"Is it all settled?" asked Philip.

"All settled," agreed Ruth. "Good-night. And thank you."

He called after her:

"I shouldn't pay any attention to what Mr. Holpen says."

There was no answer. Philip, smiling, looked again. There was nobody in the room but himself. A slight click from the closing door told him that she had gone. Had she heard the words?

3

Philip sat back in his chair. This young woman was very serious. You could reach an understanding with her by means of explicit statement, but not by means of ridicule. There was no play of mind or fancy or fun. As for the thought that she might grovel to somebody, it was preposterous. The twentieth century was the non-grovelling century. A bit histrionic, perhaps? Serious women often were, he believed. A kind of sentimentality. They wanted to impress. How juvenile to generalize! Like the special correspondent who describes what he hears from the waiter as "the general opinion." No, but any over-serious person was inclined to act. Any person in a subordinate position.

"Hell!" cried Philip, finding himself in the dilemma of theory.

Holpen had told this girl she was likely to lose her job. Why? What was it she had said? He had forgotten the words. Something—"it was *meant* to frighten me." Now, why frighten? Well, obviously not for the sake of any advantage to Philip. For the sake of an advantage to Holpen. What advantage? That was plain; it could be for one object only.

It did not take Philip more than a moment to recall other phrases. Holpen had suggested at the first meeting that the girl had been his uncle's mistress. What! That pallid old Don, undersized, insatiable . . . *again!* And this girl—was she a prude? A wanton? That dirty old man?

"It's disgusting," he said. "And yet that was his history." She had said she would do "anything." Starling had taken her from starvation. It wasn't impossible that there had been a price. Nothing was impossible, with a woman. Nothing was impossible with that old wretch!

Holpen had run away from his own hint. Why? Cowardice? Supposing she had been his uncle's mistress? Did Holpen want her for his own? Deep young man. Or rather, not deep, but intricate. The modern formula. A damned sleek fellow with a tailor and a hairdresser, sadistic with women. That would fit. Probably a devilish rent collector. A master of the threatening letter. Not a villain. Villains nowadays were *vieux jeux*—old sports. But perhaps, as here, a mischief maker. Little schemes, little tyrannies. Pinpricks and hints. And this girl . . . Philip grunted. Those two—Holpen and Miss Coulevain—knew each other better than was apparent. Were they lovers? It seemed not. You couldn't tell.

Philip thought he might be a match for Master Holpen.

"Yes," he murmured aloud, but in so low a tone that none could have heard the words. "Once poor, always poor. But I don't believe in villains. Only in slippers and sliders."

His head sank between his shoulders as he went over the conversation which had just ended, and from that drifted to other, older, less agreeable memories. Time passed. The clock upon the mantelpiece chimed eleven. The room had grown chilly. He continued sitting there, so still that he might have been asleep.

But he was not asleep. Presently he roused himself, stretching his arms in the air, and yawning.

"Slippers and sliders," he said. "And playboys. And fools. . . . I bet that seriousness of hers belongs to a sensual nature. He's playing on that. Well, she's only making a convenience of me, but I don't mind it. I wonder if I could do something to make her independent of him . . . I should have to change my solicitor . . .

"I shall probably have to do that, in any case. The world's too small."

Undismayed by the smallness of the world, which earlier in the evening had menaced him, he switched off the little light by the fireplace and went out into the hall and up the wide, shallow stairs to his bedroom, lighted thither by the stars and the pale night sky in which they were clustered.

THE GEORGIAN HOUSE.

PART TWO

THE STORY BEGINS

CHAPTER FIVE

THE CRICKET MATCH

Early in July, Sandersfold had its Cricket Week, when the town was flagged from end to end, when marquees were set up on the Sports Ground behind Grange Road, when the press of visitors became an inconvenience, and when everybody felt that Sandersfold must really be the hub of the district. Small yellow posters hung in the shop windows, yellow and green favours were worn, all the young men went more decidedly than ever into plus fours or flannel bags, and the town team was strengthened by auxiliaries from county families in order that it might battle more gloriously with every kind of intimidating stranger. England was awake.

Philip early became aware of the approaching excitement. As he walked along the High Street, the yellow bills caught his eye. He found that they bore the names of visiting teams, and that they advertised a great amateur theatrical performance which was to conclude the Week. When he bought tobacco of Mr. Hobbs, near the church, he found that Mr. Hobbs had been a hero of Sandersfold cricket in the years before the war. When he entered the trim little bookshop of Mr. Purvis, he discovered that Mr. Purvis's assistant was a googly bowler of renown, and the secretary of the Cricket Club. When he called at the bank he learned that the manager, a fine stalwart of forty, had played at one time for Somersetshire. All cricketers; all sporting patriots; all eager supporters of the Cricket Week. Such unanimity amazed him, touched him, bewildered him. This was indeed a new world for a townsman to explore.

By degrees, for the absorption of all such unfamiliar knowledge gave him secret pride, Philip learned much about the national sport. His mind went back to a day when, with less comprehension, he had closed his ears to the talk of Jenkins and Maddox, the cricketing enthusiasts of Dexter's. And when he thought of those boys his heart almost stood still. What a distance he had travelled in a few weeks! Was he the same man? Those old times were years away. They were dim. *They already seemed pleasant.* He pictured the delight he would feel in revisiting Dexter's as a free man.

House and garden, books and furniture, the trimness and elegance of everything connected with his new home, the peace and silence of the old town, roused an exultation such as he had not known for a dozen years. Each morning as he awoke, whether the day was grey or brilliant, he had heard the birds singing in boastfulness and reassurance, and although the song, now summer had come, was diminished, he still lay in bed and thought to himself: "Thank God! Thank God! This is mine. Nothing can take it from me. Oh, marvellous thought, this is *mine!*" And then, more sedately, he would add: "No more experiments. No more adventures. I must be quiet, like this old house, like this old garden. I must enjoy the remainder of my life in peace. No horrors, no emotions . . . Ordered days; the quiet life of the country . . . I shall fit into it. I shall ripen. I shall be able to do useful work . . . later, later."

There was no sound of mockery from within or without the house. It remained grave. Sometimes at night it stretched in its sleep and sent mysterious crackings through its members. But a house that has seen as much as Miss Strange's and Mr. Starling's would never smile at the dreams of a wayfarer. The utmost such a house would allow itself in irony would be the slight shrug of a chimney stack or the delicate quiver of a window blind.

And now the Cricket Week was here, and Philip had begun to anticipate the enchantment of summer days spent at ease in contemplation of the most beautiful of all games. Peace, the crack of the bat, the lovely grace of moving white-flannelled figures, the hot scent of the smooth grass, and the underlying, inexhaustible excitement of the game, all moved him to happiness. He was in a dream.

2

On that Monday morning the Holpens were as active as all the other inhabitants of Sandersfold. Mrs. Holpen, stirred by the thought of being seen among so much company, had left her room. She had breakfasted with her son and daughter. In sitting at the head of the table she had rehearsed all the effects of her entry to the roped enclosure before the wooden pavilion, all the glances that would be cast at her, all the gay remarks of which she would be the centre. She was pale now; but in the afternoon, when prepared for the game, she would be as delicately beautiful as ever. Nay, more beautiful.

What a nuisance, she thought crossly, that Lettice was beginning to look so old. And Leonard, too, was showing a little distinguished grey at the temples. Both were so morose at breakfast. She wished she had not come down, after all. She felt less vital; no wonder she lost her verve in the society of these brooding members of the younger generation.

"Young people are so dull," she thought, suddenly. Had she spoken the words aloud? A doubt made her look up. Neither Lettice nor Leonard took any notice. They were all sitting in the bare, sterilized dining room which accepted the morning sun. Lettice looked sulky, and Leonard rather white. Good gracious! What a pair! They might be mummies. There was nothing in them.

"You don't *try* to be agreeable!" thought Mrs. Holpen, accusingly. "You sit there quite stuffily. No wonder I have so little energy. I ought to be surrounded with wits. Like Madame Récamier. Of course, a dead town like this . . . I need London; the gaiety of a capital. Yes, but it's so difficult there, unless one has *done* something. One never meets people who've *done* anything. . . ."

"One never meets people who've *done* anything!" cried Mrs. Holpen, aloud. "Interesting people, bright people, people with *names.*" She became extremely exasperated as she spoke. Her own words heightened the discontent she was feeling. "This Cricket Week!" She rolled her eyes. "It's so trivial. So parochial. So——" She waved her hand, and, pleased with the gesture, she repeated it.

"So what, Mother?" asked Lettice coldly.

"Piffling," said Mrs. Holpen, at a loss.

Leonard raised his eyes from a letter which he had been reading. He stared at his mother with a familiar concentration.

"You live so much in retirement, Mother," he said, drily. "You should lead the town a little more."

Mrs. Holpen looked sulky. The tone had been too satirical for her liking.

"And here's Lettice. Lettice, why aren't you in the play this year? You were *last* year. I quite enjoyed it. Not that you were very good. You weren't. Everybody saw that. Stiff and amateurish. But it was *something.*"

"You should be in it yourself," said Leonard.

"Yes, what would they give me!" exclaimed Mrs. Holpen. "An old woman's part. Some old dowager, or servant. A *fat* woman. Ridiculous! But Lettice——"

"I didn't want to, Mother," said Lettice. "It's such a *fa-ag!*"

That was not the real reason. Memory of the real reason caused Lettice's lips to tremble. She set them firmly. Whatever her mother said, she would not speak again.

"And you, Leonard. You're good looking. Good figure. It would do you good. All you do is to go off in your car. I never see you. The county never sees you. Now, this is a *chance*. You'd . . . Your father, as a young man, used to take part. I won't say I liked it. He wasn't good. Nobody would have said he was good. He put too much into it. That looked bad. Several people tried to pity me. . . . But you're not married, Leonard. I suppose you're frightened of getting caught. My dear boy, you're too clever for that. Too shrewd. Too worldly-wise. You get it from me."

"Quite, Mother," retorted Leonard, mockingly. He passed a white hand over his well-brushed hair. "As you say."

Mrs. Holpen gave a grimace of discontent.

"Well, I hope you're coming to take me to the cricket this afternoon, Leonard."

"Oh, are *you* going?" he asked, brutally. Then, with blandness: "Of course, Mother. We'll all go. You're going, Let?"

"There seems nothing else to do," answered Lettice, wearily.

Leonard observed her drooping head. She was looking quite haggard. She ought to marry. Ah!

"I'll be home early," he remarked. Then, with pretended carelessness: "I expect Spears will be there." He watched to see the effect of his words. It had entered his head that Lettice might attract Spears. It was high time she was married, and the lads of the village were not crowding upon the scene. As for County, County preferred County.

"Oh, will he!" Mrs. Holpen brightened. "Well, *that's* somebody new."

Lettice showed no sign of interest. But Leonard smiled rather maliciously at his mother's tone.

"Yes, quite a number of eligibles for you, Mother," he lightly said, as he rose. He had no fear in that quarter. His eyes were still upon Lettice. "You'll have a happy time."

Mrs. Holpen had recovered her cheerfulness. She went so far as to smile.

"I always do," she observed, looking at herself in the coffee pot. "After all, there's something in personality."

3

At the same hour, in a room as unlike that of the Holpens, as any room could be, James Davitt was surveying his family with violently restrained impatience. The room was big and square, with a dark embossed wall paper loaded heavily with gilt frames and mountain cattle. A huge mahogany sideboard, a solid carpet, leather-seated chairs that it required muscular exertion to lift, and an abundance of vases and other nicknacks upon the black marble mantelpiece, gave this room an air of permanence, if not of splendour. The sunlight shone brilliantly upon everything, including heavy silver and substantial china.

The table was large enough to accommodate twice the number of people, but Rachel and Susan were fairly close to each other on one side of it. Opposite to them, but farther apart, were Rose and Henry. Rachel and Susan often looked with respect and admiration towards Henry, who had a perpetual crease in his forehead. That was because he was trying to look indifferent and a little bored; and it is true that his curly fair hair attracted much attention from other young women, besides his sisters. He had pink cheeks, and long curling golden lashes, and a mouth that was pouted in sympathy with the raised brows and perpetual crease or furrow aloft. Some people thought Henry looked supercilious and conceited; but he was neither.

Rose could see that James Davitt's bloodshot eyes rolled every time he looked either at his son (who was to play cricket that day, by special dispensation, and who was therefore already in an open-necked white flannel shirt) or at his prematurely aged wife, who wore a thick white shawl, looked very plump and bundled, and had a little white cap awry upon her head.

"What in God's name——" muttered James Davitt, under his breath. He had contemplated that cap until the boiling emotions within him could hardly be restrained. His real meaning was: What in God's name can be said for the perversity of an old fool who insists on wearing that ridiculous affair upon her head? But he knew that he must not dream of saying such a thing, owing to family sensitiveness. And that he must not protest against Henry's shirt or puckered brow or girlish callowness, because it would involve a scene in which his wife and at least two of the girls would possibly be moved to tears. That meant a day of strained relations, slammed doors, and general headache. "Gr-r-r!" he thundered, clearing his throat, and glaring. The knife and fork in his great hands slashed at the sausage upon his plate. His jaws worked.

An impatient speech thus smothered, James Davitt glanced suspiciously at the girls.

"All going?" he abruptly demanded. "Rose, what about you?"

"Oh, yes!" chorused Rachel and Susan. "All going."

"I'm going this morning," choked James Davitt, glaring ferociously, as if he expected them all to raise shocked protests.

"I wish we knew if Henry would be batting this morning," shouted Rachel.

"Well, we don't," growled Henry. He was lounging back in his chair and looking bothered and petulant. "So it's no good wishing."

"What, dear?" inquired Mrs. Davitt, with the gentle smile of a deaf person.

"We don't know if Henry's batting this morning!" shouted Rachel, in explanation.

"Packing? Oh, no, dear; he's playing football," said Mrs. Davitt.

"Aa-ach!" snarled James Davitt, purpling. He flung himself indignantly back in his chair, striking one of the arms of it with an open hand. Henry writhed and slipped an inch farther under the table. The girls giggled.

"Well, we shall all be there this afternoon," said Rose, cheerfully. "Except Mother, of course. She doesn't care for football."

"What, dear?" asked Mrs. Davitt.

"I said you weren't sporting, Mother!" called Rose.

"Oh, shut up, Rose!" growled Henry. "Put me off my game."

"Sh!" said both the other girls, in horror of that calamity. Rachel went on: "Are you taking your old friend, Pa? Mr. Spears?"

James Davitt made no answer. He glowered at Rachel. Then he glowered at Henry. Finally he glowered at his wife. She did not know that he was glowering at her. Indeed she was much more concerned with some plans of her own, secretly formed and of course all-important.

"James, dear, I wish you'd speak to Hobson about the car. It bumps me so when he drives it. I wondered if you'd like to drive me to Seahampton this afternoon."

"Get Hobson to take you. He's got nothing else to do," shouted James Davitt.

"What, dear?"

"Hobson!"

"But he bumps me so."

"As good as riding exercise for you."

"If Hobson drives me, I shall have to have Rose to take care of me."

There was silence. Rose felt the blood rising to her cheeks. Her heart seemed quite cold. She did not protest.

"Nonsense!" shouted James Davitt. "She's coming to the cricket."

"What, dear? Oh, the cricket. Is it cricket? I thought it was football. How silly I am. But I'm sure she'd much rather stay with me. Wouldn't you, dear? Not that horrid rough game. I always think it's such fun at Seahampton. What a pity Henry won't be there. But never mind; we'll go to Woolworth's."

Mrs. Davitt passed the napkin across her lips. She was quite unconscious of the confused bitterness in Rose's heart. She only thought what a sweet, willing girl Rose was. The best of them all, for understanding, although sometimes a little sharp-tongued. But all young people were like that. They improved as they grew older. They *mellowed*.

"That's all right, my girl," said James Davitt. "I'll see that you don't go to Seahampton." He frowned at his wife. But one bloodshot eye was momentarily obscured. It was this covered eye that Rose could see. She felt a little comforted; at any rate by the knowledge that she had his interest, but not much. Her father might be an irresistible force; but her mother, just as certainly, was an immovable object. Between the two she was unhappily stultified. Then a notion occurred to her.

"I think I shall come to the cricket this morning, Father," she said. "There won't be such a crowd."

None of them knew that under the table her fists were clenched and held tightly together, or that in her head was beating the thought: "I *will* go. I *must* go."

4

Alicia Furze said to herself:

"I'm an old woman, and this world's altogether too much for me. Here's Tom Hawke dead and buried, and I was too ill that day to go and see the last of the poor boy. If he'd not been bullied and cajoled by his domineering mother we should have been married, and I should have had children and been worried into an early grave. As it is, he's left me his little bit of money, which I shall have to hand over to his relations, because they need it and I don't. And I'm as old as the hills, and shall probably live for ever, because there's no point in it. But Tom hadn't the courage to stand up to his mother, and I wasn't the girl to snatch him from under her nose; and so here I am, with nothing to do but look on at a life that it seems to be outside everybody's power to control. . . .

"If it weren't for Rose Davitt, I doubt if anybody interests me very much now. But I love Rose, and I think she's fond of me. Is she? Sometimes I wonder even that. Why should she be? A fresh, quick young girl . . .

"You're a selfish, suspicious old woman. You don't deserve to be loved.

"Ah, but it isn't a question of deserts. Now, if I had my way, I'd give Rose anything she wanted. I should spoil her. That would be very foolish of me, and wouldn't do

Rose any good. Nevertheless, I should do it. I'm sure God means us to be happy, and to make others happy; and all this modern grabbing and grasping, that makes everybody wonder what *he* or *she* is going to get out of it, is as stupid as it's wicked. I've told Mr. Andrewes that, and he says he agrees, and that it's Christian doctrine; and he preached a sermon about it, but nothing followed. . . . People don't listen to sermons nowadays; the movies have more influence. 'Put 'em up, son . . .' 'You sure said it, big boy.' I hardly know what such phrases mean . . .

"And I don't think Rose is happy just now. There's that silly old mother, who must be a great trial to her, and that savage red-faced old father (who has a very good heart, I've no doubt, but no manners to speak of). And that perfectly ridiculous brother who ought to be put away in a bandbox and kept out of harm's way. . . . Perhaps she's just waking up to the fact that she's stifled in that house. No, I seem to feel that it's to do with this new man, Mr. Spears; but whether I like Mr. Spears I'm not sure. He's hard to know. He's a cold, frozen sort of man, they say, or perhaps he's just nothing at all; and if the child's fallen in love with him she may be very unhappy. I don't like timid men. I never did. It's a coarseness in me. Too old to change. I shall have to see him and make up my mind what to think. I ought to see them together. . . .

"But he may think nothing of Rose. She's got too much character to be easy. He's more likely to run after somebody flashy, as they all do. He's the sort that burns his fingers, and then is caught while he's blowing on them. I shall see. If Rose is in love with him, she'll suffer a great deal. She's the kind that has to look after somebody. She doesn't need a monster. She needs a gowk, poor girl. But if she's in love with him she must marry him, because I believe in people marrying when they're in love. I ought to have married Tom. I ought to have run off with him. I didn't. I've missed life.

"All sorts of people miss life. They have their chance of it; they don't take it; they regret it ever after. But they can't get the same chance back again. Only other, inferior chances. Then they snatch.

"Poor Rose. But why 'poor Rose'? She's not a fool. I wonder if she'd have let Tom Hawke's mother keep him. Haha! Yes, I wonder. Somehow I don't think she would. Poor Tom. Always a fool, but I loved him. . . ."

Miss Furze fell into a reverie in which she saw herself and Tom Hawke as young people again; he whiskered and top-hatted, herself flounced, with her hair piled and coiled on top of her head, and old-fashioned earrings in her ears. Young, young hearts under the black waistcoat and the tight bodice; and Tom was dead, and she herself was——

"Not dead yet!" cried Alicia Furze, very stoutly. "And young enough not to be sitting here killing myself with old memories. Now, what's today?

"Monday, of course. Monday, the black day. They're all alike to me now. Not black. A bit grey, I think. Yes, but it's the first day of Cricket Week. Bless my soul! It's nearly sixty years since I played cricket on the sly. These young girls think they're so novel. . . .

"We knew it all, donkey's years ago. Dame Nature's a better teacher than Herr Freud. He's the man who tried to analyze Fun, and made a fool of himself, because he hadn't got any.

"I'm going to this Cricket Match. How's that for a repression?"

5

"Mr. Spears."

Philip was startled. He had an instant's positive distaste for this thin woman who came unseen and unheard into

the room, and addressed him when he was happy in contemplation.

"Miss Coulevain."

He turned from the desk at which he was sitting in the
library. Before him was the old lawn, and beyond that a
long vista of roses. The sun was up; the day was
miraculously warm and clear. It was going to be very hot.
Bees were humming, little birds were twittering. "Mr.
Spears," and his happiness was interrupted.

"You said you were going to the Cricket Match."

"I did. I am. Are you?"

"That was what I wanted to ask you."

"You must go."

"Thank you."

Philip leaned back in his chair. She had gone. By Jove,
she wasted no words. There was something to be said for
such a woman. She had straw-coloured hair. Curious eyes,
now that he came to think of them. When she spoke, it
sounded as if her teeth were clenched. The voice was very
low, but quite distinct. An interesting woman. Not quite a
comfortable one, though. Better so. He'd said that before;
and it was still true Was she happier?

How this Cricket Match seemed to infect everybody
with enthusiasm! Even Miss Coulevain. . . . She probably didn't know a thing about the game.

A sudden thought occurred to Philip. He sprang up, and
followed Ruth from the room, overtaking her as she was
about to enter the sitting room.

"Oh, Miss Coulevain . . . I don't know what plans
you've made. I had arranged to spend the day with Mr.
Davitt. I shall have tea with them on the ground. Would
you like to join us?"

Ruth's hand was upon the knob of the door. Her face
was illumined by the great window over the stairs. It was
quite expressionless.

"Thank you," she said, quietly. "But I think . . . I've made a promise."

"Oh," cried Philip. "You're to be with friends."

She hesitated.

"With Miss Holpen, yes," she answered.

With Miss Holpen, thought Philip. And no doubt with her brother, too. Still very strange. Still very strange. He smiled, nodded, raised his hand, withdrew.

6

An hour afterwards he was in the open air, and was amused to see at once the steady trickle of pedestrians down Eden Street. Now and then a car would arrive, but it was still early for cars. As Eden Street ended at its junction with Grange Road, he saw, coming from the opposite direction, a complementary trickle. It was as though a public holiday had been declared.

A few moments brought Philip to the entrance to the Sports Ground, and once within the roughly stained wooden gates he was rewarded by the sight of an excellent pitch, a busy little pavilion, the slow swaying of a great flag at the head of its pole. You caught a slight breeze here, but it was dying. By midday the air would be perfectly quiet, save for the quiver of rising heat.

A number of seats and benches had been drawn out and ranged in a row facing the pavilion, but upon the other side of the ground. These were not yet occupied, for those who had come early were still standing idly, some of them talking and some meditatively looking around. They were of all kinds, from old-age pensioners with sticks, their brown faces weather-beaten, to schoolboys who had been lucky enough to feel not quite well that morning. There were only two or three women in the whole crowd.

Their time would come later, as the afternoon brought a more social atmosphere. At the back of the pavilion, where nets were erected, some few flannelled figures loosened their limbs in practice.

So far, nothing had moved Philip to enthusiasm. Everything was casual and imperfect. But as he strolled he felt a firm hand upon his shoulder, and looked round into the bloodshot eyes of James Davitt.

"Well, young fellow," growled James.

Behind him stood a girl in pink, one of these charming daughters, but which of them Philip did not know. Yes, he did. It was the pretty one, who had stayed with them that first evening. . . . He raised his hat and took a cool hand, observing with pleasure the gravity that gave her smile such sweetness; but he did not feel moved to engage in talk with her, because she was a stranger. They stood in silence surveying the slow movements of two men who hauled a heavy roller towards the pitch. There, gleaming, were yellow stumps.

"What a sight, eh!" said James. "It makes your heart bounce against your ribs!" He drew in his breath noisily, as some unfortunates do when they drink soup, and puffed out his chest as he beamingly swayed upon his feet. "Nothing to equal it."

"Is your boy playing?"

"Uh-hum." No more. James Davitt was instantly quelled. He would not own to any pride in Henry's accomplishments. Philip glanced aside at Rose.

"You're hoping he'll make a big score," he suggested.

"Yes. I should like him to," she agreed. "But he says the other people are awfully good. He thinks Sandersfold won't do much."

"Lot *he* knows," growled James. "Young duffer! Now, Flup, just think of it. The rot that's got into the English character. They go on the field half beaten. Psychological victims. 'Slay us; but don't hurt.' Naturally they're whacked. Then they talk about being 'sporting,' as if they were too polite to want to win. Polite! Knocking knees is what they suffer from."

Philip laughed.

"Well, perhaps they still like winning," he suggested. "Occasionally."

"Damned rare experience," grumbled James.

"You're an old cross-patch, Father," Rose rebuked him. "It's really because you're excited. Mr. Spears, he's like a mother that beats her child because it's tumbled down and frightened her. Don't let him depress you."

"I know him very well," Philip said. "His bark's worse than his bite."

"But so irritating," she smiled. "At least, to some people."

"He's like all Englishmen. They're all mystics pretending to be stupid."

"Eh?" growled James Davitt, much pleased. "You'd think we weren't the only common-sense people in the world."

"No, only the most inconsistent," said Rose. "All poets."

Philip listened with interest. He liked Rose. She had mettle.

"Here come the umpires," James suddenly cried. "Come along. Let's get round to our places."

During the few minutes of chatter, men and boys had scattered to various benches, and were now ready for the game. Two men in billycock hats and long white coats that came below their knees, and showed black boots and a dozen inches of dark trouser leg, came from the pavilion. They talked as they strolled, ignoring the sparse crowd.

What do umpires talk about to one another? Behind them came a bunch of the players.

"Oh, we're fielding," exclaimed Rose, with regret. "We must have lost the toss. I can see Henry."

Very, very slowly, as if loth to begin the day's play, some with their hands in their pockets, some throwing a ball at one another with every trick and sleight they could contrive, and some late arrivals swinging their arms and stepping high to flex untried muscles, the Sandersfold team progressed towards the pitch. By this time the umpires had separated, had placed the bails upon the stumps, and were waiting. And from the pavilion, marching stubbornly together, their pads giving their legs a curious straddled appearance, came the opening batsmen.

The sun shone; the fielding side scattered under the direction of their captain and the opening bowler. One umpire stood up close to the wicket, moving a forefinger. One batsman hammered the ground with his bat, directly in front of his wicket. He pulled down the peak of his cap; he hitched up his trousers; he glanced over his left shoulder at square leg, he stooped over his bat. . . . The bowler, a tall man with glossy hair, took the gleaming new ball, retreated, swung upon his toes, ran menacingly, alarmingly towards the wicket. . . . A golden hush fell over the ground, amid which the sharp crack of a dead bat against a living ball was heard everywhere. All grew more intense. The first game of the Cricket Week had begun.

Rose, sitting between Philip and her father, and conscious of both of them, drew her breath quickly. Her lips were pressed close together. Her eyes were strained upon the players. But she saw them only as a white pattern against a green brilliance, for she was thinking of Philip, and was intoxicated with happiness at being near him in this beautiful sunlight, passive, brimming with sensation.

7

Lettice Holpen made slow progress with Leonard and her mother from the entrance of the Sports Ground to the pavilion. Mrs. Holpen, like a weary actress who once again feels an audience beyond the footlights, had become a different woman. Stimulated by the crowd, by glances of curiosity, a touched cap here and there, and an occasional smile of welcome, she had thrown off her indolence and was quick and vivacious. She dangled a parasol across her shoulder, was charmingly made up, and was as erect and slim as her daughter. Awareness of all this acted upon her system as a tonic. In one sense Lettice, understanding it, was delighted with her. In another, criticizing, without pity, the vanity of one who was deluding herself, she found her parent the most boring of women. A slight irritability prevailed.

As soon as Lettice entered the ground she saw Henry Davitt in the long field, moving warily upon his toes whenever the ball was bowled or struck. He seemed to her now, as always, very beautiful in his easy carriage and his slightly self-conscious attitudes of grace. His golden hair glinted in the sun, he was rather flushed, his cricketing shirt was wide open at the neck. He looked boyish and fervent. That was what attracted her to him—his boyishness, and the feeling that he could be moved to an engrossed, uncritical excitement. Not her equal in wits—it did not matter; she was old-fashioned, and had no wish publicly to outshine her mate;—but ardent, ardent, ardent . . . ardent yet repressible, a man yet a permanent schoolboy, ever attractive, but blind as well as avid, not in any degree her superior. He would never be able to despise her, or penetrate her secrets. And now, in this costume, wherein his boyishness was revealed, she knew that he was necessary to her happiness. She bit her lip as she watched him.

But Lettice pictured Henry with her own eyes and in obedience to the demands of her own nature. The truth was that at this moment he was not so much ardent as cowed by circumstance. He was acutely suffering. He had been fielding for some hours, and his two spells of bowling had been so abjectly unsuccessful that he glowed still in memory of successive humiliating boundary strokes. Each of them had been seen by his father, and by others whom he would have liked to impress. Hideous mortification! The total against Sandersfold had become demoralizingly large. Already, at three o'clock in the afternoon, with only four of their opponents out, the Sandersfold players did not dare to peep at the scoreboard. They bowled, ran, and fielded the ball with none of their early nonchalance—indeed, with ferocity. Everybody knew that they had abandoned all hope of winning the match. Could they manage to save it?

Lettice herself was not very far from despair. She had endured a great deal in the last weeks, and her thoughts, as some glimmering of the truth penetrated to that active little brain, had a touch of trepidant grimness. Hers was the sad lot of a precocious pretty girl handicapped by circumstance. As a child she had been suppressed by a jealous and snobbish mother; and her first young curiosities had made almost any boy a prize. In those days she had been forced to walk alone, without the protective archness of another girl, and so lacked a foil. Leonard, who matured later, had privately told his mother, in indignation, of one escapade, so that Lettice had been starved of male companionship until she had ceased to be quite innocent in thought. At the age of eighteen she had fallen in love with the first young man to besiege her. She had stolen out to enjoy his company. They had been watched. The young man had been a Lovelace; and Lettice very amorous. Only the young man's abrupt disappearance from the district, with several fathers in pursuit, had saved Lettice from disaster.

Thereafter there had been a little gossip. It had been suspected by some mothers that Lettice was "fast," and therefore no fit companion for their sons and daughters. Lettice had received a great shock from the publicity of her first amour, and had been exasperated by censure. Her amorousness had been driven within. Accordingly, she was now, in thought, more mature than most of those whom she met. Also, like other clever girls, she had an intimidating habit of ridicule, arising from a combination of desire and reluctance. It alienated young men. The young men were not, as she came to believe, sexually afraid of her; they found her precociousness repellent and her ridicule embarrassing.

Now, driven by her own needs, she had fallen in love with Henry Davitt. It had begun with her acquaintance with the Davitt girls. She had danced with him, had driven with him chastely in his little car; she had met him with apparent camaraderie in Seahampton; she had hinted that he had better not mention at home that he had met her. This had given their meetings a delicious air of being stolen. Henry had responded to that. Quietly Lettice had increased her possessiveness. But one night a terrible thing had happened. She had brought him to the point of kissing her. Thrilling with triumph, she had laughed at his clumsiness. Fatal laughter!

Joseph himself could not have been more sensitive than Henry. A nice boy, who had virtuously closed his ears to much that had been common talk among his schoolfellows and fellow choirboys, he had grown up, as many of his generations have done (for all their bravado on paper), profoundly revolted by what he considered the uncleanliness of life. He had kissed Lettice with trembling boldness; and that laughter had been as a clap of coarse thunder in his ears. Imagining that he had been seduced, he had abandoned the rôle of lover. He had sprung into suspicious nervousness; and Lettice, humiliated, beside herself, had made the further mistake of ridiculing his timidity. Thereby she had convinced Henry that she was impure and undesirable. Since that night he had fled her.

This was why, upon this summer afternoon, with the sun beating down upon the field and all who were gathered there, Lettice was upon the verge of hysteria. She despised Henry as a prig; but she continued to think of him with emotion. She was in a sad and bitter mood of resentment and self-contempt, sustained only by a refusal to accept disaster. With seeming quietness she fell behind Leonard and her mother as they strolled towards the pavilion; and it was thus that she came face to face with James Davitt, Rachel and Susan, and the hardly known Philip Spears.

"Hullo." "Hullo." "Hullo." There were loud greetings from the girls. Only James Davitt frowned gloomily and gave her a bull-like stare from his bloodshot eyes.

Did she shrink? Not at all. She knew an enemy, and threw back her head, smiling.

"Are *you* a cricketer, Mr. Spears?" she challenged him, mockingly. "We're *all* enthusiasts, of course." She laughed, to warn him that she was not in earnest. It was like an invitation to scorn. Her widely set grey eyes assumed an expression of arch amusement. The very faintly coloured lips parted, showing pretty teeth. In her desire to please, she had the aspect of one who wooed.

"The whole town's cricket mad," responded Philip, pleasantly enough. "Unfortunately not very happy about this game."

He nodded towards the pitch, and they both stood

watching the play for a moment without further speech. Except to a Sandersfold partisan, the scene was really beautiful. The fieldsmen, though tiring, were keyed up to desperation. Their tenseness was full of grace. One of the batsmen, too, was of that charming variety to whom runs seem to be offered. He scored fast, without effort, often enough stopping his partner with a raised hand and calmly watching the ball as it skimmed the shaven grass to the boundary, while a panting fieldsman, beaten by its pace, flung up a hasty arm of signal and despair.

"O-oh!" groaned the Davitt girls, watching poor Henry sprint fruitlessly in an effort to stop one such great hit. James Davitt clucked his tongue.

"Deplorable," he muttered. "Grrr."

"We're losing, are we?" continued Lettice, with an air of innocence. "*Too* shattering."

"Aye," said James, shortly. He was in no mood for persiflage. His gesture was one of anger. "Too shattering."

The parody of her conventionalism checked Lettice's amusement.

"Mr. Spears, has Miss Furze called to see you yet? An extraordinarily *old* lady."

"I think so."

"Marvellous! No, she really *is* marvellous. Isn't she, Rachel?" But it was still with an air of raillery that Lettice spoke, as though she were ready to ridicule Miss Furze. "Well! There she is. How extraordinary!" She laughed again. "I won't say the obvious thing! You know, you ought to *know* her, Mr. Spears."

They saw Miss Furze sitting at a little distance. She was in an old-fashioned gown of biscuit-coloured silk, with a white lace collar and a large old shady hat. How different from the trim, unpetticoated smartness of Lettice! Her parasol was closed, and she leant upon it, her chin upon her hands, fixedly watching the players. Though she was old she was still very alert, and none of her movements showed the fumbling of age.

"I like her," Philip said.

"Do you *really?*" The exclamation was wondering, as though Lettice sought for that satire, that inversion of the obvious, which was just reaching the country from the towns. "Of course, she *is* rather wonderful. Somehow she always terrifies me. Like a hotel lounge. So universally disapproving. . . . Perhaps it's just me she disapproves of."

There was no bitterness; only a pouting lightness. But it might have concealed resentment.

"She's a dear!" cried Rachel, with fervour.

"Oh, I know *you* adore her," said Lettice, still lightly. And checked a further comment. "But, seriously, she's quite a character, Mr. Spears. I mean——" She shrugged. "I mean, she's lived in Sandersfold for quite centuries."

"Aye, since the place was built," growled James, fidgeting. He was glancing about with his bloodshot eyes, and clenching and unclenching his hands. "Damn!"

There was loud clapping. The graceful batsman had just made his fiftieth run. The fieldsmen joined venomously in the applause, hoping that overconfidence would now bring about his downfall.

8

Miss Furze had a very pale face, and was much wrinkled about the warm brown eyes. Her hands were long and slim, but they also were wrinkled and had lost their whiteness. She gave Philip a very direct scrutiny.

"How d'you do, Mr. Spears?" The old, thoughtful, penetrating eyes were turned from Philip to Lettice. "Do you still like your new home as much as ever? I thought you would. And you're comfortable there? You mustn't leave us."

"I never shall," smiled Philip.

"Will you come to tea with me? I can tell you a great deal about your house, because I've been in and out of it since I was a child. You may say I've seen it grow old. When will you come? Next Monday? Thank you. This is a very poor game, I think."

"Oh, what patriotism!" exclaimed Lettice. "It's because Sandersfold's losing. Isn't it!"

"No, no! We're bowling badly and fielding badly. Catches missed. Tt-tt."

"Well, they're ho-ot, poor dears."

"I don't think you're very interested in cricket, Lettice," remarked Miss Furze.

"Oh!" laughed Lettice. "How *dreadful* of you! I think it's a *deadly* game. I know one oughtn't to say such things. I'm sure I've shocked you both. Haven't I?" Laughing still, she caught Philip's eye with great coquetry. "Tennis is *so* much more amusing."

"Tiresome to watch," observed Miss Furze. "Like amateur theatricals: only tolerable if one knows the players. It gives me a headache. Well, Mr. Spears, what do you think of Sandersfold?"

"Nothing but good," he assured her.

"Even though the cricketers play badly," mocked Lettice, demurely.

She did not hear if he made any reply. She had seen Ruth Coulevain arriving. She had seen Leonard meet and greet Ruth. Philip, following her glance, also observed the meeting. Ruth had walked rather timidly behind the crowd, as if desirous of escaping notice; and was still some distance from the pavilion. But Leonard, as if he had been watching for her, was at her side. He was looking down with what appeared to be a quizzical smile, while Ruth was coldly grave. Leonard said something, to which Ruth made no reply. The air of estranged intimacy was unmistakable.

Slowly Lettice turned her eyes, not openly, but rather obliquely, in the direction of Philip. It was clear that he had seen what she had seen and that he was interested. Unable for that instant to control her tongue, Lettice said:

"Did you know your housekeeper was a cricketer, Mr. Spears?"

The malice was extreme, irrepressible; and Philip made no reply to it. Instead, he smiled. He had been struck by the extraordinary and unconscious play of expression upon Lettice's face as she watched that meeting. Surprise, curiosity, embarrassment, distaste, and even pain, had for an instant banished her look of amusement.

"Ah! They're coming in," groaned Miss Furze. "They've declared their innings closed. Now for a horrible sight—Sandersfold fighting for a draw."

Strangely enough, Lettice's answer to this was a look of indignation, of which, however, Miss Furze seemed to be unaware. She was watching Henry Davitt's despondent return to the pavilion. They all three watched. Henry, approaching, caught sight of Leonard, and lifted a tired hand. He came onward. These watchers were in his path; but as he neared them he turned his head a little away, and, following a change of direction, hastened past them and into the pavilion without showing any sign of recognition. Philip heard a smothered sound—had Lettice laughed?

CHAPTER SIX

RUTH

When the day's play was over and the crowd slowly dispersed, Philip looked for Ruth, but she was nowhere to be seen. Lettice had rejoined her mother and was gone; James Davitt, drawing in his wake the two daughters of the afternoon, had made a dismal exit. Soon Philip became aware that he alone, of all that assembly, loitered with players and groundsmen. Already the latter, in preparation for the next day's game, were sweeping and clearing the used pitch and setting little pegs to mark that for the second game. He strolled slowly homeward.

From the morning's high hopes, through the hot day of trial, to the bitter hour of collapse and defeat, this game had taken its steady, its engrossing course. It was the story of warfare in epitome. One by one the heroes had fallen. The pride of the morning had given place to the wretchedness of night. Shadows were long; the sun was sinking. Tired and spent, the players were now longing for a morrow in which their fortune might be better.

It was a short walk from the Cricket Ground to the Georgian house; but it took Philip half an hour to traverse the distance. For he had been led, by his search for Ruth, to speculate upon her actions. Why had she told him that she was to meet Lettice? In fact she had not once spoken to Lettice. Obviously the appointment—if there had been any appointment at all—was with Leonard. Yet when they were together they were out of harmony. Why?

There was no answer to such a question. He had not the facts. But what could the facts be? He was interested. More, he was curious.

Philip reached the house. It was twilight, that lovely pearly hour during which the summer day is gradually dying; and was darker indoors than out. He entered in silence, using his latchkey, hung his hat in its customary place, opened the door of the sitting room, and went straight in. Then for the first time in this old quiet house, in which everything seemed to have been arranged for the better securing of spacious peace, he became aware of raised, urgent voices. The room was half in darkness, heavy curtains partially obscuring the afternoon's last luminousness; and he stood in the doorway. Between the door and the fireplace, not close together, but apart, as if they were estranged, he saw Ruth and Leonard. They had been unaware of his entry until he was upon them.

"I never want to see you again," Ruth had said, with bitter vehemence. "Please go——"

"But my dear Ruth, that's absurd——"

Leonard stopped, turned, saw Philip in the doorway.

"Oh, Holpen, how d'you do?" cried Philip. He had spoken simultaneously, innocently, before the words he heard had carried their meaning to his mind. There was, accordingly, an instant's difficult pause before Leonard laughed.

"Ah!" he said, as if he recognized Philip with difficulty. "So sorry. We're just back from the game. Discussing it. I wanted to see you. About——"

The light from the window was in Philip's eyes, and he could not see the expression upon either shadowy face.

"I'm glad to see you," he answered quickly. "Look here, if you want to talk, why not stay to dinner? I'm sure Miss Coulevain——"

"Thanks, no. I thought I'd make an appointment. Miss Coulevain was kindly promising, as you weren't in——" Leonard glanced at the dim figure. He was perfectly cool again. "Quite a small matter," he said.

Philip nodded.

"I'm at your service. Shall I come to you?"

"Would you?"

"Tomorrow? Wednesday? Or are you going to watch cricket again tomorrow?"

Leonard laughed, easily enough.

"On no account," he cried. "I've done my duty."

"Then tomorrow afternoon? At three? Excellent."

Ruth had crossed the room and was passing him. She still wore her hat.

"Good-night, Mr. Holpen," she said gravely and closed the door after her. Both men stood silent, as if in imagination they followed her progress through the hall and slowly up the wide shallow stairs. At last Leonard took his hat, which lay upon a chair.

"Very poor game today," he remarked, casually, as he stood erect.

"A fiasco," agreed Philip. He made no effort to prolong the talk. "I saw it all."

"Oh, you saw it all," said Leonard, on his way to the door. "What stoicism! But then you're a new arrival. You'll never recapture the first fine careless rapture. To me it's an annual bore."

"Yes, everything's novel to me," admitted Philip, with a straight glance. "But one soon picks up the threads."

He closed the front door after this unexpected guest, and reëntered the sitting room, where Peter had been lying asleep during the whole of the colloquy. What a curious air the dusk had of being palpable! Philip submitted to its mysterious caress, and, still thoughtfully, seated himself near the empty fireplace. A damned odd fellow, Holpen. A damned odd pair, those two. Expressed hatred, and . . . Were they lovers?

How strange! He was unwilling to believe that they were lovers.

2

He saw Ruth again that night, but not for long. She came to the dining room as he still sat by himself at the fine table, sombrely lit, and while Sims, the elderly maid with the hatchet face, gimlet eyes, and heart of gold, who had been with his uncle for so many years, was offering him the tray with its coffee pot and decanter.

"A little brandy, sir?" urged Sims, because he was slow in taking the cup and saucer.

Philip was surprised at the pleasant warmth in Sims's voice. Still more surprised to discover that the gimlet eyes glowed with an expression that was as cordial as it was full of respect. From an impulse of responsive kindness, rather than a desire to burn his throat, he poured an infinitesimal quantity of the brandy into a small glass, and saw her smile in pleasure at the victory of suggestion.

"You mustn't make a toper of me, Sims," he protested.

Sims laughed, exposing the old decayed teeth behind a fringe of polished fangs. She was in high feather at an exchange of archness.

"No, sir. That would never do," she demurely answered, as she set down the tray.

It was at this point in the exchange that Ruth entered. She chilled them both.

"All right, thank you, Sims. Miss Coulevain, may I bring my coffee to the morning room? I wanted to speak to you."

They all went together, Sims opening the doors, Ruth following, and Philip bringing up the rear with brandy in one hand and coffee in the other. In this way they proceeded, not into the room immediately across the hall, but into a room behind it, at the back of the house, closely resembling in its size and shape the library over the way. This room was lightly furnished in a modern style, so that it was like a boudoir. A large armchair stood with its back to the windows; in a corner was an enormous divan, with cushions; the carpet was bright, there were some lively pictures, and flowers stood everywhere. An inspiriting room. Philip, who rarely entered it, looked appreciatively about him.

"What a jolly room," he said. "I see it has the same kind of French windows as the library." And indeed these windows, at present wide open, gave immediate access to the garden. "I suppose they were fitted by an earlier occupant than Mr. Starling."

"Miss Strange, I think. Not Mr. Starling. Not, at least, while I knew him."

"While I knew him!" Philip hardly observed the words at this time: later he remembered them.

"You've had your coffee, I suppose? I must drink this brandy, or Sims will be hurt."

She looked at him coldly, not understanding his reference.

"I've been wondering," Philip presently continued, "if we could give some sort of a party to the people who have been so good to me since I arrived here."

"If you wish."

"Perhaps twenty or thirty. The Davitts—Mr. Davitt is an old friend of mine; the Holpens——" He was observing her as he spoke that name. She gave no sign. "Miss Furze . . . I can't remember all their names; but we could work out a list. Miss Holpen suggested that it might be a garden party. It seems that people are anxious to see the garden. One Miss Davitt wants to play badminton on this lawn; but of course I must speak to Snell about that . . ."

Although he had been speaking continuously, he had been absorbed in watching her face and her attitude. She was dressed in black. As she stood with her head lowered, he could see the glow of her straight fair hair in the mellow light. But for that, she might have been a nun, so pale and so enigmatically expressionless was her face. He regarded the thin, pale lips, which, because they were so straight, and met so perfectly, always drew his eye.

"If you wish, Mr. Spears," she said again, quietly.

She inclined her head and waited. As he did not immediately continue, she looked up and stood erect. She had a very straight back, which was slim, but not gaunt or without shape. Her shoulders, although slight, were of fair breadth. And as she stood in this attitude, the line of her breast was breath-taking. For the first time Philip appreciated her unusual beauty. A sense of it shot through him. He was stirred to admiration, realizing how desirable she might be.

"Was that all, Mr. Spears?" she asked. For all the sign she showed, she might have been unaware of his absorbed interest in her.

Was it all? By no means. But he could not, without impertinence, speak of that overheard fragment of conversation. She was not his friend. She was a stranger, a beautiful woman whom by chance he had found in this old house. Another woman might have encouraged him to speak. Another man, more blunderingly exuberant, might have risked the sequel and ventured a cordiality.

"That was all, thank you, Miss Coulevain," answered Philip.

More than an hour afterwards, in the library, he put a question to himself:

"Did any woman, indifferent to a man, ever say she

never wanted to see him again?" he asked. That thought was so disagreeable that he made no attempt to answer it. Instead, he walked across the room and touched the walnut panelling with a gentle finger. Every room in this house had its charm for him. He stood looking from the shrouded window to the tall fireplace, from the fireplace to the dark pictures and books, from the pictures and books to the glowing table, and so to the dusky ceiling.

"Beautiful," he said. Was he thinking only of the room? Was he re-peopling it with figures from the past? Or only one figure? It seemed to him that in the seat from which he had so lately risen he could imagine the small body of his uncle. His glance moved to the chair in which, upon an earlier evening, Ruth had been seated. About the imagined figures was the shadow.

3

The next morning, when Philip awoke, it was already daylight, but very early in the morning. He had the sense of having been awakened by a sound outside the range to which he was used. He lay with his brain alert but his body completely relaxed, warm but not too warm, soft but not too soft, wrapped about in comfort.

Had there been a sound? Nobody was in the room; the door was closed; nothing visible to him was disturbed. His eyelids drooped again. Whatever the sound had been, it was nothing that need cause him any alarm. And yet he had been dreaming, and as he closed his eyes the discomfort, although not the nature, of the dream was revived.

"Shan't go to sleep again," he ejaculated. "By Jove, no."

And with that he reopened his eyes, turned over, and

looked at the door again. Just what had that noise been? Nothing, of course. The dream had been painful; some protective activity of the waking mind had roused him; he was here, safe, happy, comfortable—oh, he could think of a score of reassuring words to quieten his fears.

Yes, but what *had* that sound been? Obeying a very strong impulse, he jumped out of bed. The morning was clear and still, already warm. It was going to be just such another hot, sunny day as its predecessor, and would again give the lie to those who croaked about the English summer. Sunshine and warmth, both life-givers. . . . He leaned upon the windowsill, looking down through the thick leaves towards the garden. Good God, how beautiful it was! He lost all thought of himself in contemplation of that tender loveliness.

In a few minutes Philip left the window, wrapped a dressing gown about him, and moved to the door. His room was at the back of the house, directly over the library. Opposite to it, across what was in reality a sort of gallery about the well of the stairs, was the room in which his uncle had died. The room at the front of the house was a very long one, the old drawing room. He had an inclination to go quietly into this drawing room, in which the old panelling had been painted white, and in which there was a great deal of old furniture and a variety of eighteenth-century bijoux; but as he opened his own door he saw that the door of his uncle's room was open.

It was not widely open, but he did not remember to have seen it otherwise than closed. Was somebody there? Would it not be a good notion to change all the furniture in it, and thus banish all association with the dead old man? As Philip stood in his own doorway, considering that, the figure of Ruth Coulevain appeared in the doorway opposite. She, too, was in a dressing gown; upon her head was still a little frilled nightcap, which made her look very childish. But her face was dark with pallor, as if she were in great pain or great misery. He had never seen such a picture of unhappiness.

"Is anything wrong?" cried Philip, sharply, as their eyes met across the well of the staircase. "Were you alarmed?" Although he spoke loudly enough for Ruth to hear, his voice was low. She grasped her dressing gown. He had the impression that she concealed a small dark object. But she answered in the same tone:

"I wanted something from this room."

"Are you ill?" he asked.

For an instant he thought she was going to cry.

"No," she said. And as he made to circle the gallery: "No, no. I'm quite well." She had reached the foot of that flight of stairs which led to the upper floor, and they met there. "No!" she cried, quickly, urgently.

"Unhappy then?" said Philip, looking keenly at her downcast head. "Look here, can't I do something for you, Miss Coulevain?"

"I couldn't sleep," she told him.

"More than that," said Philip. "You must forgive me. I don't want to pry. Is there anything at all that I can do?"

"Nothing."

"I won't ask you anything." She shook her head. "It's nothing that a friend could help you in?"

"A friend," she said, rather mournfully. "Oh, no."

"Don't forget you're in my care, Miss Coulevain," he reminded her. "I feel responsible for you, you know. I feel that you're very unhappy; and although I may not be able to stop the cause of that——"

"You can do nothing," she said. "It's very good of you."

She was firm. Her foot was upon the stair.

"If at any time I can——" began Philip. He did not continue.

"Thank you. Thank you. I must go."

She looked apprehensively up the stairs. He supposed that she had heard a sound from above, and was fearful that they might be seen together by a servant.

"Very well. Don't forget."

She ran quietly up the staircase, while Philip went back into his room. What should he do? Nothing, of course. There was nothing to be done. Why, his heart was beating a little faster. Well, at any rate, they had over-passed the impossibility of raising that question. . . . It was a step. A step forward. No, she would be more on her guard than ever. Five o'clock in the morning—an unromantic hour. What had she wanted in his uncle's room? Good God, not a weapon of some sort? He dashed to the door. All was quiet. Laughing in self-ridicule, he threw off the dressing gown and went back to bed. He found that he had grown quite cold. In five minutes he was fast asleep.

Waking once more at eight o'clock, from a dream in which Ruth had been constantly present, her hand nervously fumbling at the neck of her dressing gown, he could not be sure whether he had in fact spoken to her, or whether the interview upon the landing had been a part of his dream.

CHAPTER SEVEN

SCHEMERS

RUTH COULEVAIN was the only daughter of a schoolmaster who died when she was ten years old. She was a London girl, and at the age of fourteen, just before the outbreak of the European War, she had gone out to work as a little shorthand-typist. In those days thin and undernourished, she had taken a packet of bread-and-butter sandwiches every day in a small attaché case to the office on an upper floor of a City back street, and had typed circulars, filed letters, addressed envelopes, and made herself useful in a firm that came to an end as the war began. Her employer had enlisted.

Girls had little difficulty in finding work in the war years, and Ruth had gone from one firm to another, learning the ways of offices and the ways of those who spend their lives in offices. Her mother died. Ruth, alone in the world, shared the pleasures of her kind, and was exalted by the common excitements of the period. When one day she met her first employer in the street during his leave, she tasted the joys of that lavish entertainment which was a feature of the war. Opportunity was recurrent, temptation was irresistible; and although by day she worked demurely in offices, by night she lived in the noisy recklessness of this fatal hour. At the end of 1917 she was out of employment. And after the war, when subalterns had become poor and embittered, she was penniless.

She sank almost to the level of the streets, but not altogether. Shrewdness rather than virtue saved her. Perhaps, also, egotism. She secured a post as companion to a young widow of means, and only lost this post when the widow's business was handled by a new and acquisitive husband. Again Ruth, who had become very thrifty, watched her savings disappear. She tried to write—in vain; she tried to go upon the stage, for which she had no talent—only to find that competition was relentless; and at last she was thankful to obtain scope for her old experience in temporary work with an inferior typewriting agency. Here, as a secretarial worker sent out here and there by the day, she made a precarious living, which answered her desperate need.

It was while she was working for this agency that she met Thomas Starling. And Thomas Starling was a man well-versed in women. He recognized both Ruth's hardness and her capacity for passion. He quickly discovered that her resources were gone. Playing warily, he saw that while she was, to outward seeming, a discreet and modest young woman, quietly dressed and unpainted, she was good material for his craft. She was very poor; she was unshockable; she pleased him. In three months she was his mistress; and in six months she was established at the Georgian house as his discreet friend and caretaker. Not even Sims, who at first had been naturally suspicious, had ever been convinced that her master and his housekeeper were living together in any but an innocent relationship. Sims at last ceased to dread that the two would marry. Sims had come to feel respect and liking for Ruth.

As the years passed, the amorous relationship between Starling and Ruth had declined; but the two had never quarrelled violently. Ruth, it is true, had passed through a period of coldness, during which Starling, as his powers waned, might have been ready to feel jealousy and fury. But the period had passed. He had discovered no grounds at all for jealousy. He had considered the notion of marrying her. It had abided. But always he had postponed a decision, smiling warily to himself with the thought that his hold over her would be stronger without marriage. Once married, he thought, she would deceive him with impunity, whereas now——

Just as Ruth had been able to deceive Sims, so she had always been able to convince Starling that he had no rival. And in fact he had had no rival until the last few months of his active life. And until he lay dying he did not once realize that he had always been regarded by Ruth with a chill distaste that was as carefully guarded as her every other secret.

But Ruth had a human side. Although, among all her lovers, she had been really moved to tenderness and passion only by that one who had been her first employer (the news that he had been blown to pieces early in 1917, within a fortnight of their last meeting, had made her ill for several days), she was still a woman. Although she disliked her last friend, and had been unfaithful to him without scruple, she was not dead to love. Indeed within that year she had for the first time known what it was to suffer the anguish of a love of which she would have supposed herself to be incapable. And she was now so unhappy that Philip's wild guess had been correct. It had been for the sake of securing a weapon that she had gone early in the morning to Starling's old room. Pressed against her bosom, within the neck of her dressing gown, as she talked to Philip had been the small revolver which (she had known) rested, loaded, in a drawer by Starling's bed. Only Philip's appearance and his words of sympathy had prevented her from taking her own life.

2

Now, haggard and unsteady of hand, she withdrew the revolver from its hiding place and laid it upon her dressing table, and looked long at it. The dressing gown, released from her controlling fingers, had fallen away from her neck, revealing the edge of her nightdress. She had forgotten everything save the one question: was death to be preferred to life? Despair had brought her to desperation; and to this had succeeded a state approaching insensibility. But she roused herself, for, suddenly dawning in her mind at that brief colloquy, came a realization of what Philip had to give.

She thought deeply. She moved with difficulty to the bed and sat upon the edge of it, the morning light streaming into the large square room and concentrating upon that bowed figure. With her fair head lowered, her long hands clasped between her knees, the blue silk dressing gown disarranged, and her white ankles warmed by the sun, she pondered. Her face was very white; her lips were pressed closely together; her eyes were hidden as she thought.

Once she looked at the revolver, rose, took two or three steps towards it, and pressed the backs of her clasped hands to her mouth, which had begun to tremble. The blood seemed to fly from her heart, leaving it empty. She stood thus for several moments, poised as it were between life and death. Then the rigidity slowly left her limbs; she relaxed; she staggered to a chair, and groping at its back sank to the seat half fainting.

When at last she was able to raise her head and to stare mutely into the light, a vacancy which had threatened her glance had gone. The trembling lips were again closed. The hopelessness of an instant earlier had been replaced by a hard resolution which made the shrunken face seem full of angles. The straight nose had sharpened, the chin was pointed, the mouth had become a forbidding slit, the high cheekbones were bare. She looked a sick woman of middle age, pinched and terrible, as if every past privation had left its indelible mark. Hunger and fear were mingled with malignant purpose in her expression, from which all hope of gentleness had been banished.

In the room below, Philip dreamed of one who was all love. He had been touched by her look of agony, by that defenseless air of physical slightness, by her beauty, by her proximity. If he had seen her now his dream might well have changed from fair to foul; since he could with difficulty have recognized her as the woman whom he had so lately met upon the staircase. And yet it was of Philip that Ruth now thought, sitting alone in her room with the light bleaching every hue and driving every shadow helter-skelter into oblivion.

3

Rather later in this same day, Leonard Holpen, having made no attempt to do any other work, was sitting in his office. He might have seemed, to any close observer, rather restless, but he was in fact short of work. For this reason, among others, he spread many papers upon his desk, he made many notes, looked into books, consulted files, and stood in front of his empty fireplace, with his hands upon his hips, rising gravely on his toes and sinking again to his heels. He touched his moustache, passed his hand over his smooth hair, coughed drily, and drew his face down in a legal grimace.

At last, as the result of all this hard thinking, he took from its place the black tin box that was lettered STARLING, and this he proceeded very thoroughly to ransack. The box was full of papers, carefully assorted, green-taped, and tagged with explanatory notes. Faded letters, old copies of letters sent in reply. Old leases, old threats, old squabbles over hedges and ditches, the hoarded immensities of twenty years. The late Starling had fought savagely for pennies. Here were records of a hundred battles and manœuvres. But of useful information Leonard found nothing.

Replacing the papers, he locked the box and put it away, making a few more notes as he did so. Then he spent some time in looking out of the window, down upon those who trod the opposite pavement, and who went in and out of the grocer's shop, and the fruiterer's, and the large, old-fashioned draper's, all of which stood side by side. All in vain, for Leonard recognized nobody whom he knew.

The fact depressed him. Litigation (even contentious accommodation) seemed in this town to be at a standstill. The people in Sandersfold were too damned pleasant to one another. Not a dog had been run over for a fortnight. Rents were all paid; summonses were in abeyance. Leonard felt his fingers itching to write an insulting letter to somebody who would be frightened by it. Or he would have liked to be called into consultation regarding a sale of land, or a house. A home-made will or a quarrel between sisters would have delighted him. But the local world was running unenterprisingly. Even the police were unusually benign. Failing any one of these diversions, Leonard felt that he must himself throw material into his active legal mind. "Legal mind"; he had plenty of private business in hand.

There was, for example, Ruth. He had intended to marry her, but he had expected that she would have old Starling's money. No money; therefore a problem, a "situation." Damned difficult. And she was not taking the thing sensibly. You couldn't, in these days, hold a blunderbuss to the head of a man who had been your lover. Leonard smiled. Did she *want* to ruin herself? It looked like it; but really—— Oh, well, he must find a solution of that. He had offered her a flat at Seahampton; but while his mother lived he could do no more than that. Besides, Ruth mustn't think that she was going to be a *help* to him. No, indeed. He expelled a little breath with his tongue hard against his teeth—teh!

Why the hell didn't Lettice marry?

That damned woman—his mother—would live for ever. She sucked the business dry under her settlement. It wasn't fair. She must have had something pretty strong against his father to tie him up like that. It was true that all her money had gone into the business, but it was more than tiresome——

"I'm just an office boy." Leonard spat out the words in anger.

Now how much had this fool Spears heard of the talk yesterday? That was the worst of going back to the house. It had been a mistake.

"Damn!" You couldn't help liking Spears. And yet you felt he was a tough nut. These simple fellows—— By the way!

Ping! That sharply struck bell was to summon Burgess.

Now Burgess, quite as idle as his employer, but standing erect in the outer office, which was very stuffy and dingy and flyblown, had been giving young Phipps, the junior, a little instruction in County Court procedure. This was a business completely understood by Burgess.

When the bell rang, he was holding himself very stiffly, with his finger raised, and his wig slightly out of the straight, explaining to Phipps how one should give evidence.

"Always keep a straight face, Charley," he said. "Look as grave as a judge. Look sorrowful, as if it went to your 'art. Shake your 'ed; but always speak up. Now, I——"

With his finger still raised (as if he had been addressing a jury and had been summoned to another court), Burgess ceased his instruction and marched into Leonard's room. He was not deceived by the disordered papers upon the big desk, because he was an elderly man and was rarely deceived by deliberate deceptions. Only innocence discomfited him. Still with his finger raised like a taxi driver practising suggestion, he stood awaiting Leonard's pleasure. His pale old eyes were so nearly expressionless as to be merely evasive.

Leonard, meanwhile, was busily writing something, and he did not show any sign of awareness that Burgess had answered the bell. This again did not deceive Burgess, who had known Leonard's father before Leonard was born. Such ancient tricks bored him.

"Burgess," said Leonard, in a grim, preoccupied tone. "Ah . . ." He drawled the "Ah—a-a-h." His eyelids fluttered. Suddenly he looked up. His eyes were sharply concentrated, first upon Burgess's poised finger, which dropped, then upon Burgess's twisted wig, at which Burgess immediately squinted, and lastly upon Burgess's curiously red, hairless face. "Burgess. Mr. Starling." It was like a shot.

"Sir," replied Burgess, calmly.

Leonard's manner instantly changed. He no longer barked. He smiled. His tone became kindly, coaxing.

"I wonder, Burgess, if you can carry your mind back —o-oh, a good way. I wonder if you can carry it back ten or fifteen years. Think you could?"

"It is conceivable that I might recall some important occurrence, sir," replied Burgess, with great dignity. "For example, there is the difficulty which occurred in nineteen-nineteen over the water supply. . . . I have a very clear recollection——"

"What's that got to do with Mr. Starling?" demanded Leonard.

"He was involved, sir. I reckleck correspondence passing. Very slightly connected, perhaps, but certainly——"

"No, it isn't that. You probably remember his first will, Burgess."

"The one upon which we have been acting, sir. I do."

"You remember it being made?"

"Oo, that's a long——"

"Never mind. Now, carry your mind back to the time when it was *cancelled, Burgess*." Leonard impressively shot the last two words at him. "October 'nineteen. What happened? Why was it cancelled? Why did Starling change his mind? He suddenly decided to leave everything to the town. Well, obviously the town had done nothing for it. And he never completed the will. But *something* had happened, Burgess. See? What I want to know is, what had the *nephew* done . . ."

"The nephew, sir?" Burgess gaped. In his perplexity he allowed the restive finger to come stealing up.

"This man Spears."

"O-oh!" Burgess gave a long exclamatory cry. *"Him!"*

At this, Leonard sank back in his chair, well pleased. He smiled. With the back of a finger he gave each side of his moustache a light brush.

"Him," he said, confirmingly.

"Well, sir," began Burgess. What a good thing he had been instructing young Phipps in the art of giving evidence! He was psychologically prepared. He was in form. He dropped both arms to his side. "You 'ave no documents, I suppose?" he inquired. "That is what I imagined. There are no documents, because they were destroyed."

"Destroyed?" Leonard's brows were raised. "No copies?"

"No, sir."

"Tt-tt."

"By Mr. Starling's orders, I was given to understand, sir. He came here one day to see Mr. Holpen. He was all in a fine fidget. I never saw him look so flustered. He said, 'Where's Mr. Holpen? Where's Mr. Holpen?' just like that, sir. I had to get between him and the guv—between him and the door. I said, 'One moment, sir; I'll see if Mr. Holpen's engaged.' But he wouldn't wait, sir. When I'd just opened the door, he pushed past me. I heard him say, 'Look here, Holpen——' "

"Yes?" questioned Leonard, quite excited. "What happened then?"

"That was all I heard, sir."

"Oh, come, Burgess!" Leonard regarded Burgess very archly indeed. "You're human, aren't you?"

"The door was shut, sir." Burgess pursed his lips. He looked very righteous. His lids came down low over his eyes. But he peeped. There is no doubt that he peeped.

"I'm disappointed in you, Burgess," remarked Leonard, flipping his sheet of paper with a careless finger. "All right." He appeared to abandon hope. "What happened afterwards?"

"As he was coming out, he said, 'Well, it's the finish with me,' or, 'Well, I'm finished with it all.' I can't swear to the very words."

"Hm. What did you make of it?"

"I didn't know *what* to make of it, sir," replied Burgess, in a false voice.

"Did you see the letters?"

"Well, not to say *see*. . . . I just happened to notice——" Burgess stopped. He again peeped. "Your father, sir, did it all himself. He only gave me the letters to post."

"Which you steamed open, eh?"

Burgess's mouth flew open. He gaped like a young thrush.

"Sir? I would scorn——"

"All right, Burgess. But a spirit revealed to you . . . No? Who were the letters addressed to? You noticed that, I suppose?"

"One to Captain Spears, sir. The other to a bank— Mr. Starling's bank, sir, in London. The Southern and Provincial."

"Money," murmured Leonard, thoughtfully. "You saw the replies?"

"Mr. Holpen went to London himself, sir. He did it by word of mouth."

"What? Did *what?*"

"Met the cheque, sir. Cleared the young man out."

Leonard whistled.

"Good God!" he exclaimed. "Forgery, eh?" He stared at Burgess, sighing. "How much for?"

"There was more in it than that, sir. But I never knew what it was. Something on the other side, I always thought. Only a fancy. Else why shouldn't Mr. Starling take proceedings . . . He was not what one would call an overgenerous gentleman."

"Ah. You mean Spears counter-threatened. Know what? No idea? I'm disappointed, Burgess. Bitterly dis—— But Starling didn't destroy the *will*. He never signed another. Was that conscience? Was the cheque destroyed?"

"It went to Mr. Starling, sir, from the bank."

"You never saw it? Never knew the amount? Noth-

ing about it? As far as you know, it was destroyed. Was
it a woman?"

"Honestly, I am unable to tell you, sir," answered Burgess, with agitated dignity. "Such details did not concern
me. I did not inquire as to them."

"Quite, Burgess. Quite." Leonard smiled drily, de-
risively.

"It would not have become me. Mr. Leonard, I have
been a true servant of the business, never stinting my
labour, sir——" His voice was faltering.

"This is the toast speech, isn't it, Burgess?" interrupted
Leonard.

"Sir?" The faltering had passed. There were no tears
in those colourless eyes.

"Anything more to tell me? Did you recognize Spears
when he came here? You didn't. There aren't any papers
except what's in the box, I suppose?"

"No, sir." Burgess's reply was prompt. His face was
calm as that of a dead man, but less pale.

"Hm." Leonard looked closely at him. "Well, you've
told me a lot. More than you meant to, I expect." A
curious expression flitted across Burgess's face. It was the
ghost of a smile. "Try and think of some more, and let
me know. Understand? Try and remember all you can.
I'm curious. Ve—ry curious."

"Yes, I see you are, sir," replied Burgess, still expressionless.

He shambled from the room without looking back.
When he regained the outer office he scratched his head,
which had begun to prickle all over; and in scratching
he moved his greenish grey wig still farther to one side
than it had been. He looked like an old actor—Wyndham
as David Garrick pretending to be drunk. His lips moved
silently. Presently they stretched apart in a grin that was

almost negroid in breadth. He gave a little uncontrollable titter.

2

Burgess lived in one of the small houses beyond the church, in the scrag end of the High Street of Sandersfold. He had a wife. She was still beautiful, and she still loved Burgess. She was younger than he, plump and rosy-cheeked. Her mouth had the perpetual smirk of the well-fed and the satisfied woman whose sorrows were all behind her. Shrewdness and comfort were her stock-in-trade. But she had pointed, malicious teeth, and hard dark grey eyes. The two features made her look like a tabby cat in a good home, who yet did not disdain an occasional mouse. Was Burgess a mouse of hers? No. But Burgess in the office and Burgess at home were two different people. The Burgess who worked for Leonard Holpen played the part of a grave senior with a love of phrases. The Burgess who lived at home was a quiet and determined brute who knew his own mind in an instant. His wife, who had been loved and kept in order for twenty-five years, was a happy woman. No vacillating tenderness on his part had ever undermined her respect for a virile husband.

And so when Burgess reached home that evening he found a good supper awaiting him, his slippers ready, and a plump, comfortable body, full of the afternoon's gossip, ready to chat or to listen as he preferred. Mrs. Burgess knew her husband's moods. She no longer had a tremor of fear at his coming; but the habits of a quarter of a century are powerful, and she adapted her own with rapidity. Tonight he was cheerful. She had never known him so cheerful.

"Well, what's making *you* so happy?" she demanded, jovially.

Burgess at once became grave.

"Nothing," he said. But as he spoke, that broad, irresistible grin overspread his face.

"Oh, you villain!" cried Mrs. Burgess. "You've got some mischief on, *I* know." She rallied him. She gave him a pleasant slap on the shoulder. She sat down opposite to him at the table, purring, sharpening her claws, blinking, like a cat for whom food is being prepared; and began to pour out the tea Burgess always drank with his evening meal. "I won't give you that *satisfaction.*"

Burgess tittered. He peeped at her slyly.

"You're right," he said.

"You'd frighten anybody, the way you go on. Good job I know you."

Burgess stopped tittering; but she could see that he grinned again.

"I was only thinking," he remarked. "Thinking that some people think themselves very clever. But they're not, my darling. They're not."

"Not as clever as you, *I* know," returned his wife. "There's not so many of them about."

Burgess did not answer. He did not tell his wife any more. Although Mrs. Burgess was a discreet woman, she never heard a single detail of her husband's business. Early in their married life she had questioned him about something. He had taken her by the ear and had pinched it until she screamed. All the time he was pinching, he had looked into her face with an enjoying malevolence that taught Mrs. Burgess a lesson for life. She had tended her bruised ear. She had not again asked seriously for information. She did not now ask. Only when he rose to go to his own little room did she glance shrewdly and inquisitively over her shoulder after him.

Burgess, climbing the narrow stair (for the house was a small one, and everything in it was cramped), no longer smiled. He fumbled in his pocket for the bunch of keys he carried there. And, arrived in his room, he shut the door and unlocked a small safe which stood in the corner. From the safe he extracted a curious leather portfolio, also locked, and laid it upon the table.

The room was tiny. The window was small, and the walls were dark and without pictures of any kind. It was as if Burgess used the room solely as an office, and since darkness and secrecy are natural companions he never troubled to paint or repaper his surroundings. The rest of the house was bright and clean; this room was like a mousehole.

First came copies of three letters, all in Burgess's own old-fashioned copperplate handwriting. Then abstracts of three wills. Then two documents, one short, the other running to several foolscap pages. All were in the pocket of the case which was initialled "S." The letters were all from Mr. Holpen. The first of them read:

Dear Mr. Martin. Your letter to Mr. Starling. I shall give myself the pleasure of calling upon you Thursday. Meanwhile Mr. Starling authorizes you to meet the cheque drawn to his account by Captain Spears. He is sending you a letter to that effect. Yours faithfully.

The second said:

Dear Sir. With reference to the cheque, made payable to yourself, purporting to be signed by Mr. Starling, which has been cashed by your bankers and stopped by Mr. Starling's bankers, I shall call upon you Thursday afternoon at three. Kindly make it convenient to be at home at that hour. Otherwise certain proceedings will be taken which it will be to your advantage to avoid. Yours faithfully.

And the third:

> Dear Madame. I am instructed by my client, Mr. Starling, of this town, to say that he entirely repudiates any responsibility for your condition, and that if any further steps are taken by you he will immediately institute legal proceedings against Captain Spears and yourself. Yours faithfully.

The shorter of the two documents read:

> In consideration of the fact that Mr. Thomas Starling has agreed to take no legal steps for the recovery of the sum of one thousand pounds fraudulently obtained by means of a cheque forged in his name, and in further consideration of the payment by Mr. Thomas Starling to one Annie B—— of (blank) pounds, I, Philip Spears, agree to quit the country of England and not to return, and to relinquish all further claim, now and hereafter, save as by specific deed or gift, upon the estate of the said Thomas Starling.
>
> (Signed)

The longer document was in a kind of abridged writing.

> 26th October 1919. This morn. at ten T.S. came into office demanding interview with H. Forced his way in. So agitated, I listened, and this what I heard. S. beside himself, often shouting. He said Look here H., I'm to be blackmailed. I won't stand it. These————, and many more unseemly words, confirming my view that S. is afraid, and not the thing. H. calmed him. Their voices often not to be heard, but I gathered that S. had received that morn. letter from nephew (N.B. I could not get hold of this letter. H. must have had it. What he did with it I don't know. Never seen again). A very impudent letter—threatening. It seems S. had got a young woman into trouble, and she had tried

to reach him without success. Told he was abroad.
Letters unansd. And she had somehow found nephew,
Spears (I think had known him—not sure). He had
written uncle; also tried to see. Do not know if he saw, but
if he did so without result. So, taking advantage fact that
uncle's allowance (quarterly £250, I believe; but why so
large?) always cashed bank, drew cheque thousand
pounds, forged sig., cashed own bank, handed girl, got her
out of country, now writes uncle he can prosecute if likes,
but if prosecuted will tell why cheque drawn, exposing S.
S. frightened exposure (other matters alleged) but
grudges money. H. said forgery and blackmail serious
charges. S. "Must stop him. I'm finished with him—and
her. You must get him out of country. Ne'er do well," and
so on (this not quite true, as Sp. had good mil. career,
decorated, etc. But Sp. shell-shocked or something, willing
to leave England, etc.).
H. laughed when S. had gone. H. always more careful
than S., he said to me. Nobody blackmail him (he forgets
me, but that's not blackmail, only that I know).

29th Oct

So H. goes London, settles bank, sees Sp. and woman. I
think pays two thousand (?). Sp. agrees take her distance,
no more heard.

1st Dec 1919

Re Will No. I. S. gave H. instr. destroy. H. did not destroy. Said had done so. S. had fresh will drawn, but wd.
not sign. Very ill about this time. Forgets. H. laughed one
day, said "S. thinks old will destrd, but not. I like Sp., and
documents better kept. *Too many S. documents destrd.*
already." (I agree.)

17th May 1922

This day at Seahampton was fortunate enough to meet B.
L., who used to be parlourmaid with S. Down there with
her husband. Told me a lot about S. Not at all the thing.
Always *trying*. B.L. said not successful, but I wonder. She

looked sly. I asked about the woman Annie B., not men-
tioning by name. Said I'd heard something. She asked who
told me. Very inquisitive. It appears the Captain (Sp.)
never came to Sandersf., but S. used to have flat in London in winter (I knew this), and B.L. used to go to
London with Tex to look after. (That's where anything
happened. Might have been Tex, tho'.) Captain Sp. came
there. This Annie was help there. B.L. thought Capt.
sweet on Annie. Nothing she knew of, though, she says
Annie used (By the way: was whole thing a plot? *Say
Capt. & Annie in league, black-mailing S.* Must query
this) to be "very strange at times." I said "What mean by
'very strange'?" Said "You know, strange." Did not press.
Did not know if child born. Did not know much, but
talked a lot of black stuff.

9th April 1923

Tex (S's man) died yesterday. No friend. Very close.

14 April 1925

Met Mrs. Jones, who chars for S. He had been living in
London all winter, and now coming back. Mrs. Jones and
others to clean house. Asked about servants by old Sims,
who had been alone in house all winter. Sims says S.
bringing new hsekpr, and if doesn't like won't stay. I made
an excuse to call on Sims, and sifted pretty thorough. She
knows nothing—up in arms as to new hsekpr. "Always
been good enough." I soothed. New hsekpr—"housekeeper," says Sims. Wouldn't surprise me. Been with him
in London during winter. No Tex, and Johnson, the man
who followed Tex, in prison for stealing. No more men,
the housekeeper to do all. I think this housekeeper sounds
not quite the thing. Must see her when she arrives.

28th

She has arrived. Nothing to be got there. They say she is
sweet as honey to S., but Sims does not like her. Can't say
why. "Just doesn't." (Dr. Fell, the reason why, etc.) She

is young, straight fair hair. Might be Swedish. S. very cheerful. I nearly asked if he ever heard of the Captain. It would not have *done*. Met Mrs. Jones. She has her head full of this Miss C. being not all she shd be. No *evidence*. Not a word, seen nothing, but sure in their own minds. Old cats. Personally I think her pleasant. Not sure as to S. (May 10) Yes, I think it is true. Christian names when alone. Sleep same landing, quite easy. Considering S's character, yes. Cannot make up mind re her.

12th August 1925

Open this to say H. died this morning. Young L. at office, called me home. Saw Mrs. H. Tried to pump, *as she had done many times before*. No result. Suddenly began on S. and his young woman. Said "there was something, a nephew, did something." I knew nothing. Was amused the way she persevered—like Rufus Isaacs that was (now Ld. Reading). If she had any brains she wd. make good lawyer. But took opportunity of perusing all papers relating to S. in S. box. Old will, second draft. Nothing new. Nothing about Sp. *Should like to go through S's desk*. No chance.

4 Feb 1929

S. sent for Leonard to make new will. All to Miss C. It is my belief that L. sweet on Miss C. *He was very pleased about will.*

8 Feb 1929

S. Taken ill. Some seizure. Do not know cause, told "heart." Over-excitement, I expect at his age. L. excited. Wants will signed. No luck. Has inquired. Nobody knows. My belief continues as above.

4 March

Miss C. telephones daily. L. goes. Very upset. Tries to get will signed (I believe). Not done. Very savage. Not the thing. No *gentleman*. Forced to look at him to show I knew more than he liked about dad. Sims knows nothing. She now very fond Miss C. Suspects L. Thinks Miss C. quite innocent. Never seen anything except an arm in the garden. But admits heard Xn names. Angry when I suggested Miss C. too good to be true. Admits people given up calling. I said "why." "Mind own business."

1st April!

S. dies. L. goes. In paddy. Gets out wills. Miss C. phones. Not a long talk. He whispers—cannot hear.

17

There has been conversations, much talk. L. has been there. Place ransacked, I hear. Over and over again. Very savage. I suppose thought himself secure. Now, nothing. Has examined everybody, gardener, cook, Sims, Mrs. Jones—third degree. Useless. Given up hope. Has written Sp. who would inherit anyway, owing to being nearest surv. rel. He is in America, Cleveland. Miss C. gets nothing. L. like a cat on hot bricks. But he tries to hide it. If Miss C. was housekeeper, why leave her money? I say nothing. Have always considered Sp. badly treated. What about woman? Did he take his uncle's leavings? Or was it a plant? I can't find out.

Whitsun

Sp. was in London all the time. He must have come back —we shouldn't know. He came down to see L. No likeness to S. Leonard phones Miss C. to say something about Sp. Goes to see her, but comes back cross. She stays on as housekeeper. Have been thro' all previous, and find nothing to add from certain knowledge. Confirmed in belief that S. not quite the gentleman. Must see Sp. for longer to make up mind as to him. N.B. *Can anything be done with him?* What about Miss C.? L. secretly very bitter, I think. No telephoning now.

Burgess found this document deeply interesting. As he read it his mouth fell slightly open, and his breath came

very thickly and rapidly. When he reached the last words
he nodded. No smile now distorted his face, which wore
an expression of meditative melancholy.

"Well, nothing so far," he murmured. "And nothing
to add. I don't seem to find the old ways of getting about.
Lost my looks. The girls don't like old men. . . . Sere
and yellow leaf." He scratched his wig. "And I don't see
him. What with Leonard going there, and all shipshape.
If I had an original there might be something in it. But
that is not *the thing.* That's blackmail. . . . Still, I expect he wouldn't stick at fifty pounds or so for anything
really awkward. Wouldn't improve his social status—'Oh,
he ought to be doing time for forgery and so on.' " Burgess shook his head. "No," he said decidedly. "I'm
frightened of him. Besides I've kept myself on the right
side all my life; and please God I'll die innocent. 'Except
ye become as little children . . .' "

He covered his eyes with one hand. For a moment he
was a child again, learning at his mother's knee to keep
his eye upon the main chance. If you applied these old
Biblical sayings to yourself it gave you quite a queer
sensation. You always thought of them in connection with
others. He had been kept back by scruples.

"Too honest," he thought. "No courage. I shall die a
poor man. What's all this worth?" He tapped the case.
"Nix. Not as much as a stamp collection."

The knowledge made him sad. He groaned. Then he
rose to his feet.

"We mustn't overlook Leonard," he said, impressively.
"Master Leonard." Again that broad grin spread across
his face. " 'More than you meant to, I expect,' " he
quoted aloud. He gave a contemptuous ejaculation.
"Tchah! Leonard!" he choked. "The little gentleman!"

Casually his fingers sought a rather well-filled pocket
in the case. It was the pocket marked "H." But he did

not withdraw any of the papers from that pocket. Instead, he stood erect, and in a sudden excitement tore the wig from his head and cast it across the room. His old bald head, quite smooth and hairless, was the same curious dull red as his face. He looked hideous.

"America, damn it!" he cried. "That nincompoop hasn't thought of it. America!" His head fell back. He began to chuckle endlessly, until his whole head and face was the colour of beetroot.

CHAPTER EIGHT
ROSE AT SEAHAMPTON

ROSE DAVITT, tired of directing Rachel and Susan (who never had been able to play by themselves, but had always asked "what shall I do now!" tired of rushing about with them, and tired of avoiding her mother, thought she would slip out of the house and look at the shops in Seahampton. She had half a crown, and one could catch an omnibus from the bottom of the High Street, and during the summer months the service was splendidly frequent. So she escaped.

More than that. Having gently clicked the front door behind her without telling anybody that she was going out, she ran into Cross Street. That was not the nearest way, and involved a walk along the entire length of the High Street, but Rose had an object. If she went down Hillington Avenue she might meet a dozen people she knew, and if she met them she would have to stop and talk, and explain, and get behind all the wonderment that her solitariness would arouse. It would seem so strange that she should be going without the others, and by bus, although when they were all together they often went by bus. And though the High Street had its danger they were less troublesome than the knowledge that every window curtain in Hillington Avenue might hide an observant eye. Runaways do not like observant eyes. Rose hurried.

It was a draughty day, warm, but rather overcast, and in the town, with dust blowing, it was not altogether pleasant. Rose felt that this was an advantage. Most people had stayed indoors. Had the others found out yet that she had slipped them? They would think it odd. They would discuss it. She didn't mind. She had the little red omnibus almost to herself. Only one rather shrivelled elderly woman sat behind her, and feasted herself with every detail of Rose's appearance; and this was so much a matter of course that Rose felt entirely alone. It was a lovely sensation.

A rather bumpy journey followed, and in half an hour she was in Seahampton. One felt safer in a strange place. And Seahampton was really quite a large town—crowded, of course, because of the holiday-makers, but not yet as crowded as it would become in August. Only grown-ups and very small children were there now, for the schools had not yet broken up. And the draughty wind, out of place in Sandersfold, was glorious here. It caught one's cheeks, just cool enough to be delightful. Rose felt that she would have liked to live in Seahampton. It was so exhilarating. But so was the sense of escape.

She passed from the bus stop down a short wide street which led to the sea, and battled her way across the promenade to a rail which she could grasp with both hands. Upon the beach below her a few people rested in deck chairs, their faces a lobster red. Some others were bathing at a distance. A rowing boat, manned by a crew of one, bobbed foolishly upon the water, restrained from dashing ashore by the occasional movement of stout oars. It was still early; the sun peeped through the moving clouds; the sea was like boundless quicksilver.

"Glad I came!" thought Rose. "It's awful, really." She laughed mischievously to herself. "I'm getting terrible. Not a nice girl."

A young man came and leant against the rail some yards away, but when she took no notice of him he lost his nerve and passed on. The sense that she was under scrutiny had momentarily spoiled Rose's pleasure in the scene, however, and she could no longer fight against her overwhelming wish to think of Philip Spears. She thought of him so often now that she was bored with herself for having only one subject of thought.

"You should do a little serious reading," she thought. "There are all sorts of great minds at work. . . . What's that man digging in the sand for?" Beyond the beach, as the tide receded, a strip of sand had begun to show; and in this strip a visitor had begun to dig feverishly with a child's spade. Rose watched him, trying to concentrate her thoughts upon curiosity as to his object; but the irresistible preoccupation with Philip returned in waves as steady as the beating of her own heart.

She had discovered a little more about him. A little more, and a little less. His age, for one thing. He was thirty-five. Some would say, too old to interest her. Bosh. And his "past." She wasn't really interested in that, but she had found out that he had been abroad since the war. He had *not* won the V. C. in the war. He had once been blown up, and once wounded in the leg. Nothing more. He had been ill, too. And after the war he had had a quarrel with his uncle over a girl.

That was all about the past. As to the present there was very little to add. He seemed to be very quiet. He read a good deal, or at any rate browsed a good deal. He played tennis well enough, but without much style. He had not bought a car. He liked gardening. He smoked, was not a teetotaler, but drank hardly anything, he did not gamble. He would listen to her father's long addresses upon local politics without looking bored. . . .

"What does it amount to?" she asked, impatiently. "Nothing at all. I don't know what he thinks. I don't know what he feels. Those things are only the scraps. Does he like me? Why should he? He can't remember which of us I am! Can anybody? Oh, dear! Fancy being so commonplace that you're just like one of a bunch of kittens."

That thought depressed her. The wind for a moment blew chill. Her nose felt cold.

"Well, it's no good worrying," thought she. "Yes, I know; but telling yourself doesn't do any good. You tell yourself such a lot of things. *One* tells *oneself:* 'I shall never learn how to say things'. . . . It seems to me that almost everything people tell themselves is a lie, a comforting lie. But that's to make up for all the fault-finding of others."

Again the chill. Rose had grown much more sensitive in the last few weeks. She was quite aware of that. She was a different creature, more selfish, more anxious, and yet exalted and exulting. Prettier, too, she thought. Even if—well, even if Philip *didn't* like her, she was more alive. Better to be alive and in pain than comatose! Not pain, she reminded herself. Not pain at all.

The sea no longer caught the sun. It had grown heavy and grey, a dreary waste of restless water. Very beautiful still, but depressing, agitating. Rose turned away from it abruptly and began walking. And when she did this the sun again pierced the clouds, and she was bathed in warmth, so that cheerfulness again took possession of her mind and she renewed her satisfaction in the thought of venturesome escape from her family.

After all, even Henry had escaped.

That was a new thought to Rose. But it illumined such a number of things that the discovery took her breath away. She began to remember what Henry had been saying. It had seemed, as he said it, mysterious and discomfiting; but now that she was by herself, and in a mood of glee, it became extraordinarily funny. A host of little perceptions darted into her mind and made her giggle. She forgot wind and sea, people and houses, and marched along suffused in mirth. For this reason she was unconscious of Philip's presence until she had very nearly run him down, and was then so taken aback that she could only stare. There seemed to be a lump in her throat.

"Either I must say something," she reminded herself, "or I shall bellow!"

2

For this reason she was rather more familiar with him than she would ordinarily have been.

"Hullo!" she cried. "What are *you* doing here?" How banal! However, it couldn't be helped. Better to be obvious than speechless.

"Did you think you had Seahampton to yourself?" asked Philip. He was trying to be quite sure that she was Rose. Yes, he was quite sure. The one he liked. "I was told I ought to come here and see the trippers. And the first person I see is yourself."

"Well, *I'm* playing truant," admitted Rose, still full of laughter, and now quite mistress of her demeanour. "I've shaken off my family and deserted my post. And I'm having a brisk walk before going straight home." She half glanced as if to leave him; but that was too great a feat to compass in an instant. "Then I shall resume my duties."

"I wonder whether, meanwhile, you'd mind acting as guide to the beauties of Seahampton?" said Philip.

"They don't need one. They jump at you," remarked Rose. But she lingered.

"You're shaking me off," declared Philip, briskly. "I

won't be shaken off, unless you insist. For example, what is that strange building?"

"It's the Public Library. Don't go in there. It's very horrid. All the local fossils are there."

"I'll go when I'm alone. Do let us walk. I feel so fortunate in meeting you."

"And I," thought Rose; "I'm really rather hysterical, it's clear, at meeting you." Aloud, she said: "Perhaps you don't make friends very easily, Mr. Spears."

"No. I'm diffident."

She looked aside at him as they walked. Diffident? She would not have thought that of him. He did not look diffident. His profile was very clear—not sharp, but definite. His mouth was not the mouth of a weak man: on the contrary, it was resolute. And yet . . . and yet . . . There was a sensitiveness in him that might have led to a lack of self-confidence. Was he weak? No. No! She would not allow that. It was unthinkable.

"This big building on the corner is a boarding house. The biggest boarding house in Seahampton. In August it's like a beehive. People pour out of it. We don't come to Seahampton in August. You'll find that Seahampton comes to us. Father says in thirty or forty years Seahampton will engulf us. Meanwhile it just visits and overwhelms us."

"Yes."

"It's a good thing to go away in August. But we never go. The people straggle along the High Street, and gape at your house, and finger the knob of your front door. They come over to tea in chars-à-bancs."

"I've seen the Tea Shoppes in the High Street. Are there any in Seahampton? If so, perhaps we might have tea at one of them?"

"He likes me!" thought Rose. Her heart sang, and her eyes glowed. "He *likes* me. O wonderful! O wonderful,

wonderful!" But, although exulting thus within, she maintained her calm. You would have thought her quite unmoved.

"Yes, there's a nice one," she answered. "It would be fun." Then she thought of her mother, and Susan, and Rachel . . . looking at the clock, asking where she could be, concerned, anxious, rather indignant. . . . An impulse stronger than duty swept aside these thoughts of home. She could *not* refuse. And yet how awful it would be at home when she told them what she had been doing. The exclamations of surprise, the exchanged glances, the instant conjectures. Rachel's temper . . . Her heart sank. "Thank you."

Philip wondered at a grimness in her expression. His brows lifted ever so slightly. Yes, she could surprise him. A light tongue, a light heart; but determination. Somewhere, therefore, under the air of agreeable pliancy, a very strong will, which he had hitherto not supposed to exist. He had thought her a nice girl. But had not nice girls perished in the post-war destruction of manners? Probably that was only the sensationalism of free-lance journalists at their wits' ends for a topic. He now felt respect for her. They repassed the Public Library.

"It seems very dank and noisome," suggested Philip. "I suppose to discourage trippers."

"They only look on it as a refuge on rainy days. But the townspeople use it, and there's quite a good Reference Library. On that other corner is Henry's bank—the one where he *used* to work. You know he's left home. He's now at a London branch. Poor Henry. He was so glad to get away."

"From Seahampton?"

"From home. From us. Women. He's been reading some books that one of his friends—one of the men at the bank—lent him. And he's come to the conclusion that we're all horrible. Apparently he'd never realized it until he read these books." Rose's breath caught, and she began to laugh so that the tears started to her eyes. "Of course, we all denied that we were horrible. We were indignant. But Henry said 'you can't *not* be,' and was quite angry with us for being such hypocrites."

"Angry?" asked Philip. "That sounds serious."

"We were *all* serious. Henry said he was tired of Victorian hypocrisy, and disgusted with life, and that the younger generation were going to put a stop to it. Not put a stop to it; but do something about it. I don't think he was awfully clear about what to do. We heckled him about it, but it had no effect. He said he was thankful to be getting away. He thought we'd all repressed him From birth."

"Had you?"

"Well, I musn't laugh at him; though I can't help laughing. It's unkind of me. In a way, I think we *have* been bad for him. He's been with us; and Father's kept him quiet and tried to make a public schoolboy of him without sending him to a public school. I think he's probably full of inhibitions. We all are. He's going to write a book about it all—a novel."

"Oh," said Philip. "Hasn't that been done?"

"I don't expect he'll ever finish it. He's not conceited enough."

"Has he any gifts?"

"Mr. Spears, you're on dangerous ground. We all adore Henry. I've never thought he was funny until this very afternoon, five minutes before I met you. I'm ashamed of myself for doing it now. We think he's the finest boy in the world—rather a child, and solemn . . ." She paused, thinking rapidly. "But I've just realized how funny he is—how funny we *all* are!"

And with that Rose began again to giggle, the tears starting to her eyes as she tried to restrain laughter.

"It's so . . . awful . . . discovering that you're . . . funny," she stammered. "And I believe Henry never *will,*" she added, thoughtfully. And then: "It's better if you don't. In this case, perhaps it's a mercy."

3

There are some people who receive confidences. They have an air of sympathy and discretion. They sit before us, and we tell them all. Rose was one of these people. Although she was so young and pretty, she already enjoyed the beginnings of that wisdom which is so much more rare than learning. And Philip, sitting opposite to her at a table in a teashop which had been made as uncomfortably like a repository for antiques as could be, responded at once to her poise, her humour, and her sagacity. He said:

"I expect the trouble with your brother is inexperience."

Rose looked at him with her candid, smiling brown eyes. She was no longer thinking of Henry; she was thinking of Philip and herself. She was so happy that everybody was very delightful to her, even the cracked pot which dribbled tea into the saucers and made them disgusting.

"Are you very experienced, Mr. Spears? When people are very experienced—women, at any rate—they seem to me very coarse. They have smoky voices, and they drink too much. They aren't happy; but they despise you—or pretend to despise you—for trying to make the best of your life. I can't explain. Perhaps men stand it better. You don't seem coarse."

"Perhaps it depends on the experience?" asked Philip,

rather drily. But he also was smiling now. "When you say of a woman that she's 'experienced,' I expect that's your way of saying she's a bit battered. So you're not being fair to the word. Do you like men who are 'experienced'?"

"I don't know. I don't like coarse men."

"Who does? Men don't."

"No? Do some women? Perhaps. It's got a fascination, I suppose. Perhaps I just haven't got the courage to like them. Perhaps I'm too conventional. I can see what Henry means, about our being horrible. When you say he's inexperienced, do you mean 'callow'?"

"I shouldn't dare to use such a word of somebody you loved."

"No; isn't it queer how sensitive one is! You did mean that, of course. I can think all sorts of things—I mean, that Henry is green, and that I'm stupid and nasty;—but it would be a great shock if you—if anybody else—were to say those things. Do the psychologists explain that?"

"I can't tell you. Psychologists don't come within my experience."

"Oh, yes, your experience. I want you to tell me. But first tell me if you think it's all just a sort of inverted conceit—as if instead of saying to oneself 'I'm splendid' one said 'I'm awful,' but underneath discounted the 'awful' and was complacent about one's own honesty. Made 'awful' a new, clever way of saying 'splendid.' Splendid to be so awful. It's all involved; but do you see what I'm trying to say?"

"It sounds as if you were trying to destroy your own self-confidence," Philip said, half in earnest. "How modern! One so penetrates humbug that one becomes an arch humbug. So critical that one can't believe in a single thing. It's very difficult, if you go on like that, to be sure where sincerity ends and bunkum begins. And very discouraging, you'll admit. As far as I can tell, a lot of people take great credit to themselves for cynicism."

"I'm not cynical, Mr. Spears."

"You're not cynical, Miss Davitt."

"I don't think you ought to call me 'Miss Davitt,' " said Rose, her head down, and her tongue heavy. She could feel her heart beating faster.

"Then I shall call you 'Rose,' " said Philip. "That's much nicer. But I called you 'Miss Davitt' because——"

"Yes, I know. I shall call you 'Philip.' It's settled. And now tell me about whether you're experienced or not, and what you mean by 'experienced.' "

"Will you have a cigarette?"

Rose shook her head.

"No; I've made up my mind I won't pretend any more to like it."

"Well, by experience I mean everything that's happened since one was born. In that sense, of course, *you're* experienced. You'll say it's a small experience; but it's all assimilated. That's why you're so wise."

"Hm," said Rose. "I haven't assimilated much. If you'd seen me six months ago, you'd have found me an idiot. Perhaps I'm that now. But I've shot up lately." She did not tell him why.

"All right. In one sense I've had a great deal of experience. I was in the war; I've been a rolling stone. I've met a great many people of all sorts. I've learnt more than I've been able to understand. But all that means only certain kinds of experience—narrow kinds. I'm as likely to be stupid or blind as the next man when it comes to something outside a small range. Do you understand?"

"Yes, I see what you mean. It's not the whole truth."

"You mustn't forget that the man-of-the-world is really quite a raw fellow apart from his own particular world. Like the highbrow. He seems to know a great deal. He *thinks* he knows a great deal. He doesn't know much. He's self-assured; and he despises whatever is un-sophisticated——"

"At any rate, I'm not a man-of-the-world. I don't want to be. I should like to be completely impersonal."

"Horrid. I should hate to be impersonal."

It was for Philip now to reflect. He did so.

"Yes, I expect it means one is half dead," he agreed.

"You're not half dead," Rose loyally protested. "I didn't mean anything of the kind. But I believe you're modest; and that's no good in these days. It cramps one's style. Aren't you sneaking off without telling me what you promised?" She leaned upon the table, surveying him in accusation.

Philip was not embarrassed. That was what Rose liked about him. He was always *there*. She knew he was not posing or being evasive, but that he was interested less in himself than in everything about him. An old-fashioned attitude. "I'm old-fashioned, too," Rose thought, with a nod.

"I've seen and suffered a lot. But what does it all amount to? You can't be sure. All sorts of worlds, all sorts of experience. One man's experience is another man's boredom. A great deal of what interests fashion-followers seems to me to be an amateurish examination of bilge. What shall I tell you?" Philip's face hardened. He hesitated. "Shall I tell you about my prison experience?"

"Prison?" gasped Rose, the blood creeping to her cheeks. She was breathless.

"Yes, prison. Does it shock you? You haven't heard about that?"

"I . . . haven't . . . heard about *anything*," said Rose.

"Then I'll tell you about—everything," he assured her. "First I'll look at my watch."

"No, don't!" cried Rose, her hand outstretched, almost clasping that hand he had moved towards his pocket. She was very much in earnest. If he had seen her eyes he would have seen in them a look of horror—not horror at himself or his experience, but horror at the thought that he had suffered. But he would not have been able to read that expression.

"I was thinking of you. Well, you've heard that I had some ridiculous trouble before I left England——"

"I don't know what it was."

"I'm not proud of it now. At the time I thought it the height of chivalry. It seems to me now to have been ridiculous. Perhaps I'm callous. I interfered in something. I did a silly, bragging thing, got my own way, and paid a little price for it. The details don't matter—now. They did matter. I'd been very young when I went into the army; and when I came out of it I expected a new carth. I was also conceited, high-handed. And the result was that I found myself in charge of a young woman who was going to have a baby. Not my baby. I didn't care twopence about her. But perhaps I thought I did. Enough, at any rate, to take charge of her. And in order to bring that about I'd done foolish, melodramatic things that I shouldn't have done if I'd been sane at the time. I still get hot when I think of my own idiocy. All the same, they had their effect on me—on my life, I mean. One of the conditions made by the people I'd browbeaten was that I should go abroad. I went. In the end I went to America. I was saddled with the young woman, who also managed to get into the United States. We were married."

Rose felt her heart grow cold. She closed her eyes for an instant.

"Yes," she breathed. It was a sigh. She felt as if she were dying.

"The money was soon spent. It went like water. I had no resources. And so I found work—that was easy. I'd never done anything but soldiering; but I went into business. High wages, high expenses. It wasn't easy; it was very difficult. I did various things. That's experience. You learn not to do again the things you used to think it was glorious to do—such as getting drunk, and making a fool of yourself, and inconveniencing other people a great deal. At last I found a very good job, and it involved the handling of considerable sums of money."

Rose was in terror. She tried to stop him, but could not command either voice or gesture. She felt she could bear no more. And yet that she must now hear all. Money . . . money . . . that terrible word "money"!

"And then, when, as I thought, I'd made my position secure, I was bowled over by an accusation of big and elaborate theft. It was grotesque. Really fantastic. I knew nothing about it. You *must* believe this, Rose. I'm telling you the truth."

"I believe you," said Rose, quickly.

"I was amazed. Even now I don't quite understand how it had been managed. But somehow, very ingeniously, the real thief—a man named Batocky—had contrived that if anything went wrong with his plans all suspicion should fall on me. He'd made me copy out figures, copy all sorts of things. I knew him; I liked him He had the most charming way of any man I ever met. Well, you'll admit I was very simple. I am. I trust people. Usually, with reason; but sometimes without. What can one do? It isn't a habit one decides for oneself. Anyway, a man much less simple than I would have found Batocky irresistible. He just wasn't perfectly straight, according to altruistic notions. He had the fantasy that anything he wanted ought to be his. And if not, why not, as they say. He's got an odd, tortuous mind. One minute he'd be dilating on the character of Christ, so that one was enchanted. The next he'd be rearranging civilization on a cooperative basis. The next (apparently) he'd be cooking the books. Probably insane, but irresistible. I'm sure that if it had interested him to keep to the rails he'd have been a great man; a leader and a reformer. But there was no fun in that. And he wanted quick returns. That's a modern disease. He escaped. Everything blew up. He shot himself six months later, to cheat the police. And left a grandiose manifesto. Meanwhile it was supposed that he and I had worked together, and that I'd been unlucky. There was even a good deal of sympathy and contempt for me, as a bungler. I was arrested and tried. I've no complaints to make. As I heard the story, I knew that if I hadn't *known* the truth, I should have believed myself guilty."

"Horrible," said Rose. "Oh, it *hurts* me!"

"Horrible indeed! But I was lightly treated. Everybody spoke well of me; perhaps my own stupefaction made them have a doubt. Obviously I was neither a hardened criminal nor a revolutionary theorist. I can't tell. It was like a nightmare; but worse than a nightmare, because every time I awoke the truth was more awful than the dream. I spent many months in prison. You see what it has done to me. You think I'm half dead; and you're right."

"I don't!" cried Rose, in a trembling voice.

"Don't you?" He seemed surprised. "Well, that's as may be. It's what I feel myself to be; and I suppose one thinks everybody else must have the same view. When I said I wanted to be impersonal, I was letting a consolatory voice speak. One persuades oneself that one's own defects are virtues. I was an ordinary young man, highspirited, and full of an idiotic sense of his own worth;

and now I'm just beginning to come alive again, like somebody who's been buried for several years—thanks to you, and your father, and Sandersfold."

"Philip!" cried Rose.

"Quite true," he assured her, smiling. The sadness had gone; the despair which had embittered his voice when he attacked his own desire for impersonality had gone.

"And then?" she asked. "You *must* finish, now. I've got to hear the rest, haven't I? What happened—to your wife?"

"She was never my wife. She had her child, and left us both. By that time, you see, I had no money. She died two years later, just before my arrest. She'd gone another road." He hesitated.

"And the child?"

"Still alive. With friends in America. Quite happy. They bring her up as their own; she's very precocious."

"Yes? And you?"

"It seemed as though I were just beginning to find my own feet when that frightful disaster came. It was such a blow to me that I was ill for a long time." He did not shudder; he turned pale. "I didn't want to live any longer. If I'd found any means, I should have killed myself. I thought life wasn't worth living. Well, in a good long stretch of prison you have plenty of time to think. At first I was crushed; then, as I recovered a little strength, I was desperate. Then I grew bitter and resentful—as many men of my generation, with less reason as I think, were bitter and resentful. But it may be that even prison is better than chaos. . . . It wasn't so bad after the first few weeks. The American prison system has many humane features; and a man such as myself can manage. . . . I thought things over. And over. *And* over. And

I think I grew sane. Now I know that I should never in future have the courage to do anybody a wrong. I've been too crushed; and I haven't a vengeful nature. Too much —pride, one calls it. That brings us back to your conundrum, doesn't it? Sometimes I think the world's divided into sufferers and screamers and grabbers——"

"I don't wonder you're scornful of my conundrum," Rose said.

"Oh, but I'm not. I think it a very simple presentation of a common dilemma."

"No, you're not. You might be. I was really thinking that after all you've been through you might well be bitter; but you're not bitter. Only fools are bitter. Go on. I didn't mean to interrupt."

"I came out of prison. A terrible sensation. One's bewildered. The world seems so much noisier, so much faster than one remembers. And quite as indifferent. One's lost one's place, as it were. Like a rustic visiting a city for the first time. However, it wasn't too bad. I changed my name—called myself 'Brown' . . . anything . . . I got work. You could, in those days. But I was very miserable, and did poorly. Somehow I couldn't stick to anything. I was drowsy, a little frightened. No, *very* frightened. I may have been sinking. Probably I should have ended by dying of starvation. Then an old friend of mine, named Dexter, a bookseller, very kindly urged me to come home to England. I came. I worked for him for nearly three years. Until I came to Sandersfold. If anything happened to me now I could always go back to him. At least, I think so. It's like the old woman who hides money in out-of-the-way pots and ornaments. When you've been shaken, when you've gone through a bad time, you tend to reassure yourself ever after by thinking that as a last resort you always have this or that in reserve—to fall back on—as a lifebuoy."

"But nothing—nothing evil—can happen to you now," said Rose, quickly. "That's over."

"One never believes it," answered Philip. "I wish one could."

4

They came out into the fresh air again, welcoming the fresh wind, and the sunshine, walking together like old friends.

"Odd how it shakes one up to unload an unhappy experience," Philip said. He was shy of her now, regretting his candour, his egotism, regretting (not in fear of the consequences of such revelation) the exhaustion he knew he must have inflicted upon her. "I've tired you," he cried, in self-reproach. "I've shifted my burden onto you."

"No," answered Rose, in a curious strained voice. "Given me a lot to think about. I wonder how somebody who's been protected, as I've been, would behave if she were thrown on the world. Can you tell why it is that some people crack and others don't? You haven't cracked?"

"No; I've shrunk," said Philip.

"I'm sure you're not a coward."

"I meant, grown smaller. You're supposed to get tough; but you don't. You get timid. You guard yourself —as if you withdrew your outposts and finally shut all your gates and prepared for a lifelong siege." He was thinking aloud. Suddenly he remembered her. He said: "And when you meet a delightful companion you inconsiderately open your gates and deluge her—— Why did I do it? Don't analyze the impulse too cruelly, too destructively. I did it to interest you. I didn't want you to pity me, and don't; for I'm really very lucky—now. I can't believe in my own luck."

Rose, carrying her head high, smiled.

"You think you're going to make me less proud," she answered. "It's you who are destroying—self-destroying. You're whittling away a great compliment. You'd better stop at once. You told me because something made you; and the something was *me*. You know it was." She turned confidently towards him. "You do realize that, don't you?" she asked. "It's awfully important. It would be ridiculous for you to call me 'Miss Davitt' again, wouldn't it!"

"Indeed, yes," agreed Philip. "Quite ridiculous. But then I shan't do such a thing."

Rose nodded. She had been shocked through and through. She had never before been enabled so clearly to imagine what the truth of another person's nature might be. She had learned from Philip's story immeasurable things.

"We'll just walk very briskly along the front; and then I must go home. Nobody knew I was out. They'll be thinking I've been kidnapped. What Mother will say to me I can't imagine."

"But surely—is she very strict?"

Rose laughed. The picture of her mother danced before her eyes, to which tears had started.

"She's much worse than that. She's helpless. Now that I come to think of it, Philip, I'm not really as inexperienced as I thought I was. In *your* sense, I mean. I see that I know a great deal—about human nature."

"Quite right. Knowledge of human nature is a little despised; because this is a mathematical age. But it has its value."

"I haven't suffered as you've done; but there's more than one kind of prison. A feather bed's a prison, in one way. When you wake up you find yourself stifled in it. Yes, I begin more and more to see that though Henry

was very—oh, extraordinarily idiotic, there was a grain
of truth in what he said. Mind, *you're* not to think he
was idiotic——"

"Of course not."

"He put us against him by his superior manner. It was
so annoying."

"I can imagine it. I've known it to happen before——"

"With the young, are you trying to say?"

"With the ignorant."

"Philip! Remember I warned you!"

"The unsophisticated," he amended.

Rose considered that for a moment.

"That's a terrible word!" she declared. "A most con-
demning word. Well, I believe *you're* not ignorant.
You're experienced. But you're certainly not sophisticated.
It's a relief. I'm tired to death of sophistication."

"You know nothing about it," said Philip.

"Hooh! It's evident that *you* know nothing about *me*."

"You're kind. No kind person is ever sophisticated."

This was so true, and a compliment so acceptable, that
Rose could think of no effective answer. Her great happiness had returned. The sense of it swept through her
again and again. She did not need to contradict him, or
to submit to him. She did not need to speak of herself to
him. She was happy and eager.

They went back to Sandersfold together in the little
red omnibus, and chatted of ordinary things, unconscious
of the pleased observation of Mrs. Lax, who also was returning home. And when at last she gave Philip her hand
in parting, Rose was more in love with him than ever. She
ran indoors as if she had wings.

What an afternoon of liberation it had been! How
glad she was to have gone alone to Seahampton! What
a lot she now had to remember! Oh, she was a happy
girl!

CHAPTER NINE

RUTH AT SANDERSFOLD

WHILE Rose and Philip talked so innocently at Seahampton, and the breakers dashed upon sand and shingle there, and men and women baked themselves in the fitful sunshine, Sandersfold, though left far behind, went about its business as if no such persons as Rose and Philip existed. The shopkeepers were pleasantly active, but not too active to be uninterested in the comings and goings of familiar patrons; the policeman in the High Street stalked along keeping his eyes open for vagrants, thieves, and out-of-date car licenses; children coming out of school straggled and ran races, and argued among themselves, just as if they had been grown-ups; and their teachers mingled inconspicuously with the townsfolk upon their way home to tea and leisure, and seemed almost to belong to the human species.

Leonard Holpen, although not altogether deserting the window from which he saw the life of the town, was very busy. He was attending to important matters which included the sale of some house property from one client to another, a claim against an insurance company, and the winding up of an insolvent estate. At the same moment his sister Lettice, having taken her tea alone, was beginning to write a satirical novel about a young man. She had no lack of material, and her pencil travelled very fast indeed between pauses for the assembling of epithets. Her mother, in another room, enjoyed such sun as there was, and wrote a letter in which she gave a witty but

inaccurate account of Sandersfold to an old friend exiled
in some even more desperate quarter of the globe.

In the home of the Davitts, Mrs. Davitt discussed
with Rachel and Susan the mystifying absence of Rose.
It was Rachel who was the most indignant at this absence. She was of the opinion that it was a deliberate
slight upon Rose's mother and sisters. She said she had
noticed for some time that Rose was "funny"; that Rose
often stole off alone (it was true, and Rose had been re-
proached for disloyalty by Rachel on more than one occasion); and that things were very disquieting, with
Henry being so "funny," and Rose being equally
"funny," and Father being always so grumpy. "Funni-
ness" was always troublesome; and Rachel did not know
what the world was coming to. Susan concurred. Mrs.
Davitt was the least distressed of the three; but that was
because she had a surprisingly agreeable new novel from
the library, which was as effectively causing her to nod as
any classic book in her store could have done. Far away,
at Penge, Henry Davitt was working behind the closed
doors and brass bars of his handsomely faced bank, unaware of the fact that he was being commented upon by
sisters in two different towns. He was thinking in odd
moments of the outspoken novel which he was engaged in
writing at nights in his clammy bed-sitting room hard
by.

And in the Georgian house, of which the walls repelled every assault of the draughty breeze, strange doings
were in progress. Sims was out—it was one of her afternoons. The cook—Mrs. Foster—was in her kitchen. In
the garden Snell and his assistants laboured minutely to
maintain all in its proper beauty, and in order to do this
stooped and snipped and killed and consulted together in
slow unison. You could hear their voices at times like the
gurgling of bath water. Only Ruth Coulevain, among all

those whom we know, seemed unhappy. She was distracted from every ordinary occupation.

As soon as she heard Philip preparing to leave the house, she moved to one of the upper windows and watched his departure. Secure in that, she ran down the stairs with such light steps that nobody could have known of her movements. Then, leaving the library door open so that no sound should escape her notice, she proceeded towards Philip's desk.

Her object, clearly, was not ordinary inquisitiveness, for she made no attempt to disarrange the neat pile of papers which stood there. Instead, she pulled each drawer of the desk out and laid it upon the floor, and then, shining an electric torch into the skeleton, peered into every dark recess, feeling to the extent of her reach until she had satisfied herself that there would not be any corner to which she had not had access. She turned next to the bookshelves with which the room was surrounded. Book after book was withdrawn from the shelves, and its leaves flicked over and over, slowly. All this had been done before.

It had been done twenty times before. The rugs and carpets had been lifted, and the floors tapped and tried. There was not a room in the house which had not been systematically combed, again and again. Yet Ruth still had frantic hours of search. She would be working quietly, when a voice within would bid her go to this place or that. Always, the bidding arose from the unbearable excitement of hysteria.

Only Ruth knew what had happened when Thomas Starling was taken ill; and she did not know everything. She suspected; but she was not *sure*. She suspected that Starling by some unknown means had spied upon Leonard and herself. How could he have done so? In one bitter pause over these inveterately dusty books, her nostrils filled with the odour of decay, she lived over again the crucial hours upon which her certainty rested.

2

This is what Ruth remembered:

It was a day—a short winter day, cold and dry, heavily clouded, gusty with the promise of sleet from the northeast—when Sims, as today, was out. Mrs. Foster was safe downstairs, in her kitchen, where she read an old Sunday newspaper through her smeared spectacles. Ruth was alone in the morning room, immediately under Starling's bedroom. And Leonard had come to the house through the darkness, as he had done before, by way of the garden. He had been able to leave his office, make a détour, walk up Eden Street as if he were on his way home, and (it was always dark there) slip in by way of the short lane which led to the garden entrance. Once within, he knew his way, guided at length to the window by a ray from that room.

Starling, they both knew, was in bed with a chill. It was moonless, and very dark. A single tap at the long window of the morning room had been enough to set Ruth's heart racing. One swift movement, the silent lifting of the window clasp, a whispered greeting. Thereafter she had been in paradise for an hour. But when Leonard had gone, again by way of the garden, along the edge of the lawn, and so, still keeping to the grass verge, and now facing a deluge of rain, down through the darkness to his normal world, Ruth had discovered that the door of the little sitting room was not quite latched. It was not open; it was drawn to. But it was not closed. Ruth was sure that it had been latched—usually it was locked—before she admitted Leonard. Who had opened it?

As she caught the door and threw it wide open, she had been confronted by darkness. The whole house was in darkness. The only sound in that terrible silence was the melancholy swishing of rain without. Her feet pressed deep into the soft carpet which drowned every movement, Ruth listened. All was still. She could hardly keep herself from screaming.

As last she had stepped back into the morning room, closing the door and locking it with one vehement gesture. Alone, shivering, she had tried to calm herself. But this evening she was in a fever. Leonard's coming, his caresses, her own recklessness in his arms, had excited her beyond measure. Thereafter she had been in a stupor of sensation until the warning click which a clock gives before striking had broken her happiness. From that instant, as the moment for Sims's return had come nearer and nearer, she had been impatient for Leonard to go, wounded at his intenser impatience, suddenly irritated and perturbed, on edge at the noise of the rain, the slowly beating silence of the house, the exasperation of forced parting. Now, her terror awakened, and every sensitiveness jarred, she was in extremity. For a long time, fear paralyzed her.

As panic subsided, and will and old habit came to her assistance, she had crept up to the first floor. Just so might another have crept *down* these same shallow stairs! said her terror. Ah! She shuddered. To her consternation the bedroom had been empty. The bedclothes had been thrown into disarray. He was not there. Wildly, more frightened than she had ever been, Ruth had run to the head of the stairs. There had been a sound—Sims entering the house. Click, click; and then a brilliant illumination as Sims turned on the light. At once—that broad, wide stairway; Ruth a shadow upon the stairs; Sims, elderly, hatchet-faced, white in the radiance below. The two women, thus unexpectedly confronted, had both been startled into exclamation.

Still greatly agitated, Ruth, running down the stairs, had whispered news of her discovery. "Not there? Where is he?" Sims had gasped. "Oo dear, oo dear!" She had whipped off her overcoat and thrown it aside "Tt-tt-tt." They had hastened together to the library. A light burned there; a light and a fire. And before the fire what looked like a heap of clothing. It was Starling. His hand was outstretched, resting upon the heavy brass curb. In the sinking fire some blackened waving remnants of burnt paper were still discernible.

3

As she remembered that scene, Ruth even now shivered. She rose to her feet and stood looking towards the fireplace, imagining she saw the little huddled body, the grey face, the old quilted brown dressing gown with the discoloured ankle protruding from under its edge. An impulse made her go forward, stoop where Starling had lain, start to her feet, put her hand against the carved mantelpiece as if she were minded to tear it from the wall. . . . Fury seized her.

Together on that winter night she and Sims had struggled to raise the old lifeless body. They had carried him to a couch; and while Sims had run to telephone for the doctor, Ruth had smeared the purple lips with brandy, trying to force apart those ugly teeth, hideously gapped and yellow. Sims had screamed for Mrs. Foster, and had then hurried out to bring Snell from his cottage near by. They had all three helped Snell to carry Starling to his bed; and by the time this had been done the doctor had arrived.

From that moment Ruth, frozen with certainty, had

been in terror lest Starling should recover speech or the use of his right arm. As long as he lay silent and help-less, he could not tell them what he had seen and heard—if he had seen and heard anything at all. "What non-sense! What nonsense!" Leonard had angrily cried. "Why on earth wasn't the door *locked?* Fatal neglect!" And again: "He *couldn't* have come in. Ridiculous!" But Leonard was really as frightened as she. His fear showed itself in blame, in harsh refusal to believe. If Leonard had been cool, Ruth herself would have been incredulous. How suppose that Starling could have entered the room and withdrawn without attracting notice? It was absurd!

But since Leonard had shown fear, Ruth's terrors grew. She knew well how one could slip about the house un-observed in the darkness. Starling was light; he knew every stair and every inch of the way. And it would be characteristic of him that, having seen his betrayal, he should creep away again, malignantly secretive. What hatred Ruth felt for him! All the pent hatred of years, intensified by fear!

The suspense had been almost unendurable; the need for circumspect action so pressing (it cut her off from Leonard, and caused her to see him only, if at all, after the first days, in the presence of servants or the doctor) as to heighten the horror; and the death of Starling had been such a relief that she had slept in exhaustion after it for eighteen hours.

But there had followed a further trial of another sort. Leonard, Ruth found, was greatly troubled over the de-struction of those papers of which only charred and indecipherable fragments had been found. He had then revealed to her the fact—of which she had been unaware —that Starling had desired a will to be drawn in her favour. He had been greatly preoccupied—too preoc-cupied for love. He had searched for the will, and at last had insisted upon seeing Starling, in the hope that the dying man might by some gesture or glance indicate its hiding place or the nature of his own secret. All in vain. If Starling had known what Leonard's object was, and if he had been able to command his expression, he would have shown his teeth and gums in a grin of delight. But Starling seemed to comprehend nothing. He lay in almost total silence, as one absorbed in the struggle for life. He was apparantly quite unaffected by Leonard's presence.

The search had become more desperate still after Starling's death. Over and over again they had tumbled the contents of the house, hunted the cupboards, desks, shelves, and lifted the carpets. They had tapped the walls for hiding places such as an old house might conceal in every room. But without result. And with the inevitable abandonment of the search, and the summons to Philip Spears, Leonard's affection for Ruth had grown less demonstrative. He had come to the house, it is true; they had still been lovers, using the old caution and the old means; but it was plain that behind these snatches of love-making which had become a necessity to Ruth there lurked in his mind an uneasy calculation. At last he had suggested removing her to Seahampton.

The offer had been refused, with good reason. He had then temporized, saying that she must stay in Sandersfold, that she must wait . . . wait . . . Would she stay at the Georgian house for the present, as housekeeper? If it could be arranged? He spoke much of his own difficulties, his mother, how careful they must be. Ruth's blood had grown hot at his concern for everything but herself. And yet she was not unskilled in men, not unused to their tortuousness of explanation in such matters. All was clear to her.

It was Ruth who wooed. Let her but find a way! She had known that Seahampton would be the end. A flat there, visits that grew fewer, reproaches, coldness, money —nothing. She had experienced all the moves before, when she was young, and when it was a matter for unconcern. It was different now. She was older. Too old to relish the familiar finesse. She loved Leonard; she was without resources; she must keep him. For how long? It was a lengthy game, and a losing game. Leonard could not, he explained, at any rate in his present circumstances, marry; and marriage was essential to her. Otherwise, Seahampton or Sandersfold, she would sooner or later lose him to another woman.

The weeks had passed. Philip had arrived. Meetings with Leonard had grown more rare, precious agonies for Ruth. At last the day of the cricket match, his announcement that they must part. It was a mistake to continue these affairs beyond . . . Good God! He had been with her two nights earlier, while Philip slept! Was *this* her lover! This man of reason! "I never want to see you again. Please go!" Philip Spears had interrupted them. Then, so desperate was she, Ruth would have found release in death.

But even as she bade him go, the busy mind behind her white forehead had belied the angry tongue. She had passed through absolute despair afterwards; but then and since she had refused to abandon hope. If she had had money, she believed that Leonard would have married her. It was true. If by any means she could now obtain money——— Alternatively, a new way opened to her. It was clear that Philip Spears was conscious of attraction. She knew every sign of dawning interest. Well?

Revolving these alternatives while Philip and Rose discovered the charms of comradeship, Ruth sank down at last with no further power in her limbs. She was in a state of violently suppressed hysteria. She could not cry. She seemed to have cried away all her tears in the night.

All she could do was to grip her handkerchief so tightly in rigid hands that presently under this extreme strain the fine threads parted, and she had unconsciously torn the handkerchief into infinitesimal pieces.

4

It was now that the evil determination was formed. She would have telephoned to Leonard, but she knew that if she attempted to do this she would not penetrate beyond Burgess. That horrible old voice would answer. "No, Miss Coulevain . . . I'm sorry Mr. Holpen . . . Not today, I think. . . . Should I give him any *message*, Miss Coulevain?" A frightful anguish of despair seized her at the knowledge that she could not speak with him thus. Not only the barrier of his mood, but the common humiliating barriers of business were employed. The perception maddened her. What, must she lurk in wait for him—— No, no! She could not stand in the shadow like a beggar . . . importuning . . . "Sir, sir . . ." That was unthinkable. She could never plead with him again. Never!

After agony, cunning. Since need was so great, she must find a victim upon whom to wreak vengeance for her own suffering. The victim was to be Philip, to whose temper she had already in the weeks of his stay at the Georgian house brought a remorseless analysis. Philip was a proud man. A proud man is scrupulous. He was a simple man. A simple man can always be deceived for a time—for long enough. He was a good man. A good man is always tender, passionless, movable by sympathy and pity. Was he a weak man? Cold-eyed, she considered that. Vulnerable, at least, as good men are, as proud men are.

She could no longer keep still, but was compelled to move about the room in a sort of madness, throwing wildly from her path any object which she touched or saw in that tempestuous progress. The neat pile of papers upon Philip's desk was flung in a shower in every direction; the last book in which she had fruitlessly searched was torn across and dashed to the floor. As it struck the heavy carpet it made hardly any sound, but lay there with its old wrenched pages forlornly gaping. And, as she stumbled about the room, in a fury she tore and tore again at the threads of her handkerchief, as one possessed.

The mood of active hysteria passed at length. She fell into sullenness. There were still no tears, but she became aware of what she had been doing, and felt remorse for it, and stooped blindly, picking up the disfigured book and the disordered papers, and trying to restore all to a jumble of order. Then she gathered together the fragments of her handkerchief, holding them crushed into a little ball, and staring with an expression of horror at her clenched hand and the threads protruding from it. Quite mechanically she went to the open French window and stood looking straight out into the greenness which had been made more intense by the grey skies above. The leaves were constantly in motion, swaying and whispering as the wind caught them, in a disorganized and irregular rhythm. The sound drove her to such an extremity of agitation that she restrained herself only with great effort from screaming.

This effort caused her to begin to tremble violently, so that she was shuddering until her teeth chattered. Her lips were grey. She was quite forgetful of her surroundings. Everything about her grew very dark, grew clearer again, and, darkening, came closer and closer, threateningly, until she felt that she must suffocate if this horror persisted. She could not breathe. A great faintness and sickness seized her, and she lost the power to stand. Falling she caught at a chair, and knelt sprawling by its side, holding it desperately while the perspiration started to her brow and about her eyes in a chill discomfort.

What had happened? She had never known anything like this before, such deadly sickness and faintness. Had she been poisoned? It might be so. She would die. She was dying. Or it might be that the strain of all these weeks of love and torment had made her seriously ill. Good God! Her hands flew to her face. She did not know what she was doing. She was beside herself, moaning, gasping, horror-stricken, not only by the pain but by the thoughts which gave her no peace.

CHAPTER TEN

MOVES

PHILIP, returning from Seahampton a little exalted and disturbed as a result of what had been, in fact, an exhausting resurrection of the past, let himself into the house and was soothed by its air of reassurance. He strolled into the library, and was about to pass into the garden, when he perceived Ruth kneeling by a chair, clinging to it, and half fainting. Her face was ashen. Her eyes were closed. When he called her by name she did not seem to hear his voice; and when he strode forward and tried to lift her she did not respond to his supporting arms.

"Here's a go!" thought Philip, unconsciously paraphrasing the Heir of Lynne. "And what a grip!"

He desisted from his attempt. Ruth groaned. In vain did he ring the bell to the kitchen. Sims was out; and Mrs. Foster had fallen fast asleep over her Sunday newspaper.

How ghastly she looked! Something must be done. He again put his arms about that tense body and loosed the clasp of her fingers. Struggling, he lifted her with difficulty, received her dead weight, and let her sink gently back upon the couch. He chafed the cold hands; and then ran to bring brandy from the next room. They were still alone, he bending over her and carrying the brandy to her lips, she with her eyes closed, her hands, like a child's, upon his hand, her teeth clenched, when the telephone bell in the morning room rang. Neither was aware of it. The bell continued to ring in a distant wheezy whirring; and they remained unconscious of the sound. For this reason Ruth did not speak to Leonard Holpen, who telephoned.

As last Ruth's eyes opened and her lips parted in a sigh. She no longer repelled the hand which carried the restorative, but drank greedily.

"More?" demanded Philip. He was looking keenly at that deathly face. She drank again. Afterwards she stared surprisedly, first at her own pale hands and then at his brown one. And as she did this, and raised her glance to his face, a slow colour came into her cheeks. All rigidity ceased. Her head dropped. Once more, with an effort, she brought her hands feebly to his; but this time it was in gratitude. Thanks could never have been more humbly rendered. The lids again fell over her burning eyes—a first instinctive movement of secrecy.

"That's better," Philip said. "Lie right back. I won't ask you to tell me what happened."

"I . . . don't . . . know." Her voice was thick.

"Head clear?"

A long pause. At last:

"Mm. I felt so sick."

"Well, I've rung that bell a dozen times. Just why there's no answer, I don't know."

Ruth made weary movements. She tried to speak.

"Sims . . . is out."

"I see."

"She's . . . won't be back yet. Mrs. . . . Foster's there." Still white and without strength, Ruth let her head droop back onto the head of the couch.

"You stay there while I rout out Mrs. Foster. I shall telephone to Dr. Henty."

"Oh, no!" She cried out at that, struggling up. "Good God, no!"

Philip, already moving away, was arrested by the urgent alarm of the cry. What? He turned, and saw her sitting upright, but swaying, as if she might fall forward. He was instantly back by her side, his arm about her shoulders.

"Look here," he said, firmly. "Lie back. Put your feet up. Don't move. I'll get something to keep you warm." He lifted her again, this time with more ease, and as if she were a child; and laid her comfortably upon the couch. From a chair near by he took another cushion to put behind her back. Presently, after some hunting, he found an old motor rug which lay upon the divan in the morning room, and this he put over her legs. "There! You'll be warm, at least." He stood proudly regarding his handiwork.

She groaned. Her lips moved. He hardly heard the words.

"You're . . . so kind."

Philip grunted.

"Yes; but the doctor would be kinder."

She frantically shook her head. Strange; was it Henty whom she disliked? Or *any* doctor? Well, damn it, she would have to see a doctor. Philip did not mind which of them.

"All right. All right," he cried reassuringly.

He left her in quietness while he ran down to the kitchen. It was the first time he had been there apart from the first ceremonial visit. Mrs. Foster had awakened, and had cast aside the Sunday newspaper. With a clean overall about her comfortable figure, she was crossing the kitchen, holding a colossal saucepan before her, as Salome must have held the charger.

"Oh, my law!" she cried, in heightened tones, upon hearing the news. "What's done that, then? Goo' gracious me! I never heard the bell nor nothing, sir. . . .

My salts is upstairs. Well, well! Dear, dear! . . . Well, what had we better do? I'm all of a tremble. . . . Shall I get my salts? They're upstairs. . . . Ah, *there's* Sims, now. . . ." Her flutter subsided a little.

Philip noted that Sims was the brains of the staff. It did not surprise him to learn this, because he himself had faith in Sims; but surely a *cook* should have more presence of mind? He did not know that Mrs. Foster was still drowsy after her nap, and still dreamily preoccupied with the extraordinary mass of crime recorded in the Sunday newspaper. Sure enough, Sims had returned. He hastened up the stairs and intercepted her as she was mounting to her room. "Sims! Sims!" How reassuring was that prompt, "all-there" response to his information! Sims with a head clear, and both lungs full of fresh air, was to be relied upon. Good.

"What d'you think, Sims? Doctor?"

Sims was decided.

"No, sir. Not if she's upset. Doctors is all very well if you've got a disease, and they know what it is. If you're upset bed's the best place."

"But, 'upset,' Sims. She's ill."

"Upset, sir," responded Sims firmly. She fixed him with her gimlet eyes.

"All right." Philip returned the glance. "What do we do next?"

"Get her to bed, sir." Sims was brief. She was in charge, and Philip knew it. The practical woman will always command respect from men, until she assumes the rôle of boss, when she calls for deposition.

By the time they returned to the library, Ruth was sitting up; but her shoulders were bowed, and she shivered as if she were very cold.

"Sims says 'bed,'" announced Philip. "No doctor yet."

Ruth slowly nodded, without expression, and suffered

herself to he helped to her feet. Each took her, to this end, by an arm; and, supported, she walked feebly across the room and out to the foot of the stairs. Here a new difficulty arose.

"Here, take *our* arms, m'm," said Sims.

The exchange was made. Philip could feel that she leant heavily upon his arm, and held it tightly against her breast. He could see the long white fingers pressed into his sleeve, and could feel their clasp upon his forearm. Thus the trio progressed to the second landing, and to a door previously unknown to him. There was a pause. Then Ruth's voice, stronger than it had been, and without thickness or hesitation:

"I'm all right now, Sims. Open the door, will you?"

She was better. Already she reasserted a social difference. It was unmistakable. Sims moved quickly.

Alone, for one instant, Philip supported that burden. His arm was about her body, and she leaned against him. He had a first glimpse of a white room, very airy and suffused with light. And he could not mistake the close pressure of her breast against his, which bore the weight of her body, nor the tightened clasp of her fingers upon his shoulder. It was almost an embrace.

"You're so kind," she murmured, in a changed voice through which warmth ran like returning blood. "So kind to me."

Sims was there again; they were within the room. Philip was once more upon the landing alone, and smiling. The changed tones—one for Sims, the other for himself; the relaxed body; the farewell touch . . . How quickly the afternoon was forgotten. It did not once occur to him as he descended the stairs to think of all that had happened at Seahampton. That might have happened a dozen years ago.

2

Later, as he dined alone, the moment of murmured thanks was a cause of slightly exhilarated amusement to Philip. It had slipped lightly into his memory, as so many other things had done, and was working there unseen, composing a portrait and an estimate of character. Not wholly favourable; but rose-hued. Upon his return from the sea he had been conscious of a release of emotion; and he had been in a mood of readiness to respond to adventure. Adventure had arrived. A distinct advance had been made. Towards what? He did not know. Now, well pleased, when he had learned from Sims that Ruth was better, and fast asleep, he ruminated upon all that had happened.

"You're still against the doctor, Sims?" he asked, while Sims stood over him with the coffee tray.

"Dead against, sir," responded Sims, jerking her head up and down like a toy. "She'll be all right."

"Overworked?"

Sims did not answer for a moment. Then:

"Nursing, and all that," she said, almost intimately.

"I hadn't thought of it," Philip answered, self-reproachfully.

"Not your place to, sir," Sims remarked.

"Well, I don't know."

"No, sir. You haven't hardly settled down. But some others might of—that *knew*." She did not press brandy upon him tonight, but set down the tray, retreated a step, and stood in her black dress and white cap and apron with hands loosely before her. "I think she rather expected something, too, sir. From——" Sims jerked her head faintly. "From Mr. Starling, sir."

"Something? I'm stupid."

"*A* something," revised Sims.

"O-oh!" Philip did not exclaim; he drew his breath. "Yes, I see."

"I knew they was looking . . . hunting, you might say. She was upset. And then perhaps a bit of disappointment, too."

Philip looked at Sims in silence; and Sims looked at Philip. She did not speak any more. Instead, having said much in few words, and having resolved to say no more, she went quietly out of the room.

Philip sat on, reflecting. Sims was a major communicant. He admired her immeasurably. Yes, there might be others, besides Miss Coulevain, who had "expected something." He laughed a little, thinking of Starling: "They didn't know him!" Well, as far as "something" went, that could be remedied; and it should be remedied. Why not?

"Of course, I've got no more right to all this——" Philip waved his hand. "This" was the Georgian house, Sandersfold, the friendship of Rose and James Davitt, the guardianship of Ruth and Sims and Mrs. Foster and the unseen Mrs. Jones. "No more. And no less," he continued. "No *less,* mark you!" he repeated. "As long as we live in a capitalist world. Even a capitalist world in a funk."

What a series of events there had been in his recent life! Wave after wave of surprising fortune. First the kindness of Dexter, who had summoned him home. "I must have starved to death. Did I deserve any better? You'll never get a man to admit that." Then the coming of his quite unexpected inheritance. The arrival here at a house that answered his every dream. Davitt . . . his new friend Rose . . . And now, what?"

"A bit of disappointment." What? Holpen, of course. What did Sims know? She hadn't heard the words of dismissal, as he had done. But she might have heard other words. Or was "disappointment" merely at the absence of legacy?

She was very beautiful, and very desirable. Very beautiful and very desirable. Unconsciously, forgetting the untasted coffee which stood before him, Philip smiled as he filled his glass again with Mouton-Rothschild. He was quietly, secretly elated this evening. He held the wine aloft, so that he could watch the rich colour of it against the light. How beautiful it was: beautiful and desirable. . . . Sacrilege to speak of the two in the same terms! And yet, though she had now this strong attraction for him, he was not infatuated. The simple and the subtle resemble each other in this, that both assume virtue to be the natural state of man. But they do not therefore close their eyes to detail.

3

From the window, presently, Philip could see the corner of the Lion opposite, and a portion of the nearer end of Larch Street, a few moving pedestrians, all in a pale light, and turned to resist the buffeting of the wind. Just so, at Seahampton, had he and Rose turned. He remembered again the emotion of the afternoon, was embarrassed afresh at the thought of having spoken too much, and released from his embarrassment by truer perception of cause and effect. Rose, so sage, was staunch; and she had encouraged him to open his heart. He liked her tremendously. He liked her prettiness, her candour. . . . She had a purity . . . She was a child, just growing into womanhood; the loveliest period of life, even today, when the world is a bewilderment to the seeking heart. She was beautifully honest. . . .

His mind strayed into appraisal of Rose.

At length he went out of this room and into the library, whence the disorder of that scene of fainting had long ago been removed by zealous Sims. But he stood for some moments looking at the couch upon which he had laid Ruth. He could feel the pressure of her breast against his own. The whispered words. His eye fell upon the book at which she had torn in her fury of the afternoon, and he picked it up, observing the violence with which it had been handled. Feltham's *Resolves*. Was that her reading? Or was it some symbol of a detested rivalry? "Upset." "A bit of disappointment." Very beautiful and very desirable. . . . How desirable? Desirable enough for love? For marriage?

Setting down the book, he moved to the window, and was drawn to the windy garden, where the leaves were beating together in tempest as if they were the breakers upon an open shore. He felt on his cheeks the strong warm breeze which was increasing as the heat of the day passed, and strode across the lawn, inhaling the thousand mingled scents of the evening.

Here and there he went among the paths, down beside the drowsy roses and into the dusky shadows beyond, past apricots and luscious plums that grew upon the old wall, past the greenhouses and delphinium borders, past the pond from which a giant goldfish leapt at unseen dancing gnats, past the Dutch garden, and so to the broad open patch with which hitherto he had made no acquaintance.

At first there were no longer any trees, for this was the kitchen garden, and he could discern little except orderly rows of vegetables, like soldiers on parade, straight lines from every angle. The wind was very strong, but it was less noisy, and it flung itself upon him as he stood unprotected. Exciting! Philip laughed as he almost lost his balance. This struggle was fine fun; it stirred him and made him set his teeth. But he was glad at length

to seek the protection of the wall, and during the rest of
his walk he continued in its shelter and shadow along
a narrow strip of grass bordering the plots.

"You're so kind. . . . So kind to me. . . ."

Half meditatively he surveyed the lines of the vegetables, delighted with their regularity and the general
trimness of the ground. It pleased him to know that in
this part of the garden, no less than in that part of it
which normally would meet his eyes, the same scrupulous
order was observed. He made a mental note, indeed, to
congratulate Snell, the head gardener, upon his excellent
work; and he wished that he had thought to do this
earlier. A further cause for self-reproach! He had been
too ready to accept what he found. One consequence of
such luck as his was that the inheritor did not appreciate
his debt to ministrants.

"A mistake," thought Philip. "I must remember in
future. It's important."

His speed had slackened as he considered this matter,
and when he resumed his brisk walk he noticed that the
light had failed. He had now to strain his eyes in order
to see across to the other side of the garden, and shadows
were deepening everywhere. They came like clouds. You
had your glance fixed upon one point; you looked away;
you tried to recover that point in vain. It had been
swallowed up in the encroaching darkness.

"I can't see!" muttered Philip. "I'm blind."

Owing to his preoccupation, he had quite unexpectedly
reached the end of the long high wall running down that
side of the garden next Eden Street. Before him was
a big five-barred gate, and beyond it a gravelled entry
through which a large vehicle could come with ease.

At the same instant he thought he could just discern
something more—perhaps the figure of a man—at the
other side of the gate; but in this baffling light he could

not be sure. If a man stood there, it was probably either Snell or an under-gardener, whose name he did not remember; and with the thought that it was Snell he went forward, still upon the grassy path, towards the gate. His feet, of course, made no sound on the grass, or only a slight rustling which was drowned by the roar of the wind.

"That you, Snell?" called Philip.

There was no answer. He could no longer see the figure, if figure it had been. As he reached the gate and looked over it into the lane running into Eden Street, nobody was there.

"Dreaming," he murmured. "Idiot!"

That irritated him; because it suggested a defect, or a state of bemusement. So he was not satisfied, and went out into the little lane, and along into Eden Street. It was the first time he had been this way, and he was interested to see that although the lamps were alight and already moth-beset, the street was deserted. Only at a distance, walking quickly, but without haste, a tall man was disappearing through the beam of a street lamp into impenetrable dusk. At the time Philip made no guess at the identity of this man; upon his slow journey back through the garden he wondered whether it could by any chance have been Leonard Holpen.

4

Ruth, lying in bed, groaned. It was night. The breeze still violently stirred the trees, and caused them to sound like breaking waters. She could not sleep. Her head ached, and her eyes burned. Although it was dark, the wind-driven sky was light and clear, and she could see the familiar objects in her room, dimly but with recognition. She lay awake for what appeared to be hour after hour, staring about her, and soon tossing to her other side, and over and over, until the bedclothes were dishevelled. When, finally, she sat up in bed, she grew so sick that she crept once more between the sheets, shivering, and holding her hands to her breasts. Although she had so lately been ready to take her own life, she was now afraid of death.

Her throat was so parched that she could swallow only with difficulty; but she was afraid to move, for fear that terrible nausea should return. At last she could endure no more, and rose staggeringly, as if she had been long ill. The night air from the open window was sweet, and when she had had a drink of water she wrapped her dressing gown about her and lay back in a chair by the window, exhausted. She was better. She could think more clearly. It was necessary that she should think very clearly indeed, and plan, and picture to herself the consequences of her plan, lest the plan itself miscarry.

So absorbed was Ruth that she did not observe how the short remainder of the night passed, and how the birds began to chatter in the morning greyness. Her first awareness of the new day came when her eye was caught by a sparkle among the topmost leaves of the mulberry tree. The sun was rising. A weary sigh shook her. She moved her cramped limbs, stood erect, swayed. But the faintness passed; and presently, as all about her became bright, she went to the dressing table, meeting in the mirror her own haggard gaze. Slowly she examined the traces of that night's suffering and pressed steady fingers to the pale cheeks.

She could hear slight noises from the next room, as if somebody were moving there. A lock clicked. The heavy tread of Sims passed her door. Listening, she knew that Sims had gone down the stairs. By now she would be as far as the next landing, as far as Philip's door. The sounds ceased; she had gone beyond, down, down past the library. . . . Silence.

If Sims was unheard, could not Starling have been unheard?

5

Philip had been reading, sitting in the shadow of a tree, and watching the little points of sunlight as they dappled the grass before him. Once he had seen a purple beetle clambering through the grass, and had followed its progress for several minutes until distance and the intervening blades of grass had hidden that mighty effort. At other times he had noticed how a dull-breasted robin, hopping wide-legged and cocking its tail, had driven a clumsy, nervous starling away by a mere threat. The starling hurriedly prodded the lawn with its beak, absorbed and exploring; the wagtail darted hither and thither, sideways, forward, and with tiny malignant flights; the chaffinch was stolid; the sparrows humdrum. None of them could run as lightly and sweetly as the thrush, or look as innocent. . . . The beautiful bird; the eager, alert, and graceful bird. . . . His book slipped a little. Smiling, he recovered it, and lay back in his chair, looking straight up into the deep green of the leaves above his head. Was not this peace paradisial? Or did his happiness spring from some other source?

Last night's wind had diminished with the coming of a new day; and now it hardly made an undersong for the busy life about him. He had heard Snell and some other, invisible, person talking in low, growling voices; but they were gone, and he was alone, dreaming, lying idle.

Quite suddenly, he knew that somebody was near him; and as he started into awareness he saw that Ruth had come from the house with a basket and scissors. She

was passing near, walking slowly and with languor, her
head low and her body listless. Philip sprang up. He
should have remained attentive, for no grace could have
been greater than Ruth's. But his thought was of her,
and not of his own epicureanism.

"Miss Coulevain!" he called. "Good-morning. How
are you?"

She stopped. Why had she nervously started? Surely
she had seen him?

"Good-morning," she said.

"Are you better?"

"I'm better this morning, thank you."

She did not look better. She looked very ill.

"I don't think you ought to be bothering about flowers," Philip told her, abruptly. What hollows there were
under her eyes! They were as if bruised. "Suppose you
leave them? Look, *I'll* pick you some. . . ."

Ruth shook her head. She did not respond to his smile.

"I must do something," she said, in a low voice.

"Do you really feel better? I don't want to be fussy;
but I should have thought a rest was indicated. You've
been working too hard. Why not take a little holiday?"

If her face could have been paler, he would have supposed that she blanched.

"Oh, no!" she cried.

"Well, now, why not?"

"I couldn't." Her quick glance at him had been like
lightning. Not a friendly glance, and not resentful either,
but incalculable.

"No answer," said Philip, promptly. At that, he saw,
she smiled. Her face became lovely. But she was immediately serious again. After a pause, and rather breathlessly, she answered:

"I have too much to do. I'm quite well. I've nowhere
to go. I couldn't leave *you*."

"Oh," said Philip. "You couldn't leave me."

There was a faint turn in her lips—expressive of a dryness, perhaps, or it might have been a half-smile. Not to be read, at least.

"I don't want to go away," continued Ruth, quickly.

"We'll see," said Philip, watching her. "You mustn't be *really* ill."

"No."

"You don't think you're really ill *now?*"

"The heat tries me."

"Yes; and the continual strain," said Philip.

She started. Then she returned his very direct gaze. She had singularly beautiful brown eyes, of unexpected clearness.

"There's no strain," she answered at once. Then, more slowly: "You know I'm very happy working here. I don't want to go away."

Philip had not forgotten their former talk.

"All right. I shan't insist. Let's go and see what flowers you're cutting. . . ." He stretched out his hand for the basket. As his fingers touched its handle she slightly resisted.

"Please, Mr. Spears," she said. He smiled.

"You know it'll get quite heavy after a time."

Her eyes sent curious guarded glances about the garden.

"It will look bad," she protested. "I wish——"

What? Philip had an instant's displeasure. A frown contracted his brow. It was gone.

"It will be so much better if I carry it," he said, blandly. "And less tiring."

Through some clumsiness, undesigned upon Philip's part, their hands met as the transfer took place. Then both continued to walk slowly, side by side, in the sunlight and the warm breeze. Each moment the air grew more delicious. Bees hovered and butterflies danced; a robin followed them, settling each instant upon a vantage point, and expectantly watching for earth to be turned. Echoes came very clearly across the garden. All was tranquil. Even Ruth, as Philip could tell, had relaxed, and was as if secretly smiling.

6

That day passed; and the next, which was equally fine. Out of doors the traffic had increased with a continuance of this halcyon weather, and cars busily stopped outside the Lion and before the moon-faced petrol pumps. But within the Georgian house and in the seven acres of its garden everything was undisturbed. The routine of house and garden was maintained. Only the relations of those who dwelt in the house varied and recombined, like the coloured glasses in a kaleidoscope. Nothing there was ever still; thoughts and emotions played one with the other, in endless reaction.

Towards the end of the second day Philip, who had been walking in the garden after supper, found himself in exploratory pursuit of the faint scent of burning wood. He had followed his usual route without discovering its cause; and, being near the house, again crossed the lawn, this time in the direction of the orchard, where apple and pear trees already bore in miniature the fruit they would presently yield. The rather long grass beneath the trees was pleasant; he was tempted to stay strolling there, smoking and imagining. And as he walked he met Peter, the big cat whose presence in the house (as the warmer weather came) he had of late rarely noticed. The phenomenon was explained.

Peter came towards Philip, waving high in the air his long plume of a tail, and threw himself down in the grass, rolling upon his back, grasping Philip's fingers in gentle paws, and as gently biting them. Then, becoming excited, he bit more fiercely, was filled with consternation at his own excess, licked, bit again in sportive nonsense, jumped to his feet, scampered to a distance, and rolled in repetition, enjoying the fun, and ready to continue playing for as long as he could persuade Philip to bear him company.

It was Philip who first tired; and when he announced that he would play no longer, he saw that Peter had followed him, and had run up the trunk of a tree, extending himself along a branch and lying and clawing there with his mouth open and his tail swinging from side to side. As if this were not enough, Peter presently darted right up into the tree, and danced out upon a long, springy branch high above the ground. He was quite without fear, and made faces as if he would gnaw all the apples off the tree.

"You'll fall, Peter!" called Philip. "You idiot! Who'd catch you?"

Finding that Peter was altogether reckless, beside himself with play-acting, and fearing that the fun might end in accident, Philip left him, coming at length to the farther side of the vegetable garden, where a wall (this time a low one) checked his progress. When he looked over this wall, which he could do by standing upon tiptoe, he could see another garden; and there, although it was by this time growing dusk, was Snell, his head gardener, bending over a small frame, hard at work. This must be Snell's own garden, for Snell lived near by, and Philip knew that his garden adjoined that of the Georgian house. Since Snell had not seen him, he passed on without a hail; and now at last, beyond the orchard, and midway to the sheds, he reached the carefully made smother fire whose scent he had noticed earlier.

How ingeniously it had been built, so that while the fire at its heart burned steadily it was to outward seeming

no more than a heap of cold twigs and rubble. Only from
the top of it floated a thin feather of smoke, drifting
with the wayward evening breeze. This was another example of the gardener's skill, so little recognized by those
who idly accept the results of his labours. This and the
rows of vegetables, the beds of asparagus, finished and
now becoming a jungle of tender green, the orderly
frames, the beautifully trained wall-fruit trees, gave Philip
a pleasure that was wholly æsthetic. A great man, Snell,
who knew how everything in a garden should be done,
and did it in that way and no other. When one saw his
greatness one saw oneself insignificant in contrast.

"What am I now? A parasite?"

How discomfiting.

"We won't think about it at the moment," said Philip,
pushing away discomfort. "Later. I'm a lily of the field.
Once a worker. I don't defend the laws of inheritance."

He stood looking back in the direction from which he
had come. There was no sign of Peter. The dusk had
swooped. Bats were fluttering; he could just detect their
flight. Night was at hand. Very well, he would find his
way indoors. But first he would go and see if there
was any sign of that figure which he thought he had
seen at the five-barred gate the other evening.

There was no sign of anybody standing there. He
peered over the gate. The lane was empty. What a glorious scent the garden had in the evening, at the end of a
summer day! He was in no hurry to go indoors. It would
be colder there, and very lonely. A house to which one
returned at this hour, from the companionship of so
many invisible friends, was always lonely and chilling to
the spirit. His pipe was drawing well. He would sit here,
upon the seat under the wall, just where the vegetables
gave place once again to the flowers. The roses were here,

and were filling the air with perfume. It was like an enchanted scene, grey and still, full of silent life.

He sat dreaming. Even when his pipe had been smoked
to the end, and he had knocked out the ash, he continued
in the warm darkness to yield himself to its rapture.

7

How long he had been there, he did not know. He was
aroused by the sound of quick light footsteps upon the
path, and discerned a ghostly figure coming towards him
from the direction of the house. It was Ruth Coulevain.

"Don't be alarmed, Miss Coulevain," he called. "I'm
sitting on this seat. I advise you to do the same."

"Oh!" It was the little cry which may or may not be
an expression of surprise. She stopped at a distance; then
came forward more slowly, a grey indistinct outline.

"Were you tempted by the evening?" asked Philip.

"No," she answered, in a low tone. "I was stifling."

"Not feeling ill again?"

"Thank you, no." She at last seated herself, at the distance of a couple of feet from him. The seat was only
a rough bench, but a back had been added to it, so there
was crude comfort to be had from its support. They were
silent for a space.

"I don't know if one hears the nightingale in Sandersfold?" continued Philip, at length, idly. "You haven't?
It's a night for him; but he's house-shy, perhaps with
reason. Birds are helpless at night, and I don't know if
he's any exception. I've been playing with Peter; he
alarmed me by climbing trees."

"Yes." It was a listless voice that answered. He could
imagine, from her constrained attitude, that she was
listening, or wishing him to go. Perhaps his presence
there had been unexpected? A complication? Well, she

should bear with him, for all that. Before he could speak again, however, she had drawn her breath quickly. "I was a little nervous, too," she said.

"Of what?"

"Oh . . . thoughts," she answered.

"Loneliness, perhaps?" He thought she nodded. "Well, let's have a talk. Banish thought. Tell me something about yourself."

"I? Oh, no." After a pause: "I don't know anything about myself."

"No? That's better than knowing too much. Thoughts can terrify, can't they? Facts are simpler. Try facts. Are your parents living? . . . Nobody? I don't wonder you sometimes feel lonely. I do, myself. I think you said Mr. Starling was kind to you."

"Very kind." The words came after a moment's hesitation.

"Did you like him?"

"No." It was bitter.

"Hm." He grunted.

"Did you?"

"I wonder if anybody did. It's a horrible thought. I wonder how many of us are really liked. Depends on 'us,' you'll say."

"You'll always be liked," she said. "Because you're kind. With a woman it's less easy. People don't like me."

"Oh, come! I like you."

"I should have said 'women.'"

"I can understand that. It might arise from a sense of disadvantage. That's the greatest cause of dislike."

"I can't believe that. But thank you. I'm glad you like me. I don't know why you should."

"I think you and I could be friends."

"Master and servant?" she asked quietly.

"I said 'friends.'"

"No." It was the smallest of words, so decisively uttered.

"You'll admit that we're better acquainted than we were?"

"But never friends," she insisted, in the same quiet voice of finality.

He was baffled by this difficult and uphill effort on behalf of ease.

"I don't agree," he went on. "You'll see how well we know each other in six months."

Her head was shaken. She half turned towards him.

"That will be too late," she said, in a strange tone.

"Let's demolish time! Be a friend now! Tell me what makes you unhappy. Let me try—if I can—to remove the cause of it." Philip bent towards her. He was smiling and trying to detect an answering smile upon that half-seen face. No smile came; but there was a responsive turning of her body. "Come, now's your chance. We're alone. If one can't be candid at night, in darkness, among the flowers, all's lost. Don't you agree? Come, a bold throw. Won't you let me help you?"

They were appreciably nearer to one another as he delivered this coaxing appeal. He was quite aware now of the rise and fall of her breast. She was in a light grey dress, with a darker jacket of the same colour over it, which she must have slipped on when she came into the garden. He could not see the colour of her hair, but her face might have been of marble. At last she said:

"If I were to ask for your help——"

He caught her up.

"I should give it with rejoicing. Do you realize that it's years since I was able to help anybody?"

As if Philip had not interrupted, Ruth said:

"You'd refuse it."

"Nonsense."

She put her hand suddenly upon his as it lay upon the seat between them.

"No!" she cried, in a clear voice. "It's impossible. If I thought I could take from you, I would. I can't. There are good reasons."

"How mysterious. Surely you can tell me what they are?"

He turned his hand, and so clasped hers, which was quite cold. He felt it quiver.

"No," said Ruth. "That's not possible. And I must go indoors now. I ought to have been there long ago."

But her hand remained in his.

"Listen," said Philip, quickly, and very much more seriously. "You're missing your chance."

His altered tone produced a further change in her. She said:

"I've always done that. I've had so many, haven't I! Let me go now. I've left the house open."

"Sims is there."

"Sims went to bed before I came out. You can see her window."

"I can't." Philip looked towards the house. "I can see nothing. I can hardly see even you."

"Thank God for that!"

"Why do you thank God?"

There was no answer. When she spoke again, it was in direct assault.

"I wonder what you *do* think of me," she said, slowly, as if between her teeth. "Of *any* woman; but of me in particular. You'd be afraid to tell me, for all the darkness. . . ."

There was enticement in her tone. It was like a practised caress.

"I'm less than ever afraid in the darkness. But I should prefer the light."

"Yes? Why?"

"I think you extraordinarily beautiful——"

"A moment ago you couldn't see me at all." Now, indeed, she was smiling in a curious demure way, her thin lips hardly turned at the corners.

"I can remember. But in that respect I should prefer the light, as I said. For purposes of inventory. Extraordinarily beautiful and secret. I think you may be a voluptuary. I doubt if you would be so quiet if you hadn't experienced a good deal of life; and that's why I'm surprised to find you here in Sandersfold, where you have so little scope. There must be some explanation, which I promised not to try and find out. Am I offending you?"

"Not at all." She was deeply interested, and was listening intently.

"But, since you *are* here, I'm disposed to exclaim at my own luck."

"Why?" she interrogated, sharply. He recognized that she had the gamut of the coquette, if not of the harlot. He was unperturbed. The die was cast.

"Various reasons. One of them this moment." Ruth laughed—a smothered laugh. "I look forward to learning a lot more about your character. At present I see only that it isn't all on the surface, although I don't know how deep it lies. And I see that you're very resentful against life (there may be reason). And I think you the most provoking obstinate person I've ever met——"

"Do you? Am I?" She leaned towards him. He released her hand and put an arm about her shoulders, as it was clear that she had intended him to do. She made no show of resistance. Far from being rigid, her shoulders pressed back against his arm, in just such voluptuous surrender as he had imagined. Her face was very near to his.

"Why are you so obstinate?"

He heard her laugh.

"I wonder!" she said, in the same deep, caressing tone. "Do you think you could guess? Perhaps from—disinclination."

"Is it from that?" asked Philip.

"I wonder," she said, in a voice that might have made him shudder. "My God, I wonder!" she repeated. "Of course it is, you darling!"

She was in his arms, as purposeful as he. Her arms strained him to her breast. Her cheek was raised; it was against his own. Her mouth was eager for his kiss.

"Apparently not," observed Philip, before he kissed her.

"Why waste time *talking?*" she ferociously demanded. Her breath was warm upon his lips, her body heavy in abandonment to the embrace. They were surrounded by the warm darkness, and the night breeze was laden with intoxicating perfume. Philip heard an owl hoot, as if in laughter; but thereafter he was conscious of no other sound than her quick deep breathing and the rapid beating of her heart.

CHAPTER ELEVEN

THE GARDEN PARTY

ALICIA FURZE was dressing to go to the garden party at the Georgian house. Although she had no need to consider with much anxiety the question of what she should wear—for she always had either a pale grey or a biscuit-coloured silk dress for summer afternoons—she was long upon the task. That was because her sight was less good than of old, and her fingers less apt; and because all the time she was dressing she had in mind recollections of many parties which had taken place in the past. No longer did her hands go straight to a brooch, or straight to a button. They wavered, while her thoughts said: "The first time I wore this brooch . . ." or, "It was a button like this that Annie Jones swallowed at school sixty-five years ago," or, without any obvious connection (but some connection there must have been, since the mind is less chaotic than modern writers wish us to credit), "I wonder what it really was that old Dr. Dobbin said to Mrs. Lambe when she threw his medicine at his head."

She was waiting for the Davitts, who were to call and take her on to the Georgian house. Naturally, it was of Rose that she thought most often, for if the truth must be told she had a curious sense that Rose was in temper rather like herself. She believed that human nature did not alter; but that fashions in thought and morals changed in cycles. This decade free; that uncertain; the next Puritan; and so on. And her notion was that *if* Rose had been an only daughter, and *if* Rose had been born seventy-seven

years ago (instead of twenty-two) she might have let
Tom Hawks stay with his mother, as Alicia had done.
But, again, that if Alicia had been born in the twentieth
century she would now be just such a one as Rose, and
by no means inclined to allow Tom's mother to get the best
of it. Was the greater independence of today a good
thing? Was it not likely to be succeeded by an era of
strictness?

"Now why can't young people be happy?" asked Miss
Furze, as she arranged her broad lace collar and cuffs.
"I suppose it's because they don't know what they want.
And they're too proud to let that be seen. Or if they
know what they want—but, however, that's not possible.
People should all live twice, as those dreadful people say
they do. Theosophists, I think. . . . I don't like this
rackety music. It's like pepper; for jaded palates. . . .
They're all overexcited, children who've stayed up too
late. . . . Rose isn't like that. Yes, but that family!
Those girls will never get married. At any rate, not until
Rose marries. She might start a landslide into matrimony! And a good thing, too.

"I haven't seen Rose with that man. If a man's timid,
he pretends to be indifferent. If he's not timid, he's ruth-
less. Everybody pretending. Everybody. I liked him,
though. I don't think he's timid. What's the matter with
him? A man oughtn't to be considerate. If he's considerate
to women, he's taken advantage of by women. Hm.
Hullo, there's Rose."

She had gone to the window of her room upon the
first floor, and now saw Rose walking briskly, alone, along
the road. It was a quick, rather nervous walk. That was
dangerous. She walked according to her mood, which
varied much from grave to gay, and this afternoon, as
Miss Furze could tell, she was in high spirits. She looked
very slight and very pretty, in a light green dress and

a little green hat cocked a trifle upon one side of her head, so that a fair curl made its appearance above a single visible ear.

"Not too robust," thought Miss Furze. "Healthy enough. Oh, dear, she's pretty. She's as pretty as a spring flower. Who could miss it? Do the men like these pasty faces and dirty lips that make one think of decay?" She shuddered. She had seen more than one dead woman in her time. Death horrified her. She was not afraid of it for herself (because she was that anomaly, a religious woman without conviction of sin), but she was horrified at the thought that Rose must die one day, and all this serene loveliness pass.

"My dear, I'm glad to see you," said Miss Furze, as Rose came straight up to her room. "You look charming; but that's not the only reason. I've been getting gloomy."

"It's the thought of going to a party, Alicia," laughed Rose.

"It's the thought that I shall never again look as pretty as you," retorted Miss Furze. "It's a pretty frock, and a pretty hat; and a pretty face, too."

Rose knew all these things; but the compliment was perfectly welcome.

"Don't flatter!" she cried sternly. "But why should you be gloomy, Alicia?"

"I've been thinking we ought to have two lives. One for experiments."

"Yes, this is an experimental age," said Rose, oracularly.

"None the happier for that," retorted Miss Furze. "People are so conceited."

Rose shook her head.

"You're being naughty," she reminded her friend. "Who are 'people'? You and I? We're 'people.' I mean, to others. Isn't it funny to think of everybody being 'I' to herself! I never get over it. I think you're rather restless, Alicia. A modern woman. You're impatient."

Miss Furze liked to be teased—by Rose.

"Yes," she agreed. "I'm fussed. I'm not myself. It's because I've been lonely. You haven't been to see me; and it's been raining. Where have you been?"

"I've been to London, where I saw a play, and the shops, and the funny 'people.' It wasn't a good play. So few plays *are*. Or novels either, for that matter. And I've been to Seahampton, where I met Mr. Spears. And I've been to the Girls' Club, because I was bullied into it by Mrs. Paget. Alicia, I haven't any fancy at all for good works—at least, for improving the culture of the poor. It seems such cheek, somehow!"

"Yes," said Miss Furze. "And do you like Mr. Spears?"

"Very much," admitted Rose, frankly.

Too frankly, thought Miss Furze. With too great an air of candour. Well?

"I like him, myself," she agreed. "But I can't quite make up my mind about him."

Rose was demure.

"Perhaps you will, this afternoon," she suggested.

"In that crowd? No. Everything will be perfunctory. Did you talk to him?"

"Yes. He's quite a chatterbox." Rose smiled. With what happy archness! "You ought to be kind to him, Alicia," she added, more seriously. Who was to discover that her heart always beat a little faster when Philip was named? She hoped, nobody. Not even Philip? Philip least of all. "But I'm sure you will be."

Miss Furze knew then that Rose was in love with Philip. Her lips were closed. She looked once at Rose, an embracing glance of wisdom; and averted her eyes. She spoke of him no more. At least, she asked no more questions. Whatever her faults, Miss Furze was a lady, if that word nowadays has any but a ribald significance.

"I'm sure I shall be," she responded. "At my age it's one's only weapon."

For a moment they were not at all serious. Miss Furze's heart rose at the sense that Rose was happy. She could— surely?—not be happy without reason. That must be taken for granted. She was wise, not likely to deceive herself. . . . And yet—— Miss Furze held her tongue. It was no time for repressive cautions. They were out of date.

2

As Rose and Miss Furze, walking slowly, reached the corner of Hillington Avenue, they met the rest of the Davitt family, en route. James and his wife came first, and Rachel and Susan marched arm in arm, a habit they had when Rose was absent. When she was with them they were like two of the three balls of a pawnbroker's sign or two of the three legs which represent the Isle of Man. Henry, of course, being stationed now at Penge, was not with the party. He was busily engaged with great books at a big desk, behind closed doors; and he was thinking of Lettice Holpen, from whom that morning he had received a dry letter; and soon would go home to write his scurrilous satire upon modern life, as to which he was so well informed.

"Tt-tt," clucked Alicia Furze, at sight of the quartet. "Reminds me of my schooldays, when we all walked two by two, very primly. And, as I live, I see Mr. and Mrs. Paggles farther along! They're hurrying. All want to arrive at once, like a school treat. Rose, my dear, never develop a love for doing things en masse! It's a sign of degeneracy. So sheeplike. And you know what happens to sheep. Well, Mrs. Davitt, how is your cold?"

"What, dear?" asked Mrs. Davitt.

"Cold!" cried Miss Furze.

"Are you? You should wear a shawl. I always do. I have it on *under* my coat."

"Aa-ch!" cried James Davitt, abandoning his wife. "Come along, Rose. I've seen that bore Paggles. He'll be on us in an instant, while your mother dawdles. I've heard all his stories; and all his opinions; and one day I shall tell him so."

Davitt looked very fierce. His moustache bristled. Rose had a disrespectful memory of the words "quills upon the fretful porcupine."

"He's bound to catch us, Father," said she. "They're coming at such a rate. You'd better compose yourself. Think of something pleasant to say to him."

"Well, what?"

"Ask him to tell you his story of the boiled mutton— say you only *half* remember it."

"But I could tell it him backwards!"

"Sh. Here they are."

Mr. and Mrs. Paggles were upon the party while Mrs. Davitt was still engaged in giving Miss Furze a consummate record of recent symptoms. They rushed up. Hats were raised—Mr. Paggles raised his afresh as he enthusiastically shook hands with each member of that sluggish group—and smiles were exchanged; and it is a remarkable thing that while Mr. Paggles was detested by all who knew him, his wife, Mrs. Paggles, was generally liked throughout the town. She was small, and demure (not at all sly), and grey-haired; while he was tall, scraggy, and overfamiliar. His carriage was a perpetual half-bow. He was a born usher.

"Going to the garden party? Splendid! How do, Mrs. Davitt, Miss Furze . . .Younger each day, I see. Haha! Well, now, Davitt, you're the man I want to talk to.

Do you know the Council's going about the building of these cottages on the Whippingham Road, and using tiles when they're twice the price of slates? Who's responsible? Who's responsible, eh? Some jiggery-pokery there, isn't there? With Snatch on the Council! I tell you, I've written a stiff letter to the *Mercury*. Signed it. 'Large Ratepayer.' Didn't I, Madame! '*Large* Ratepayer.' With rates as they are . . . I've said—now, how was it? I said 'Sir.' No '*Dear* Sir' for me: just 'Sir.' Short, you see. Curt. I've got no use for the journalistic fraternity. And then: 'Having resided in Sandersfold for the last twenty-five years, I *think* I may presume to know something of its *domestic economy.*' 'Think,' d'you see? 'But, sir, does the Council know anything of *any form* of? I trow not.' "

"Come on. Let's get on," growled James Davitt, taking that eager arm, and drawing Mr. Paggles ahead of the women.

" 'I trow not,' " repeated Mr. Paggles. "Else why should they now . . . Sir, this is a very travesty of economy . . .' "

He spoke in a loud, high voice which hit the houses upon one side of Eden Street and bounded off them and back to the long wall opposite, so that the noise was like that of rolling high-pitched thunder. If Mrs. Davitt had not been causing Mrs. Paggles to raise her voice also, they would have heard his every word. Mrs. Paggles was saying:

"I told Mr. James I wouldn't have minded his saying a good word for the modern young man; but for the modern *girl*—no, I said. Nothing could be too——"

"What a drum and fife band!" growled James Davitt in Rose's ear. He had relinquished the arm of Mr. Paggles on a pretense of remembering something which he wanted to say to Rose. This was his message. "Don't marry a bore, my girl."

"Marry . . . marry . . . marry . . ." thought Rose, with a little gasp.

They came to the corner of the High Street. Already, three or four cars were standing, parked outside the Georgian house; the front door stood wide open. Entering, they had a first glimpse of the garden through just such an arch as the Dutch painters used in many a scene of beauty. It took Rose's breath away. She grew confused, and doubting in her delight.

"By Jove, this panelling, eh!" exclaimed Mr. Paggles, running his hand over it as he cast bright eyes about him. He had been an auctioneer, but was now retired. "Lovely! Lovely!" He smacked his lips boldly and bravely. "How d'you like it, Miss Rose?"

They tramped onward, through the library, and out by the open French windows to the lawn, where other guests were already assembled.

"Just look at these books!" cried Mr. Paggles, in what he believed to be a confidential tone. "All old. All old. Fine old calf." But he shook his head as he spoke, for he had found that fine old calf no longer had much prestige among buyers of books. The knowledge bewildered him, as many things nowadays bewildered elderly people with fixed standards. And, in face of shelves full of old books Mr. Paggles was suddenly beset by the thought that he might have difficulty, if still in business, in raising the bids. The world was frighteningly unfamiliar to him. "Old calf's not what it was," he tried to whisper into Rose's ear. "It's all this 'uncut.' "

Rose was not listening. She had no interest in old books, or, at present, for panelling, distant ceilings, or carved mantelpieces. Some consciousness of these antique delights

she must have had, for she was by no means insensitive
to domestic or decorative beauty; but they were of less
importance to her than the scene without, which was
radiant. There upon the wide lawn, of which the grass
was so fine and so free from every intrusive weed that
it might still have been growing upon the hills of West-
morland, were Philip, Ruth, Mr. James the vicar and his
wife, and a dozen other residents in the town. All were
talking and laughing, and she was never to forget the
picture they presented, so instant was its effect upon her
mind.

She stopped abruptly in the doorway. Her heart
jumped, and thereafter continued beating at a gallop.
How near to one another Philip and Miss Coulevain were
standing. Not as if she were a stranger to him. As if
she were the hostess . . . with some understanding . . .
As if something—he was changed. He was quite different.
Not the clothes, or the difference of situation. Not just
because he was at home, instead of being wind-stricken
at Seahampton. Different within. A stranger. Unknown.
And *she:* her summer dress revealed her figure, her hat
shaded the pale face, she was laughing; but at the same
time was everlastingly glancing, with a kind of tense
restlessness, towards the house and the new arrivals. . . .
Not at ease: why?

Such a moment of violently destroyed happiness Rose
had never known. She might have fallen from a great
height, so complete was her dizzy sense of shock. In spite
of all her natural self-control she half stumbled as the
message of her intuitions brought disaster to every smiling imagination of the day. But as she stumbled she
knocked against Rachel, who took her arm and drew her
onward, down the steps and towards the group on the
lawn. Rachel had seen nothing. Nobody but Rose had
seen so clearly what was toward. But she had certainty.

She made her way between her sisters (for Susan was quick to make a third in the usual trio) across the lawn, and met the others, and shook hands with Ruth, and said a few incoherent words to her, as pale as Ruth herself. Only to Philip's face she found that she could not raise her eyes, in spite of her longing to do so; and from him she turned away with what might have been thought a cold smile of indifference. She was in despair.

3

What happened subsequently, Rose had no means of knowing. She wandered in the garden by herself, or with Mr. James, who was a kind old man greatly interested in flowers. He would see a flower, and, still talking, would totteringly stoop, assume a pair of horn-rimmed glasses which had each time to be taken from his pocket in a case, and read the name ticket or examine the foliage. She did not understand a word that he said; she only answered "yes" and "no" at random, and while he stooped stood very straight, with her hands clenched, staring at nothing. Indeed she was quite blind. Mr. James, engrossed in his jubilant tour, supposed that she was as enthusiastic as himself. He was a blind good man, who thought well of everything because he still believed in the creed he taught, and he did not hear what Rose said, but charitably supposed it to be orthodox. All passed without confusion.

But presently, as they came down through the last rose pergola and found themselves in the kitchen garden, Mr. James caught sight of Snell, the head gardener. He went to speak with his old colleague and parishioner, while Rose, finding herself near that gate over which Philip had lately seen a man looking, slipped through it, out into the little lane, and so, without aim, to the town once more. It was broad daylight; there were numerous pedestrians; she turned down past the Sports Ground, discovered herself remote from observation, and with colour at last causing her cheeks to burn, walked on and on into the windings of an unfrequented road.

Meanwhile the Holpens had arrived. They came into the garden and were more obtuse than Rose had been. Mrs. Holpen, it is true, ignored Ruth, but gushed to Philip. Lettice was more cordial, and stood chatting for a moment. She said: "Isn't it all gawgeous!" Leonard, standing behind Lettice, observed Ruth with a calmly quizzical stare of which she gave every sign of being unconscious. However, when Lettice discontinued her talk and joined Rachel and Susan, Leonard spoke to his hostess in a low tone.

"You're very official," he commented, smoothly.

"Am I?" Ruth could be as smooth as he.

"Quite impossible to speak to you at leisure," he continued, "I suppose."

"In the circumstances, yes," she answered.

"I'm still in your black books!"

"Yes, I'm quite of the same mind," she said, with a cold smile.

"But you won't remain obdurate."

"Oh, yes, I think so." She half moved away from him. He saw that a nerve just below her throat was quickly throbbing, so that he knew she was less calm than she pretended to be. And he shook his head very faintly in menace.

"It's unwise," he said, "to quarrel with me. You'll find it so."

He received, at that, a quick glance of lightning, in which indignation and contempt gave fire to distaste. But although he winced he did not immediately accept dismissal. The truth was that he believed himself, as far as

Ruth was concerned, to be in an impregnable position. He was undeceived. Philip, stepping forward, joined the two. The three of them stood together, Ruth smaller and slimmer than they, and of course more fair by contrast with their darkness; Philip lean as whipcord; Leonard better-groomed and more noticeably clothed in the mode.

Whether his coming had been dictated by jealousy, Philip did not know. He did not stay to consider that. He had wished, it is true, to escape Mrs. Holpen; he had wished to interrupt a conversation which, as he thought, was possibly causing distress to Ruth. And so he allowed Mrs. Holpen to engage in talk with a County visitor, took two steps away from the more elderly contestants, and was at Ruth's side. Her arm, as his fingers lightly clasped it, was stiff. It yielded, however, after an instant's resistance. He could have sworn that she trembled. That was curious; but he paid no heed. Instead, he said in a low tone:

"Ruth, dear, as Holpen has had so much to do with our affairs, don't you think we owe him a small confidence?"

Leonard's expression changed. He was still debonair, but he was unsmiling. His glance grew keen.

"Confidence?" he cried.

"We were married this morning."

Leonard's mouth fell open. He stared—at Ruth. All colour left his cheeks, and returned an instant later.

"What's this?" he demanded.

Ruth was smiling now—a smile that showed her regular teeth.

"You've surprised Mr. Holpen, Philip," she said, in a breathless tone.

But Leonard had recovered. He, too, smiled.

"Indeed you have!" he said. "Well, well! Well, well! I congratulate you both. Very surprising; but—how *right*, how *convenient*." He was sneering.

"You mean, how *simple*," suggested Philip, drily. "How *fortunate*."

"Yes." Leonard turned upon him. "The *mot juste*. How simple!" He seemed greatly amused. "And how fortunate—for both of you. Yes, I congratulate you both. This morning, you say? Where; at Seahampton? It wasn't noised here, I think. . . . Excellent. Excellent."

"We felt sure of your approval," explained Philip, who was puzzled by Leonard's air of sneering enjoyment; but determined to face it boldly. "Apart from Sims, you're our first confidant."

"You couldn't possibly have a better. Or one who's more delighted. Capital! But so sudden! Now, am I to spread the news?"

"No." The interjection came from Ruth.

"Not?" He was all bland surprise.

"We'll do that ourselves, I think," said Philip. "More formally."

He still lightly held Ruth's arm, as if to show that he did not choose to be parted from her at the moment, but his attention (for, after all, he was indifferent to Leonard, whose congratulations might have been withheld, for all the importance he gave them) had been distracted by the sight of Dr. Henty, who arrived at this moment.

"Here's our John Bull," he remarked.

"And my friend," added Ruth. "My good friend." They both moved towards the doctor, leaving Leonard standing quite alone in the centre of the lawn. Leonard, following them with his eyes, continued to observe Ruth.

"Poor boy," said a high, amused voice in his ear. "You look quite thunderstruck." It was Lettice, who had been a spectator of the scene from a distance.

"I feel it," murmured Leonard. "They're married!"

"No-o-o!" Lettice laughed aloud. "I say! Quick work. He's been more agile than you, my dear."

Leonard gave his sister a peculiar look.

"Yes, hasn't he?" was all the answer he made. Then, as she laughed again, he walked away from her, down the garden, and out of sight, leaving Lettice in solitary enjoyment of his discomfiture. As he went he did not see Rose, who was returning to the party, a little pale, a little dusty as to shoes, but with her head high in pride and anguish. But Rose saw Leonard, and was thankful to escape his notice. Her one thought was to join her sisters and to go home as soon as possible, in order that she might endure alone the first profound distress of her life.

PART THREE
CONSEQUENCES

CHAPTER TWELVE

SUMMER PASSING

IT WAS two months later. The summer was beginning to stale, although as yet no very strong winds had caught the rain-loosened leaves and sent them flying helter-skelter to nourish the earth. In the outer world men were starving and food was rotting; capitalism (some said, civilization) was staggering downhill under a load of no-confidence; but in Sandersfold, where every interest, or almost every interest, was that of the quiet life of the district, the outer world seemed far off and hardly at all terrifying. Sandersfold accepted the change of season: that was all.

In the High Street the rush of August visitors from Seahampton had passed. Dwellers in the town could once again walk the streets in pride, without danger of being pushed under the wheels of motorcars by phalanxes of trippers. Afternoons were more precious (they were shorter); one or two chilly evenings had already brought about the lighting of fires and the discovery of smoking chimneys. Residents and diners at the Lion were already arguing as to the comforts and discomforts which *might* attend the installation in that hostel of central heating. The big drapers were preparing to hold sales, football boots filled the windows of the shoe shops, little boys rushed home muddy from rough tussles in front of goal, young women of all classes were considering new styles of costume and headgear, harvest festivals had been held and apples were being stored. And a faint melancholy was to be observed in the demeanour of every person over forty years of age. Sandersfold was settling down to a long autumn.

A small lean woman was leaving the grocer's shop three doors down the High Street from the church. She was dressed in a long coat that descended to her ankles, and wore a curious green hat which might have belonged to a member of Robin Hood's foresters but which had in fact belonged to Mrs. Valancourt of Fiveways, a large house outside Sandersfold. As she left the shop with a few coppers loose in one hand, and a small handbag and heavy marketing bag in the other, Mrs. Lax's sharp grey eyes peeped very rapidly up and down and across the street, so that she saw and recognized everybody who was within range; and when those eyes encountered the eyes of another woman who was coming from farther down the High Street, she stopped. This was a friend indeed.

"Well, Mrs. Teviot," she greeted the other woman. "Good-evening."

"Good-evening, Mrs. Lax," was the reply. "Quite a stranger, ain't you?"

The friends surveyed one another. Mrs. Teviot was dressed very similarly to Mrs. Lax, but her hat was of purple velvet (which she liked because it was a quiet colour), and in this light it cast a mauvish pallor over her broad and not especially lively face. The colour resembled that ghastly hue which dominates the royal mausoleum in Berlin.

"Stranger!" protested Mrs. Lax, in her dry, feeble little voice with its country burr. "It's you that's the stranger. Haven't seen you anywhere. Don't you go to the pictures now, then?"

"Oh, dear, I'm tired!" responded Mrs. Teviot, with a

giant sigh. "It's me back—well, I don't hardly know how to hold myself straight. I really don't. No, I haven't been to the pictures. I don't like these talkies—yah, yah, yah, through their noses, and no roof to their mouth. B'sides, Ted's made a new wireless—get Vienna and Warsaw as clear . . . It's wonderful."

"What's the good? You can't understand what they say."

"No, but it's wonderful."

"Keep it," said Mrs. Lax. "A nice book's better than all."

"Never was a reader," admitted Mrs. Teviot. "No, I never was. Nor's my Ted. I doubt if he's ever read a book in his life. Can't settle to it. How're you?"

"Very well, I thank you," said Mrs. Lax. Her thin lips hardly moved when she spoke. She was still looking about her, as birds do, although she was facing Mrs. Teviot and by no means inattentive to her friend. All their talk had been friendly; although they had disagreed, they spoke of themselves impersonally, not arguing, but remarking phenomena. That is the scientific spirit of the age. Mrs. Lax continued, still impersonal: "You heard what's happened, then."

"Where?"

Mrs. Lax jerked her head down the street. Mrs. Teviot pondered. She was giving nothing away.

"Don't know as I have," she admitted. "Where d'you mean, Mrs. Parsons?"

"No-oh!" drawled Mrs. Lax, in scorn. Such news was at least a fortnight old. Her glance shot across the road and up to the first-floor window of a building opposite. She did not fail to see—she never failed to see anything— that somebody was standing at the dingy office window, looking out; but she did not mention her discovery. It went to form a detail in her collection of odd knowledge.

"Why, that's *old* news, Mrs. Parson's twins. They're all right now. The *second* one——" her voice was lowered. Presently: "No, I meant Starling's—well, Starling's that was. Haven't you heard? She's expecting."

"She's *not!*" Mrs. Teviot's shadowy brows quite disappeared under the brim of her hat. Mrs. Lax almost stooped in order to see where they had gone. Mysterious nods passed between the ladies. "Oo, isn't it quick! Who told you?"

"Missus Jones. She goes there regular now, since *he* come. Every day. Says he's noice."

"Well! Why, they was only married——"

"Perhaps that was why they never told nobody they was getting married." It was a luscious thought. It held then both spellbound for a moment. Mrs. Lax handsomely resumed, however: "Though Mrs. Jones don't think so. No more doesn't Mrs. Sims. She think it was because they don't like fuss and bother—and him so fresh come, and her not being sociable."

"Did she tell Missus Jones, then?"

"No, well, how I come to hear of it——" Mrs. Lax lowered her voice still further, until Mrs. Teviot had to listen hard in order to follow what was whispered. "Missus Jones come to see me the other evening—well, she wanted to borrow my big saw, then. She said Mrs. Sims ask her if she'd *noticed* anything——"

"Well!" whispered Mrs. Teviot. "Had she?"

"She says 'No.' I *said* to her: 'Good gracious, it's too quick . . . What you dreaming about?' It appears Mrs. Sims overheard something said. Made her look rather sharp. But however——"

"What she hear?" asked Mrs. Teviot.

"Not spoken out. Just 'if it's a boy,' or something. So she told Mrs. Jones."

"Mm," murmured Mrs. Teviot. "It's quick. But they got plenty money. Does Mrs. Jones say they get on all right?"

"Sweet as butter, she says. Very polite."

Mrs. Teviot shook her head.

"Oo, *polite*," she murmured gloomily. Her lips were pursed.

"He's got good manners."

"Mm. What's happened to the other one, then?" Mrs. Teviot slowly swung a little, and indicated by the faintest movement of her marketing bag the building opposite, in the first-floor window of which Mrs. Lax had already noticed a standing and observant figure. "I see he's over there."

"I know he is. He don't go. Mrs. Sims think they both thought she'd have something left her. But I'll tell you. My husband, he had to deliver coal there one morning. Of course, he goes up Cutthroat Lane to the garden gate. He see Mr. Snell, the gardener, and Mr. Snell ask him if he ever come that way at night. Seems Mr. Snell thinks somebody's been coming in that gate. . . . He's never seen who it is; but he's bin watching, in case it's somebody after his apples—some boy. But the funny part of it is, he says one night, just soon after the new one come, he thinks he see Mr. Holpen come out of Cutthroat Lane——"

"What!" gasped Mrs. Teviot. "Mr. Holpen!"

Mrs. Lax enjoyed her triumph. When her mouth stretched a little you could see that she had lost most of her front teeth. This was why she hardly parted her lips in speaking, and why she preserved so demure an expression.

"I don't say he *did*," she reminded Mrs. Teviot. "Snell don't say he did. It's only what he *thinks*."

Mrs. Teviot looked away from Mrs. Lax, as a cat

occasionally, in moments of tension, looks away from an opponent. The tip of her tongue moistened her upper lip. She considered for a moment. This was extraordinary news indeed. What could she say to supplement it? To gain time, she said:

"But what could he want there?"

"Don't know." Mrs. Lax said the words with lip-licking satisfaction, as if she were joyously lying. Again Mrs. Teviot thought carefully. At last:

"*I* was told as Mr. Holpen's got no money, only what his mother lets him have."

"O-oh!" cried Mrs. Lax, in a hushed whisper. She was always generously ready to pay tribute to a friend's valuable information. "A-ah! I wonder if that's it."

She had no malignance at all; only a tremendous inquisitiveness, and a scientific habit of putting two and two together. She was a sort of inductive philosopher, a sociologist in a small field.

"What?" Mrs. Lax had gone quite beyond Mrs. Teviot's power of combining facts. Mrs. Teviot's mental tempo had been slowed by association with a dull and voluble husband.

"Why," persisted Mrs. Lax, with a side glance across the street. "Him. And *her*. Nothing coming of it. He'd like anybody with money——"

"S-sh!" Mrs. Teviot was in a panic. She felt that they were heading into scandal. "Oo, don't you say I told you. Missus Baker only said it——"

"Oh, I won't say. Nor you say what I told you— about the baby."

It was as if each put a finger to her lips; but although each face wore an expression of solemn relish, there was no indication that the two heads, so close together, had moved.

"Maybe it's all nothing," suggested Mrs. Lax, presently, in a false voice. "You don't *know*."

"I wonder," sighed Mrs. Teviot, obstinately. "I know I shall keep thinking about it."

"Well, don't *talk*," advised Mrs. Lax. To change the conversation—but in a sense to keep it upon the same theme—she said: "I see *Miss* Holpen the other day. She was talking to Mr. Davitt up Hillington Avenue—the *old* man. They were talking, as if she'd stopped him or something. He did just look disagreeable."

"Ted says it's all bark," put in Mrs. Teviot.

"Well, he's got teeth," observed Mrs. Lax, drily. "I dunno what he does with 'em. I know she looked uncomfortable."

"She's got nothing. Well, I *know* that, for a fact. It's all *Mrs.* Holpen, Mrs. Baker says. Mrs. Baker sews for them. Says Miss Holpen wants to go away to London; but she's got no money. Says there's always rows in that house."

"Why doesn't she get married, then?"

"Opportunity's a fine thing," observed Mrs. Teviot.

The two women fell silent, for this was not a profitable diversion, and neither knew of anything which could compare, for interest, with what had already been told.

They looked up and down the High Street together, and saw a boy ambling along—young Tommy Sadler, out of work again,—and a girl in a new pair of shoes which hurt her. She had thick ankles, and had sketchily painted her lips in an effort to look smart. No spoken comment was needed upon such ignominious failure. A lady in a smart little car drove herself up to the grocer's shop and went within. Neither Mrs. Lax nor Mrs. Teviot looked at the car, for they were engrossed in the lady; but Tommy Sadler, idling this way, stopped to examine its wheels, the maker's panel, the dashboard with its enchanting gadgets.

The renewed sight of Tommy, who lived in a neighbouring house to her own, reminded Mrs. Teviot of a woman next door who had been stricken with illness. She did not mention that she had cleaned the woman's house, done her shopping, nursed her, and given the husband part of her own dinner; but instead dwelt upon some details of bed linen, a dirty cupboard, and the sick woman's stupidity.

In return, Mrs. Lax described what had happened to a child who had fallen into his mother's washtub in trying to get bubbles for his pipe, and who had been rescued in the nick of time. She did not say that the mother had been gossiping with Mrs. Lax as she hung out a basketful of clothes, or that she herself had effectively rescued the child while his mother had been hysterically angry. She laughed a little at the picture of the draggled boy, and made Mrs. Teviot laugh also; but without any but the most humane enjoyment of the incidental disasters of life. At last she returned (as they had both longed to do) to the earlier, important, topic.

"Funny them getting married at Seahampton, then," she observed.

"What, *them?*" Mrs. Teviot heavily moved her head. "D'you like these marriages in registry offices?" she asked. "I don't. Church for me, every time. It's all so much like getting a wireless license. Seems to take away the sacredness of it——"

"Go on!" rather jeered Mrs. Lax. "Old married woman like you."

"Well, it does. You can't wonder there's all these divorces if there's nothing sacred."

"Well, what I wonder is why they have to get married at all. If it's nothing but a makeshift. 'Stead of 'For

ever and ever,' 'For just as long as I choose, and not a
a minute longer.' "

"And then that little scrimpy honeymoon. It was in
the paper."

"Yes, funny," repeated Mrs. Lax, with her quiet smile.

"There's a lot of things funny," suggested Mrs.
Teviot.

"Yes, isn't there?" agreed Mrs. Lax.

They were gradually drawing apart now, like ships
leaving a quay. They were a foot away. You could not
detect any movement, but could only recognize that the
space between them had widened.

"All sorts of things," remarked Mrs. Teviot. "If you
got a sense of humour."

They nodded. The speech had been a sort of Nunc
Dimittis, or God Save the King. The foot had become
eighteen inches. Both smiled a farewell. Two feet. They
had positively parted, Mrs. Lax to trudge down the High
Street to a sweetstuff shop, when she bought a bar of
chocolate for the lately bubbled child, and Mrs. Teviot to
enter the shop from which Mrs. Lax had so recently
emerged. Each felt soberly elated by the encounter which
had taken place. Neither remembered to look again in the
direction of Leonard Holpen's office upon the first floor
opposite.

Had one of them done so with attention, she would
have seen that the observer was still there, benignly
watching them. She would have seen that it was not
Leonard Holpen himself, but an elderly man with a wig,
one of whose hands was concealed under the tail of his
coat, while the other idly tapped the air in a sluggish
rhythm. But she would not have been troubled, because
old Burgess was known in Sandersfold as a character
who had been forced by age to relinquish the gambols
and pursuits of the virile.

2

Nobody, in fact, now took much notice of Burgess. In olden days, when Holpen senior had roamed the countryside full of masculine enterprise, Burgess had performed various feats of adjustment. Now his occupation was gone. He had lived through the time when men kissed and did not tell; and he had emerged into an age when men tell but do not kiss. He had no great respect for the new age. If one descended to individuals, he had no respect at all for the son of his old employer; but it must be admitted that this was a matter of personal distaste, and was not a general ethical judgment.

When Leonard was out, Burgess always went into the private office, glanced around, and went to the window. He loved to do this. The sight of men and women walking gave him great satisfaction. When they stopped to talk, he wondered what they were saying. But as he was no expert in lip-reading, he never knew.

However, the shoppers this afternoon included others besides Mrs. Lax and Mrs. Teviot, and Burgess had the satisfaction of seeing Rose Davitt stop and look into a shop window. The sight of her made his mouth water. He could not restrain himself from making a sort of kissing noise with his tongue against the hard palate of his denture—"tee-tee-tee." The prancing forefinger wavered. The hand to which it was attached fell to his side. He grew very intent, quite still, like a cat by a tree which holds a bird's nest. But he had no evil schemes; his catlike watch was no more than the tribute of a superannuated satyr to virginal beauty.

"Aye," remarked Burgess. He thought how he would have liked, as a younger man, to kindle such quietness to flame. But he did not, as a younger man might have done,

underrate the difficulty of such a task. Nor did he fall
into the error of thinking that Rose was insipid. As he
looked at her, his eyelids steadily lessened the amount of
iris visible in his pale old eyes. His lips fell apart. He
was so absorbed in contemplation that he heard nothing.
He did not hear footsteps in the outer office, or the pushing open of the door, or Leonard's quick entry into the
room. And consequently he was for a time unaware of
the fact that as he watched Rose, so Leonard watched
him (but with a different degree of intensity).

At last something broke the spell. Burgess looked
round, caught Leonard's eye, started, and responded with
what dignity he could muster to the contemptuous jerk of
Leonard's head towards the outer office. He slowly made
his way across the room, closed the door very softly behind him, and left Leonard the master.

"Now, what's that old devil been after?" thought
Leonard, smoothing his hair with both hands. He went
in two light strides to the window—just in time to see
Rose, who had been into the shop, come out again and
step briskly away. She was in a light coat of a pale
crimson, with a small hat of the same colour set firmly
upon her little head, and she was made, from the slight
elevation upon which Leonard stood, to appear slimmer
and smaller than she really was.

"Oh!" exclaimed Leonard, aloud. "Oh!" He gave a
faint chuckle. "The old sinner!"

He turned from the window and sat down at his desk.
The shadow of that chuckle remained upon his face. He
turned his hand, with the tips of the fingers pressed into
the palm, and examined his nails with care. Rose Davitt,
he thought. Anything to be done there? Davitt must be
a warm man. And he was choleric. Leonard shook his
head.

"No," he said. "Too many of them. No use for Brother

Henry. Nor Sister Sue. Nor Sister Rakehell. As for Ma, she'll live for ever. I can do better elsewhere."

A faint half thought of Ruth Spears (née Coulevain) crossed his mind. That, he felt, was over. And well over. Just as well. She'd have been a nuisance. No money; greedy; exacting. Just as well it was over. All the same, he remembered with a twinge the surprise she had given him. He had not seen her since. Nor Spears.

3

After Leonard had gone home, Burgess returned to the front room. But it was getting late, and there were hardly any shoppers to watch. Those who still dawdled were the slatterns, who had run out of butter or cocoa for their supper; or the do-nothings, who eyed shop windows as a cheap treat, but never bought; or inconspicuous strangers, who were filling time until the next omnibus for Seahampton was due to start.

"All trumpery," thought Burgess. "Not at all the thing."

He turned discontentedly from the window. There was nothing for him to do. He might as well go home. Aye, there was no pull either way. Nothing to do here; nothing to do at home. Was the safe locked? It was. The desk? He tried the middle drawer. It was. Master Leonard was as careful in that as his father. Not the man his father had been. Uppish. Bumptious. Unlike his father, he never confided in Burgess. It was a grievance. Burgess knew that he could have given Leonard much information. A little flattery would have kept him sweet and loyal. It was not forthcoming. Leonard was jealous; he was suspicious. Also mean. The old man had not been mean. Leonard got that from Mrs. H., who was as tight as a miser.

What about the waste-paper basket? Burgess was by

no means superior to waste-paper baskets. They had often afforded him a pleasant half-hour. Sometimes a useful fact. No facts were useless. In winter, when there were coal fires, confidential notes were burned; but in the summer they were often torn into small pieces and cast adrift. There was no fire as yet; were there interesting fragments? Nothing, apparently. Envelopes, all formal; a circular or two. . . .

Burgess, having placed the basket upon Leonard's desk in order that he might look through it more easily, was stooping to set it in its customary place (it would be emptied in due course by a charwoman), when his eye was caught by the second drawer down upon the right-hand side of Leonard's desk. It was slightly open. He had felt the top drawers, and had supposed that as they were all controlled by a central lock any examination of the others would be superfluous. Now his eyes glistened. Something more to go through! He could have rubbed his hands in glee.

"But I ought to have seen it at once!" muttered Burgess, annoyed with his own blindness. "I'm getting old."

He pulled the drawer open and his face fell. It was empty, save for a pair of brown kid gloves—Leonard's gloves. They must have been there for months. What a blow! He was about to replace the drawer as he had found it, when an impulse made him pull it right out, go down upon his knees, and peer into the blackness from which it had come. He knew that sometimes a paper will get lodged at the back of a drawer. An important paper.

At first he could see nothing at all; but as he peered he thought the corner of a sheet of paper was showing at the back of the space. He put his arm into the hole, and his fingers touched something. Very gently he seized the something. It was a paper which had been in the top drawer, and which, as that drawer had been rapidly shot home, had gone to the back, and over the back, of the drawer. It yielded to his touch. He drew it out, rather grimed from having been lodged in a dusty corner, but intact. Burgess turned over his discovery and whistled. It was a thin envelope, apparently empty; but it had been through the post. He carried it to the window. He whistled again; and gave a backward skittish kick of his old heel in satisfaction.

The envelope was addressed to Leonard in a handwriting which Burgess well knew to be that of Ruth Coulevain—now Mrs. Spears. And the envelope had never been opened. He examined the date of the postmark. July— more than two months ago. July—he could see a figure "1," but the figure which followed was blurred. Why had it not been opened? A quarrel. He had been told to say that Leonard was out if Miss Coulevain telephoned. She had telephoned more than once; and Burgess had lied to order. At last she had ceased to telephone. The tale was clear. They had broken with each other. Here was another proof of it. Aye, and a proof that things had been hot between them.

Burgess's face was like a mask, or like the face of an old actor. He put the letter into his pocket. He then closed the drawer until it was exactly as it had been when he found it. He then returned to his own office. This was treasure indeed! He had never previously happened upon a letter from Ruth. With hands that trembled a little— another lamentable sign of old age—he lighted the small gas ring upon which he was in the habit of boiling a kettle for his necessary tea. There was enough stewed water in that kettle for his purpose—the less the better; and it would soon boil.

But unopened. Why unopened? Burgess could never have left a letter unopened. Unanswered, yes; but unopened, no. That argued either indifference or such

emotion that another letter would be unbearable.
Thoughts of unanswered letters took Burgess a long way
back in his life. There had been quite a number of delicate
matters in his own younger days, as well as in the days
of Leonard's father. Days when life was really freer
than it is now, for all the modern talk of freedom.

"Freedom!" thought Burgess. "Too much reggalation.
All talk, and no do. Everything's paper now, like the
money."

He enjoyed a pleasant ramble among old conquests
while he waited for the kettle to boil. It prevented him
from feeling impatience. Conquests and defeats. True,
the contrast irked him, for some of the defeats rankled,
and some of the conquests had been trash, and a recognition of lost powers made him sigh; but if an old amorist
may not mumble over his amours in senility, his lot must
indeed be hard.

Very soon Burgess heard the kettle singing. Very soon
the first shiver of steam came from the spout. Humming
merrily, and in a very good temper, he held the letter aloft
with a skilled and experienced hand. He knew this work
as well as he knew anything. He was an artist at it. He
never had torn an envelope in his life; and the number
of those with which he had dealt successfully was incalculable.

But he was still trembling. Damn it; he was growing
excitable over a letter! Old age, old age! He peeled this
one open with unsteady hands, and drew the enclosure
from it with the greatest care. Only a single sheet. Only
a few words without signature. "I *must* see you. I am
going to have a child." Burgess's mouth opened. He
swallowed quickly. He experienced a new respect for
Leonard, who in spite of all was his father's son. His
smile stretched widely across his face.

Unopened until now. Why? More than two months old, by the postmark. Before the marriage. Before——

"Oh, dear, oh, dear!" said Burgess, laughing so heartily that he tottered. "The pity of it! I'm afraid there has been some slight error of judgment on somebody's part. Hee-hee-hee! What a mis-*fortune!* What a mis-*fortune* for all concerned! Thank heavens it's only me that knows about it! In wicked hands it might be a trouble. Thank heavens indeed!"

He refolded the letter, replaced it, resealed the envelope; and again placed it in his pocket for safety. But he was bent double with silent merriment.

CHAPTER THIRTEEN

ROSE AND LETTICE

In these weeks of fading summer, without understanding the cause, Rose Davitt became aware of a change in Lettice Holpen's manner to her. Lettice had always been superficially pleasant to the Davitt girls, and exclamatorily glad to see them whenever they met. She had never, however, shown much interest in their doings. Only Rose had noticed this. The others were content with so little. While *Lettice* talked, the Davitts were to listen delightedly; when *they* talked, she became like the Gilbertian gondolier who "allowed his attention to wander." Rose had seen Lettice, as they chattered, looking at her sisters with bored hardness and even with cruelty.

Also, whereas the Davitt girls knew a large number of residents in Sandersfold, and remembered their names and circumstances, saw them at church and at parties or larger gatherings, asked after their health, and were generally interested in a hundred innocuous relationships, Lettice, although she knew many of these people by sight, and even to bow to, was always aloof in manner at the time and slighting or scornful in after-comment. Rose had not heard her speak pleasantly of anybody.

Towards Rose, at their first acquaintance, Lettice had begun by being condescending—the young woman-of-the-world anxious to impress the bread-and-butter miss. When this claim had worn thin, Lettice had grown a little insincerely intimate—dropping her voice from its high-pitched, pseudo-aristocrat drawl to a commoner style, uttering contemptuous criticism of others (as if she and Rose alone were emancipated), and taking quick offense at Rose's own careless adolescent smartness. Finally, and for months, Lettice had been guarded, satirically smiling, defensive, apparently convinced that Rose "disapproved" of her.

Now all was changed. Lettice came often to the Davitts' house, running in at times upon no pretext at all, braving all James Davitt's growls and snarls, and listening patiently to his wife's trifling conversation. She was cordial to Rachel and Susan; but it was to Rose that she offered confidences. It was as if she had discovered that Rose was not quite such a fool as she had always thought. Such discoveries are occasionally made in every society. But friendship then only arises if the translated fool responds to the flattery of attention, or if the previously exclusive person reveals attractive qualities of her own. As between Lettice and Rose, friendship could not have arisen if Rose had not felt herself in need of a change of society.

Her father, though he understood more than the others, was too often set stormy for comfort. Henry was away: in any case he lived in a state of indignation with the world which Rose could not share. Philip was lost to her, and she detested his wife. Alicia Furze was too old. She had left Rachel and Susan far behind. Rose therefore did not withdraw from Lettice; rather, she was touched and pleased at finding herself sought by somebody so ingenious.

Rachel and Susan, having lost their idol, Henry, and their leader, Rose, lived in a baffled state of good works. They threw themselves with demented energy into the social labours which Rose disliked—working parties, visitings, girls' clubs, teas for old people, teas for young people, and the collection of funds for this purpose and

that. Their talk grew big with town concerns. They no
longer waited for Rose to direct or even to join them, but
were out and about upon virtuous errands at all hours of
the day. James Davitt could not understand what had
happened to these girls. He said to Rose:

"Here, I say. You appear to have a little sense, Rose.
What the devil are they up to? They're like virgins of
fifty! They craze me. I meet them everywhere, carrying
soup and cheer. What's in it?"

Rose could have told him a great deal; but she did not
do so, because she loved him and because she was still
engaged upon her own pilgrimage. She could have said
to him, like an accusing angel:

"Well, Father, they're what you and Mother have made
them. You've kept us all infants, and now we're beginning
to struggle out of the cradle. Henry's gone; I'm going;
Rachel and Susan, being a little older, and perhaps in
some ways nicer, are trying to run about in the nursery.
They're playing little games. If they knew as much as I
do, they'd be playing with dolls."

But Rose did not make this speech. She smiled at her
father and said:

"It's all right, Father. They need occupation. You must
be prepared for all of us to be a bit restless, these days.
The whole world's restless."

James Davitt listened. He understood more of Rose's
moderation than she realized.

"But they're making fools of themselves. You're not,
are you?"

"I may be," Rose answered him, soberly. "I'll tell you
when I know."

"You frighten me, Rose," cried Davitt. "Are you
happy? Damn this world!"

"I *shall* be," said Rose. "And so will they if you leave
them alone."

"Grrr," answered James Davitt. He took his stick from the stand in the hall and went out for a fierce walk by himself.

2

Henry was coming home for the week-end. It was an uncommon thing. As a rule, he gave them to understand, he spent his spare time in relishing his new freedom from home constraints. But what he really did with his week-ends and his spare time, the Davitt family did not know. It was enough that they missed him from the nest. Even his father, to whom Henry's departure had been a relief and a loss.

Rose knew more than the others, because Henry had developed a habit of writing to her. They had all showered letters upon him during his absence, and he had replied in brief general proclamations. He was well, happy, busy, in satisfactory digs, getting on all right, and so on. Only Rose had received additional notes, and these she latterly did not show to her sisters.

"Henry doesn't write to you now, does he?" remarked Susan, with satisfaction.

"Very seldom," admitted Rose.

"He soon got tired of *that*," Susan said, in triumph.

Rose knew that Henry was working hard. He wanted now to do his job well, but even more than this he wanted to escape altogether from the job. Routine work exasperated him, he said. He needed more money. Now that he was away from home, and had to pay bills from his salary, he was suddenly poor. He had also learned what income he would receive when, if ever, he became a branch manager. The facts made him whistle with horror. And since his removal to London, Henry had changed a good deal. He no longer played cricket; he had no intention of playing football. He was writing a novel, poems, essays, and short stories. Nobody at home knew this except Rose.

In his letters to her, Henry spoke much of one Molyneux, a fellow clerk two or three years older than himself. Molyneux said this, Molyneux thought the other. Molyneux cared only for what was first rate. He was scathingly critical. Only two or three among living writers were worth reading, Molyneux said: most of the others, and most of the old writers, were complete duds. Women were all strumpets, biologically backward, either intellectually pretentious or purely sensual. Everything in the world was filthy and decaying; communism was as hopeless as capitalism; intellectualism as crass and material as the Victorian ideal. There was no hope in science. Poetry was dead. Everything was terrible.

But Rose would like Molyneux. He was a wonderful chap. And she *must* keep Susan and Rachel out of his way. They would *ruin everything*. It was a pretty hazardous thing to bring him home, in any case; but Molyneux had consented to come, and Henry hoped that Rose would do her best to make the week-end "go." They would probably be out most of the time, anyway, as Molyneux loathed stuffiness, and his idea of a happy day was a twenty-mile tramp, bread and cheese and beer for lunch, and his old pipe to gnaw for the rest of the journey.

Rose, in the manner of those sickened by the reported perfections of strangers, already hated Molyneux very heartily. She imagined him a crushing bore. But she loved Henry and was determined to give him as pleasant a time as possible. She could do little to reduce the horrors of Molyneux's bedroom, for that would have involved throwing a great deal of furniture into the street, stripping the walls, and rebuilding part of the house. But she made sure that he had some conventional books to deride, a giant ashbowl, plenty of matches, writing paper, ink, towels, and coat hangers. She ordered, further, some dozen bottles of beer, revised all the cook's menus, and gave Rachel and Susan no nerve-racking advice as to behaviour. In this she showed deep wisdom.

At a quarter past four on Saturday afternoon, much too early, Rose set out alone for the station. Having been warned by Henry not to bring the car, as Molyneux hated cars and much preferred walking, she marched with a sinking heart up the road and through the big cobbled station yard, where three or four highly polished and very old cars with extraordinarily low bonnets stood pretending to be taxicabs. She knew by sight every one of the drivers, who touched their hats cheerily although she had never engaged one of them and had hardly ever seen one of them engaged by anybody else. She was then engulfed in the rambling railway station.

Sandersfold station had character. It was so old—or it looked so old—that one had trouble in believing that it had not been built to receive Stephenson's Rocket. There was a very large booking hall which always looked dirty, and in which the clock was ingeniously kept two minutes fast, on purpose to frighten late-comers and make them run. But as the late-comers well knew the clock's habit, they did not run, and were not at all frightened. In order to reach the principal down platform it was necessary to use an antediluvian tunnel under the lines; and the dank, earthy chill of this tunnel made everybody who used it experience a moment's reflection upon mortality. Whether this was a calculated effect on the part of the railway company, none knew.

Rose, emerging into pure air, found herself upon the platform and looked quickly about her. Ticket collectors, porters, a postman with a truckful of sacks, old Lady Snickle with a footman in attendance, Mr. Morris the estate agent, and Mr. Sneyd the corn chandler, were the only people whom she knew by sight. The men saluted her, and Lady Snickle stared appraisingly as if at a filly.

"I expect she thinks I'm a 'gel,' " thought Rose. "Well, in that case she's an 'old gel.' I shall look at my fields."

She did so. All about the station were agreeably broad meadows, fringed with tall elms and hedgerows, and still, after the English manner, lavishly green. A pleasant wind blew from the southwest, wandering and threatening rainclouds rambled overhead, and weak sunshine hopefully penetrated the clouds, without effect. It was a lovely pale day, all mauves and light greens, and the kind of day to provoke washy watercolour drawings. Rose was delighted with it. She could have continued to regard the scene with satisfaction for much longer than the term of her waiting; but in less than ten minutes the London train rushed into the station. Rose, who had taken up her stand near the ticket collector's box as the train approached, saw Henry jump down from a very distant carriage near the engine. He seemed to have grown. He wore no hat. How changed! Rose held her arm aloft in greeting. She saw him joined by another, smaller man, also bareheaded. That must be the redoubted Molyneux. How much fault would he find with the Davitt family before the week-end was over? And, in retaliation, how much fault would the family find with him?

"What a world!" thought Rose, uncontrollably. "So warm-hearted!"

Yes, Henry was indeed changed. At home he had always worn, unless at business, an astonishingly baggy suit of plus fours. His legs then had resembled the legs of a hen, and in looking at him strangers received the disagreeable impression that his braces had broken. Now, Rose wondered what had happened to her Henry. His hair was much longer; his legs were clothed in dirty grey flannel trousers; his coat was of shapeless and severely worn light brown tweed; and the case in his hand was far too small to hold another suit. Molyneux again?

Molyneux was dressed in exactly the same style. His trousers were, if anything, dirtier than Henry's. But Molyneux, although he was rather dark, did not look at all dirty. Rose was surprised by him. She had expected six feet, burly, blubber-lipped, square-toed manhood, a moustache, and a pugnacious air. Or else—such is the elasticity of the human mind—a thin, lady-like, supercilious creature with offensive manners. She saw a smallish man, clean-shaven, stocky, round-headed, with longish straight rumpled hair that needed cutting. He did not look at all clever or assertive: on the contrary, he had a rather stupid, piggish face, with only partially opened eyes, a snubby nose, prominent lozenge-like teeth, and a highly nervous manner which disconcerted her.

But Henry was brimming with delight at seeing Rose. If he had changed, his manner to her was much improved. It was still abrupt and a little casual, but showed affection.

"Molyneux insisted on being near the engine," he explained.

"One always gets less *motion* there," cried Molyneux, in a highly emphatic voice. "Besides, if there's an accident one's generally killed outright. One has a horror of being maimed. Have you, Miss Davitt?"

He certainly, thought Rose, was not speechless.

"I think I'd rather be maimed than dead," she replied, hesitantly.

"Oh, *would* you? I should hate it. So horrid to think of oneself as imperfect."

"I never think of myself as anything else," said Rose, laughing.

Molyneux took a quick glance at her. That reply was not what he had expected. It was against the rules. She saw that his small eyes were not those of a bull, and not those of a terrier; but there was enough of the pig in them to give her a little discomfort. Nor did she like his overemphatic way of speaking. It seemed an attempt to give pungency to the commonplace. But she could tell that he had no wish to be disagreeable.

"Oh, charming!" cried Molyneux, as they came out into the station yard. "These fellas are all the real thing. Extraordinary how yokels have adapted themselves to motors! Have you ever thought of that? One talks of 'chawbacons' and 'hodges,' but they're not so slow, after all. Don't you think?"

"They dunno much," Henry observed. "See them fiddling with their plugs and carburettors."

"Still, from driving cows, old man." Molyneux was not shaken. "Cows to cars, eh?" He did not laugh. The square, lozenge-like teeth showed a good deal. The words, as he said them, resembled one another almost indistinguishably.

They emerged into the road leading to Cross Street; and Rose could tell that Molyneux was interested in his surroundings. With some reason; for although this road was not much more than a wide track between fields, with coal-order offices standing about like loafers in its precincts, Cross Street was very narrow, decidedly old, and quite picturesque. Molyneux's round head was constantly turned from left to right, without subtlety, but with great attentiveness. Swiftly Rose penetrated to a truth about Henry's friend. He was a little slow; but he was honest. She had thought he might be a pretentious fraud. He was not. He seriously thought all he said, and he was always thinking; but he was not a clever man, and was content to dogmatize when he might have persuaded. She believed he would get into trouble with her father.

"Henry, you mustn't start Father on politics," she

suddenly said. "Be careful, won't you? He's rather touchy just now."

"Oo," grumbled Henry. "It's Molyneux you ought to warn."

"But I'm so peaceable!" declared Molyneux. "What is he, a Tory?"

"A Liberal."

"Oh, dear. A washout. I'll be very careful. I don't want you to think I'm *tactless,* Miss Davitt. I'm a monument of tact, really. But how anybody can cling to these shibboleths—how anybody can *not* see that Liberalism has begun to stink, I cannot imagine. Of course one knows that old men are hidebound; but even Communism's out of date. The world moves so rapidly. Oligarchy, Republic, Aristocracy—the thinking world's tired of such terms. Would it matter if one rather took that line with your father?"

"Don't do it until Monday morning, at least," suggested Rose. "He might quote Burke and Gladstone to you."

"What fun! Could one tell him they've helped to make the world a ruin?"

"I'm not going to give *you* any advice, Mr. Molyneux," said Rose. "You'll have to fight your own battles. But Henry's our ewe lamb——"

"Rot!" said Henry.

"Quite so," agreed Molyneux, beaming. "That's understood. Miss Davitt, I'm sure we have a great deal in common. I *feel* it. We must talk about this chap——" he indicated Henry—"our Ewe Lamb——"

"Hell!" cried Henry. "That'll stick."

"Silence!" thundered Molyneux. "We're already talking about you. We must decide what's to be done with him. Because, really, some of the things he's written are not at all bad——"

"They're not?" asked Rose.

"Oh, no, quite tolerable——"

Henry was as red as fire. But he was grinning. Molyneux was chattering readily, rather nervously. Hence his jocularity. Rose was glad that they were so near home.

"By the way, Lettice is coming tomorrow afternoon," she said to Henry.

His acknowledgment of the news was inaudible. After all, if he did not want to see Lettice he could always take Molyneux for a tramp in the neighbourhood.

3

That is what he would have done, if Molyneux had been movable. But Molyneux preferred staying at home. Molyneux drank beer abstemiously with and between his meals, smoked his pipe only in the garden, and made himself generally agreeable. Molyneux was a success. His opinions as reported by Henry had seemed violent; but his good nature was such that nobody minded his opinions. He resembled those revolutionary philosophers whose habits are so chaste that their minds are left free for anarchy. Molyneux engaged Rachel and Susan in delighted argument, was extremely nervous and respectful of James Davitt, followed Rose ingratiatingly whenever he saw her, and was overwhelmed by Lettice as soon as she arrived on the Sunday afternoon.

Lettice was beautifully dressed in brown, so that the delicate slimness of her body was emphasized. Her hair, now long enough to be "put up," was archly arranged, and her hat was coquettish. With her straight nose, flat cheeks, and thin, rather small mouth, she looked demurely sophisticated; and her response to Molyneux was so rapid that Rachel and Susan, fearing an instant elopement, stared amazed. They were not old enough to be shocked. And Lettice was too cold in bearing to give the notion of physical vulgarity.

"Rose has promised you to me for weeks!" Lettice declared, ardently.

Molyneux blinked and leapt. His voice grew shrill.

"I ought to be able to give Henry the same noble character," he replied. "I can't. Henry!"

"Too bad!" cried Lettice. "There's a biological difference." Rose had never seen her so gay, or so audaciously sparkling in her glances at Henry. She was instantly flirting with both men. Ah, this was what she needed. An audience—a male audience. "What do you make of the boy?"

"Young. Young," said Molyneux, showing his teeth. "But with possibilities."

"Really?" The tiny arched eyebrows moved slightly upward in mock surprise.

"Some. Some. Is that your own notion?"

"I can't think."

"We must have a long talk about Henry, Miss Holpen."

"Oh, dear, how dull!" Lettice grimaced boldly. "Only Henry?"

"And other things, of course."

"But isn't your idea of talk rather advanced, Mr. Molyneux? You must remember we live in rural innocence."

"I assure you!" Molyneux hopped in delight from one foot to the other. He had crimsoned with satisfaction. "I'm the most discreet person——"

"I was afraid of it. You're disappointing me horribly!"

"Then *you* shall talk; and I'll only interrupt."

"But what can a country girl tell an omniscient youth from London?"

"That remains to be seen."

Rose stole a glance at Henry. He was looking at

Molyneux with admiration. What rapier-play! Her eye passed next to Rachel and Susan. They were delighted. Rose knew that she could safely leave all five to their self-entertainment. As she went, she heard Lettice say:

"But what have you been *doing* to Henry?"

"Doing?"

"He looks like a poet."

"He *is* a poet——"

That was enough. She marvelled at Lettice's determination to keep the talk for ever hovering about Henry. It would please and embarrass him; it would keep him near; she would be able to criticize him obliquely to any extent, and woo him, laugh at his timidities, lead him back to her arms. . . .

"I couldn't do it," thought Rose. Her face grew suddenly hot. If she had wooed Philip as crudely, would she never have suffered? Was it all as crude, as *crude* as that? "Make haste," said her heart; "make haste upstairs, where you can be alone, to forget Philip." Forget him! She did not want to forget him. All she wanted to forget was a cruel suspicion of his weakness.

Molyneux: what a chatterbox! Henry: what a green idiot! Lettice: what a mixture of crude art and simplicity! But if they got what they wanted?

4

When, a little later, Rose descended for tea, she found the party more moderate. The high-pitched would-be-smartness of that first moment had sunk to a murmur. Rachel and Susan, still engrossed, had ceased to smile, and were looking anxious; Molyneux was moving his hands about, putting them on his knees, pulling his nether lip, sinking back in his chair, and crossing and recrossing his legs. He was excited. Rose heard him say:

"Well, I sympathize. I sympathize. That's all I can tell you. If you want my advice—and mind, I only offer it for what it's worth—I should definitely say, 'Go while the going's good.' Clear out. Don't you agree, Henry?"

"Er," said Henry. "Well, ye-es, I do." He was less enthusiastic, as if he had a private reserve.

"Yes, I should. What's the objection? What's the alternative?"

Lettice looked up and saw Rose. She brightened. She made haste to absorb Rose into the group. Indeed they all brightened at her cheerful presence.

"What do *you* say, Rose?" asked Lettice.

"Yes, let's hear wisdom!" cried Molyneux, gallantly.

"Shall we go?"

" 'We'?" Rose went forward.

"Definitely, yes," repeated Molyneux. "Both of you." He beamed.

"No!" shouted Rachel and Susan, in horror. "Not Rose!" Susan added, speaking very rapidly: "Don't listen to him, Rose. Don't listen to him!"

"Obscurantists," muttered Molyneux. Rachel said:

"He's simply terrible. He's got no respect for anything. He says there oughtn't to be a word 'home' in the language."

"Why should I respect anything?" demanded Molyneux, delighted. "Here's a world that's finished. It's done. You should get rid of all your antiquated ideas of safety and duty. Move about. Make the future!"

"I'm sick of the future!" cried Rose. "I believe it's become a Juggernaut in reverse gear. We shall end up worse than we ever were."

"But the present's a total wreck!" cried Molyneux. "Anything's better than that."

"Oh, be quiet!" admonished Lettice. "Rose, Mr. Molyneux says we're petrified in Sandersfold——"

"He didn't. It was *you* who said that!" shouted Rachel, indignantly.

"Did I? Rose, I told him Sandersfold was dead. Nothing happens here——"

"It does!" shouted Rachel. "Heaps!"

"Yes, I know. Bones and dust and rubbish; teas and mothers' meetings. Nothing exciting. Nothing real. He says we ought to leave Sandersfold to its fate, and go to London, and be emancipated, whatever that means——"

"Oh," said Rose; "but that's all so old-fashioned. The really smart thing is to marry, have babies, and hang them out of the window——"

"We've got no babies," declared Lettice. "So we can't expose them." She sent a lightning glance at Henry that only Rose understood. "But we *could* go to London and see what all the fuss is about."

"One minute," interrupted Molyneux. "You say emancipation's old-fashioned, Miss Rose. It is. The thing to do is to use it. With courageous selfishness."

"Father to pay the bills?" asked Rose. "I hate being selfish at other people's expense."

"Ach, you're a Conservative!" screamed Molyneux. "That's his duty. In a properly constituted world the State would endow every woman——"

"How nice to have a little money!" cried Lettice.

"Well, *I've* got none," grumbled Henry. Rose saw that his face had fallen. He looked almost sulky.

"Cheer up, little man," observed Lettice, reaching out her hand quickly and touching his arm. She was more arch than ever—apparently she had some reason to feel triumphant. Henry reddened. "Rose, the point is, shall you and I go and try to find work in London? And keep ourselves. Why not? Other girls do it; they're independent. Don't take any notice of Mr. Molyneux. He's only a one-man rabble. But London! Rose, dear!"

She looked prettier than ever. She was pretty and beseeching.

"We'll talk it over quietly," said Rose. "It's been in my mind for some time."

5

Henry and his friend had returned to London. They left disquiet in Sandersfold. Molyneux had argued to his own satisfaction; but he had impressed them less with his argumentativeness than with his abounding vitality. Lettice's "one-man rabble" had been deemed a fitting sentence. Henry, while painfully avoiding solitary conversation with Lettice, had been at her mercy more than once during Sunday. She had shown great restraint.

Lettice, indeed, was not ill-pleased with the week-end. She had sized up Molyneux as a bluffer, a man who talks hard and immorally because he is too timid to do anything but earn his living. A big talker is a little doer, she thought. Only the sterile are doctrinaire. In ten years he would be a dreary bald-headed drone. As for Henry, she had better hope. He was less frightened of her, if still nervously circumspect. He was working hard—a good sign. But he was doing this at a distance. Somebody not herself might step in and reap the benefit. That must be prevented.

"Look here," she said guardedly to Rose, on Tuesday afternoon. They were in the garden at the Davitts', and sat talking while Rachel and Susan frisked upon the tennis court. "What do you suppose one could live on in London?"

"I'm vague," Rose answered. "We'd better go and see.

I don't expect it's very nice in a cheap boarding house.
There are hostels. We can look at some advertisements."

"No, I mean a flat. Where one can have people to see
one."

"Men?" demanded Rose. "Of course: how silly!"

"Anybody. And have parties. And furnish for oneself
—you don't need much. A bed, a chair or two, some
cushions. . . . And make coffee when one needs it."

"And sit on the floor? Lettice, you've been reading
books! Chintz and cushions and Heal china. . . . Lash-
ings of gin and vermouth. You're thinking of Chelsea, I
know."

"What if I am? Don't you think it would be nice?"

"Lovely. At least, it sounds like an endless picnic. I
don't know who washes up. But it might cost a good deal
for one; and as for two——"

"Do you think if a girl marries she ought to give up
her job?"

"I've got an idea that marriage is a bit of a job."

"Yes; well, why marry? That would save a lot of
divorces. But if two people are earning money, they can
make enough together to keep them in comfort; whereas
if only one is earning, they may always be too poor. I
don't mean that I want children: I don't. I'm just thinking if I *did* want to marry, and *if* the man I wanted to
marry wasn't well off——"

It all seemed artless enough; but Rose did not respond.
Lettice continued:

"Trying to get money out of my mother is like trying
to get butter out of a dog's mouth. You've no idea how
stingy she is. She's got every penny. Len's not much
better off than I am; but he's got his profession. I suppose when she dies I shall get something. But she may
live twenty years. Aren't mothers and fathers tiresome!

They make a virtue of bearing you and bringing you up. It's only self-indulgence in the first place, and social vanity in the second. When it comes to letting you be happy, they jib."

So far Lettice had been general. She reached her points:

"Yours are different. Rose, how well off *is* your father? Of course, there's four of you . . ."

Rose faintly flinched. She had been listening innocently. This direct calculation of a quarter interest was so open that she was startled. Did she *want* Lettice to marry Henry? Lettice gave herself away a good deal.

"I don't know anything about Father's money," she answered, steadily. "It's all in house property, I think. He says he's as safe as anybody can be. But what he has, I don't know. Somehow it never comes up. We don't spend a lot. He doesn't like the idea of us working."

"But if you were to marry, Rose. Would he give you a dot? Or only a house?"

Rose smiled.

"I shall never know," she said mischievously, "if no one ever marries me."

Lettice was diverted from her inquisition. She said:

"Isn't it awful! The young men are such saps; and the older ones, if they've got any money, are such sticks! And I want to *marry*. Even if I go to London, I don't want to have just a trickle of affairs. They *sound* all right, while they last, but they might leave you high and dry in the end. Don't you think so?"

"Well, I *have* wondered what one of these splendidly unmoral girls in novels will do when she gets older."

"Commit suicide, I should think. Or marry some old widower with half a dozen brats. Or go on the streets. Rose, I've been very disappointed over Mr. Spears— over his marrying Ruth Coulevain."

Philip! The introduction of his name was so unexpected that Rose felt her heart jump. It beat hard; it was choking her. She sat very still, hoping that she might not betray her distress.

"Why? Because he was so 'eligible'?" she asked, as quickly as she could.

"Well, he was good-looking, and wealthy. I'd have married him if he'd asked me. He could have had any girl in Sandersfold."

"Even if she'd wanted somebody else?"

"She wouldn't have."

"She might. It's horrid to mix love and money. Yet lovers seem to come up against money all the time. It ought *not* to be so."

"Don't be silly. What d'you mean by love?"

"Well, I should think if you were starving you'd think more of that."

Rose was quite ready now. She was as calm as Alicia Furze would have been.

"I never thought of marrying him," she answered, truthfully.

"No, but feel physically attracted by him? I don't know him; but I could imagine he *is* attractive. Of course, he's rather old for you." Lettice looked speculatively at Rose, half closing her eyes in a sophisticated expression. Rose countered with a smiling:

"Well, he's not quite a Methuselah!"

"My dear, you're perfectly right. Oh, why didn't he ask *me* to marry him!" exclaimed Lettice, with fervour. "Why doesn't *somebody* ask me? In spite of all that's said and written about modernity a girl like you or me can't go up to a man and say to him: 'Look here, it's your money I want.'"

Rose laughed.

"No, but you can beckon him with your eye," she said.

"No good. He doesn't come. He thinks he's being vamped; and flies to some really nice little hypocrite. Oh, Rose; I'm so sick of everything. It all seems so hopeless. Do you think Ruth is attractive?"

"She must be," replied Rose, coolly. But these swoops of Lettice's agitated her very much.

"Yes, she must, mustn't she?" Lettice became thoughtful. She was remembering that scene at the garden party, when Leonard had rushed away in anger. Leonard had wanted Ruth. No denying it. She returned to Rose, and (how far intentionally?) stabbed: "The trouble about you is that you're too calm and sensible. You wouldn't excite a man. He'd think of you as a sister to assist him. Now I excite the wrong sort of man. The others I scare. They're frightened of me, the fools. We shall both be old maids, mark my words. Or else get into a mess with some man who's already married."

Too calm and sensible! A sister! Rose hardly heard what followed. The words went straight to her heart, wounding desperately. He had been so glad to tell her about himself, and so frank. . . . She had supposed one couldn't be so frank unless one loved a person. And now here was an explanation. Calm and sensible. Too calm for love; sensible enough to receive a confidence. No more. This was the truth that Lettice spoke.

She did not believe it. He *must* have understood her better. Something had happened. No, it was the truth. What bitter malice lurked in truth! What almost unendurable pain!

"As for you," announced Rose, trembling, although she spoke with outward calm and good sense, "I shouldn't give up hope. You may still find somebody who isn't afraid—in Chelsea!" She smiled. "And as for me, I must try to be less calm and sensible. I must follow Mr. Molyneux's advice, and live dangerously."

"What, with *him?*" asked Lettice. "What *is* his Christian name?"

"I don't know," asked Rose. "Has he got one?"

CHAPTER FOURTEEN

ENCOUNTER WITH A STRANGER

IT WAS a Saturday afternoon in late September, and the garden at the Georgian house was in its last period of brilliance. Roses glowed, hollyhocks mounted ever higher, late monkshood displayed deep blue cowls against a noble green, tall yellow perennial coreopsis and large pink and crimson cosmos spread their sturdy lightness about the borders. In contrast to the strident dahlias, zinnias, and salvia, tender-hued stocks and asters and cherry pie took the eye with quietness; and every tree was florid with abundance. Yet over the whole garden, rich though it still was in life, brooded the hint of decline. "In a month," said this profusion warningly, "chill winds and falling leaves will begin; the soil will be damp with mist and rain; the summer will be ended."

Ruth Spears (as she now was) had left the house and was walking in the garden. Whether from a sense of coming autumn, or from some preoccupation with secret things, she shivered once as she went, and brought her hands together, and locked them as if in anguish. Although she held herself very erect as she walked, her head was bowed; the expression upon her face was reflective and cheerless. Sometimes she stayed for a moment to examine something which had caught her eye, but when she did this she was always inattentive, and immediately afterwards began abruptly to walk again with two or three quick steps. Her progress through the massed bril-

liance was thus slow and fitful. Her whole demeanour
suggested irritable melancholy.

Indeed she was a sick woman. She could not bear to
stay in the house. It had become an exasperation to her,
so much was it in contradiction of her own mood. Its
quiet heightened the strain of nervous tension from which
she suffered. She had roamed from room to room this
afternoon, always as if seeking oblivion, without ever
finding it, always as if she hoped to receive a message
which would free her from the constant torture of
thought. For a time she had stood and looked out upon
the picture to be seen from those discreet windows com-
manding the High Street of Sandersfold. But all movement there had ceased, and the street was a blank. She
could have screamed aloud as the last hurrying woman
disappeared, leaving herself alone. It was like a deser-
tion. The silence was an oppression. She had hastened
from this room to the morning room.

But in the morning room her solitude had been greater
than ever. She had looked around, as if stupefied, at all
this familiar furniture, so associated in memory with
snatched passion and the horror of a single evening's
panic. Then, as if awakening, she had stumbled towards
the open French windows and into the garden. Even there
she could not escape from her thoughts. They tore at her
mind until, from alternating weariness and excitement,
she came close to hysteria.

She would have reëntered the house, sought out Philip,
and made some excuse to remain in his company, partially
solaced; but Philip, she knew, was busy in the library
with a stranger. She could not go there. Besides, Philip
was one of the causes of her distress, an element so disturbing that it was the thought of Philip which made her
lock her hands together in fierce effort to retain self-
control.

Philip attracted and repelled her. She thought of him now, while moving among the borders, as silken steel, flexible but unbreakable. He did not hide from her in cold reserve, or continually face her in suspicion. He was not indifferent to her. She respected him. She trusted him. But, since she could not understand him, she despised him. Perhaps she only *wished* to despise him?

Men had always been at Ruth's mercy. She had deceived them into a triumph of passion; and had meanwhile enjoyed experimental amusement at her own power. Poor blundering shy gross boys, for the most part. Not Starling: he was malignantly satyr-like: but by so experienced an eye as her own he could be read as easily as any of her earlier loves. Except that she loved him, Leonard was no different from the rest. Why did she love him? Her own greater need of love, revulsion from Starling, above all an uncertainty of the future, something in Leonard himself—a weariness, a coldness which called for effort. . . .

But Philip escaped her. He was never to be solved. But then she was still in love with Leonard, and she carried Leonard's child within her. She had no joy in her achievement of marriage with Philip: that had been no victory, but on his part an inexplicable act of mercy. She had willed it, but he had voluntarily offered it, disarming her, robbing her of an excuse for voluptuous contempt. Her relation to him was therefore still undefined, and but increased the complexity of her tormenting thoughts. What was her future to be? When the child was born, would they find a way of life together? What a maddening sense of impotence she felt!

Even Philip's present engagement, which forced her to be alone and self-tortured, was one that angered Ruth. He was shut up in the library with the proprietor of the small bookshop in the High Street. The object of the meeting was a discussion of plans of assistance. The bookshop did not pay; its proprietor was a youngish man with insufficient capital, who had intelligence but no acumen. Ruth had tried to dissuade Philip from entangling himself, but in vain; and annoyance at his determination was now a minor trouble to her, an exaggeration of that more serious impatience which had larger grounds.

Ruth did not see why a bookseller who could not make his business pay should expect to be helped by one of his customers. She had said, quietly enough: "He'll involve you. Why *shouldn't* he smash, if he's not competent?" Philip had smiled. He had said: "I'm sentimental about booksellers. And this chap *is* competent." There could be no more discussion.

There could be no more discussion, because Ruth knew she had no ultimate power over Philip. Knowledge of that, while it forced her unwillingly to admire him, drove inward the anger she felt at her powerlessness, and increased the sickness of her mind. She would end by loving or detesting her husband. Circumstances would decide between love and detestation.

2

If it had been possible to make a diagram of Ruth's progress about the garden, she would have been shown as turning round and round in a series of imperfect circles. She did not observe where she went, but obeyed only the impulse which urged her to restless movement. During the whole time she never once passed the end of the flower garden, but followed the paths mechanically, and stopped, and went on again, without more than superficial awareness of her surroundings. But once, when she had stopped, and, without knowing it, had plucked a flower and torn it deliberately, petal by petal, until only the head remained, and her hands had been moistened by its sap, she raised her eyes and looked into the distance.

Still screened by the privet hedge at the limit of the flower garden, she caught sight of a man who stood or moved just outside the five-barred gate at the bottom of the vegetable garden. For an instant Ruth's heart stopped beating, for it was here that she had several times— though never in daylight—met Leonard in the early days of their love. She stared. The man was no longer visible. In a moment he reappeared; and she looked as closely at him as the considerable interval of space allowed.

She did not recognize this man, although it seemed to her that she had seen him before. The heavy beatings of her heart subsided. It was not Leonard. Ruth did not deceive herself as to her feeling for Leonard; at thought of him she was seized by despair. But who was this man who so mysteriously came and went?

She remained in her place of concealment because of the man's strange behaviour. He was apparently walking, or pretending to walk, in the little lane beyond the end of the garden, for he appeared at the gate, stood for a bare fraction of time looking sideways towards the house with a quick jerk of his head, and immediately disappeared again. He was making no attempt to conceal himself, and therefore Ruth felt no nervousness; but there was a slyness in his bearing which invited suspicion.

As she watched, she considered. Had the man some appointment—for instance, with Snell, the gardener? But Snell had gone home. Sims and Mrs. Foster rarely went into the garden at this time of day. The lane was so short, and it so obviously led only to the garden of the Georgian house, that it could hardly be a tempting general promenade. Who was the man? Why was he so mysterious? Was he waiting to speak to Philip? Another beggar? Could he be a messenger for herself? From Leonard?

As this imagining occurred to Ruth, the stranger paused by the gate. She saw him look quickly behind him, and as it were press himself against the gate, as if to screen himself from somebody at that moment passing the end of the lane. Then he skipped away, peering in another direction. But as he was an elderly man, who (though nimble) was of substantial build, there was something indescribably ludicrous in his movements, which brought a smile to Ruth's face for the first time that afternoon. She was also rendered very curious indeed. An elderly and respectable-looking man who wished to avoid notice, and who yet showed himself boldly at the gate. That was odd. Ruth moved from her screen, pretending not to notice the stranger, but allowing him to observe her presence. She retired behind the screen once more. The effect of her action was immediate. The elderly man did not resume his walk. He remained quite still, his arms resting quietly upon the top of the gate. Even now he was singularly sly, for the position he had taken up was at the end of the gate, rather in the shadow of the wall, and as Ruth supposed out of sight of any who passed in Eden Street.

She walked down towards the gate. The stranger did not move. He awaited her.

3

Two or three minutes must have passed by the time Ruth came within hearing of the man who stood by the gate. But as she approached she saw that he was clean-shaven, very much like an old actor, and soberly dressed in a frock coat, a tall stiff winged collar, and a hard felt hat. He raised the hat from his head in respectful salutation to herself, and disclosed a fine head of greenish grey hair. And when he smiled, a row of very regular, rather discoloured teeth could be seen. He had something the appearance of an undertaker's mute, with his long coat and black tie. His eyes were very light in colour.

"Are you wanting to see somebody?" called Ruth, pausing at a distance.

"Madam," began the stranger, with sublime grimace, "if I might make so bold as to have some words with you." He bowed again with the grace of an impresario. "A few words only . . . of some interest to yourself."

"What is it?" Ruth went a few steps farther. She spoke, as always, in a low voice, as if between clenched teeth. She looked at him suspiciously. His air was too ingratiating. He was like the kind of old man who with honeyed words accosts young girls in a city street. She distrusted him. She had often dealt scornfully with such old men.

"May I have the privilege?" He smiled again, and again raised his hat.

"I don't understand you," said Ruth. "Why are you so mysterious? You should have come to the front door if you had some business."

The stranger opened his mouth to speak, checked himself, looked around in fear of eavesdroppers, smiled delicately, and whispered. A long, penetrating whisper.

"Madam, my name is Burgess. Mr. Holpen's managing clerk."

Ruth started. Her cheeks coloured faintly. She stood quite still. Leonard!

"You have a message?" she asked, distinctly. But her self-command was less. Outwardly, it was perfect.

"Not a message," called Burgess, in the same whisper. "Oh, no, not a message. I came on my own initiative." She heard only a thick hissing—"neesha." He closed his eyes as he pronounced the word. His manner was unctuous. "Very private. Concerned with *you*."

He made no effort to enter the garden, but stood back from the gate as if to suggest that she had nothing to fear. He had taken off his hat, and stood humbly awaiting her approach. But he had succeeded in arousing her interest. There was much that he might have to tell. She was insecure. . . . She was ill. Presently, after hesitation, Ruth went near to the gate. She had dropped her voice. She looked steadily at the stranger.

"Now," she said, with a great air of coldness. "You have a message for me. What is it?"

"Not a message," repeated Burgess, humbly. He stared up the garden. What was this? Blackmail? Her heart began to throb. "Mr. Spears," he continued—"is he at home? I would *rather* . . ." He smiled again. "I think *you* would rather there was no possibility . . . So private . . ."

"My husband's engaged." Ruth was breathless. Her eyes closed for an instant. She had leapt at last, with certainty, to the object of this call. It was a threat of some kind. What was her defense? Not Philip's incredulity. She had no defense. Damn Philip! A wave of hysteria passed through her. Only her own wits. "What is it you want?" she demanded.

"It's about a *letter*," whispered Burgess, in an old man's confidential tone. "A letter you wrote . . . So confidential. I thought it was such a pity for it—one never knows what might happen—such a pity if it should come into Mr. Spears's hands. When everything is so pleasant." He beamed. "You mustn't suppose—oh, you mustn't for one moment suppose that——"

"A letter I wrote?" Ruth faced him imperiously, although her lips had blanched. "But I haven't written to you."

Burgess looked at her, smiling. He raised his right

hand, wagging his forefinger gently and persuasively in the air.

"No," he said. "Not to me. To Mr. Holpen."

What was that? A letter of her own to Leonard? Good God! They were notes. How explicit? Ruth was in terror.

"You'll have to show me the letter," she told him. "I don't know what you're talking about."

"No; but you *will* know," said Burgess, drily, "madam."

"Did Mr. Holpen give you the letter?"

"No," answered Burgess, comfortably.

"Then I don't quite see what you have to do with it."

"Only to give it to you, madam."

"Thank you."

"But that's not the only thing," Burgess whispered. "Oh, I can tell *you* something rather advantageous, as well. I *think* you would be interested. If you could spare me a very few minutes. I think you and I could help one another, Mrs. Spears. Really, I do."

"Is this blackmail of some sort?" demanded Ruth. "I'll call my husband, if it is."

"Oh, madam, what an injustice!" cried Burgess indignantly. "You call an act of kindness 'blackmail'?"

"What is the letter? What can you tell me? You're so long-winded!"

Burgess pursed his lips together. He wagged his forefinger. He abandoned unction and began to speak in a practical tone.

"If I was a blackmailer, madam," he said, "I should go to your husband. Mrs. Spears, I know a number of things as I ought not to know. That can't be helped. They stick to me. I don't use my knowledge. Nobody's ever been the worse off because of me, I assure you. But I know a lot of things, if you follow me. I know all about you and Mr. Holpen——"

"Has *he* sent you?" asked Ruth. She could hardly stand. She was forced to rest against the five-barred gate, to support herself. "Don't you think I'd better telephone about you to Mr. Holpen?"

Burgess smiled.

"You 'aven't been very lucky with your telephone calls lately, madam," he reminded her. "Not to Mr. Holpen. I'm the gentleman who's had the disagreeable duty of, if I may say so, putting you off. Mrs. Spears, to cut a long story short—I can see you're not yourself, and I don't wish in any way to incommode you—madam, I'm married myself, and though we have never been blessed with family I have a loving wife who does what she's told, and I'm thankful for it. But I've got this letter of yours. I'll give it back to you in pure Christian kindness of heart. I will, really."

"Yes?" said Ruth, with painful dryness.

"Yes, I will," insisted Burgess, in a pleasantly earnest manner. "I swear I will. And I'll tell you something to your own advantage. Still kindness. Still free and cordial——"

"What's the price?" asked Ruth.

A spasm crossed Burgess's face. It might have been a fleeting smile.

"Well, madam," he said, "I leave it to you to say whether the finder of such a letter, who does the right thing with it, might not deserve a little reward. There! Can I say fairer than that? Think of the contrast. If I was to take it to Mr. Spears——'"

"You'd get nothing at all," Ruth said, bitterly.

Burgess winked at her.

"The letter is one you wrote to Mr. Holpen—telling him something was going to happen. That's worth a lot of money to several people."

Ruth now knew what the letter contained. It was within her recollection.

"I see that you could do me some harm," she said, looking directly at Burgess.

"If you please, madam," agreed Burgess. "Quite inconvenient, I think."

"Though you don't know my husband." Her lips were trembling.

"I don't think he would like it, madam," said Burgess, very respectfully. "They don't like such things as a rule. Somehow."

"But you would give me this letter. How did you get hold of it?"

"By misfortune," confessed Burgess. "By misfortune —no intervention of mine, madam, I swear it—that letter was never opened by Mr. Holpen."

"What!" cried Ruth. "But you've read it."

"I must confess that," agreed Burgess. He looked ashamed. He hung his head. "Madam, I ask you to forgive——"

"Never opened." Ruth felt sick.

"Mr. Holpen had thrown it aside," Burgess told her cruelly, and watched her mouth fall open in unconcealed misery. She was indeed haggard. No beauty now. "He told me, madam, that when you telephoned he was to be out."

"Yes." Ruth did not know that she had spoken. "And he was in?"

"I'm sorry, madam." Burgess cast up his eyes. "I had my instructions. Against my will and inclination." And then, as if he had received from above an inspiration for a change of tone, he said, very confidentially, with a brightening smile, "But, madam! Leaving all that aside. In our profession all sorts of little ways are necessary. . . . Leaving that aside. Would you like to know something about your husband, Mrs. Spears? About before he came here. Before—well, before he *was* your husband, if I may say so. . . . Very curious. . . . I can tell you some things——" He nodded, beaming again with encouragement. "It's always useful. . . . They're no use to me, because I should regard any use of them as outside my activities. They're no use to anybody, except you. But of course I know a good deal about you and your affairs, because Mr. Starling was a client of ours, and hadn't no secrets from Mr. Holpen—Mr. Holpen senior, that was."

"It *is* blackmail, I see," said Ruth, unsteadily.

"So help me!" cried Burgess. "I swear it's nothing of the kind."

"I've got no money."

"Get it!" He grew excited, intimate. "That's what I meant by saying that we could help each other. Listen, you've been in a bad place, what with Mr. Starling and young Leonard. . . . I sympathize. I've been in bad places myself. . . . You had to do the best you could for yourself. Cruelly treated, you've been, madam; and likely to be, again, if that letter was to miscarry. But I can tell you some things that'll make Mr. Spears eat out of your hand. Oh, madam, it's so simple! For your own sake, let me give you a word of advice. And if you was to remember me, why . . . Get a settlement. Tell him you want money of your own. What? Only two months married, and a baby coming! He'd do anything you asked—now. Say you're worried about the future. About the child. Tell him you've got some debts. . . . Take my advice, Mrs. Spears; get a settlement before you give him a well-grown seven-months child. That's a crucial moment. A crucial moment. He'd be very funny, madam, if the child was too big for his months. Hehe! But this is where I can help you, d'you see? I've had to deal with husbands before now. And if he's tough, ask him how

he enjoyed his holiday in Sing Sing! Ask him how he'd
like to be known in Sandersfold that *his child* had a forger
and embezzler for a father. Eh, Mr. Spears?" His hands
were in the air and shaking with the excitement of his
own eloquence. He might have been testifying to a
miracle. His beaming smile held no malice, but only
triumph at a benevolent intention. "That'll give you the
whip hand, I think," he concluded, in high glee. He
laughed hoarsely. "Eh, madam? Eh? Oh, I'd like to be
there to hear you frighten him. I would, indeed!"

Ruth was clutching the top of the five-barred gate with
both her hands. Her head was turning. She could hardly
see the genial features before her, but only knew that
Burgess was a frightful grinning nightmare. She tried to
stand, to run away. It was impossible.

"You're ill, madam. I'm sorry," said good-natured
Burgess. "I had to take my chance. Will you allow me
to give you my arm up the garden? If Mr. Spears is
engaged. You'll understand that as to the letter I shouldn't
wish to see Mr. Spears."

Ruth's voice was thick. She said:

"I won't have you inside this place. I'd rather crawl."

"But you'll think it over, Mrs. Spears," coaxed Bur-
gess. "Think over what I said. It'll be all right. Look here,
I'm a gentleman——" He foraged in his pocket. "There!
Just to comfort you. There's the letter. There's the letter.
Not the original, but a copy. Say no more about that.
You shall have the original next time. Tomorrow. To-
morrow evening. . . ."

He pressed something into her hand, but she was so
confused that she did not take it. Something white fluttered to the ground.

At the same moment Burgess uttered an exclamation.
"Oh, excuse me, madam. Somebody's coming. I'll call
again. I'll call again—tomorrow evening. Be strolling here

about nine." He was gone. Clinging to the gate, Ruth saw that Philip and another man—his bookseller—had appeared beside the hedge which divided this part of the garden from the other. She crouched down, groping for the dropped letter. When she was at last able to stand upright the two men were no longer in view. Nor was Burgess anywhere near. She found herself clutching what appeared to be an empty envelope.

CHAPTER FIFTEEN
PHILIP VISITS MISS FURZE

PHILIP awoke upon that Sunday morning with a feeling of dissatisfaction. He lay still with his face to the light, watching the movement of leaves against a very pale sky. At first his mind went back to his conversation with Mr. Purvis, the bookseller whose business was too small for his expenses, and he tried to tell himself why Mr. Purvis was a failure. There were difficulties. Here was a town of ten thousand people, visited often from Seahampton during holidays, and not robbed of trade by any enterprise upon the part of Seahampton rivals. . . . Mr. Purvis's shop was attractive. Mr. Purvis himself was small, quick, and agreeable. In any other business he would have made money. He loved books; that was his trouble; he was a failure.

"I'm a failure myself," thought Philip, grimly. Some men were born failures. But Purvis was not so born. At least, he had a competent air. He was quiet, did not talk too much, had alertness and assurance. What more was needed? There must be a kink somewhere in his character. Nobody could be as competent as Purvis seemed. Was it all façade? Philip did not think so. He thought Purvis a genuine article. But perhaps too inflexible? Alas, not quite good enough? Yes, but flexibility could be as great a fault as overconfidence. Was not flexibility next door to flaccidity?

"Flaccidity. Is that *my* fault? I've never had any driving ambition. What a godsend *this* has been to me! I wonder. I should still have been at Dexter's. I was half dead there. And yet it was pleasant and interesting, and I'm dissatisfied here. Dissatisfied with myself." How lucky those men were who had definite ambition! A niche, a line, an aptitude for some particular career or trade. A writer was always enviable; a man who cultivated the soil was always enviable; a scholar, a craftsman. Philip thought: "I'm nothing. I'm war-spoilt, prison-spoilt; and too old to recover. Is that true? No whimpering when one's got a fortune, eh? But I wish I saw something ahead." There were various definitions of what hell was. Dante had said, profoundly, "the gratification of the evil choice." How about "the inability to make a choice"? Or, simply, "Idleness"?

He sat up in bed. Unless, presently, he found occupation which was suited to his present condition, he would petrify. How about buying Purvis's business and working in it? Books—he loved books; he could afford, as other men could not afford, to run the business at a loss. Purvis was opinionated. He thought he knew what books people ought to buy. Well, he *didn't* know. Little fool! No, by no means a fool; but wanting in some sort of tact. Call it imagination; but imagination upon a practical plane. Tact, discretion, charm. Purvis had no tact. You would not want to go to the shop for a chat. No "snail's-horn perception of beauty" there. Purvis had a feeling of superiority—mental superiority, probably; but more probably the conceit of the half-baked—and an obstinate determination in favour of his own opinions. Damn it, the man was a highbrow!

Philip laughed. "Common enough," he thought. "What am I doing except prefer my own opinion?" He left the subject of Purvis. That would come round again, like a recurring decimal; but the words "obstinate determination" had produced a flash of anger in Philip, and he knew that this flash of anger had reference, not to Purvis, who amused him, but to Ruth, who was his wife, and no laughing matter.

Ruth, who wanted him to have nothing to do with Purvis. Why not? Money, of course. "Damn the woman; she's mean!" He knew why she was mean. She saw the money being taken from *herself*. She had the instinct of a miser. And a dominating miser, too. As hard as nails. Her attitude was: "Why give it to Purvis? He'll only lose it for you." But she had the same obstinate determination as Purvis—by which Philip meant (although he did not admit as much to himself) the same implacable stupidity. Was it only in reference to money? He thought not. A personality; but a personality less by nature than by consistency.

Ruth was in the room across the great landing from his own, lying in the bed which had once been Thomas Starling's. She had now occupied this room for a month, ever since she had told him she was going to have a child. Was that not odd? Philip could not help thinking it curious that she, an ardent voluptuary, should have become nunlike from the moment of this discovery. How seriously she took the burden of motherhood. Or else how suddenly her passion for himself had subsided. He smiled.

Seriousness, pondered Philip. She had communicated her news without elation and without a tremor. She had said one afternoon, as if in very carefully rehearsed phrase: "Philip, I think I'm going to have a child." Philip, whose mind had been busy elsewhere, had answered (but of course he did not realize with what self-command): "I say! Are you pleased?" And he had received the reply: "I don't know. Not altogether, perhaps." Something more had followed, without warmth. From her tone, the child might have been immaculately conceived; but this tone, Philip considered, was defensive. It might have been adopted to conceal excitement. He thought it was. If so, the concealment was perfect.

Philip remembered this now. It was true that his wife was a strange woman. It was true that there was no child-ishness in her, but in daily behaviour a composed frigidity. Yet she was amorous. "The truth is," he thought drily, "she's serious." Anything more than that? His intuitions carried him farther; but he could not formulate them while the spell she cast was still potent. In coldness, yes; in bitter anger, yes. Not now. While his present mood lasted he was inhibited from judging her. He could only speculate. In a year or two, perhaps after the child was born, she would lose whatever constriction it was that made her for most of her waking life a stranger.

What was she really like, under her calm, and apart from her capacity for passion? He did not know. She had intelligence. But her interest was not easily aroused. If he discussed any general topic with her she showed the intelligence, but no originality of comment. No sympathy; or no range of sympathy. She was indifferent, collected . . . only concerned with tangible things, such as money. Money. . . . Either her mind or her heart was frozen. Not her body. Did he like being married to her? With irony, two months after marriage, Philip recalled her own words as to the baby: "I don't know. Not altogether, perhaps."

What was the time? Six o'clock: too early to disturb her. She had been particularly silent the evening before, as if suffering. He lay down again. Now, as to Purvis . . .

2

Sims reported. Mrs. Spears had a sick headache, a little better. . . . She was staying in bed. Would Mr. Spears go and see her for a few moments after breakfast?

"He will," thought Philip, blandly. To Sims, he said: "How does she seem?"

To his surprise Sims shrugged very faintly as she answered.

"I think it's her spirits, sir," was what Sims said. "She seems low."

What Sims meant to convey by that, Philip did not understand. He ate his breakfast in silence. When he entered his wife's room he gave no sign of having received such a hint, and the light in the room was so poor, owing to a lowered blind, that he could hardly distinguish Ruth's features. She lay white and terribly listless, and although her face as he kissed it was cold as stone, her hand was burning.

"I'm sorry you're so feeble, old girl," Philip said. "Any pain? Or just the head?"

"The head," she answered, in a very low voice. "You'll forgive me, won't you?"

"I think it's a good idea to keep quiet. Don't worry about me. You haven't got anything on your mind, have you?"

"No." It was almost too quick.

"Not the baby, or anything?"

"No."

"I can't see you very well. It's odd asking questions of somebody you can't see. You would tell me, I suppose?"

"What makes you . . ." The pallid face turned wearily upon the pillow. She did not complete the sentence. He heard a sigh. But he knew that she had not been impatient. Indeed, before he could speak again, the burning hand had slightly pressed his own and been withdrawn.

"Just a wish to explore every avenue, as the politicians say. Not to make your head worse."

The head moved again upon the pillow. A feeble nodding. Her eyes were closed.

"You're very . . . kind to me." It was hardly audible.

"Yes. Ought a wife to say that to her husband?"

"No." Her eyes opened.

"I'll go. I'm pestering you with questions. Is there anything I can do?"

"Stay with me . . . a moment. Just quietly. . . ." The hand moved near to his own, and he sat holding it, conscious that although it lay softly within the clasp of his fingers there were a thousand nervous stirrings so enclosed. He did not speak. He could hear the quick ticking of a little clock which he presently discerned on the bedside table. Endlessly lively little thing! Tick-tick-tick-tick, whatever happened. It was frightful to think of such imperturbability. Ruth's breathing was not audible to him. She was painfully still. He bent slightly towards her, observing how thin her face was. Not a happy face; the face of one who was never happy, because never secure. . . .

"What are you thinking about?" Ruth asked, unexpectedly. He had not known that although her eyes seemed to be closed she was watching him.

"About you. If you were asleep."

"What were you thinking?"

"That you didn't look very grand. We might go to Scotland. Get you away for a bit."

"Hm." There was a faint, noncommittal murmur.

"Did you think you'd get up later? If so, we'll talk about it then."

"Philip, if I wanted some money, would you give it to me?"

"All I have. Didn't you know? I've got that matter in hand. I've talked to Cross, the manager at the bank. The winding up of the estate's been the trouble. Do you want some immediately?"

"I might. What 'matter'?"

"When we know what's to come in, you shall have some of your own. There's so much that's long-winded."

"Thank you." How mysterious she looked. He could have sworn that an expression of contempt had transformed that pale face for an instant. Of course, he could not see. But if contempt first, then satisfaction afterwards. In so dim a light one could fancy anything the mind suggested. Philip said:

"If it's money that's—I mean, if you've been worried about money——"

"Yes. I've been worried about money. All my life."

"But that's over."

"You have, too."

"Not all my life. In fact at one time—when I was a boy—I used to have more than was good for me." He saw her head shaken again, as though she thought such a thing impossible. "It's quite true; and a bad thing for the character. And anyway money's a bore, you know. If you've got too little, or too much, you're always anxious about it; and if you've got enough, you're very exceptional. Eccentric."

Ruth did not smile. Her eyes were tightly closed. In a very low voice she said:

"Yes, very exceptional, I should think. And if you don't care about it, you're very exceptional, too."

"D'you mean 'contemptible'?" He spoke idly, pinching her fingers. But that had been his reading of her dry tone.

There was a pause. She shook her head, and lay as if she were unconscious. At last:

"I think perhaps I can sleep now."

"And dream of money bags—full!" laughed Philip.

"And dream of nothing at all," answered Ruth. "It's better. And rarer. You've done me so much good."

He went quietly out of the room.

3

Philip would not have visited Miss Furze that day if she had not insisted upon it. But an invitation from Alicia was hard to refuse. At nearly eighty, she had a beautifully gentle assurance, and some of the charm of a very young, unaffected girl. That was because she had a quiet heart, and because her liking, when given, was an honour. Philip had met Miss Furze near his own house two days earlier; and she had stopped him. "Mr. Spears," she had said, with earnest charm, "you must do what I ask you." "Miss Furze," he had answered, "you need not ask; you shall command." "Come to tea with me on Sunday. And come alone. I want you to myself. Yes?" "Yes." She had pressed his arm with her gloved hand. She had nodded. Being nearly eighty, she could do this; but for that intoxicating moment she looked twenty.

Now Philip was upon his way to Miss Furze's house. It was hot to sultriness. The streets of Sandersfold were still buried in post-prandial silence, for Miss Furze took tea at four o'clock. Apart from a few strolling lovers and a purposeful girl or two in her best clothes, Philip might have been the only human being abroad in that shuttered solitude. And first of all he thought for a moment of the English Sunday, when London is for the greater part of eight or nine hours dead, and the main roads to the sea are crammed with hot and glittering cars, and towns not upon the direct route to any popular resort awaken to echo the hum of wandering vehicles. But secondly, and in reality without interruption, he thought of his wife, whom he understood and by whom he was mystified.

He remembered her phrase about the child: "I don't know. Not altogether, perhaps." She had been watching him. She was a curmudgeon. "I've been worried about money—all my life." Poor woman! Yes, "poor woman," not "poor child" or "poor girl." Had she ever been young? Had she ever played? He could not imagine her otherwise than as she was, talking in that low-pitched voice, always as if between her teeth, and without warmth. "I don't know. Not altogether, perhaps."

He was still smiling at his memories, and the sedate ambiguity of some of Ruth's words, when the door of Miss Furze's house was opened by a little elderly maid with the face of a very shrewd and perturbed monkey; and as Emma, this maid, was always pleased to see a frank smile, she responded with a smile equally genial. Emma was as clean-looking as a nursemaid. She knew a million things which are ignored by metaphysicians, and which she was never suspected of knowing, even by Miss Furze; and indeed she absorbed knowledge through the pores of her skin (for she had few brains, and those were of poor quality). In some respects she knew more than Philip—especially about Philip, who certainly knew very little of his own character. She also knew who were Miss Furze's favourites. And Emma smiled back at Philip. The tea party had begun well.

4

But when Philip heard the sound of a voice coming from Miss Furze's drawing room upon the first floor he had a qualm. Had not Miss Furze given him to understand that they would be alone? He had looked forward to a tête-à-tête. This would be no private and delightful exploration of ideas and ancient history. It might well be such a crush of bright chatter as would destroy all his happiness. He would go sorrowing back to his sick wife.

"Oh, Miss Furze!" he said reproachfully—but to himself, in the depths of his sinking heart. Before he could speak aloud, Emma had whipped open the drawing-room door, and—still smiling—had announced him. "Mr. Spears." You could have heard a pin drop, so abrupt was the silence. How singular! As if a pistol had been fired. Philip took two steps into the room. Although Miss Furze was not quite alone, she had only one other visitor, Rose Davitt; and it was Rose whose voice had suddenly failed before Emma's bombshell.

The two ladies were sitting at a little distance from a very small fire which burned in the grate. This room was a long one, and it was papered and painted in pale grey, so that in spite of the hot day and the little fire it seemed quite cool. Every picture on the walls was a pale water-colour, framed in a thin band of gold (a psycho-analyst who did not know that the pictures had been gifts would have supposed the frames symbolic of a wedding ring which Miss Furze had never worn); the carpet was pale; the cretonne chair covers were old-fashioned, pretty, and frilled. Miss Furze sat in her usual armchair with the high straight back, and was dressed in grey silk with a full skirt and a lace collar—a lovely picture of the past. Rose, in a russet walking costume, was, Philip would have said, much as usual. But although he felt so much affection for her, he had not yet grown especially attentive to her appearance. She always had clear eyes, a clear skin, and the direct look of a young woman with a clear conscience. Nor did she now show anything but calm pleasure at his coming. She was, if anything, rather graver than usual.

"Come and sit down, Mr. Spears." Miss Furze patted a chair standing vacant by her side. (Rose was upon a low chair at the other side of the fire.) "You didn't know Rose would be here; but she's a friend of yours, I think.

She's a friend of mine. I wanted your help, for the silly girl has an idea in her head."

Rose, shaking hands and laughing, said:

"Alicia means 'a bee in her bonnet.' "

"So I do," agreed the old lady, with a shrewd glance. She thought: "I like him; and she loves him. She's quite changed since he came. And he's a fool not to have known it. Such fools, always!" Aloud, she said: "How's Mrs. Spears? Not hurt, I hope, because her husband goes out to tea with an old woman?"

Philip thought: "She doesn't like Ruth. Well, I guessed that. However, this is dislike." He said:

"She's in no state to object, Miss Furze. She's in bed."

"Hm," grunted Miss Furze. "I'm sorry. You're not worried about it? You don't want to run away? All right. I'm glad you've come. If that's inhumane of me, you must put it down to my years. I can't tell you how much I'm dreading the winter."

"Poor Alicia!" murmured Rose.

"Oh, I wasn't pleading," grumbled Alicia. "I'm past pleading, with you. . . . He doesn't understand what we're talking about. Quite mystified. That shows how secret you've been——"

"I haven't seen Mr. Spears——" protested Rose, sparkling.

Emma trundled in with the teapot, a hot-water jug, and a hot dish, smiled at Rose, and trundled out again.

"Rose, you pour out, please."

Poor Rose! She had hoped to avoid that. One could talk lightly, however confused. But one could not pour out tea, and pass cups, and hand scones, with the same air of confidence when one's mind was disturbed. Bother! "Come on, girl!" thought Rose. "Don't make an absolute *idiot* of yourself!"

Fortunately Miss Furze had her own plan for the conduct of the party, and engaged Philip's attention at once.

"Listen, Mr. Spears. This child is bent on leaving us. On going to London to work. Do dissuade her from doing any such thing."

"It's no good my saying I don't want to go," said Rose. But then it was quite impossible for her to say that her inability to stay was due in part to himself. "I've got to the point of feeling useless here. And of course that's not true, either."

"I wondered if it would strike you," drily commented Miss Furze.

"What are you going to do in London?" asked Philip.

"Find some work. And grow up."

Philip exchanged an expressive glance with Miss Furze.

"We've lost her," he said.

"You're on her side then," groaned Miss Furze. "Apart from selfishness. I'd hoped better of you, I think. What's going to happen to the world, Mr. Spears? When all our clever young ones can never come back to us! She's going to do what they all do. She's going to cut off her nose to spite her face. When she's lost her nose she'll forget us——"

"Never!" There was more feeling in Rose's voice than she had wished; but indeed this attack by her old friend was very hard to bear in the presence of one whom she loved better than anybody else in the world. "If I don't move I shall get crotchety."

"Go or stay, it's the same with the young ones," cried Alicia. "Or so it seems to me. They make themselves unhappy, and then pretend it's the superior thing to be unhappy. But really it's quite a superior thing to be happy. Wouldn't you agree, Mr. Spears?"

"I'm still crushed by the knowledge that we shall lose

her," parried Philip. "But I agree that she won't be happy if she stays. It's a blow. I thought she was happy. I thought she'd found the secret we all want to know——"

"So did I," thought Rose. Aloud, she said: "You needn't be afraid, either of you. I'm not going to be silly or stuffy. You'll see. You know that people always want kittens to stay kittens. They *can't* stay kittens."

"We're talking about different things," said Miss Furze. "I want you to stay in Sandersfold, where you can grow up naturally. You insist on going to London, which is like a forcing house. That seems to me conventional. You think it's unconventional——"

"No!" declared Rose. "I only think it's educational. I think you've got the idea that London's all cocktails and night clubs, just as you think Chicago's all gangsters and Paris all restaurants and monuments. You think it's all vulgar Bright Young People, and you're afraid I shall turn into a raffish rake. But I shan't."

"All wrong!" contradicted Miss Furze, with spirit. "If you were like Lettice I *should* expect that. I expect it of her. She'll go to pieces, and think herself clever. That doesn't disturb me. What I'm afraid of is that *you* may lose health and spirits. I think you may run with the crowd, and learn to despise us, without learning to admire anything else very much. That's so easy."

Rose turned imploringly to Philip.

"Philip! Help me!" she said.

Philip was unprepared. He had been shocked at the news, and was now saddened by a feeling that these two had really reached an inevitable parting of the ways.

"I think we shall have to trust her, Miss Furze," he announced. "You and I are both frightened of change."

"We're frightened of coming sorrow," said Miss

Furze. "Don't you remember what Housman says?" She quoted:

> *" 'If young hearts were not so clever,*
> *Oh, they would be young for ever.' "*

Nobody spoke for a little while. They listened to an aëroplane flying overhead. It was safer to be on the earth; and that fluttering roar disquieted them all.

"True enough," agreed Philip, at last, returned to the quotation. "But Rose is Rose. We mustn't forget that, in calculating the chances."

"I don't forget it," said Miss Furze, sadly. "I think of it all the time. You must remember us sometimes, Rose. We don't like to be forgotten, you know."

That was all. Forget . . . forget . . . Rose did not answer. She was forced to keep her head low for a moment. They did not know how much they were <u>hurting</u> her.

5

"Now I want you to tell me some more about old Sandersfold, and particularly about my house," Philip said, a little later.

Miss Furze, sitting by her little fire upon that sultry day, bent forward and stretched a wrinkled ivory-coloured hand towards the embers. She, too, was thankful for a diversion. Her voice was more like that of an old woman than usual. She thought for a little while before responding.

"I always loved your house, Mr. Spears," she said. "I always wanted to live in it. I suppose it doesn't really matter where one lives."

"I understand you," answered Philip.

"I think I should like to make a little house all afresh," put in Rose. "Of my own."

Philip smiled towards her.

"You're afraid of this child growing new-fangled, Miss Furze?" he asked.

"You think of her as a child," said Miss Furze, taunting in her turn.

Rose flushed.

"I'm afraid you do," she admitted. "I shall live that down."

"The house," continued Miss Furze. "I mustn't say any more about Rose. It's like turning the dagger. I used to go there long ago, when Miss Strange lived all alone with three or four servants. She wasn't a very cheerful old thing. She'd been disappointed in love, and couldn't get over it. Although I believe the young man wasn't worth pining for. They aren't, you know." Miss Furze smiled as she mischievously said this; but she said it with a half meaning for Rose and herself. "I heard of him from others. A weak, foppish creature with a lisp and fidgeting hands. She once took a miniature of him from her secret hiding place in the mantelpiece, and said, 'I'll show you the portrait of the finest man that ever breathed.'"

"Of course, nobody would say that now," cried Rose. "They'd say, 'He's an awful idiot; but rather a darling.' They might stop at the 'awful idiot.'"

"It means the same thing," retorted Miss Furze, with relish, "however you say it. It means, 'He thinks a good deal of me, and anyway he's mine.' At any rate the miniature was of a man that even a painter hadn't been able to make look good-tempered. I always thought he must have been very stupid. In fact I hated him on hearsay. We can't borrow the rose-coloured spectacles; so we use our own, and they're yellow. Mine were yellow enough that day. And as she was putting the miniature back it somehow slipped and fell into the fireplace, and broke the glass. I thought she would die. She very nearly did. I gave her water and chafed her hands. To no purpose. I was terrified. I rang the bell, but nobody answered. . . . Finally I collected every scrap of glass and put it in my hanky, and she pressed the bits to her heart in a frenzy."

Philip had a sudden memory.

"Is this the library?" he asked. "I wonder if that bell doesn't ring."

"The servants were all gossiping in the garden, it appeared."

"You see, you won't alter human nature!" Philip told Rose. "The room's haunted. History repeats itself. But Miss Furze, what is this secret hiding place you speak of? I don't think I know it."

"Oh," said Miss Furze. "It's in the mantelpiece. You still have the old carved mantelpiece? Yes, it's there. Let me see, I fancy there's a spring." She looked towards her own mantelpiece. "I'm almost sure there's a spring that you can feel if you put your hand up the chimney. To the right. Somewhere about here." She illustrated. "I don't expect there's anything there now."

"I might like to keep something there."

"Oh, what?" begged Rose. "Have you any secrets, Philip?"

"I wish I could keep my conscience there."

"Is it such a burden?" She was laughing. It was extraordinary how happy she felt. Nothing mattered when she was with him. Was that unnatural? Immoral?

"I think I shall have to leave mine with Alicia when I go."

6

Philip and Rose walked back together to the Davitts' house.

"I won't come in, as Ruth's not well," he said. "Will you be able to come and see her before you go?"

"I'm going tomorrow morning," Rose said. "I may be back for next week-end. Or later. I didn't say anything to Alicia because she's very distressed, and I'm very fond of her, and felt I couldn't bear it."

"Then this is good-bye for the present?" asked Philip. "I can't say that I really welcome your plan, you know. I think you must do what you want to; but I wish you weren't going."

They had almost parted. The distance to her home was nearly traversed, and they were alone in the long, respectable road which was as straight as monotony itself. Rose felt that she was choking. Now that it was good-bye, parting seemed impossible. She turned to him, driven by such anxious and tender love that she could not restrain her tongue a moment longer.

"Philip. Forgive me. Are you happy?" Why ask? Idiot! Idiot! Her eyes were suddenly large and very bright indeed. The corners of her mouth drooped. She was so blanched and strained that her secret was open to his unseeing eyes.

Philip said:

"Yes, I'm happy. I've got a great deal to make me happy."

"But that's not quite the same thing."

It is a little difficult to ask such questions in open street in a small English town, when one may be observed from windows along the route. But Rose was constrained to the task. She could not part from him as a stranger.

"I'm not satisfied with myself," Philip candidly answered. "I feel useless."

"Like me."

"Oh, but you're useful. You bring happiness wherever

you go. It's unostentatious, but irresistible. I don't do
that."

Rose brushed aside his reassurance as to herself. She
was scornful.

"People like me because I'm young and good-tempered.
That means nothing. I want them to like me because I'm
Rose."

"I like you because you're Rose," Philip said, quietly.
"So does Miss Furze."

"I shall howl," murmured Rose. This was all quite different from what she had expected. Their talk had taken
a wrong turning and might lead to unthinkable confes-
sions, ever to be regretted. She desperately sought for
something to say of a less personal nature. "Philip, what
did you mean when you said the room was haunted?"

He hesitated. She thought his face showed something
of constraint. Because it had reference to Her? But he
answered:

"You remember the day we met at Seahampton." Rose
was instantly alert. He was to tell her something terribly
important in its implications, however trivial in itself.
"When I got home, I found Ruth fainting in that room.
I gave her brandy. I chafed her hands. I rang the bell.
Kept on ringing. Nobody came. Isn't that an odd coinci-
dence?"

Rose smiled benignly. She thought: "He's an old
goose." Then: "Yes, but if I understood! If I understood!" She became excited at the knowledge that a secret
lay hidden in his words. For this reason, when she spoke,
her tone was rather dry.

"Very. Had she broken a miniature?"

Philip shook his head. Helpfully, he admitted:

"She'd torn a book. Not quite the same thing."

Rose could ask no more. Neither good manners nor

fear of his opinion restrained her, but a sense that she dared tiptoe no closer to what she believed a secret of immense importance to herself. After all, had he not told her a good deal—now and earlier? Had he told Ruth as much? Never! What did Ruth know of him? That cold and selfish woman!

"You feel useless?" she asked. "I don't think you're useless. But I wish you had a lot of friends—to laugh at. A lot of activities. You need them. I need them. I wish you'd seen a young man Henry brought down here."

"A young man," repeated Philip.

"Only because I should have liked to see you together. To know what you thought of him."

"Was it he who suggested London?"

"He was ridiculous." She was silently laughing at the memory of Molyneux. "You'd have made mincemeat of him. The real reason you feel useless is that you've got nothing here to get your teeth into. Philip, I think *you* ought to come to London!"

She had recovered. She was able openly to laugh at him.

"I'll see." Philip had misunderstood her. "Whatever happens we shall still be friends, shan't we?"

Rose did not answer. What could she have said?

CHAPTER SIXTEEN
DISCOVERIES

As PHILIP, still light-hearted as a result of his conversation with Rose, strolled homeward, he heard the early bells ringing for evening service. Ding-ding-ding, they said, upon a thin, high note, rather depressingly. Soon, like ants, the good people of Sandersfold would come straggling into line, all in their Sunday best, armed with prayer books and explosive coughs for a bout with organ, choir, and Mr. James's simple, rather throaty discourse. But Philip, although he liked Mr. James, preferred the words of other divines, such as Jeremy Taylor. . . .

He turned in by the little private lane, intending to reach the house by way of the garden; and by this action he caused panic to a prevous occupant of the lane. There was a sharp scurry, as of a rabbit among leaves. Philip hardly noticed it. Here, upon his left, was a thick hedge, dividing the lane from meadowland; and upon his right, beyond a shallow ditch bordered with tufts of long grass, was the turn of the garden wall. The scurry became an unmistakable rustle—no longer a rabbit, but a hippopotamus. Philip saw an elderly man stooping down near the five-barred gate and fiddling with his boots or his socks. Was this not a very strange place for such a man and such an occupation? Philip thought it was.

The man looked over his shoulder at that moment. He was most sedately dressed in black, top-hatted, and with the unctuous air of an old, even ducal, family servant. Philip could imagine him behind a salver, or carrying a noble decanter. . . . He saw the man's bootlace trailing upon the ground.

"Good-evening, sir," mumbled the old man, in an old, indistinct, but courtly voice. "I trust you will kindly pardon me for trespassing."

Philip, nodding, responded to the greeting, and was then struck by a sense of half familiarity with that curiously red face and those pale and evasive eyes. He had seen them before, in a different scene. Where?

"Good-evening. Are you in trouble?" he asked pleasantly.

"My boot, sir . . . I retired here . . . A small pebble, I think. Quite painful to the foot, sir, a pebble; and still some distance, if I may say so, to church." He cast up his eyes.

"Quite," agreed Philip. "Probably you should lace your boots a little tighter."

He had passed. He had unlatched the gate. He looked back. The elderly man had removed his boot, and stood upon one leg holding aloft a foot encased in scarlet half-hose. No cleft was visible.

"A piece of coal, sir. A piece of ordinary unburnt coal. No doubt it had lodged at home."

Philip nodded again and went on up the path through the garden. Coal in a boot in September: that old chap must have started fires early! There was something peculiar about him. He wore a wig. His eyes were like overripe gooseberries in full flight. How prudish to come up a lane to investigate the contents of his own boots. But if one wore scarlet socks perhaps, in a conservative town, the precaution was warranted. Who was the man? Surely it was Holpen's clerk? What the devil did he want? By Jove: Sims? A flirtation? There was no sign of Sims. No, no. Sims was above conversations at the back gate. There was no sign of anybody at all. Perhaps

the old rogue had spoken the truth? Philip walked
through the sweet-smelling garden and directly into the
library, thinking no more of Burgess.

2

He had thrown down his hat, and was about to go upstairs in search of Ruth, when he remembered what Miss
Furze had said about the secret hiding place from which
Miss Strange had taken the unlucky miniature. That was
odd, wasn't it? A secret hiding place. It accorded with
his hopes. He wondered if he could find the spring. The
mantelpiece was tall and of walnut. There was no elaborate carving upon it, but certainly in the centre there was
what seemed to be a panel. He must admit the panel. It
was undeniable. Well? Philip peered at the panel.

About it were several straight lines, or indentations,
which (if Miss Furze's memory was not at fault) might
very well have as their object a confusion of the eye and
a concealment of the join. The panel was possibly
eighteen inches long by five or six in height. That was
large enough to be of some capacity. Now, as to the
spring! He ran his fingers in a gingerly way under the
edge of the woodwork. No result. He bent down and tried
to see something in the darkness behind. Nothing was to
be seen. Again he ran his finger along, but this time with
more assurance.

It took Philip some time to discover the catch, because
he had forgotten to ask Miss Furze if this was in the
form of a small knob or a cavity. It proved to be a knob,
but a knob now so stiff that he had almost abandoned the
effort to move it when he heard a faint click and the
panel in the mantelpiece shifted slightly.

"Hurry!" cried Philip, pressing the knob a little harder.
Nothing further happened. He pushed the panel, which

resumed its former position as a part of the mantelpiece.
He again pressed the knob. Again there was a faint click,
and the panel detached itself almost imperceptibly from
its surroundings. This was evidently as far as it would
come of its own accord. With great care, he put the tip
of his pocketknife and the tip of his left-hand middle
finger to the sides of the panel. It immediately yielded
and became a solid drawer of perhaps a foot in depth
from back to front. A drawer, moreover, which was by
no means empty!

"I say! I say!"

Really excited, Philip brought the drawer to his desk.
It was dusty, but not coated with dust. He saw that it
contained a number of loose papers, a few more papers
in a rotted elastic band, a pocketbook, and two small
boxes which looked as if they might hold rings or
brooches.

"Treasure!" he cried, exultingly; and opened one of
the boxes. There lay three gold sovereigns. "What a
hoard!" He was scornful. The other box held a ring of
no interest, and a small folded piece of paper which,
when unfolded, disclosed a lock of brown hair. In his
own mother's handwriting were the words, "Philip's,
April 1898." The ring must have been hers. He had not
thought of his mother for a long time. She had been dead
for nearly fifteen years; and he had hardly seen her for
three or four years before that, owing to his absence at
school. A ring, a lock of hair, two words in his mother's
handwriting, and three sovereigns. Philip's enthusiasm
was damped. He set these discoveries aside with disappointment.

The papers, however, were more interesting. Taking
first the bundle from which the rotted elastic band fell as
he touched it, he saw that this consisted of various old
letters. One of them was from himself, in a schoolboy

handwriting, returning thanks for a postal order for five shillings; others were from his mother; one was a rough copy in pencil, now a little rubbed, of a letter, apparently, from his uncle to an unknown correspondent. It was a very peculiar letter, which Philip with difficulty deciphered. It ran:

> Dear H. I do not understand your inquiry as to finance. You have my assurance that all is in order. I have been making certain readjustments which will be to our common advantage, and you will find that some benefit will accrue to you in the result. As for P. you need have no fear that he will be a sufferer as the result of our arrangement. I enclose a copy of my will showing that I intend him to have everything at my death, and meanwhile I undertake that his allowance shall be ample. I hope this will set your mind at rest. I may say that as a result of the arrangement into which you *quite voluntarily* entered at the time of your husband's death you and P. have greatly benefitted, as you will continue to do. I therefore do not at all appreciate the rather querelous note of your inquiry. Do you not *trust* me? Please let me hear no more of this. I am glad you are better. I am none too well. Your affec. T.S.

The date was of January, 1914.

The letter quivered in Philip's hand before it was thrown down. Excitement sprang up in him as he realized that this letter must have been written, or drafted, to his own mother. What was its plain meaning? That his mother had entrusted her all to Starling. That instead of being indebted to Starling as he had been led to believe, for his schooling and his early allowance, he had certainly been cheated out of his father's money!

But where was the record of that trust? It was not here. It had not been among his mother's papers, because they had all been in Starling's care after her death, and were now destroyed. Philip glanced at the pocketbook. It was something that had been discarded, and was empty except for the counterfoil of a forgotten postal order. Damn it! Could this have been the order which he had acknowledged? Absurd; and yet with such an old devil——

He searched through the bundle. There were possibly more than a dozen of his mother's letters, written upon very flimsy, shiny paper, with watermarked rulings, in a clear but angular hand. The letters all ran to six or seven pages, but they seemed to consist solely of statements about health, lodging, and religion. There was no single reference to money. Possibly his uncle had destroyed the "querelous inquiry." Too incriminating! The pencilled draft possessed, therefore, only a literary interest. But it was exciting! It was illuminating! It angered him.

Philip was to be still more intensely excited, however; for among the loose papers, which he had somewhat tumbled in drawing out the boxes and the bundle of letters, was one which made his heart quicken and his cheeks burn. It was a cheque drawn in his own favour, and endorsed by himself, bearing Starling's signature. A good copy, but a forgery; the result of a mood of bravado and folly hard now to imagine, but fraught with bitter shame. Long years of shame and self-contempt.

"Good God!" muttered Philip, staring transfixed at the cheque. "It's enough to make a man kill himself. You silly, blasted fool! Always! Always! Then and now. As much now as ever. And I know it. I know it." Long afterwards, he added: "What an old devil to have kept it all this time!"

Philip continued to hold that cheque in his hand, and to stare at it. As he did this all the memories associated with it came back, flooding his mind with sensation. At the time, he had not long been discharged from the army, and he was then so much affected by the horror of his war experience that he had been half crazed. He had dreamed each night of the sights and sounds and smells of warfare. He had found in the thunder of London traffic a continuous nervous strain that drove him to eccentricity. In this state he had gone to his uncle's flat. . . .

Now, standing in the quiet room at Sandersfold, with the cheque in his fingers, he lived again in that period. Pictures rose before him; he heard snatches of talk, voices, noises; he recalled forgotten sensations. In all his pictures stood old Starling, his uncle, a little man with baggy skin under his eyes, and vicious teeth, and a wide, malignant grin. The dwarf! The hateful, lecherous dwarf! Philip could see him yet, and hear the drawl of his sneering voice.

Quiet. Quiet. What hatred he had felt for Starling. How, when that child had come to him one day, with her yarn, he had fired into this hatred. He had believed the yarn. Although he had afterwards discovered the girl to be a liar, he still believed she had told him the truth. Inveterate sentimentality! It ran through his life, through his character. He had always been thus. Self-contempt was very hard to bear. He flicked the cheque with his free hand. It fluttered to the desk.

If Starling had kept the cheque it was likely that he had also kept some record of the whole affair. Malignant to the last! Was it not so? Philip rummaged among the papers. Yes; here was a history—three closely written quarto sheets, signed in full. An indictment! Oh, how noble were the words: "Because he was my sister's only child, I decided——"

"I hope he's in hell! I hope he's in hell!"

Hysterically, Philip almost shouted these words. Before he knew what he was doing—but some part of his brain must have functioned very deliberately while he was still too agitated to be aware of it—he had stepped to the window, struck a match, and burned cheque and memorandum to ashes. His fingers did not feel the scorching of that quick flame, so hot was his mind; and as he threw the ash down, and watched the flame die, and saw the black skeleton flicked here and there by the breeze, he drew his breath as a man does when he is awakening from deep sleep.

3

It was long before Philip could bring himself to return to the examination of that fatal drawer. When he came as far into the room as his desk, and saw the drawer lying there, he stood for some minutes unable to touch it. Even then his impulse was to return the drawer to its place, where its remaining contents might moulder undiscovered for the rest of his life. Had he not destroyed the evidence of his own folly? Could there be anything else before him which called for his knowledge?

Very few papers remained. Not more than half a dozen. They were untidy, because he had sought with clumsy hands for what he had just burned. But they were there. Unless he now completed his scrutiny he would always, every time he entered this room, look first to that panel, and be troubled by memory of what he had found and what he had left unread. His fingers hovered restlessly above the drawer. At last they dropped, as if at random.

The first paper he lifted was stiff. It was of the kind upon which legal documents are engrossed, and was rather soiled and bruised, as if it had been carried much with other articles in a pocket. Caught up in this was another sheet—of notepaper, this time, and notepaper similar to that which lay in the drawer close at hand. A letter, without envelope, open to the eye. Philip glanced hurriedly. The writing was Starling's:

> Dear Ruth. I am leaving you my money. Made up my mind yesterday. Nobody else to leave it to. On no account give *one farthing* to my nephew, Philip Spears, who disappointed me some years ago. He may try to upset, but cannot do so. He has *no claim* on the estate. You have made me pretty happy on the whole, though you are a greedy devil for love. It will be your ruin yet. In fact I'm not sure if I *will* leave you the money. Keep clear of young Holpen. He's no good to you. He's pestering me about the will. I know what that means. Sell the house. T.S.

Philip stood very erect at his desk. He had read the paper at a glance, without doing more than grasp its purport. Now he tore open the stiff, soiled sheet of paper, and was as one dead.

> This is the last will . . . Starling . . . To my dear friend Ruth Coulevain . . .

The will was signed. It was witnessed. Two names were affixed; those of Thomas Baxter and Martha Baxter, at an address in Clerkenwell, London.

No sound came from Philip. He stared at the will. Then at the sheet of paper which had been caught up in its stiff folds. Then back at the will. The whole house was silent.

4

He did not move for a long time. At last, laying down both papers, he stepped away from the desk with unusual quietness and care, and crossed to the fireplace, where he stood to all seeming deep in thought. He was not thinking. Before him, but forgotten, was the dark cavity from which the drawer had been taken; behind him the open window, through which a clear but paling light shone upon the disarray of his desk.

So everything belonged, not to him, but to Ruth. So she had been Starling's mistress. Holpen had been right. Holpen had warned him at their first meeting. And everything was hers. The clothes he wore were not his own. And she had been Starling's mistress. It was bitter.

There were other things in this dossier. There was a hint as to his mother's money. There had been the cheque; but, without knowing that he was destroying Ruth's property, he had burned that. He had had no right to burn it. He no longer had any rights here.

She was carrying his child. She loved him—perhaps. Would she not, as he would have done, forgive his unknowing usurpation? Of course. Ah, but his pride had suffered, would suffer. He had no right, no *right* to anything here, to his peace of mind, this house, this lovely haven of quietness. All was hers. "On no account give one farthing . . ." She had been that foul old man's mistress. She had been greedy of *his* love. Christ! He could kill himself!

The day Holpen had first brought him here she had been in the front room, standing by the fire. So straight, so gentle. How cold! Holpen had made her blush. What had he said? Sims had hinted "a disappointment." Of course she had expected this—the money, the house, everything. That must have been a disappointment indeed! Instead of owner, humble housekeeper.

How had he treated her? "You are so kind." Yes, it had been he, then, who could be kind. He had been *kind*. He had made her, *kindly,* his wife. Well, was that a sin? He had kindly planned that she should have an income separate from his own. How kind! How kind! But it had not been his to give. What a joke! Yes, but she'd been Starling's mistress.

However, Ruth would forgive him for his kindness. She would be able to afford to do so. The world need hardly know that any change had occurred in their fortunes. If it knew, the world would laugh, and call him "lucky dog." It would say that a blind sense of his own advantage had moved him; for, after all, if one cannot inherit oneself, it clearly must be the next best thing to marry the heiress. Even though she be the late mistress of the testator. Such things are not unknown in the great world.

Everything belonged to Ruth. What would she say? What change would it make in her attitude to him?

This was decisive. He must find work at once. He had had Ruth's money. The amount was assessable, and must be repaid. He would not take money from her. No, by God! Not from that old satyr's mistress, greedy for love!

He mechanically went back to the desk and put back into the secret drawer all the things he had taken from it, with the exception of the will and the draft letter addressed to Ruth. These he left upon the desk while he carried the drawer back to the mantelpiece, adjusted it, and pressed it home. No trace remained of any operation. Only, outside the window, one last piece of burned paper danced, and on the desk the will and letter lay side by side, both soiled from contact with Starling's pocket. Philip lifted them with fastidious fingers. He had not felt the flame of the burning cheque; but these two papers, with which the dead man had come so closely into contact that they bore some of the filth from his pocket, were so abhorrent to him that he could hardly hold them.

Nevertheless, it did not occur to Philip to do otherwise than take the papers straight to Ruth, the person most concerned in their contents and their possession. He went up the shallow stairs holding the papers before him, and stood for some moments upon the silent landing before advancing to her door and knocking for admission.

5

The room was still darkened. Although the blind had been drawn up, and the window was partly open, the mulberry tree threw a monstrous shadow, and the light was fading a little. Ruth was in bed, just as he had left her; and at his entry, as though she had not heard the knocking, she moved quickly in a startled plunge.

"Hullo, have I disturbed you?" cried Philip.

"Oh!" she cried, in a shuddering gasp. "It's you, Philip. I thought . . ." Her voice faded. She closed her eyes again, and lay watching him.

"How d'you feel?"

The head moved.

"Wretched. But I've had some sleep. You saw Miss Furze?"

"She asked after you, and was sorry to hear you were ill."

"Hm. Kind," murmured Ruth. "Did you come straight home?"

"Yes. I came in through the garden——"

"Through the garden?" Ruth's eyes had opened.

"Yes. Up the little lane. There was an old man there tying up his boots. That old clerk of Holpen's. I can't imagine what he was doing—the boots were a pretense, of course."

She had grown haggard in an instant. Or were his eyes deceived in this light? She said:

"Did you speak to him?"

"He told me he had found coal in his boot. I think he hoped to throw it in my eye."

"Extraordinary." Again that shuddering gasp. "Has he gone?"

"Oh, yes, I think I frightened him away. Look here, Ruth, I found something still more extraordinary. You ought to see it at once. Read that!"

He recaptured the papers, which he had dropped upon the bed, and held them out to her. Instead of stretching out her hand, Ruth seemed to shrink back. A look of terror settled upon her face, which was almost as white as the pillow upon which it rested. She was staring at him. At last, very reluctantly, she accepted the papers.

"Where did you get them?" she asked, in a whisper.

"Read them," said Philip laconically. He rose from the bed and went to the window, standing there and looking out until he thought Ruth must have had time to digest the will and its accompanying letter. He had heard her sit upright in the bed with a quick spring, and had heard the bed lamp switched on. When he turned round from the window she was still staring at the papers, ghastly in the glow of the electric light. Her face seemed full of shadows, distorted and malignant.

At his movement she looked up quickly, a changed woman. Her tone, when she spoke, was no longer a murmur, but a harsh and bitter cry.

"How long have you had these?" she demanded.

"Five minutes," answered Philip. "I've brought them straight to you."

"Where did you find them?" It was peremptory.

"In the library mantelpiece."

She seemed unable to hear what he said. Her face was wrinkled, as if with impatient deafness.

"What?"

"Miss Furze told me——"

"Oh, for God's sake, not all the rigmarole——"

Philip stopped, his anger mounting. He looked steadily

at her. She was as if beside herself, clawing the bed-clothes, and trembling. If he had faltered, she would have been as savagely merciless as a fighting cat. He did not falter. It was Ruth who faltered under his scrutiny.

"Miss Furze told me there was a secret place in the mantelpiece. She showed me where the spring was. When I got home I tried it. There's a drawer. These things were in it. Some other papers, too."

"What other papers?" She was quieter.

"Letters, a ring, a lock of hair——"

Ruth sank against the wooden head of the bed. He could see that her whole body was shaking with great violence. Her hands were trembling so much that the papers flapped against one another; and her teeth chattered. Philip, seeing a woollen bed jacket hanging over the back of a chair, would have put it over her shoulders; but she shrank from him with vehemence, and sat there as if in ague, her eyes starting wildly from her head, and her bare shoulders jerking. At last she said, with a sobbing breath:

"You . . . you've read them?"

"Both," Philip answered.

Again she struggled for breath.

"Yes?" she asked, as if she had not heard. "Yes?"

"You know as much as I do. We'd better leave it all till tomorrow. No?" She shook her head, but was unable to speak. "You're ill, my dear. You're not fit. We can't——"

"We must."

Philip shrugged. She was so ugly, so devoid at this moment of all attractiveness, that he looked at her with repugnance. It was impossible to him to conceive of delight in her caresses, or to imagine that he had ever known such delight; but she was still a woman, and therefore to be gently treated.

"All right," he said, quietly. "You'll have to see Holpen. He'll have to get the will proved. That means more delay. That's all. Everything's yours."

"Yes, yes, yes!" she cried. She looked like an old woman, shaking there, her face yellow in the white glare of the electric lamp, her eyes glittering. There was a long silence of estrangement, in which each might have heard the thickened beating of the two hearts, like distant drums. The beating steadied and died down. At last: "You must let me go," she said.

A shock ran through Philip. He felt his heart leap. His blood seemed to chill. He could not immediately answer her.

6

In all the physical agitation that Philip saw, there had been no hint as to the nature of those thoughts which ran fierily in Ruth's brain. She had lost modesty. She could not see herself, and was careless of what Philip might think of her. She was entirely indifferent to him. She knew, indeed, that he was before her; but she was conscious of him not as a husband in whose arms she had lain, or as a man whose blood she might yet have kindled; but only as a chill and insignificant bringer of tidings. She was engrossed in the tidings and their implications. Philip, for all he meant to her, might have been a figure seen dimly in a mirror. She thought:

"Safe! Safe! I've got the money. Nothing else matters. Everything's changed——"

In imagination she was in Leonard's arms. Downstairs, in the morning room. That night when she had found the door unlatched, when she had listened in the darkness, paralyzed with fear . . . So Starling had not destroyed the will. He hadn't seen them after all! That whole nightmare was gone. Had he not seen them? What papers had he destroyed, then? He'd destroyed papers. Oh, thank God! Safe! And Leonard . . . Leonard . . .

Philip was standing near the bed, looking at her. He spoke. What did he say? Philip? He was nothing. He was like Death. His face was accusing. She saw him as a silent figure, judging her. What right had *he* to judge her? The thief! The thief! Ah, but he's been beaten! He must go. She must get away from him. That was over. The terror was over. The joy had come! "I'm safe. I can snap my fingers at everything. The devils! And Philip— the devil of kindness! I must go to Leonard. I must find him." Aloud she said:

"I must see him now. What time is it?" She did not wait for the answer. "I must get up." She swept aside the bedclothes, indifferent to Philip's eye, and careless of the fact that he must recognize her condition. "Yes, yes, I must go to him."

Then she paused. No. She was cold; her teeth were chattering. She couldn't go. She couldn't do anything now. The bedclothes were pulled back about her body. What was Philip doing? He was coming towards her. He would snatch the will from her. He meant to do so. There was hatred in his eyes. She feared him; and shrank back, clutching the papers to her swollen breasts.

"What are you talking about?" asked Philip, in a puzzled voice, coming nearer, and half smiling. It was the smile that made her afraid of him, for she could not read it, and supposed it to indicate some evil purpose.

"Let me go! Let me go!" shuddered Ruth. "You must let me go?"

Philip said, in a tone of contempt:

"You're ill. You don't know what you're saying."

"I know what I'm saying!" Ruth cried loudly. She saw his face come nearer, very dark and colourless, and seeming to be impassive. She saw him shake his head. He said, very slowly, and coldly:

"No. You don't. What you're saying is ridiculous."

Again that horrible convulsion of fear shook Ruth. She must go to Leonard at once. She was frightened. She must send this man away. He was terrifying her with menacing coldness.

"I can't help it!" she cried, in a loud, trembling voice. "You've got to let me go. I must get away from you."

Philip, knowing nothing of what was in her mind, but seeing and hearing only her agitation and her vehement exclamations, himself greatly excited by all that had occurred, said clearly:

"You've forgotten that we're married."

Ruth laughed.

"Look at these!" she cried. The papers crackled in her raised hand.

"Yes, I see them. I saw them before you did. Don't forget that I could have destroyed them. Have you thought of that?"

"You wouldn't!" exclaimed Ruth.

"Why not? It's the sort of thing you seem to expect."

For a moment the conviction that he was going to wrest the papers from her filled Ruth with unreasoning terror. She screamed.

"No!" she cried out. "You can't! You shan't!" She made as if to spring from the bed.

"Of course not. Don't be ridiculous," Philip said. "You must be quiet. Look, I'm quiet enough, aren't I? I'm the one who's lost the money. Not you. You've got what you wanted. That was all you wanted, wasn't it? You've got it. There's nothing more to worry about. But you say I must let you go. What do you mean? What about the child? Have you forgotten it's mine as well as yours?"

"What?" Ruth stared. Her voice was hoarse. Her jaw dropped. But then the tenseness of her expression relaxed into a slow smile, which deepened until her whole face was lighted up with a kind of laughing exultation. Philip, watching her, read the changes at first with wonder and at last with certainty.

"The child's not mine!" he said, swiftly. Everything was clear to him. "Ah! Holpen's! Why on earth didn't I think of that!" His anger rose so suddenly, and swept him with such fury, that for a moment he could have struck her—even strangled her—if another, still more powerful emotion had not imposed its restraint. Upon that first impulse his hands were raised in such a threatening way that Ruth screamed again, chokingly, as one in a dream may do, and struggled away from him, towards the other side of the bed.

Philip drew back at the sound of the scream.

"You fool!" he cried, bitterly. "You got into a mess, didn't you! You imagined you'd be on the streets. What rot!" His face had grown very pale, so that it was grey beneath the sunburn. He was cold with anger. The child; Holpen; her terror of poverty—he saw every stage of that simple cunning. "You made a convenience of me; it's been done before. Now you've no more use for me. All right. Certainly. But you'll get nothing out of Holpen. He's not the sort."

"He'll marry me now," Ruth said. She was elated. She was smiling—grinning, rather—a horrible sight as she dreamed of coming triumph.

Philip's anger was gone. He contemplated her with contempt. He knew of her now that she had been Starling's mistress, that she had been Holpen's mistress, that she would have been his mistress if she had not needed to secure herself from ruin. Behind that reserve of hers, that air of being fine and withdrawn, of yielding a secret treasure with proud reluctance that rose to ecstasy, there was nothing but cold, lecherous avarice. She was a harlot.

And yet that was not all the truth. The infatuated confidence of her last words, the wide, exulting smile, which distorted her face more hideously than the former wildness and terror had done, brought inescapable understanding to Philip. In some base, horrible way, spirit among the corruptions of her nature, she loved Holpen. She had insatiable passion for him, and even now her smile showed that she was living in memory of that passion.

As anger had given place in Philip's mind to contempt, so contempt wavered before the onset of pity. The two emotions struggled together for mastery. He watched the smile fade from her lips, and saw how, under his steady scrutiny, she quietened and grew piteous. Unconscious that he did so, Philip shook his head.

"You poor, you poor, poor fool," he said in a low voice. "You're ruined."

And with that he turned and walked out of the room, leaving Ruth lying back against the head of the bed, half fainting, in sudden misery, her eyes glittering.

PART FOUR
THE CURTAIN DROPS

CHAPTER SEVENTEEN

VISITORS TO LONDON

ROSE leaned back in her place and smiled at Lettice, who sat opposite. The train had started while Rachel and Susan were still chattering simultaneously. Behind them, James Davitt had scowled, and Leonard Holpen, debonairly ironic, had stood with his eyebrows raised to the last. But the platform and its burden had withdrawn; even the tower of the church of Sandersfold could no longer be seen; Lettice and Rose, with an old lady unknown to them, were en route.

Above Lettice's head was a coloured photograph, taken early in the century, of visitors to Seahampton. The men all wore boaters, and the women blouses and long skirts. Behind them, dreary stucco houses and old horse flies were like petrified remains. The horrors of an English seaside town caught in the act of growing were made manifest. Rose turned quickly from the photograph and looked out of the window. Meadows slowly circling; the green pastures of England, enchantingly lovely. . . . A rustling caused her to look at the old lady, who was peeping greedily into a paper bag. What a wizened, hungry face! The face of one perpetually starving! Presently the old lady seized something within the bag and popped it into her mouth, glancing furtively at Lettice as she did so. At Lettice, not Rose. Rose was too impersonal to impress old ladies in railway carriages; they hardly realized that she was there. God bless them! The old lady wore a black straw hat and a black home-made cloak and black curly boots. Where could she possibly be going? London? Her hair looked as if it had been dyed black, and it had been inexpertly shingled. She was ravenous. Her cheeks, hollow from the lack of supporting teeth, moved like the nose of a nibbling mouse. Finally, clawing up the exhausted paper bag, she threw it under the seat and swept away her crumbs with one grand sweep of a black gloved hand. She looked like a dyed, very faded cockatoo.

Lettice began to talk to Rose in that loud, affected voice which some Englishwomen use in railway carriages. It was a very aristocratic voice; she referred to personal things hintingly. Rose flinched.

"They'll go home and have an inquest on you," Lettice said. "Looked gloomy enough, I must say. Did you ever see anybody *like* Leonard! My dear, he's discreet. More than that, he's sly. D'you know what he's been doing?" Rose, shrinking, confessed inaudibly that she did not know. She wanted to say that cookatoo-like old ladies with hollow cheeks and black hats have ears and long noses; but Lettice, driven by an impulse unknown to Rose, must publish a dozen secrets. "Well, he hasn't been at home in the evening for *weeks!* D'you know the Pudgells? Don't you? They've got that big place on the Yewmouth Road. He's been there. *Some* attraction." She laughed. "I tried to get out of him . . . what it was. D'you think I could?"

"No, of course not," said Rose.

"You *do* know the people?" pressed Lettice, as if she wanted to enlarge upon their importance. "They've got quite a big place. Ride, and all that."

"I've seen them. They're always at the Church Fête."

"Yes. Charlotte was at the gifts stall this year. I didn't take a stall. They wanted me to. Oh, I don't know; all that sort of thing seems so . . . d'you know . . ."

Rose thought: "Yet she's my friend. She doesn't talk

like this at home. I wish she'd stop. It's so hinty and ostentatious." Then she laughed a little, within, at the memory that Philip had called her usefulness "unostentatious." What a gander the man was! All men had a strain of solemnity in them: if you loved them, you laughed at it. All men: Father, Henry, Philip. As for all the *other* men, such as Leonard Holpen, they were somehow common. There was something frightfully *cheap* about Leonard, hair oil and all. He very narrowly avoided being a pukka sahib, which apparently was the most vulgar thing in the world. Lettice seemed fluttered about this Charlotte Pudgell business. So there must be something in it. The Holpens would be delighted. A good match. And yet Charlotte Pudgell was an expressionless and stupidly patronizing girl with a thick waist and a bad carriage. She was insipid, but had a slug's sense of good feeding. There would be photographs of her in the London evening papers. If she was very pushing, there might be a London wedding, with bridesmaids dressed as ancient Egyptians, and the bride's mongoose on a string, and some poor totterling from the cradle as a mascot. Horrible antediluvian processionalism and display. But Lettice liked it. She was a snob; so was Leonard. He had a mean sense of his own advantage. No morals, but a fear of opinion. Was that all morals were? It didn't do to be too censorious.

"What's the matter?" demanded Lettice. "Homesick? You *are!* I know you are! But you'll soon get over that, my dear. We'll have a glass of sherry when we get to town. It's an infallible pick-me-up. What's this place we're coming to? Not stopping, thank goodness. I was asking Len about Charlotte this morning. I think it's a case. I wonder if Mother would cough up anything. She ought to. My dear, she must have pots and stacks! . . . Never spends it, you know. . . ." There was a pause. "I say, did you read the Ludwig books? I adawd them. What I like about his style—he's got such economy of *words*."

Rose closed her eyes, smiling.

"Headache," she said. At the moment she believed she had a headache; but it was only boredom. She saw Lettice subside. She saw the old lady fish in her large handbag for another packet of food—this time some raisins. Behind her closed eyes she thought until the soft dumping of the train over joints in the rails lulled her to sleep, and she then dreamt that Philip had kissed her by mistake and was very apologetic for such a misdemeanour. It was an amusing and embarrassing dream from which she awoke with regret to find Lettice and the old lady in conversation. The old lady was doing all the talking, in an aged toothless tone, saying that she was going to stay with a daughter at Fulham, and that the daughter had a little girl with whooping cough; while Lettice, not looking at the old lady, was coldly returning repressive monosyllables. What coquetry! As if Lettice had not all along regarded the old lady solely as an audience!

2

London, when they reached it, seemed to Rose rather grey and heartless. That was her mood. She had left behind her so much that she loved. Even the big scarlet omnibuses which had their standing places in the entrance yard at Victoria, although they gave a welcome splash of colour to the scene, were monstrous. The sky was very near, like smoky cotton wool. Was it to be like that all the winter? However, it was no good grizzling. They were here, now. Stop all gloomy thoughts! . . . "What's that policeman doing? He's bending over somebody on the pavement. Somebody in a fit. . . ." Something strange and terrible was happening every instant in London!

From that moment Rose was captivated by the interest of all she saw.

They were to stay, at first, in a medium-sized, featureless hotel near Oxford Street; and their route took them past Buckingham Palace, into the land of clubs, and by way of the roundabout at Piccadilly Circus. All in motion, all curious and full of contrast. Rose, by no means a regular visitor to London, began to crane her neck and recover her spirits. This, after all, was a great city—some thought it the greatest in the world; and a great city is great only so long as it is alive. How remote, and small, and quiet Sandersfold had become! Sandersfold, now as usual going, quite self-engrossed, upon its leisurely way, the shops emptily open, the loiterers straggling, under a blue sky, and the trees, however dusty, still, by contrast with the trees of London, verdant and lovely.

The hotel was reached, and the view of a dingy well in which their window was but one of a hundred windows caused Rose's heart to sink to her shoes. "No matter," she said to herself, "it's a dull day; it's not the same when one's just left home for the first plunge into a new and exhilarating life; you'll feel better when you have a little place of your own. Or if you don't you'll be a silly, feckless, cowardly creature who had better run home again and stay in Sandersfold for the rest of your life, a creeping withered spinster with a grievance against everybody."

"Well?" demanded Lettice.

Rose, with a jump, found that the braided porter, having set down their luggage, had withdrawn. The door was closed. In a mirror set in the wardrobe she had a glimpse of her own woebegone expression, and of Lettice, very observant, already with a look of satiric suspicion curling her thin and sensitive lips. The walls of the room were very close and very straight, as if they were the walls of one among a thousand piled boxes of iron. . . . These perceptions came at a single glance. Rose pulled herself together.

"Grand!" she answered, gaily.

3

The train despatched, Leonard disembarrassed himself of the Davitt crowd and marched back to the little sports car in which he had driven Lettice to the station. He was smiling with great satisfaction. Not for a long time had he been so pleased. There was much in his work that had a good aspect; but Lettice's going was quite an acceptable item in the budget. He was not wholly sorry that she had gone. No, my boy, *sorry* was hardly the word to use when one was jubilant.

The reason for this jubilance was that Leonard had not, latterly, been idle or indiscreet. He had seen clearly. That is always a satisfaction. He had moved quickly and surely. That is always a cause for even greater satisfaction. He had triumphed. Not vulgarly, or in the vulgar sense of that word when it is applied to a love affair, but in the true, the satisfying sense which implies solid gain. Triumphed. A cash value to triumph may seem sordid to prigs and idealists; but to one who loves money it is certainly something positive. Such a one's heart feels warm and plump under his ribs.

And so Leonard, who had been ridiculing the Davitt girls, and old Davitt, all the time he had been with them, and noticing a pimple on Susan's neck and a moisture in James Davitt's eye with that malicious unkindness which by some is thought peculiarly modern wit, turned triumphantly from his sister and her friend, and the concourse of mourners. He laughed slightly to himself

as he left the station, showing his regular teeth and raising his shoulders in a faint amused hunch. It was a laugh
of satisfaction and ridicule, combined. The Davitts were
ridiculous, particularly old Davitt with his tears; and
Leonard was successful. He did not fail. He calculated in
advance. Hence the shrug and the laugh.

There was some satisfaction to be gained, also, by
racing the engine of his car as he swept in a wide curve
from the station approach. The roar caused people to
look up. Well, what they saw would bear inspection,
wouldn't it? A successful young man in a good humour,
driving his car with verve, knowing his own value, and
smiling. What more could they ask?

Old Davitt was cracking. The girls were getting careless about their appearance. Not Rose, but the others.
Soon they would be dowdy. A great mistake. If the old
man was cracking, there would be some complications
there. Leonard supposed the widow would get the bulk, in
trust. Those two, Rachel and Susan, would get more and
more religious. They would starve themselves, make their
own dresses, grow hideous, and in fifty years leave fortunes to the missionaries. What a waste! But Leonard
could not wait for fifty years. By that time he would be
dead.

As he drove home he glanced at his wrist watch. He
would be late at the office. But he did not want to park
the car. Very well, he must be late. He would telephone
Charlotte from the office. The point was, his mother was
pleased about Charlotte. She was on tenterhooks to know
if it was coming off. He was keeping her there. It would
do her good. She would be all the sweeter. He said:
"Look here, Mother; you know very well that old Pudgell won't agree to anything unless my income's all right.
You'll have to make up your mind to that." She had
quailed. Well, he knew what his mother's income was. It

was all tied up to her. But she was so keen upon County
that she was fumbling at the ties. Once they were loosed,
they were not easily caught up again.

Still laughing to himself, Leonard garaged his car and
walked briskly towards his office.

4

The girls had not realized; but the train in which they
travelled to London had carried another passenger from
Sandersfold whom they would have welcomed as a companion. This was Philip Spears. On Philip's part there
had been deliberate avoidance. He had run into the station
very late, having had difficulty in getting there; and, seeing that familiar group about a door to his left, had by
instinct turned to the right. By this means he escaped
their notice; and he had no sooner flung himself into a
smoking carriage than the train started. He crouched
back in order that the waving trio, with Holpen in the
background, should not see him.

Philip's object in going to London had been, first to
see his old friend Dexter, and then, possibly, to see Dexter's solicitor. He needed legal advice as to his course;
and Holpen as an adviser was for the time being impossible. Ruth would see Holpen. He would have liked to be
present. For there was no doubt that the situation was
piquant. The more Philip thought of the situation, indeed,
the more bitterly piquant it became.

True, he had lost his inheritance. True, Ruth's child
was not his. But they were married. That gave him a
curious advantage. Did he need it? His first impulse,
which had been to leave the house at once, allow himself
to be divorced by Ruth, and thus conclude the unsavoury
and humiliating situation, had cooled in the night. He
had cooled with his impulse. He had resolved that he

would do nothing without consideration. It would be necessary that he should know where they both stood. If Ruth were high-handed, he would resist. But he could not go to Holpen.

Holpen had not injured him. In Holpen's place Philip thought that he would almost certainly have remained as silent as Holpen had done. After all, at their first meeting Holpen had hinted at the relationship with Starling. Not—perhaps excusably—at the relationship in progress with himself. And that relationship had been broken before the marriage, as Philip knew. What then? Still chiefly concerned with his own affairs, and suffering from a most serious wound to his vanity as a male, Philip was particularly thoughtful at Ruth's preference of Leonard to himself. However base, that was *love*. He could not escape from it. Perhaps, to salve his vanity, he emphasized it.

While Rose, in another carriage, was dreaming that Philip had kissed her, Philip, tortured by shames innumerable, but without mercy to himself—or only showing such considerateness as a sensitive man would show to his most contemptible rival—was finding those soothing jolts which a well-sprung train communicates to all its passengers so many hammer-beats. They drove home his sharp self-condemnations. They exasperated his distresses. But he sat through them all, white-faced, with set lips, not wholly crushed, and not altogether without ironic enjoyment of his own calamitous situation.

5

The rest of the day was spent by Rose and Lettice in examining small flats. They had never seen such small flats as some of these were. They had never dreamed that small flats could be so dark and so extravagantly dismal.

At one time Lettice, as they emerged from one examination, said indignantly:

"For 'Small Flat' see 'Hole.' "

" 'Square hole,' " supplemented Rose, cheerfully.

" 'Dirty hole,' " corrected Lettice.

They looked at small flats in Bloomsbury; they looked at small flats in Chelsea. All were partly furnished; none was furnished in such a way as either Lettice or Rose could command. They lunched at a teashop, and were so full of dust from small flats that they had no appetite. Finally they went to Hampstead; and here, to Rose's inexpressible relief, they were lucky enough to find something which pleased them both. It was high up in a red brick house, and the rooms were insignificant; but there was fresh air, the place was clean, there was no art-y furniture, and the two beds were beds, and not campstools.

"I think," Lettice said.

"I *have* thought," replied Rose.

They closed. "True," thought Rose, "Hampstead is rather far from Henry. But then we haven't come to London to be *very* near Henry. Or at least *I* haven't; because the boy doesn't want a sister clinging to him all the time. Has Lettice? Sometimes I seem to think *not*. Perhaps I shall notice tonight."

They had arranged to meet Henry in the evening, at Charing Cross. They were, as newcomers, overpunctual, and had to wait. Henry did not appear; but Rose espied Molyneux's bare head a moment after their arrival ("Gosh, Molyneux!" "Heavens!" was the exchange); and presently the two young men came strolling up.

"Hello!" "Hello!" "Welcome to London!" "All right?"

Again Rose was pleased with Henry's greeting; again she observed that Molyneux talked volubly from a kind of nervousness. In that throng and din (for Charing Cross is a crowded station, and the trains are so close that all their puffing and hissing is many times swollen by proximity and echo) it was impossible to hear what he said. He shouted and gesticulated. Rose nodded. But she did not hear. On the whole she did not want to· hear.

As they emerged:

"Good!" cried Molyneux. "Now we can talk. I don't know if you've noticed; but this is the seven-o'clock crowd. They're all different. Five, six, seven, and eight. All going to their little. breeding hutches. Come and go, male and female, boxed up together, respectable and stupid . . . curtains at every window to shut out the light and shut in the foulness——"

"To you, the curtains must be the worst offense of all," Rose said.

"Flags of hypocrisy," said Molyneux. "It disgusts me. All living beyond their means. Hire purchase beds, smoky chimneys, bad cooking, fear . . ."

They had reached the Strand, and a man running passionately into the station for a train which had already left winded Molyneux in the middle of his address.

"I think you're a sentimentalist," said Rose. "You're so troubled about what some people consider happiness."

"Pigs and rats are as happy," declared Molyneux.

Rose was laughing at him and enjoying the sense of walking through the crowd. It made her feel rather excited, as if she might lose her way without ever being wholly lost. She glanced back to see that Lettice and Henry were close upon their heels, missed Molyneux from her side, looked about to discover where he had gone, and, to the surprise of all her companions, ran after a man who was passing, caught him by the arm, and began talking breathlessly, radiant as a star, quite forgetful of those to whom she belonged.

"Good Lord!" muttered Henry. "I say, Rose!" She did not hear.

"Who's this bloke?" demanded Molyneux, in disgust.

Lettice had been about to speak to the deserted pair when, to the astonishment of both young men, she too advanced gaily towards the stranger and joined in the conversation. She seemed as pleased in his company as Rose had been. That is very disconcerting and discomfiting to any cavalier or cavaliers. Young women do not always realize this. Rose and Lettice clearly did not do so.

Henry and Molyneux turned to one another in surprise. They did not speak. They strolled past the little group and by common consent pulled up a few yards ahead, carefully nonchalant, and blind and deaf to everything behind them. No sociability marred their aloofness. But Molyneux, from the corner of his eye, took careful stock of the stranger. Tall, thin, dark, clean-shaven. . . . Hm. . . .

The man wore a hat—symbol of middle age; he was neatly dressed—symbol of the bourgeoisie; he was short-haired and inconspicuously good-looking—symbol of ordinariness; and, damn it all, on very friendly terms with Rose—symbol of complication so undesirable even to free-thinking swains that Molyneux was forced to swing a cold shoulder in the stranger's direction.

"Know him?" he asked, in a low voice. "Never seen him? Bet you what you like he's St. George and the Dragon."

Henry scowled. He was suspicious of everything.

"He's from Sandersfold," he said at last. "I've seen him there. Knows my dad."

Philip Spears, coming moodily along the Strand after a tiring and dispiriting day, had been wondering how he should spend the long hours of the evening. He had just left Dexter, and for a time was oppressed by all the old feeling of cowed misery which he had known upon his return to London. When, in such a mood, he heard a voice, felt his arm plucked, and turned to see the flushed and sparkling face of Rose, there leapt in him such a quick, warm wave of blessed joy that he was incapable for an instant of giving expression to it.

6

A quarter of an hour later, five cheerful persons were seated round the coarse white cloth and dull cutlery of a Soho restaurant table. If the food had been leather and sea water it would have been acceptable to Philip, with such happiness about him, with Rose at his left hand and Lettice at his right, Henry next to Lettice and Molyneux beyond Rose. Nor were the others less lighthearted; for an additional male member of her audience spurred Lettice to do her best, and the two younger men showed how really good-natured they were by accepting Philip cordially as one of the party.

There had been some amusement over the introduction by Lettice. She had said to Philip:

"This is Henry; and this is Molyneux. He's a Liberal without prefix or suffix, if you know what that means. It means that he hasn't a degree or a title. He hasn't even got a Christian name."

To which the party had responded by guessing Molyneux's Christian name. "Rumpelstiltskin" had been the favourite; but others had been nearly as appropriate. Molyneux greatly enjoyed being the centre of such controversy. He rejected "Marmaduke," "Lionel," and various other elaborate names, and he and Henry kept the truth to themselves. Nevertheless, the silliness of high spirits served well in making everybody feel at ease; and

Rose was thankful enough for any folly that rendered her joy inconspicuous.

The talk turned once, and once only, upon a topic of moment to Philip. Molyneux was in a reasonable mood (a little anxious to please the stranger, whom he recognized as an imperturbable senior); and when he had shown his contempt for everything in the Sermon on the Mount, which Philip, who was more familiar with the Sermon than Molyneux, found still an effective rule of life, he ventured only a few words upon the subject of inheritance.

"Nobody ought to inherit money," said Molyneux. "When a man dies, the State should grant his widow a life pension of twenty per cent of the estate. But able-bodied men should all work for their livings."

"I should agree to that," said Philip. "What about minors?"

"I haven't worked it out," responded Molyneux, modestly. "But I should send them to school at the State's expense."

"Do *you* agree, then, about inheritance?" asked Lettice, wonderingly. "But——" She checked her tongue, and looked from Philip to Rose. "Oh, well," she smiled. "I suppose it's all right. But I'm looking forward to getting a little presently, myself. Molyneux, what would you say I ought to do with that? Cancel War Loan?"

"Keep it," Molyneux said. "Be a realist to that extent."

"Would *you* marry an heiress, Mol?" asked Henry, unexpectedly.

"Shouldn't marry anybody," retorted Molyneux. "Why should I? Marriage is done for. Why, because two people are physically attracted to each other, should they want to box themselves up in some miserable little hovel and spend the rest of their lives in chains, bored to death?"

"Hark to the Lion!" cried Lettice. "I'll bet you five

pounds, Molyneux, that you'll be married in two years.
You've got all the look of a marrying man. Hasn't he,
Mr. Spears?"

"That would be an ignominious end," said Philip. "I
think he'll make a good husband and father." .

Molyneux flushed with pleasure. He was a timid creature who knew nothing of women.

When the meal was finished, it was late enough for the
girls to be taken back to their hotel; but Rose had the
opportunity of a few words with Philip as to the reason
for his visit to London. As a consequence, she learnt
with astonishment, indignation, and something like rapture, of what had taken place. In the hurry she had no
opportunity of learning that which would have made her
still more astonished and indignant, for Philip confined
himself to the will and the prospect of his being once more
a wage-earner. But what she heard entitled her to give
him the address at which she would be living after tomorrow, and to exact a promise that he would write to
her. With this she was forced to be content. The party
came to a pleasant end.

All the same, Rose did not altogether escape distress
that night. For when she and Lettice were at last alone
together, Lettice remarked in a strange voice:

"I don't know if you know it, Rose, but you rather
give yourself away with Philip Spears. You positively
gape at him."

Rose, still absorbed in her dream, stared.

"What did you say?" she asked.

Lettice repeated her intimation.

"I thought I'd better mention it," she said, kindly; and,
indeed, her intention had been good throughout. "Makes
you a little conspicuous."

Rose grew scarlet. For a moment she felt quite sick.

CHAPTER EIGHTEEN
RUTH AND LEONARD

WHILE Leonard was garaging his car, and while Rose and Lettice and Philip were travelling to London by the same train, the Davitts were walking home, all rather miserable at parting. Rachel and Susan walked together, and loitered a little over some cheap shoes in a shop window in Cross Street, with the result that James Davitt walked on, redder in the face than usual, muttering under his breath a number of remarks as to women, children, shopkeepers, and railway stations. He soon outdistanced his daughters, and they lost sight of him.

Davitt saw his family disintegrating, and he was heart-broken. Now he was alone; for, apart from Philip, Rose was the only person who understood him. But he did not want to go to see Philip, because that meant seeing also Philip's wife, whom he disliked. Philip's wife, Davitt thought, was the sort of woman who needed a weekly thrashing to make her human. But of course Davitt had never thrashed anybody, and would have interfered with any thrashing attempted; so his belief on this point was quite theoretical.

The wish to see Philip was so strong that when he came to the scrag end of the High Street, which runs to the west of the church, he turned along it, marching and glaring ferociously at all the children who were absent from school (so that they slunk indoors), and all the

loiterers (so that they straightened themselves and pretended to be looking for work), and all the early house-
wives (who stared virtuously back, giving, as the saying
is, as good as they got). And in this way he came abreast
of Leonard Holpen's office, although on the other side
of the High Street, and was surprised and relieved to
see a figure, which he knew to be that of Ruth Spears,
entering that very doorway.

The sight gave Davitt wings. He brushed aside an
amiable old man whom he knew and who always took
his constitutional at this hour, and strode forward to the
other end of the High Street, past the petrol pumps and
the Lion, until he came to the Georgian house. He was
then distressed to learn from Sims, who answered his
thundering knock, that Mr. Spears had that morning left
for London. He gave a great frown at Sims, whom he
had known for many years.

"Why's he gone?" he demanded abruptly, as if to say,
"Now, none of your lies!"

"Couldn't say, sir," replied Sims, with the air of one
who says "You won't get nothing out of me, you old
man!"

"Mm," growled James, very suspiciously.

"He was all packed, ready, before breakfast," said
Sims, with a straight look.

"Packed!" cried James. "Packed!"

There was no answer. The two of them exchanged a
burning look. Satisfied, at last, that Sims could tell him
no more, James touched his hat abruptly to her and turned
away. He walked more gently back along the High Street,
but he struck his walking stick several times in anger
upon the flagstones. Why couldn't the fellow have told
him? Why was that woman going to Holpen's? There
was something in all this. The world was crumbling.

2

Ruth had not seen Davitt. She had not seen anybody or anything. Having spent the whole night without sleep, she was incapable of recognizing a single face among all those which swam before her as she hurried along the street. She had tried to telephone to Leonard the previous night, but had been told by a servant at his home that he had been out all day. She had telephoned again this morning, to be told that he had left the house. Dressing herself, therefore, with care, she had determined upon visiting him at his office. That was why James Davitt had seen her as he passed.

Her tread upon the bare wooden stairs from the street was so light that her arrival was unheard. She had climbed the stairs with difficulty, for her breath was short, and she had to hold the wide, sticky rail at the side, and once had to pause and rest awhile as she mounted. Recovering a little, she turned the handle of the door quietly and entered. There was nobody in the outer office. A voice from the inner room caused her to start and listen intently. The voice, which was rather sonorous, went on speaking. It was not Leonard's voice. Her heart sank.

"Too many reggerlations in these days, my boy. They talk about this being a free country; but all these reggerlations about the school age, and the age of consent, and the licensing hours . . . It doesn't do to say these things *anywhere,* mark you. You have to remember that we're in a sort of sense representatives of the Law; and the Law, my boy, is a mighty engine . . ."

Burgess! A faint colour forced its way into Ruth's cheeks. A slow, malicious smile dawned upon her lips. She bent forward, very slight in that dark cobwebby office, but with the cruelty of a watching cat. Burgess!

He was not speaking to Leonard. He must be speaking to a youth. He would not dare to speak in that way to Leonard. Nor to herself. He had cringed to her, although he threatened. He should cringe again, and spend the rest of his life in cringing. So much was certain. He could no longer threaten. He should pay for having threatened. He had frightened her; he had made her ill. That was a long time ago. Much had happened in the interval.

He had been waiting for her on the previous evening. He had waited in vain. She enjoyed her coming triumph over him. He would cringe, as he had waited, in vain. Ruth was pitiless in the repayment of injury. She never forgot or forgave.

There was the sound of steps. The two of them, who had been in Leonard's room, were returning to the outer office. Ruth waited, composedly expectant. Burgess would be surprised to see her. She thought he would come first, and braced herself to meet his glance, again with a smile of relish; but it was the pasty-faced boy in his shabby black suit who entered. He looked half starved and furtive, as if the burden of so many secrets alarmed him at his own shadow. Burgess had remained behind.

"Mr. Holpen?" asked Ruth.

The pallid boy gaped at her. He stammered, being unprimed with instructions about her, but somehow aware that she was not favoured in this office. He said:

"He hasn't arrived yet, madam." Then he gave an uncomfortable glance over his shoulder. Presumably he sought Burgess's aid. Was he in the secret? Was he trying to signal? Ruth's heart hardened towards him. If he was in the secret, he too should be punished. Then Burgess came. He was saying: "You'll find as you get older——" He appeared in the doorway, benign and ready to resume his monologue. His jaw fell. She could see him jump. The jaunty carriage, and the beaming smile of complacency which was wreathing his reddish face, instantly disappeared.

"Mrs. Spears!" Burgess drew himself up. He was all caution. His finger rose unbidden in the air. "This is an unexpected pleasure." Turning aside, he snapped his thumb and jerked his head, so that the boy disappeared into Leonard's office. Then Burgess, with marked quickness and lightness of step, came close to Ruth, shaking his head. "You ought not to have come here, Mrs. Spears," he said, in a peremptory whisper. "It's not the thing. You know perfectly well that Mr. Holpen won't see you —he's away just now—and it's obvious I can't spare time to talk to you in office hours. Surely you can see that for yourself, don't you? You ought to have come down the garden last evening, like I told you to. I was there, and I'd brought that letter, as I promised; but you didn't come. That makes matters more difficult, you see. I shall have to consider my position. I mean to say, you can't expect me to hum and ha in a case like this. Why didn't you come? I can't have you treating me like that, you know, when I'm trying to do you a kindness. However, I mustn't stop to listen to you now, as I'm busy. You go straight home, as I tell you; and come down the garden tonight, Mrs. Spears. I'll be there, and I promise you I'll bring the letter if you'll go straight home. Did you see your husband, like I told you?"

He was rising above her and bustling her out of the office, using his greater height and longer reach to bully her back, without touching her, and to open the door.

"You go right away now," he continued. "You go right away now, and wait at home. Not here. Why, good gracious me, do you want the whole town to know about that letter? No, no. Not at all the thing. Madam, I'm frightened of that boy's ears. He hears everything, and if he was to hear . . . Besides, if Mr. Holpen was to know you'd been here, he's quite capable, madam, of——"

"Have you finished?" asked Ruth, coolly. "I'm not going. I'm waiting to see Mr. Holpen. Don't try to hustle me, Mr. Burgess."

"Go on, get out," Burgess said, in a rough whisper. "You do what I tell you. I'll come and see you later."

"I'm waiting to see Mr. Holpen."

"I tell you he won't see you. He's away."

"He's on his way here now. To see me."

Burgess's face showed one flash of anxiety. Then he smiled, with his old air of geniality. The pale eyes were quite hard. Although he saw with trepidation the smile upon Ruth's lips, he could not afford to betray the smallest sign of lost confidence. He was unaware of the fact that he had betrayed himself.

"No, no," he said. "That can't be." He shook his head firmly. He now grasped the door handle, and drew it towards him, raising his chest again to overawe her.

"By the way, that letter," said Ruth. "It's no good, you know. That's all changed. Mr. Spears knows all about it. I've told him. If you try to use it you'll be in a very dangerous position. Very dangerous, I must warn you."

"Oh, no, madam," smiled Burgess. "You're mistaken."

"We'll see what Mr. Holpen thinks," said Ruth.

"You won't see Mr. Holpen, Mrs. Spears."

"I hear him coming up the stairs now," cried Ruth.

Burgess slipped between her and the door. He was through the door and out upon the landing in an instant, holding the door firmly closed. But when Ruth, finding herself imprisoned, realized his object, she ran quickly into the inner office, and across the room, past the pasty-faced boy, and unlatched the private door opening onto the same landing. By this means she discovered Leonard and Burgess in whispered colloquy upon the landing, in semidarkness.

"Won't you come in, Leonard?" asked Ruth, very coolly, holding the door open. "I've been waiting to see you. Leonard, the will's been found! The will's been found!"

She drew it out, and triumphantly waved it in his face, laughing in excitement at his discomfiture and the shock of surprise which Leonard and Burgess had both received.

3

At Leonard's entrance, and as the boy stole out of the room by the other door, closing it softly behind him, Ruth backed away towards the light, which was behind her. She saw Leonard come through the doorway and close the door. She saw him hang up his hat. She saw that for a moment he kept his face turned from her. He was evidently discomposed by her presence and her ecstatic cry, and was trying to plan very swiftly what his demeanour should be. At last he gave a short laugh and looked at her.

Ruth kindled. He was the same as ever. She looked anxiously at his shining black head, and his spruce clothes, finally at his eyes and his lips; smiling as she completed this swift survey with proud delight. He was the same. That was all she had needed to know. Leonard, for his part, had made a very quick, furtive examination of Ruth. By Jove, she was with child! he thought. He had not known that. He had not seen her for weeks. He had heard that she had given up telephoning after her marriage. It had threatened to be a nuisance; but he had stopped it. What did she want? She'd lost her looks. Some of the old charm . . . Most of it had gone. That was the worst of marriage.

"This is quite a surprise," Leonard said, with an air of joviality. He showed his teeth as he smiled; but Ruth knew that he was watching her critically. She knew that she looked haggard; that was the child, and the worry and fright and excitement of the last two days.

"You don't ask me to sit down," she murmured.

"Please do." He remained standing.

"Leonard, I'm a client," cried Ruth. "Look!"

She threw onto his desk the will which Philip had found in the secret drawer. Leonard picked it up, opened it out, and looked sharply at the signatures. Then, apparently, he read the will through, for his sleek head was bent and his eyes were fixed upon the paper. In reality he was trying to make up his mind as to what he was to do and say to this woman who no longer had any interest for him.

Ruth, sitting quietly in the chair by the desk, began to tremble violently. She was holding her hands clenched together, and watching him, her lips curved in a fixed smile, her eyes hawklike and eager, keen to notice if there had been unsuspected changes in him since they had met, to discover his thoughts, to catch the first words he might utter. He was different, after all; there was a line by his mouth that suggested greater purpose. He was the same, but subtly older, more mature; not quite the boy of her first ardour. She had taught him a great deal. She would teach him more. But why didn't he speak? Or look at her? What was it? The will? For God's sake! As Leonard remained silent, she struck her two hands together, bruising the knuckles by her fierceness. Her feet moved convulsively. At last:

"Yes, it seems all right," Leonard said, but in a dull, dubious tone. Quite perfunctorily.

"Well?"

He looked quickly at her.

"Well, I don't quite see what it does," he answered. "I mean, you're married to Spears."

"Ah, but that's——"

"Of course, there's no doubt it improves your position. You can keep him short, if you want to." His teeth showed as he smiled neatly.

Ruth interrupted him, with impatience. She did not want this.

"Leonard; that's finished. He found this. He gave it to me."

"Really. Rather sporting of him. But what d'you mean, 'finished'? You're married to him, aren't you?"

"We'll get unmarried."

Leonard shook his head decidedly.

"But why?"

"So that you and I—ah!" Ruth rose elatedly from her chair. She was young again, using all her charm. "You stupid old boy! Didn't you see that!"

"Oh, no," Leonard said, in a hard voice.

Ruth stared. Her hands dropped to her sides.

"What?" She was incredulous.

"You don't realize what it means. Look here, my dear; you're married."

"Yes, but of course I shall be divorced. Quite simple."

"Not at all simple. Surely you see that I, a solicitor, can't be mixed up in a divorce suit? It would ruin me."

"You don't come into it," she laughed. "I shall divorce Philip."

"Well, the man's a fool!" cried Leonard. "Why should he allow it? You'd have to pay him something pretty handsome——"

Ruth shrugged. It had not entered her head that Philip need be considered in a matter of such importance to Leonard and herself.

"He'd do it for me," she said, calmly. "Of course he would."

Leonard grunted.

"I doubt it," he said, sceptically. "Oh, no. Put that idea out of your mind. You'd far better stick to Spears. He's a very decent fellow. You get on all right with him, don't you?"

Ruth began slowly to understand what he was saying.

"But, good God! D'you know the child I'm carrying is yours?" she asked. "I'm four months gone with it."

Leonard's lips closed firmly. His eyes narrowed.

"I don't think we can consider that," he said. "I mean, it's not an argument."

"But I tell you it *is* so. I *have* told you, but you didn't answer my letters, and I couldn't see you . . ." Her eyes flashed at the memory of so much suffering as she had endured.

"I don't doubt your word for a minute. I only say you're better off as you are. You're very well off, you know. A husband, a fortune——"

"But the child's *yours,* Leonard."

Leonard shook his head. He was smiling.

"A child born in wedlock is the husband's," he said. "That's the law."

Ruth rose to her feet. She staggered a little.

"Oh," she said, with ominous quiet. "That's the law, is it? I'm glad to know." Then her anger overwhelmed her. "Leonard!" she cried. "Do you mean to tell me that you refuse? You're playing with me!"

"Not a play," declared Leonard.

"I offer you all I have."

"No."

"This makes no difference? You mean you've changed? You're finished with me?"

Leonard cleared his throat with a little cough.

"I'm afraid so," he said coolly. But she saw that he had flushed.

"Oh, thank you." Her head was bent as if in demure thought. She sighed. "Then I think you'd better give that back to me." She held out her hand for the will, which he gave her. "I shall get somebody else to act for me as to that."

"Perhaps it would be better."

"Leonard!" Ruth was reproachful, cajoling. In reality, a tigress. Her eyes flashed at his unresponsiveness. She came nearer; he retreated a step, mercilessly quizzing her, with his eyebrows satirically nicked, until even she could not misunderstand further. She took two quick paces towards the door, and he followed her with the impersonal courtesy of his profession. She said, thoughtfully: "I can't help wondering why you've changed." Then: "I haven't, you know."

"You've changed a great deal," said Leonard. He saw her eyes flash again. Lazily, he went on: "And then, of course, time passes. You had your chance with me, you know."

"You mean the flat at Scahampton?" she asked, almost gaily. "Yes, what a pity for you I didn't agree to that. But how lucky for me!"

"Yes, you didn't agree to that, did you?" Leonard said.

"No. You came to my wedding party, instead."

Leonard smiled.

"You'll have to come to mine," he said. "Next month."

Ruth was rigid. She was suffocating.

"You liar!" she said, in her old level voice. He was holding open the door for her. She saw him smile again, with complacency, and slightly shake his head.

"No," he answered. "It's true. Look in the *Times* to-morrow."

He was bowing. His head was upon a level with her own. Like lightning, Ruth spat in his face, and was down

the stairs and out in the High Street before he had
recovered his balance.

4

There began for her now an awakening to reality of
which her mind was with difficulty capable. During the
rest of that day she sat alone in the morning room in a
sort of stupor. When Sims called her to luncheon she
remained silent, and neither went to the dining room nor
acknowledged Sims's entreaty that she drink some chicken
broth which had been brought to her. Sims said: "Think
of the little baby, ma'am," and was rewarded with a
stare so distant that she was alarmed. She went away,
leaving the broth, which, when she returned, was still
untouched. "You'll make yourself ill, ma'am," protested
Sims. "I *am* ill, Sims," Ruth answered in a strange voice.
She thought: "He's no good to me. It's finished. He's
going to be married. I believe that. Something happened;
he never meant to marry me. He'd have married me if I'd
had the money. It's the money that has been the trouble
all along. Starling meant it to be. He did it in devilry—
hid that will where nobody would find it, thinking that I
should get nothing. He must have seen us. He tiptoed
in there and hid the will. The devil!

"It's the child that's the root of all this. If I hadn't
been upset, thinking Starling had seen us, I shouldn't
have forgotten. It's the child that's the cause of the trouble. Starling and the child. If Starling hadn't hidden the
will. If the child hadn't been coming. If Leonard had
opened my letter. My God, he left my letters unopened!
I hate him for that. I hate him for that. He was finished
with me then. He never cared that—" she flicked her
thumb—"never cared *that* for me. He knew about the
will. He knew Starling had made the will. I know he did.

"Philip's a better man that he is. He didn't know about Starling. He didn't know about the will. He brought me the will when he found it. I've sent him away. But Starling did it on purpose. He hid the will. He hid the will. And Leonard knew it had been drawn. We all looked for it. I knew. I knew all along that Leonard didn't want me when the money was lost. I've been deceiving myself. I knew it. He knew it. He didn't open my letters. Burgess opened them. He let him. He probably let Burgess try to blackmail me. He's no good to me. The child's his. A child born in wedlock is the husband's.

"I hate him. Once the money was gone, he'd got no further use for me.

"I've had a rotten life. All the time. Weaver was good to me. He was the only man who's ever treated me decently. He was good to me. The others weren't. They were nothing. They had what they wanted. But they're all no good to me now. Philip's gone. He won't come back.

"It's Leonard. I loved him; but he didn't love me. Why? What went wrong? The money, and the child. The child's his. He knew it. He knew that was true. He didn't attempt to deny it. The beast! The coward! I spat in his face. I'd like to kill him. He's made me suffer. I'd like to kill him. Kill. For what he's made me suffer.

"He was lying about the marriage. 'You *can't*, you know. You can't *do* it. I say you *can't!*' " She was screaming as she sat there. "Who is it? I must find out. No, he was lying to get rid of me. 'Sorry, little girl; I'm getting married! Have to break off our nice time.' No, he wasn't lying. It's the sort of thing he'd do. She's got money, you see. Well, I've got money, too, haven't I? Haven't I?" She screamed "Haven't I?"

That led her to raise the crumpled will and bring it close to her eyes. She could hardly read the words, because it was getting so dark. It was getting dark early tonight.

It would be sunset by seven. Good God, it wasn't that!
A storm must be gathering. No, the sky was clear; the
sun was shining. Yet it was dark in this room, in her
eyes. Was she blind?

It had been dark that night—that fateful night. Leonard had tapped at the window; she had let him in, and
drawn the curtains. "It's all right; he's in bed. Keep very
quiet, my love; he's in the room overhead. But he won't
come, and Sims is out, and old Foster's asleep in the
kitchen, dozing over the paper, as deaf as a post. . . .
Only you and I in the whole house that matter." He had
held her in his arms, they had kissed fiercely and silently,
pressed close in each other's arms, their hearts beating,
beating . . .

Ruth closed her eyes. She was lost in a dream of that
hour, of the house in darkness, and only a dim light in
the room where she and Leonard had been together. A
dream that faded, and was renewed, and lost itself in a
confused multitude of dreams. . . . And then, with a
muffled exclamation of terror, she awoke to find the room
indeed in darkness, and the door slowly, silently opening,
as it must have opened that night when Starling crept
down the stairs and spied upon them, and drew the door
close and stole away to the library to destroy the will and
ruin her.

"You poor, poor fool. You're ruined!" A-ah!

It was Sims again. "Ma'am, won't you take something
now? It's getting late, and you've had nothing to eat all
day." "Yes, Sims, I think I must have something now.
Has Mr. Spears come home yet?" "No, ma'am. Did you
expect him? He took his bag, ma'am. I thought he was
going to be away." "Oh, yes, of course. I'd forgotten,
Sims. He won't be back tonight. He had to go to London
on business."

Sims was going, and Ruth was alone again, thinking,

thinking. Philip would never come back. He had said he would never come back. He always did what he said. He would not come back if he said he wouldn't. Who cared? It was Leonard she loved and hated. "Leonard. I love him; but he doesn't love me. Why? What went wrong? What was it? He wanted the money. He didn't care about me; it was the money he wanted. The child's his. He knew it. He knew before I told him. He *had* read the letters. That man lied. He lied. Leonard knew all along. He was finished with me. He's going to be married. I spat in his face when he told me. I'd like to kill him for what he's made me suffer. I'd like to kill him for that. Yes, kill. I'll kill him. I'll kill him.

"I tried to kill myself. Philip stopped me. I'd have done it but I saw Philip, and knew he'd save me. But Philip's gone. My God, he hates me now, as I hate Leonard. I thought he was going to kill me. He didn't. . . . Yes, come in, Sims. What's the time, Sims? It's very dark. . . . No, I shan't want anything more. You can go to bed when you want to. I'll leave the things here. I'll lock the front door. Good-night, Sims."

Ruth sat there in the dim light of the morning room, stirring the chicken broth, which she did not drink although the smell of it made her mouth water. She was brooding still upon the thoughts which had churned all day in her weary head, exhausting her mind and bringing it to a state of excitement that was close to madness.

5

It was a very dark night, and Leonard Holpen had driven home along the main road back into Sandersfold in his little car. He had passed a pleasant and satisfactory evening with his Charlotte, who, if she lacked the ardour of one whom he had known some months before, would, he felt sure, prove in due course a suitable and ambitious wife. Not a flyer, but sound, Leonard thought, with reasonable happiness as he steered his little car through the darkness and between the tall hedges which fringed the road upon either side. The hedges were a brilliant staring green in the rays of his headlamps. Driving at night exhilarated him. He would not have minded if the journey had been many times longer, for the air was warm and soft, as if rain were in prospect.

He was very well pleased with his day. It was better, he felt, to get rid altogether of Ruth, who might have been a complication. Better than having a professional concern that brought them together, and laid him open to siege. That was too dangerous altogether, as things were. A woman in love, with a grievance, is always dangerous to the man she loves. Well, she might still be a complication, mightn't she? He thought not.

Charlotte was a sensible girl, quite modern. She had already asked him if he'd had any experience of women, and he had been fairly candid. He had admitted experience. One woman, in particular, now married. Quite finished, of course. She had expressed herself contented. So if Ruth tried to make mischief she would find herself in the cart. She would have to leave Sandersfold. What a little brute to spit in his face! The memory of that episode—disagreeable as it had been at the time—made him laugh slightly as he turned into Sandersfold. His teeth gleamed. He was not ill-pleased. She'd been angry, all right. Absurd. She was very lucky to have Spears. He had long passed any jealousy of Spears.

He was still occupied with these thoughts when he ran through the darkness of Larch Street, into the Crescent, and round to the little garage at the back. There was a hedge beside the gravelled roadway, and his headlights made this hedge and the interior of the garage

more brilliant than ordinary daylight could do. He kept
the lights on as he switched off his engine and brought
its sputtering roar to instant silence. Then he moved round
to turn off the petrol, and raised the car's bonnet in order
to reach the tap. He was silhouetted against the reflection
of the lamps, a big black moving shadow.

But as he lifted the bonnet a movement outside the
garage caught his eye. It looked as though a slight figure
was standing there in the darkness. He did not recognize
the figure, but thought that he could not be mistaken in
thinking it that of a woman. Ruth? Good God! What
had she in her hand? Christ! It gleamed!

"Who's that?" Leonard called. Something caused him
to duck as he ran towards the figure. Bang! There was
a sound of an explosion and a rattling of plaster and
metal. "Here! Stop that!" Bang! Bang!

He had reached the figure and thrown his arms about
it. He felt the rough cloth of a coat, and the muscle of a
firm arm and the resistance of a fierce and energetic body.
He knew the familiar scent of the hair with which his
face came into contact. "Stop it, you fool! Stop it!" he
cried in a fury. "You're mad!" Bang! Bang! There was
a cry, a shriek! Then Leonard was thrown violently to
the ground. He was conscious of an instant's violent
pain, and all was lost in oblivion.

CHAPTER NINETEEN

ROSE BUYS A BOOK

THIS is by way of epilogue. It is about something that happened nearly a month after the events described in the chapters immediately preceding, and it has as its setting a late October day in London. The day, a Saturday, was windy, but clear. For once, London looked as air-swept as New York ordinarily does at this season of the year, and every outline was distinct against a sky in which small clouds were flying.

At Dexter's, the bookseller's shop on the north side of the Strand, between Bedford Street and Southampton Street, a number of people were standing about. Some were buying books, some were examining them with no intention of buying, and one or two were waiting to be served, like cattle at a meadow gateway. Everything was marked by an air of leisureliness; but the shop was crammed with books from floor to ceiling, for this was the height of the autumn season; and the service was brisk and efficient. Near the door a youth was receiving money for a book from an elderly man who had several other books, bearing the label of the London Library, under his arm. This was Jenkins, a young Welshman, whose voice when he spoke had a slight sibilance. Near him, his friend Maddox was listening to an elderly lady who whispered in his ear particulars of a work with the title of which she was unfamiliar. Over in a recess was a taller, older assistant, a very dark man with a refined

and sensitive face, who was explaining to a bearded
stranger why a book was more expensive than the stranger thought it should be.

Out of doors the Strand traffic roared, the breeze blus-
tered, and a constant flashing of vehicles in the sunshine
sent bright reflections into the shop's darkness. The hour
was nearly two. o'clock, and already lurking figures could
be seen beyond the farthest shelves, instinct with desire
to pull down the shutters and close Dexter's for the week-
end. One customer drifted out of the doorway and into
the Strand's brilliance. One reader gave an abrupt nod,
as if satisfied, and went smartly away. And at this
moment there walked into the shop a young woman who
was dressed in a long brown tweed coat, and whose
cunning brown hat, of the same shade and material as
her coat, revealed a small and expressive face, some light
brown hair, a single ear, and two well-opened brown
eyes. She was not a tall young woman, but her figure was
slim, and she carried herself in such a way as to suggest
independence, buoyancy, and good health.

Both Jenkins and Maddox caught sight of this young
woman. The older assistant, who had his back turned, did
not notice her. But Miss Sparkle, who was sitting in the
cash desk, became as a cat watching a mouse. Not the
smallest movement made by the visitor escaped Miss
Sparkle. From the tiny button on the top of her hat to
the inches of silk stocking above the heel of her shoe, this
lady was appraised from the darkness with an exactitude
worthy of Scotland Yard. Whereas the observation of
Maddox and Jenkins was sidelong, emotional, and hopeless, that of Miss Sparkle was direct and devouring.

At last Jenkins bowed from the door the customer
who had detained him; only to be intercepted as he turned
by one who had decided after all to buy the book of which
he had read a gratuitous chapter. The whispering old

lady was supplied with a copy of *The Culture of the Abdomen*, which she needed for an obese son-in-law; and Maddox rushed to the cash desk for change. All three, Miss Sparkle, Maddox, and Jenkins, were flurried by some of the excitement of the racecourse. All three saw the charming young woman take a single step towards the older assistant in the recess and, as it were, mesmerize him into looking in her direction. Trade was suspended for a second, an age. The assistant turned.

They saw this cool assistant's face change. They saw it lighten into unguarded joy. They saw the bearded man dismissed with finality. They saw their colleague go straight to the charmer.

"What luck!" murmured Maddox, enviously, to Miss Sparkle.

"D'you think so?" asked Miss Sparkle, coldly. She glanced aside at her own reflection in the window of the cash desk and tilted her chin so as to eliminate a fulness beneath it, and at once resumed her exhaustive analysis of the stranger's costume, complexion, and bearing.

"I want a copy of *The Martyrdom of Man*," said the stranger.

"It's not what you think it is," he replied. "Rose!"

"I know," said the customer, with calm. "Will you wrap it up, please? And hurry up, Philip. I want to see you. How long will you be?" The last three sentences had been spoken so low that not even Miss Sparkle heard them. Philip Spears, with one quick glance at the lady, disappeared.

"Being attended to, madam?" asked Jenkins, with an extraordinary sense of daring and ingenuity. He beamed; he archly smiled; he rested his hand with careless grace upon a pile of books. Miss Sparkle's lip curled. Men! She threw a dark glance into the distance, after Philip. Even he!

2

When, a quarter of an hour later, Philip left Dexter's, he hurried along the Strand with purpose so unmistakable that the crowd parted to let him through. Under the clock amid the bustle of Charing Cross Station, deafened by the hoots and whistles and roaring of the trains and maddened by the scuffle of a thousand distraught humans, he saw none but a single figure, in a long brown overcoat and a brown hat. She raised her hand. He was at her side. No greeting passed between them, a fact strange enough to be remarkable of two people who now saw each other for the first time for several weeks.

"Look here," Philip said, unceremoniously. "Shall we go and lunch somewhere?"

"Please," Rose answered. Her glance at him, unobtrusive though it was, had all the penetration of Miss Sparkle's. It told her: "He wants me. He knows. Thank God!" As if no such thought had ever occurred to her, she added: "Somewhere quiet." They walked a few steps and out of the station. Rose was very subdued. She did not look at him directly as she said: "I hope you hadn't made any other plan, Philip."

"None," Philip assured her. "But if I'd made a hundred it wouldn't matter."

He spoke in a tone that brought the colour to Rose's cheeks. She lifted her head. Her heart swelled. For a moment she felt blinded by the sunshine.

"I only heard from Father this morning. Where to find you, I mean."

"Yes." Philip was apparently not listening to her. He put his hand lightly to her elbow as they crossed the Strand, but dropped it again when they reached the other side. They were pushed by the crowd, but neither noticed

the crowd or the shining scarlet omnibuses which reared
above them. It might have been thought they were silent
from familiarity or constraint; but in fact they were silent
because what they had to say could not be shouted amid
this din.

"I asked for the Winwood Reade out of nervousness,"
Rose said. "I couldn't think of anything else. I used not
to be self-conscious, but I'm getting it—very. I suppose
it's the studio atmosphere. I could feel eyes boring into
me in that shop."

"Only Maddox and Jenkins," laughed Philip. "They're
really engrossed in this afternoon's football. Yes, and
Miss Sparkle. She's a dear."

"Oh?" asked Rose. "She's got eyes like gimlets."

"Have you been living in a studio atmosphere?"

"That was only a sneer. I've been to one or two parties.
Awful. Philip, why haven't you written to me?"

"I couldn't," he answered, briefly. "Everything was
too intolerable."

They did not speak again until they were in a small
restaurant in Greek Street, where the tables were set
far enough apart for privacy, and where most of those
who had been lunching had departed or were about to
depart. As they took their places, it was for Rose to look
again at Philip, who, now that he was opposite to her,
was for the first time constrained. She was outwardly
more composed than he, but the reality was otherwise.
Both were shaken by this meeting and by thought of what
had happened since their last meeting. There was some
hesitation over the choice of the meal, and it was at last
only chosen with the aid of a black-moustached waiter
to whom meals were significant. A month before, at
another restaurant, they had dined and talked; and on
that night Ruth and Leonard Holpen, struggling together
for possession of a revolver, had both been mortally hurt.

No wonder Rose and Philip were silent. At last they were alone.

"Did you mind my coming today?" asked Rose, directly, with an anxious glance. Philip looked into her eyes with a faint smile. He did not reply to her question. There was no need to do so.

"I didn't write to you, because I didn't know your address," he said. "And I didn't ask your father for it because I couldn't bring myself to do it. I've had a good deal to see to."

"Of course."

"There were the inquests. I've put the house into the hands of agents. I never want to go to Sandersfold again. I'm helping Dexter until Christmas. I thought it wasn't fair to burden you——"

"Yes, burden," said Rose, quietly.

The waiter was bustling about their table, with rolls and glasses and the wine list. They could not speak the truth when it might be overheard by a busy-minded stranger.

"How's Lettice?" asked Philip.

"In her element. She's been tremendously quick to make friends and get about."

"Quicker than you?"

"I'm not quick. She loves it."

"She won't go to pieces, then, as Miss Furze thought?"

"You don't got to pieces nowadays. You toughen."

"Hm. You don't like London, then?"

"It's in my blood. I want to visit it. Not to live in it. Lettice is happy to live in it."

The waiter had hurried away. He had the moustaches of a general, but the feet of a camel and the eyes of a little pitcher with long ears.

"Yes," said Philip. "I wanted to come running to you,

to tell you another episode in the life of an indefensible cretin."

Rose shrank.

"Not now, Philip. Don't tell me now," she begged. "I don't feel very—quite up to it."

"I don't want ever to tell you," said Philip. "There's no need now. Except that——"

"No, there's no need," insisted Rose. "I want to hear whatever you want to tell me. But not *explanations.*"

Philip listened to her emphasis upon that word and understood its meaning.

"You don't realize what you mean to me," he said.

"No." Rose looked away. Her heart was full. "No, I don't."

"What!"

The waiter was back again, this time with plates and hors d'œuvres.

"You like some a dis?" he demanded, with a winning air. "Dis? Dis?"

When he had gone:

"It's wonderful," observed Rose, breaking her long roll, "how Lettice has picked up the latest thing. She's already got her hair brushed back from her forehead, and earrings——"

"Is that the fashion?"

"Victorianism."

"But not Victorian sentiment?" asked Philip.

"Pseudo-Victorian dress; and pseudo-Augustan god-lessness. All stucco."

He was impressed at her determined knowledge.

"Does the stucco cover Victorian sentiment?" he asked.

"I don't know what it covers. Not a multitude of virtues. And very few sins."

"Oh, isn't your own costume a little Victorian?"

"One must be dowdy in the vogue."

"Rose. Before that wretched fellow comes back again,
I must tell you——"

"He's coming," she said. "But I want you to tell
me."

"I love you," Philip hastily told her.

"What?"

"I love you. Yes, yes . . . that's quite right, thanks.
Yes, thank you. Yes . . ."

The waiter whisked a corkscrew from his pocket,
opened the wine, poured it out, and set the bottle down
with a flourish. During this performance he had occupied his Latin eyes with expressively benevolent glances.
The language of the eyes, to which also he had reduced
Rose and Philip, is used best in silence.

"Thank you, sah!"

"I did hear," said Rose. "I heard you the first time.
I wanted to hear it again." Her nose was wrinkled, as
if she were going to sneeze; she blinked several times.
"Damn!" she murmured, choking. "What a frightful
idiot I'm getting!"

But Philip only knew that she was talking under her
breath, and could not hear the words.

"Speak up. I can't hear you," he said.

"No; and I don't mean you to," answered Rose. She
laughed a little. "The truth is, I was swearing. At least, I
don't expect it's regarded as swearing now. I've learnt
more swearing since I came to London than I ever did
at school. Everybody's so Freudianly keen on showing
his worst side that the good's quite overlaid."

"I don't think you're as cheerful as you sound," suggested Philip.

"Well," began Rose, "I am."

"Is it because of me? A reluctance? A resentment? I
feel very abject before you."

"You're ridiculous. But when I'm happy the tears come into my eyes in floods, and I don't want to disgrace myself before our waiter. It isn't Victorianism; it's just sloppiness."

"Well, I think Victorian sentiment was the best thing about Victorianism," said Philip.

"You know nothing about it. Nor do I. And if we weren't in a restaurant, and if this awful creature weren't bringing me some sort of bijou, or bonbon, as a treat, I should throw myself in your arms. I might swoon. Thank you. Thank you. It's lovely. What a hypocrite I am! Philip, you should have written to me. You nearly broke my heart by not writing. If I hadn't known you, it *would* have broken my heart."

"You don't know me," Philip said, grimly.

"Better than you know yourself. Tell me some of the good things. I know all the others."

"I wish you did."

Their eyes met. On both sides they were clear and honest; in both pairs of eyes there was a mixture of candour and reserve. The honest eye is often deceptive; but not when it expresses a condition of mind.

"I'm not going to tell you what I know about you, Philip," said Rose, very truthfully. "A lot of it I couldn't express. But I don't want it cluttered up with your own ideas. I'll tell you this——" She lowered her voice. She did not look at him. Her eyes were cast down, and her cheeks were flushed. "I fell in love with you the moment we met. I couldn't help it. Pop! It's no good pretending; I did. I've never wavered. *Never.*" Her eyes rose significantly in a flying glance. "Whatever you did, I should swallow. I'd know that somehow you were all right. However wrong. See? That's character, as opposed to behaviour. Got it? You couldn't say as much about me."

Philip had listened to this speech with his head bent

forward to catch her softest word. His eyes saw the blood moving under her skin, coming and going as she spoke. Her simplicity and candour and good will touched him inexpressibly. He was awed by them. He knew that she was, in fact, so essential to him now that if, after this, any obstacle should come between them, hope would depart from his life.

Rose sat back. Her lips trembled into a smile and back to seriousness. There were tears in her eyes.

"Couldn't I?" asked Philip. "If not, the fault would be in me. My dearest, you're terrifying."

"I'm terrible," agreed Rose. "Are you going to risk it?"

3

They came out presently into the October sunshine and strolled through the Soho streets and down Piccadilly into Hyde Park. The leaves had begun to fall, and a few were scattering down, but there were a good many left upon the trees, and the grass was very green. In the clear afternoon air sounds came very distinctly, and children who were playing on the grass shouted much in merriment. Dogs passed, half strangled by the pull on their collars, and peeped up into Rose's face, very slyly and waggingly, or looked with longing at the tumbling children, whose play they would have liked to join. A few riders were cantering in the Row. There was a general aspect of holiday.

"You haven't said what we're going to do, or where we shall live," said Rose. "Or anything at all, now I come to think of it, except that you love me."

"You can decide for yourself."

"I don't want to decide things for myself. I want nice things to happen naturally, without all the fidgeting and bossing we get nowadays."

"You think it's all boss or be bossed?" asked Philip. "Well, I think so too."

"Did you know how much I'd learnt from you? When I met you first I was a trooping girl. I'm still silly——"

"Yes," said Philip. "You're silly."

"I'm not at all silly. I'm wise."

"Yes; and you're wise," agreed Philip.

"I'm an idiot. And an egoist. *That* will have to be squashed."

"One thing I hope," said Philip, "is that you won't ever be serious. I mean, solemn."

"No. But then I'm not a sensualist. Nor are you. That's why you think yourself ineffective, which you aren't at all, by the way."

"Fascinating!" cried Philip. "You'd think we'd never want for entertainment. We'll talk about ourselves. You invite it, and I invite it. Both negative characters."

"Negative fiddlesticks!" cried Rose, indignantly. "I say——" She looked quickly to right and left, glanced at Philip. They were in a path beside which shrubs grew tall and bulky. Nobody was in sight. In an instant his arms were open and she was within them, as sweet as a bird. They exchanged a little quick kiss; then, cheek to cheek, they both laughed. A park keeper came round the corner of the path, turned aside his head, brushed his moustache. Rose and Philip, not arm in arm, but apart, walked sedately on, as if nothing had happened.

THE END